An excerpt from *Second Chance Rancher* by J. Margot Critch

"Where are they?"

"Where are what?" Wes asked.

"The annulment papers," Daisy answered.

"I haven't signed them yet."

"What? Why not?"

"Have dinner with me. I want to talk to you about something."

"You can tell me right here. Why didn't you sign them?"

"I didn't want to."

"You didn't want to. You don't get to decide that on your own. We got drunk, hooked up and got married. We live in different countries, have different lives. We need to put what was the stupidest thing we've ever done behind us."

"I didn't sign them because I wanted to see you first."

"Why?"

"I need to be honest with you. I haven't stopped thinking about you—not once—in the three months since we said goodbye."

"Evie Hartmann. Nice to meet you."

His voice was low and warm, the scratchy timbre of a man who indeed found it nice to meet her.

But she wasn't Evie. She was clumsy Mia, the almost divorcée who never *ever* managed to look good for a first meet with an impossibly handsome driver of a car she'd just hit.

"I'm really sorry. I didn't mean to hit you."

"It doesn't really matter how we got here." The man a few feet from her smelled innately masculine, like spice and cloves and rain all mixed together in the most intoxicating packaging she'd ever smelled. African American, fit as hell and dressed for business, the man with beautiful shoulders flashed a sure smile at her. "I just want to keep this out of the press."

Out of the press? Who was this guy?

"Antone. I'm Antone Williams."

Reality hit her. The wide receiver for the Texas Horns?

If only she really *was* Evie and could think of something clever to say.

"I signed an autograph for the cop. I don't think this has to go any further." Antone smiled.

"Well, uh, thanks for that."

"I didn't do it for free." He winked at her. "There's a catch."

* * *

J. MARGOT CRITCH
&
KATIE FREY

SECOND CHANCE RANCHER
&
FAKE DATING, TWIN STYLE

Recycling programs
for this product may
not exist in your area.

ISBN-13: 978-1-335-45755-4

Second Chance Rancher & Fake Dating, Twin Style

Copyright © 2023 by Harlequin Enterprises ULC

Second Chance Rancher
Copyright © 2023 by Juanita Margo Bishop

Fake Dating, Twin Style
Copyright © 2023 by Kaitlin Muddiman Frey

For questions and comments about the quality of this book, please contact us at CustomerService@Harlequin.com.

Harlequin Enterprises ULC
22 Adelaide St. West, 41st Floor
Toronto, Ontario M5H 4E3, Canada
www.Harlequin.com

Printed in U.S.A.

CONTENTS

J. Margot Critch currently lives in St. John's, Newfoundland and Labrador, with her husband, Brian, and their little fur buddies. A self-professed Parrothead, when she isn't writing, she spends her time listening to Jimmy Buffett and contemplating tropical locales.

Books by J. Margot Critch

Harlequin Desire

Heirs of Hardwell Ranch

A Rancher's Reward
Second Chance Rancher

Harlequin DARE

Sin City Brotherhood
Boardroom Sins
Sins of the Flesh
Sweet as Sin
Forbidden Sins
A Sinful Little Christmas

Visit the Author Profile page
at Harlequin.com for more titles.

You can also find J. Margot Critch on Facebook,
along with other Harlequin Desire authors,
at Facebook.com/HarlequinDesireAuthors.

Dear Reader,

It's been my pleasure to return to the world of Applewood, Texas, for the second book in the Heirs of Hardwell Ranch series.

This time, it's older brother Wes's turn to go through the highs and lows of love when he returns to Hardwell Ranch to work and fulfill his grandfather's inheritance demands. But that isn't all bringing the former black sheep back to the small town. He's also there to reconnect with his family and his roots, and of course there's the issue of his wife, Daisy. There is still quite a bit unresolved from the last time they saw each other during their impromptu quickie Las Vegas wedding. Torn between his life in London and his love in Applewood, for Wes, returning to his roots is the key to a happy future, which I believe is something we can all take away from this story.

I'm still absolutely gobsmacked that I get to write these books for Harlequin Desire and all of you. Thank you for coming on this journey with me, and I hope you love Wes and Daisy as much as I do.

I love connecting with readers. You can likely find me on Twitter, @jmargotcritch (even when I should probably be writing).

Happy reading!

J. Margot Critch

SECOND CHANCE RANCHER

J. Margot Critch

As always, this one's for Mom.

One

"I told you, Bryant, I'm going to be out of the office for six months," Wes Hardwell said, regretting the impatience in his voice, as he spoke to his business partner on the phone. He navigated his way through and around the throng of tourists in the lobby of the Las Vegas Boulevard hotel where he'd been spending the week.

Half-way across the world, Bryant didn't seem to notice of care about Wes's temperament, though. "You were serious about that?"

"When have I ever done anything I wasn't serious about?"

"It's just that you only go back to Texas when you're under obligations. Like your grandfather's engagement party."

Little did Bryant know that what had happened at that party was only one of the reasons for his upcoming extended stay in his hometown of Applewood, Texas, where his family ran Hardwell Ranch, one of the biggest, most profitable ranches in the country.

The entire family had gathered to celebrate his grandfather's engagement to his soon-to-be second wife, Cathy, when the old man had tapped his crystal champagne glass.

"So that's why I'll be leaving Hardwell Ranch and all of its assets in the capable hands of my grandchildren," he'd said then. "To be entitled to their shares," Elias continued. "Each of my beloved grandchildren will have to return to the ranch for a period of six months, to work the land and show that they deserve to profit from its operation." His grandfather had often lamented that his own children had found other callings in their lives, instead of working at the ranch. With their blessing, Elias turned to the next generation—his grandchildren—in hopes that the inheritance obligations would help keep the family involved in the ranch. Wes knew it was just a way for his grandfather to make his new wife happy by retiring, but still keep an eye on the place, and his fingers in the business.

When just about everyone in the family—his brother, father, and grandfather—had expressed their doubt in his returning to Hardwell Ranch, Wes knew he had to return. He wasn't close to his family and mistakes he'd made as a teenager still haunted him. He had serious amends to make with the ranch, his family and his past.

Bryant guffawed on the other end. "So, you're actually going to go back there? What, are you looking for a payday? Have you been hitting the craps tables hard with the company money in Las Vegas?"

Wes laughed, but then sobered. His few trips to the casino floor so far hadn't exactly been profitable. "It's not about the money, but, yeah, I've been thinking about it. I'm still a Hardwell, and the ranch is as much a part of me as the name."

Wes and his brothers were raised in High Pine, the town which neighbored Applewood, where his father ran a medical clinic. When he was a teenager, it was obvious that his younger brother, Garrett had been the golden child—he'd worked at the ranch with Elias, helped in the community. But Wes was bored and did what most bored teenagers do—he rebelled. He skipped school, hosted alcohol-fueled parties. He and his friends had even stolen a car owned by their math teacher and went on a joy ride on the back country roads.

After being what some—*everyone*—might call an out-of-control teen, his father had sent him to live at the ranch with his grandfather, in the hopes that some hard work and being surrounded by nature would be good for him and help settle him down. It didn't work. Even though he'd still somehow maintained good grades in school, the move to Applewood hadn't tamed him much. Not being interested in ranch work, like a moth to a flame, he found yet another group of troublemakers and he'd gotten up to the same types of antics. If that hadn't been enough, on one occasion, his discarded still-lit cigarette had ignited several hay bales and the ensuing fire could have potentially done a lot of damage to the ranch.

That had been his turning point. He could have taken anger from his family, but the disappointment on his grandfather's face as they'd surveyed the damage had done him in. He buckled down and used every privilege at his disposal to make something of himself, then secured a spot at a top university in England. That was where he'd met Bryant, and together they started a communications technology firm, which had brought them both massive success.

"What about work?"

"I've been thinking a lot about it, but it shouldn't be a problem. I'll take the next three months to tie up any loose ends in London and prepare everyone for my absence. Then I'll head to Texas to do my six months on the ranch. The time-zone difference might be a bit tricky between London and Texas, but it's not like I'm going to the Amazon rainforest," he said. "It's Applewood. We do have internet there, you know. We've got phone, email, videoconferencing. I'll be connected."

"So, you're doing this, yeah?"

"Yeah. I feel like I have to." Even though he had nothing to do with the operations at the ranch, Wes had started off with a strong foundation because of an education that had been paid for by his family, some good luck in his investments, and successful business deals, meant he didn't need the money, but returning to the ranch was something he had to do for himself.

"Well, if it's something you've got to do, I'm with you. I'll take care of things on this end."

"Thanks, I appreciate it."

"And maybe I'll take a weekend to see you roughing it on the ranch."

Wes cringed. He knew that Garrett, his brother, and Dylan, the ranch manager, would surely make him work his ass off, but the main house of Hardwell Ranch also contained luxurious household amenities, so Bryant wouldn't have anything to sneer at. "Yeah, maybe we'll even put your ass to work."

"I don't think so." Bryant laughed. "I'll leave that to you."

"I'm sure you will."

"So how about you? Are you having a good time in Vegas, while I'm handling the business here?"

Wes stopped walking and leaned against a marble pillar to finish the conversation. He'd been attending a conference that focused on green technology, and it had been eye-opening to see the many ways his communications tech company could help the environment. He was looking forward to returning to London to share the things he'd learned.

"The conference has been great," he began. "Too bad you couldn't make it. I'll send you today's notes and information."

"That would be great."

"And I made some good connections with the CEO and the board at TotalCom."

"Oh, really? That's huge." TotalCom was an international giant in the telecommunications world, and it had been Wes's goal to get an audience with their CEO.

"It is. TotalCom and some board members are planning a European visit in the next year. I'll set up a meeting when they do."

"That would be great. That's why you're out there. Connections."

"And that's what I do. I'm headed to my room now, so I'll—" Before he could finish his statement, he cut himself off when he looked up and saw a woman sitting on a barstool, no more than ten feet away from him, bringing a lemon-colored martini to her lips. Hers was a vaguely familiar face, bringing to mind his stay in Applewood. But he didn't believe in coincidence; it couldn't be her, though. He looked closer, squinting, and leaned forward slightly. Although, it just might be...

She turned to take in the crowd, and he saw he was right. He would recognize her anywhere. It was Daisy Thorne, Applewood's town vet, and one of the most beautiful women he'd ever seen in his life. He wondered what twist of fate had brought her to Las Vegas, at the same time, in the same hotel where he was. He didn't question it too long. She was sitting alone. But there was no way she was in the city alone. She had to be waiting for a date—her boyfriend or husband.

She was wearing a short, black dress, cut very low, that displayed her ample cleavage, and dangerously high black pumps. It was a far departure from the jeans and flannel he'd seen her in on his last visit to the ranch, when she'd paid a house call to check on some livestock, and it was far more scandalous than the long, formal dress she'd worn as his sister-in-law's, Willa's, maid of honor. He watched as she swiveled slightly on her barstool in order to cross her long, shapely legs underneath the bar.

Before Wes could stop himself, he started walking toward her. "I'm going to call you later," he told Bryant, before sliding his phone into the inner pocket of his sport coat. Whether she was there with another man or not, he was going in. He could at least say hi to a woman from his town, right?

He wasn't normally the type of guy to chat up a woman sitting alone, but he couldn't pass up the opportunity to say hello to the most beautiful woman to come out of his hometown. "Hello, there. I thought I recognized you."

She turned to face him, and he could see her brow furrowed in irritation at being approached by a random man at a bar. Her eyes roamed his face for an instant, as she was no doubt trying to place him. But then her eyes widened in recognition, and the corners of her full, ruby lips turned upward. "Wes," she said, shocked. "What are you doing here? How are you?"

"I'm well," he responded. "And yourself?"

"I'm good. It's been a while. Well, a few months at least."

"Yeah. Not since the wedding. As you know, I don't get to Applewood much." They hadn't interacted on his last trip home, but he'd noticed her, had been unable to take his eyes off her. And it sounded like she'd noticed him as well.

"Twice in one year is way more than usual."

"It certainly has."

"Especially with what big, worldly city boy that you've become.

He grinned, rested an elbow on the bar and looked at her face, not allowing his gaze to drift farther south to the expanse of flesh that the cut of her dress exposed.

He pointed to the empty stool next to her. "Mind if I sit?"

"Of course not," she said, using her foot to swivel the chair toward him.

As he took a seat next to her, he grazed his thigh against her foot. He tried to ignore the frisson of energy that shot through his body at the contact. "It's nice to see you again," he said.

"Likewise."

"What brings you to Las Vegas?" he asked.

"Well, I had a veterinary convention here, but it ended today. I thought it would be fun to stay a few days. You know, for a little vacation."

"Well deserved, I'm sure." The bartender approached them, and he ordered a bourbon on the rocks. "From what I heard on my last trip home, all the ranchers in Applewood sing your praises."

He saw a faint blush color her cheeks and she looked away. "They keep me pretty busy. What are you doing here?" she asked. "You still live in London, right? This is a long way from home."

The bartender placed his drink in front of him, and he picked it up. "Same as you. I'm here for a convention as well."

"What are the odds?" she asked. "Well, except that Las Vegas hosts hundreds of conventions a year, I guess."

"It helps." She finished her drink and put the empty glass on the bar. The bartender was in front of them almost immediately. "Let me buy you another?" he asked.

"I thought you'd never ask." She turned to the bartender. "I'll have a beer," she said. "Blue Moon, no orange slice, please."

"No more martinis?"

She wrinkled her nose. "Nah, I was trying something new." She tugged at the hem of her dress, and his eyes went immediately to her thighs. "I thought I'd try being glamorous." She sighed. "I bought some dresses, and got my hair and makeup done to hit the town, but really, I feel more out of place than a fish at a rodeo."

He chuckled and let his gaze roam down and then up her body again, lingering slightly on her toned thighs, exposed by the short skirt of her dress. "Well, you look beautiful. It was all worth it."

"That's kind of you to say."

The bartender returned with her beer, and they clinked their glasses together in cheers, before drinking. Over the rims of their glasses, their eyes connected. Wes knew that her intention matched his own and he knew where the night was headed.

"When are you heading to London?" she asked him.

"It's supposed to be tomorrow."

"Supposed to be? Too bad you're not staying longer." In his mind, Wes had already rebooked his flight home for a few days later. It might be a bad idea, but it wouldn't be the first time he did something he shouldn't. He watched Daisy over the rim of his glass. "I think I could be persuaded to stay."

"Good."

He shifted closer to her, close enough that he could smell a hint of her perfume. It was a multifaceted smoky, vanilla scent that was somehow heady and feminine, and smart, and reminded him of the outdoors on a warm evening. "So, you stayed in town to try some new things. What is on the list?"

Her smile was slightly self-conscious. "I don't know. It's not a list, per se. I grew up in a strict family and was focused on my studies in college and then building my practice. It's all been worth it, but here on my own, with no work commitments, I just wanted to cut loose a little."

"Any ideas how you want to do that?"

In a move he knew was deliberate, she brushed his calf with the toe of her shoe. The bolt of lightning that shot through him at her touch was almost enough to knock him from his chair. "Maybe. You have anything in mind?" She set aside her glass and leaned her elbow on the bar, resting her chin playfully in her palm.

He trailed his fingertips up the underside of her forearm, her skin delightfully smooth. Wes had had every intention of heading back to his room, doing some work, going to sleep at a reasonable hour. But all reason flew out the second he touched Daisy's skin. "I'm sure we can think of something."

* * *

Daisy pulled a small gasp between her teeth and leaned closer to him. She knew it would be a bad idea to pursue anything with Wes. But the more she thought about it, the more appealing the idea seemed. They could hook up in Vegas, have an unforgettable night—or two—together and then they would part ways. She knew him—a little—and she knew his family. She could trust him. Then she'd go home to Applewood, and he would fly off to London. He rarely visited Applewood; and she could avoid him when he did.

She batted her eyelashes in a way that she hoped was seductive, but probably looked ridiculous. "I have to admit, Wes, I had a crush on you back in the day."

He laughed, and his deep chuckle made her chest flutter. "Did you, now?"

It had been true. He had come to Applewood when they were teenagers. He was the hellion with the bad reputation, and she was the minister's daughter. Didn't exactly equal a match made in heaven. "Look at you. How could I not? But you barely knew I existed."

"That's not true."

"Please. At what point did our paths cross? I was such a good girl back then." It was true. She'd grown up in a conservative household, where dating had been strictly prohibited. But when she left her parents' home, opting to go to veterinary school out of state, she'd branched out, met people, dated guys, and not always good ones. Her track record with men wasn't exactly one to brag about. And she knew she was close to making a mistake again.

He put his hand on her knee, and the contact almost shocked her. "How about now. Our paths have crossed tonight." He leaned in and put his lips to her ear, his mouth skimming the edge. "Are you still a good girl?"

A small, shocked breath squeezed out of her lungs. She turned her head ever so slightly, bringing her lips a hair's breadth from the pleasurably rough five o'clock shadow on his cheek. "Not always."

He didn't skip a beat. And she heard, felt, the rumble of his low groan. "Are you staying in this hotel?"

"Yeah."

"So am I."

"Why don't we go upstairs?" she asked. "We can compare rooms."

She turned her head, and they stared at each other for just a few seconds. The lights and noise of the bar and casino fell away. She pressed her lips against Wes's. She forgot about wanting to do something different. Looking back to her past was what she wanted.

Wes cupped her head, and he deepened the kiss. His lips made promises that she knew his body would keep. Before she lost herself entirely in the middle of the crowded bar, she used every bit of will she possessed and pulled away. "Let's go."

Two

Three months later

The horse's hair was sleek and shiny in the sunlight as Daisy slid her hand over the mare. In appreciation, the mighty creature snuffled in her ear as she nuzzled Daisy's cheek.

"Animals always seem to know who the helpers are," Garrett Hardwell said. She hadn't noticed her best friend's husband come up behind her, but she should have known he'd be nearby. Not much happened on Hardwell Ranch without the boss's knowledge.

"Leave it to horses to know how to read a person. But Marmalade is a special one," Daisy said. "She's very smart. Smarter than some people I know. She knows that we've helped her reclaim her life." Daisy had always had a way with animals, and that was why she'd chosen to be a veterinarian. Daisy loved animals, and they loved her back. In response, Marmalade went for another nuzzle, but was overenthusiastic and ended up butting Daisy playfully in the head.

Garrett chuckled. "How's she doing?" he asked her, with a hopeful beat in his voice.

She patted the horse's muzzle. "I think she going to be fine," she responded. "Her leg has healed nicely, and it looks like she's getting stronger by the week. I'd say keep taking her for gentle walks and keep up with the veterinary physiotherapist. No riding yet, but I'm confident she'll get there."

Garrett blew out a breath and smiled at her, while stroking the horse's side. "That's good news, and it's all thanks to you. I don't know if she would have survived without you."

She smiled. Words like that made all the hard, long, and sometimes discouraging days worth it. "I just did what I could." Since leaving veterinary school, Daisy had worked as the town vet in Applewood, where she was trusted with the lives of the household pets and the livestock at the many ranches, not just in Applewood, but the entire area. But overseeing the recovery of the horse standing next to her had been one of the most satisfying cases yet. She'd helped deliver the mare several years ago, and the horse was trained at the Hardwell facilities for racing. But during a fateful race last year, she'd broken her leg, and Garrett had taken her in when the owner contemplated putting her down. Together, she and Garrett, and his staff, had nursed her back to health, and now she would live the rest of her days, comfortable and happy on Hardwell Ranch.

"Thank God you were here," he said, patting the horse's flank.

Daisy, bashful when faced with praise, looked away. "You saved her life," she said, stooping to pick up her backpack, which held her travel medical kit. "I fixed her up."

Ever the gentleman, Garrett took her backpack from her hand and slung it over his shoulder. "We all greatly appreciate it."

She smiled at the praise. This was why she'd returned to Applewood after finishing school. She loved being a part of the community. Her position had let her become close to almost everyone in town. They began the walk to the main house, where she'd parked her car. She and Garrett had always been friendly—she'd been seeing to the Hardwell horses and livestock since she'd settled here. But since her best friend, Willa, had married Garrett, they had become friends.

"Do you have a busy day ahead of you?" he asked, making conversation on their walk.

"I've got a couple of stops at ranches and farms before I head to the clinic, then a couple of appointments for domestic animals, but my staff can handle those if I don't get back in time."

"So, you're saying it's a very busy day."

"They're all busy days," she confided. "And nights, too."

"Willa was telling me how in demand you are."

"That's true." She didn't take many vacations. The

last time she'd been able to get away from the clinic was for the veterinary conference that she'd attended in Las Vegas just three months ago. She thought back to that week-long trip. She had started it out being professional, organized and well-planned, but how quickly it had gone off the rails for her. And it was all Garrett's brother's fault.

"Ever thought about bringing in another full-time vet?" Garrett asked her, pulling her away from her loud internal thoughts and back to reality. "It would certainly give you lots of time to have a social life."

Daisy laughed. "I think Willa is rubbing off on you," she said. Her best friend was always on her to stop working so much. She'd done wonders on her husband, former workaholic Garrett. But that wasn't for Daisy. The one-time she'd given herself a little free time, tried to cut loose a little, it had ended up a complete disaster. Sure, they'd had a lot of fun together, say nothing of the incredible nights, but what they'd done the night before they parted ways was something that had followed her back to Applewood.

She shook her head in amazement of how stupid she'd been. What would her family say if the truth got out?

Garrett laughed and checked his watch. "Oh, damn, I didn't realize it was so late in the day," he said. "I've got to get to the main house."

"You and Willa have plans?"

"Not really. But my brother should be here any minute," he said casually, not knowing that he was dropping a bomb on her.

"Oh, really?" she asked, her pulse thundering in her ears. "Wes or Noah?" she asked, trying to appear unaffected. Her body tensed as she braced herself for the answer, while trying to keep moving with him. Willa hadn't mentioned either of her new brothers-in-law arriving, and God knew that Wes hadn't called her himself. Maybe it was Noah, one of the Hardwell brothers who, like Wes, had left the ranch. Though instead of going abroad, he'd headed for Key West, where he now lived on the beach, making a living as an artist.

"Wes," Garrett told her. "He called last night, telling me he was coming to town for a bit."

"Wes?" Her mouth dropped open, but she quickly recovered before Garrett noticed the way she stood ramrod-straight and tense. *Think of the devil.* The reason her Las Vegas trip had gone so wrong was going to be at the ranch *any minute*. She had to get out of there. "Wes is coming? Why? For how long?"

Garrett shrugged but didn't seem to notice her change in demeanor or her sudden interest in his brother. She hadn't told anyone about their indiscretions and terrible mistakes, and from the lack of questions coming from his family, she'd assumed he hadn't, either. "He's coming to work the ranch. Supposedly for six months, as per the conditions of Elias's living inheritance." Then he scoffed, "but who knows how long he'll last."

Daisy attempted to swallow the lump in her throat. She hadn't seen Wes since their unforgettable weekend—even when she tried to forget it—in Las Vegas. Some big mistakes had been made that weekend, and she thought she would be able to put them behind her, but with Wes coming to Applewood, she would have to deal with any unfinished business between them head on.

With the radio appropriately playing an old honky-tonk song about horses and women and heartbreak, Wes Hardwell drove his luxury rental car through Applewood. The landscape hadn't changed much since he was sent to Applewood to live with his grandfather as an unruly teen. He hadn't cared much for what the ranch had to offer as a child. Back then, he was more content to hang out with his friends, or cause trouble, while his brother Garrett, who now ran the ranch and the business since Elias's retirement, visited the ranch every weekend and any time he could, working and learning the ropes. Wes, however, after spending most of his time carousing and causing trouble, had cleaned up his act and opted instead to move to London for college, and he stayed there after graduation, to work with Bryant, and create Intel-Matrix Communications, a communications technology firm. All of his time, energy and a lot of money went into building it and keeping it on top likely contributed greatly to the burnout he was now suffering from.

Now older, wiser, more mature and part owner one of the most successful communications technology companies in Europe, Wes regretted not spending that time with his grandfather and brother as a younger man. He'd fallen in love with London. The noise, the lights, the crowds—even the weather had called to him.

It still did, but he knew in his heart that if he did not seize this opportunity to come home, get back to his roots and right his past wrongs, he would regret it.

He drove past Daisy's veterinary clinic and felt his fingers clench around the steering wheel. He had something important to share with her, and he hadn't wanted to do it through email. The mistake they'd meant to put behind them had remained unfinished because of him. It Talking to Daisy was one of the first things on his list to take care of.

As Wes got closer to the ranch, the pit in his stomach grew bigger. This would be his first time spending an extended period there since his teenage days, and while he'd initially looked forward to it, he now wondered if it was a good idea.

Despite the tension that radiated through him, Wes couldn't help but smile at the scenery. Spring was the perfect Texas weather. It was time he got back to nature, back to his family. And not to mention—back to the woman who, after one short weekend together, had completely turned his life upside down.

He made his way up the long gravel road to Hardwell Ranch. The fenced land opened up to a crossroads. Seeing a couple of the ranch hands on horseback looking to cross the road, he stopped the car and waved them on. As he was officially on Hardwell land, he assumed that they were some of his brother, Garrett's employees. The horses trotted across the narrow road as the ranch hands checked out his luxury rental car. Hardwell Ranch, and the entire business, was very successful, but the vehicles of choice of the ranchers were generally trucks, four-wheelers and, of course, horses. Wes, however, preferred something smaller, sleeker, to differentiate himself.

When the road was clear, he carried on, climbing the gentle grade to the ranch. When he passed the last fence of the property, he exhaled, unsure if he was making the right decision or not.

The past couple of years had been so busy for him. He'd worked close to every day and then the burnout came. He'd hidden it from everyone, even Bryant, and figured that the trip to the ranch gave him a great opportunity to restore his energy. He crested the hill, and the main house came into view. He parked between a truck, branded with the Hardwell logo, and a car he recognized as Willa's Mini. Wes got out of the car and pulled out his suitcase.

Garrett walked out of the house, and Wes smiled and waved. Despite everything that was going on with Daisy, and how hard the ranch work would likely be, this trip would be a good opportunity to reconnect with his brother. "You made it," Garrett said, holding up a hand. He kept his distance, neither of them making an effort to embrace. They'd never had a close relationship like that.

"I did."

"How was your flight?"

"Uneventful. As was the drive from Austin."

"Good to hear."

There was an awkward silence between them that was hard to ignore, as if neither of them could settle on what they wanted to say.

Garrett crossed his arms over his chest and looked at the car. "You got a rental? I could have picked you up. Or sent one of the guys."

"Uh, yeah. It was no big deal. I picked it up at the airport in Austin. It's due back in a couple of weeks, but I can extend the rental if I want."

"You're only staying a couple of weeks?" Garrett looked at Wes's one suitcase. "Planning a short visit? What happened to six months?"

He shrugged. Garrett's rapid-fire questions made him bristle. "I said I could extend the rental if I wanted it. It's not a big deal. I took a six-month sabbatical from the business, but you could say it's more of an open-ended trip."

"Three visits in one year. It's unheard of. I never saw it coming."

If Wes started to talk about what else had brought him back, he might be there all afternoon, and Garrett likely had work to do. That other reason he found himself in Applewood would require a long explanation. He wasn't getting into that until he saw Daisy first. He shrugged. "It was time to get back to the country, get back to my roots. Those ridiculous inheritance demands just came at a good time."

"It's too bad you just missed dad and Elinore they left for the Caribbean a couple of days ago."

"Yeah, I tried, but I couldn't get away from London any earlier. There will be time to spend together when they get back in a month. I'm here for six, remember."

Garrett scoffed. "You're actually staying for the full six months?"

"That's the plan."

"What about your work?"

"It's not ideal, but I can telecommute, and Bryant can take care of anything that needs to be dealt with in person." When he realized that they were still standing outside the house, his brother in front of him, his feet spread, arms still crossed, Wes felt his irritation climb. "What's with the interrogation, Garrett? Am I welcome to stay here, or would you like me to get a hotel, or something?"

"Of course, I don't want you to get a hotel, dumbass." Garrett gave a rueful smile. "You're always welcome here."

"Thanks." Wes nodded as he entered the house.

"If only we could get Noah home this easily."

"Yeah, right," Wes cracked. Noah, their youngest brother, a painter living his best beach bum life in the Florida was just as unlikely to return to the ranch than Wes, himself, had been."

"Take your choice of the rooms upstairs," Garrett instructed from behind. "With Elias and Cathy spending most of their time in Arizona these days, nobody else is staying here right now." Wes knew that most Texas families would not approve of the men referring to their grandfather by anything but that title, but once Wes, his brothers and cousins became adults, Elias insisted they call him by his first name.

"Will do. Thanks." He began to climb the stairs.

"Welcome home, Wes," Garrett said.

Wes stopped and turned and looked at his little

brother. "Thanks," he said with a nod and headed up the stairs.

Bypassing the large bedroom his grandfather and his wife used while at the ranch, Wes pushed open the door to the bedroom next to it. It was the bedroom he'd stayed in when he'd come here as a kid, but the then bare-bones room sure hadn't been so nice or luxurious at the time. It had seen a lot of updates over time.

Wes wheeled his suitcase to the foot of the bed and looked around. The bedroom was large, included an en suite and a walk-in closet, but had been updated with new fixtures, furniture and a flat-screen television that had been mounted on the wall. He looked out the window. The room faced the back of the house and had an amazing view of the vast acres of land. Rolling hills and mountains in the distance, and open blue sky as far as he could see. Wes had a great flat in London with a killer view of the city, but he could probably fit most of his entire place in this one bedroom. He wasn't used to so much space.

He opened his suitcase and picked up the envelope that had been delivered to his condo two days ago that included a short letter from Daisy, asking him to sign the papers enclosed and return them. It had surprised him to see them, but against her wishes, he didn't sign them. He wanted the chance to see her in person first. The timing had been right, and had aligned with his plans to return home, but those papers were the greatest reason for his return. He knew that he should have signed them and been done with it, with her, but no matter how much Wes sat, with his pen poised over the first stick-on arrow, he just couldn't bring himself to sign. He needed to see Daisy first, to make sure they were making the right decision.

He looked up from the papers and out the window and whom did he see but the woman herself—Daisy Thorne. She was speaking to one of the ranch hands. He had to talk to her. But not here. Not around his brother and Willa, or anyone else who might want to have a listen to their conversation. He'd have to go to her. And soon.

She was his wife, after all.

Three

Daisy bit back a yawn and sat heavily in her office chair. It had probably been the first time she'd been off her feet all day. She removed the scrunchie that held her ponytail and shook her hair. Beyond her desk, she looked out the window. The sun was setting…and she'd left her house just after dawn that morning. Multiple house calls, followed by an afternoon of appointments, had left her exhausted. Thankfully, the clinic was unusually quiet. It wasn't normally the case, but there were no animals kenneled or needing overnight care, and with her assistants gone for the day, her animal hospital was finally empty. She reveled in the blissful quiet for several moments. It was finally time for her to head home—her deep soaker tub and a bottle of cabernet were calling her name.

After checking her email and messages, she closed her laptop and picked up her backpack. She turned off the lights and headed for the door. She loved her job, but some days were harder than others. Some days she was stretched so thin that she didn't know when she'd ever get a moment to rest. Not that she should—the last time she'd taken some time off, it had ended in disaster. It seemed that anytime she wasn't consumed by her work, her brain shut off and all common sense went out the window. She paused and she finally had a moment to think about Wes. Luckily, she'd gotten off the Hardwell property before he'd arrived, although it would only be a matter of time before they met face-to-face. He hadn't mailed the divorce papers; it was probably his style to hand them over in person. That time would come sooner or later, as he was likely home to work at Hardwell Ranch for six months. *Unless*, she mused, *he realizes he can't handle it and gives up after a couple of days.*

She shook her head and forced herself to get past it. Three months ago, she and Wes had made a terrible, irresponsible, drunken mistake in Las Vegas, and they had to deal with the consequences. She'd done that by sending the divorce papers to him, after he'd failed to take care of it, even though he'd vowed he would just before they parted with a cordial handshake at the airport. He'd promised that his lawyer would contact hers and they'd get the divorce as quickly as possible. She hadn't heard from him since then. Daisy comforted herself with the fact that whatever he was doing in Applewood, and for how long, it had nothing to do with her. He only had to hand over the signed divorce papers. Anything else he did wouldn't concern her in the slightest, she lied to herself.

After locking the clinic door, she turned from the door and gasped in surprise when she saw that she wasn't alone in the parking lot. There was another car parked in the lot, and a man standing next to it. She exhaled. It seemed that she hadn't managed to avoid Wes Hardwell, after all.

"Jeez," she said, as her heart rate returned to normal, when she realized that the man wasn't a threat to her. Not a threat to her physical safety, anyway. "Give a girl a heart attack," she said to Wes as she headed for her own car. "I heard you were coming to town." She got closer and saw that he hadn't changed much in the past three months. He was wearing jeans and T-shirt—casual, but still as sexy as hell. "What are you doing here?"

He put his hands on his trim waist. "Would you believe me if I said I came to see you."

"No. I'm pretty sure you're here to fulfill your grandfather's inheritance demands. Because we've already dealt with everything we had to. There should be no reason for you to come and see me. All you had to do was send the signed papers."

He shrugged. "I was heading here, anyway, so I figured that I should deliver them in person."

"Instead of arranging for them yourself?"

He cringed. "I got busy."

"You got busy," she said in a flat voice, folding her

arms. "We're all busy. But somehow, I found the time in the past three months to get it done."

"I know, and I feel badly that I let it go on so long."

"So—" she looked into the car, searching for an official-looking envelope "—where are they?"

"Where are what?"

"The divorce papers. Did you file them?"

"I haven't signed them yet."

"What? Why not?"

"I told you, I've been busy."

"I'm sure you've found the time to sign your name on other documents."

"Maybe I wanted to see you first."

"To do what?" She didn't want to admit how much his one casually cocked eyebrow made her belly flutter.

"It's just…" He opened his mouth to say something else, but then closed it again. He hooked his fingers on his belt loops and looked away. He chuckled. "Never mind. Can I take you to dinner?"

"Why, Wes? All the business that we had has been completed—once you sign the divorce papers, that is."

"Just one dinner, and I'll sign them."

"I'm too tired for dinner. I'd have to shower, find another outfit, do my makeup."

"You look amazing just the way you are."

"Forever a sweet talker. Why do you want to take me out so badly?"

"I want to talk to you about something."

"You can tell me right here." He crossed his arms and said nothing. "Why are you being so cagey?" she asked. Then her eyes widened. "Oh, my God, you're pregnant!" she joked.

He jolted and then cracked a smile before chuckling at her joke. "No," he told her. "I'm not pregnant."

"So, what is it?" she asked, crossing her arms. "Don't put it off any longer. Again, I've had a long day and I'm exhausted. Just tell me what it is, so I can go home."

Shrug. "I didn't want to sign them."

"*You didn't want to*... Wes!" she admonished. "You don't get to decide that on your own. We got drunk, we hooked up. For God's sake, we got married. We live in different countries; we have different lives. We need to put what was the stupidest thing we've ever done behind us." She let out an exasperated sigh.

Wes seemed to be waiting to see if she was done, then asked, "Is it my turn to talk yet?"

"Go ahead."

"I didn't sign them because I wanted to see you first."

"Why?"

He took a step closer to her, leaving only scant inches of space and charged air between them. "I need to be honest with you. I haven't stopped thinking about you—not once—in the three months since we said goodbye at the airport, and I watched you walk to your gate."

"Wes," she began, "we decided that's what was best. We should have annulled the thing in Vegas."

He held up his hands. "I agree with that. I'm not saying that we shouldn't end the thing. But what we had in Las Vegas was good. We were hot together and you can't deny it."

The killer was…she couldn't deny it. Her three days with Wes, even including their drunken wedding, had been the most incredibly sexy time of her life.

"You aren't denying it."

"I'm not."

"So why don't we keep it going?"

"What?"

"I'm here in Applewood for an extended period of time. Why not try to recapture some of that spark. I think I'm feeling it right now."

The way her entire body contracted with desire didn't surprise her. In the past three months, she'd thought about him, how he touched her, how he tasted, every single night. Not only that, but with Wes, she'd also been carefree. That weekend in Vegas, she'd had no responsibilities but chasing the next height of pleasure. And he'd brought her there…many times. It was one fun weekend for them, they'd thought. Little did she know it would all come back to haunt her when she arrived home a married woman, with her "husband" living on another continent.

"Are you insane?" she asked with a smile. "That weekend in Las Vegas—that was a fantasy world. It wasn't real life. We can't have what we had there anywhere else."

"Why not?" he asked as he rested his hand low on her hip. "Since Vegas, I've only thought of you. I haven't been able to work, sleep, do anything without the memories of you rendering me useless. I know you feel it also."

She opened her mouth, closed it again, unable to form any words, unsure of what those words would even be. "You don't get to decide that on your own."

"You don't remember how good we were?"

"I didn't say that."

"There's no harm. Neither of us is seeing anyone."

"You need to sign those papers," she warned.

"And I will," he promised. "But there's no reason why I can't have a little fun with my wife in the meantime, is there?"

"I'm not your wife," she said, exasperated. She'd known Wes to be stubborn, but this was ridiculous. This interaction just proved how dangerous he was—just his proximity was enough to make her forget everything for the promise of just one night of passion. And with him in Applewood, his mere presence was enough to take her over. "At least, not in any traditional sense. We got drunk and thought it would be fun to get married. We had one hot weekend and then it was over."

"We did, didn't we? Had a hot weekend," he added, a cocky half smile on his lips, as his fingers found her waist, and he pushed her lightly to rest against her car, effectively trapping her. His touch was almost enough to make her sigh—she hated that he had that power over her. This is why she hadn't reached out to him, sticking to communicating through certified mail, in the three months since they'd gotten married. Because part of her knew it would end like this—them face-to-face, and her in danger of losing her head completely. This close to Wes, she might be liable to agree to anything he wanted.

"And then we parted ways," he said with a frown. "I went to London—you came here."

Mustering all of her strength, she stepped away from him, giving herself the space she needed to think. "Why, Wes?" she asked again, finally. "It's been a long day. I'm too tired for any BS. Tell me the reason you're here. Is it the ranch?"

He was silent and looked at the ground, as if he wasn't sure what he wanted to say. "I came back now, not only to work at the ranch—I could have done that anytime—but mostly it was to see you. When I looked at those divorce papers, I realized that it wasn't what I wanted, and I wouldn't sign until I saw you again." He paused. "I wanted to be sure. I liked the idea of you being my wife."

"This is unbelievable," she muttered. "We were drunk, Wes. Sure, we had fun, but what is this? The world's worst hangover?"

"I can see you're reluctant."

"I'm not reluctant, I'm in shock. What am I supposed to say?"

He chuckled. "Well, I was hoping you'd say yes and then we could go back to your place." She shook her head in disbelief. "Or we could go back to my guest room at the ranch, if you'd prefer that."

"You think you can swoop into my life, and I'll fall into bed with you. Just until you realize you're done with Applewood again?"

He shrugged. "A man could hope. I'm here for you, not Applewood. Hell, maybe you'll come home to London with me."

She looked at her clinic. Maybe he was right. He did things to her no one else ever had. And she knew he would never stay in Applewood. For a brief moment, she could see herself ripping up those divorce papers and following him to England, all the way across the ocean, just for his touch. What if he was right? What if she did pack up her life and move to there to be with him… *No!* She dismissed the thought altogether, and turned to him, her resolve firm. "Wes, I can't pack up and leave. I have a business. I'm the only vet here. Not to mention, my friends and family are in Applewood." She looked at Wes as she spoke. He was just as sexy as the man with whom she'd shared an intense history and started a too-brief affair—*ahem, wedding!*—after one-too-many tequila shots at a lobby bar in Las Vegas. Her body responded to his intense gaze immediately.

"So that's it, then?" he asked, folding his arms across his chest again. The material of his T-shirt stretched over his shoulders and showed off exposed corded forearms. His physique might be from expensive gym memberships and CrossFit, and not from the actual physically demanding work that many of Applewood's men did, but it had the desired effect. "We really had something, though, didn't we? You can't pretend that weekend didn't mean anything to you."

"What we have is chemistry," she responded, "and the same tendency to make bad decisions."

"Bad decisions make better stories, though, don't

they?" He leaned in a little closer and she could smell his cologne. It brought her back to their wild weekend in Las Vegas. Ringing bells, blinding lights, crowded streets, but she'd noticed none of it at the time. She'd been enraptured by him.

She looked up at him, and in an instant, because of his low, deep-voiced words, she was under his spell. "That's true."

"And the chemistry," he added. "We'd be fools to let it go, wouldn't we?" He leaned in and brushed his lips against hers. But before it went too far, before she got in too deep, an old farm truck rumbled down the road in front of the clinic, breaking the spell he held over her.

With this newfound resolve, Daisy took another step back. She might be wildly attracted to him, she might even be his *wife*, but she and Wes were more different than night and day. They had no future together. He was strong-willed, bullish and had no plans to stay in Applewood. Meanwhile, her life—her business, her friends, her family, everything she knew—was in Texas. She wouldn't be going anywhere, no matter how sexy he was, and how seductively he asked. No matter how much that small kiss threatened to blow up her entire life. She was off kilter, confused, aroused, and it was all the fault of the man in front of her. Her life would be a lot easier if Wes would sign the divorce papers and go to Europe and let her forget the momentary lapse in judgment in her past, and before she made any others. But if there was a way they could make this work...

She scoffed. There was no way that Wes Hardwell

was looking to start something serious with her. But she could put the challenge forward. "How long are you in town for?" she asked.

"That depends on you."

She shook her head. "You're unbelievable." Then she thought of the way to get those papers signed, get him out of town and out of her life. She smirked at him. "I thought you were here to work. Unless you were never planning on staying the whole time. What were Elias's terms? Work at Hardwell Ranch for six months?"

His eyes narrowed. "What does that have to do with anything?"

She shrugged, enjoying seeing him off his game. "I don't know. Probably nothing. But that's my condition. You have six months, Wes," she began, "sign the papers and leave them with me. You're so eager to relive the few days we had together in Las Vegas? in me over. Work at the ranch, stay here, commit to it. You told me in Las Vegas that you haven't always connected with your family. Use the opportunity to get to know them again. Show a commitment to your family, the ranch." She paused. "Show a commitment to me. Prove to me that you want some kind of future with me, and that we just don't have potent chemistry between us." She was bluffing, of course, expecting him to scoff. This was a good plan. Foolproof. There was no way he would stay in Applewood that long. And there was no way in hell that he would consider working the ranch for that amount of time. He had his own life in England. He would surely sign the divorce papers, turn tail and leave.

He checked her out, as if contemplating the conditions she'd just given him. Instead, he grinned, and her own smile fell. She knew in her mind that she was about to lose, but on the flipside, maybe her hormones would win. He stuck out his hand. "You're on."

Shaken, she tilted her head to the side. "Huh?"

"I'll stay. And I'll thank you for the invitation. Prepare to be won over. Now shake on it," he told her, nodding his head at his extended hand.

Numb, she shook his hand. "You're going to move here?"

"I was planning on staying six months, anyway. If you need me, I'll be over at Hardwell Ranch," he said, backing away from her, instead of answering her question. Then he winked. "See you later, sweetheart."

Wes was in his car and gone from the parking lot before Daisy got into her own car. On the short drive to her house, Daisy's mind was aflutter, and she was so distracted she almost missed her own driveway.

She walked up her front steps, opened her door and was greeted by Ozzie, her Great Dane, who, even though she'd paid trainers a truckload of money to teach him to behave better, jumped on her. He was so large a dog that his paws rested on her chest. She opened the door to her enclosed backyard and let him out. While he sniffed around the bushes, Daisy picked up her phone and called Willa. As Wes's sister-in-law, Willa might have some insight into her current predicament.

Before she could dial Willa's number, however, she noticed a call notification and a new voicemail from her mother. With a far-too-dramatic sigh, Daisy pressed the play message button.

"Daisy, it's your mother," she started as she always did by identifying herself—like Daisy wouldn't know her mother. "We're hosting an informal lunch fundraiser on Saturday, and we'd like to see you there."

Daisy closed her eyes. Her mother's gatherings, while the purpose of the events was to fundraise for the church, her mother often saw them as a way to scope out acceptable suitors for Daisy. There were dozens of things that Daisy would rather do on her day off, but as a dutiful daughter, she felt she couldn't say no.

"No need to bring anything," her mother carried on over voicemail. *"Just your lovely self."* Daisy was about to disconnect from her voicemail, but clearly her mother wasn't done. *"Oh, and wear a nice dress,"* she told her. *"Something pretty. You never know who will be there."*

"And there it is," Daisy said to herself, before thumbing to her contacts list. Standing in her kitchen, she dialed Willa's number, she opened a bottle of wine and poured herself a glass. She needed a drink. Although, alcohol was what had gotten her into trouble in the first place.

After several rings, Willa answered the phone. "Hey, Daisy. What's up?" Daisy could hear the ever-present smile on her friend's face. Since marrying Garrett, Willa had never seemed happier.

"I…" She trailed off. How could she start this conversation without giving away too much information? She hadn't told a living soul about her wedding to

Wes—not even her best friend. "Well, I ran into Wes today."

"Oh, yeah?" she said casually. "Garrett told me he'd arrived. I haven't seen him yet, though."

"I was wondering if he'd told you guys about why he'd come home."

"As far as I know, he's here to work at the ranch for his inheritance." Willa paused. "Why do you ask? What do *you* know about it?"

Daisy exhaled a heavy breath. Where would she even start? Willa was her best friend, but Daisy still argued with herself over how much of the story to tell and decided to fill her in on everything that had gone down in Vegas. "I don't want to get into it over the phone," she said. "Can you come over?"

There was a pause. "Are you serious? This sounds juicy. Of course, I'll come over."

She only had to wait five minutes for Willa to arrive at her home, and Daisy had a glass of wine waiting for her.

"Thanks," Willa said, accepting the glass. "I've already informed Garrett he might have to pick me up if this conversation requires more wine."

"It just might." Daisy paused and drank. She then looked at the glass and poured even more. She drank again from her too-full glass. "Let's go in the living room." They walked over to the couch and sat. "Okay, first things first—you aren't allowed to judge me."

Willa laughed. "I can't possibly promise that. But as your best friend, I promise I'll do my best depending on what you're about to tell me."

"Okay, do you remember three months ago, when I had that veterinary conference in Las Vegas?"

Willa and Garrett had dog-sat Ozzie for the week she was gone. "Yeah, sure. What about it?"

"Well, Wes also had a conference there. At the same time."

Willa gasped. "Did you hook up with Wes?"

If only it had been that simple. "I just happened to run into him in the bar of the hotel we were both staying at. What are the odds, right?"

"You'd better keep going," Willa warned.

"Anyway, it turned out that we both had a couple of extra days booked in the city. So we had some drinks."

"You slept with him!" her friend shrieked.

"Well, let me finish."

"Well, hurry up and give me the rundown on this situation."

"Yeah, we slept together." She sighed. "But that's not all." She took another gulp of wine.

"You're killing me over here. Do I have to pull the story out of you?"

"Okay, after several nights together, we had way too much to drink, and we thought it would be fun idea to get married."

Willa's eyes widened as they sat in stunned silence from Willa, and Daisy just had to fill it. "Come on, you have to have something to say."

Willa drank heavily from her wine glass. When she lowered her glass, she was smiling. "Man," she said. "Some people just can't handle Vegas."

Four

Wes was up with the sun the next morning. In the city, he was always an early riser. His typical routine at home normally consisted of getting up, downing a coffee—despite living in the UK for years, he'd never developed a taste for tea—heading to the gym and starting his day in the office by six thirty. On the ranch, however, he opened his eyes, not recognizing the bed, or the bedroom around him. With the lack of city noise, the utter quiet was jarring, and it took him several seconds to recall that he was in Applewood. At Hardwell Ranch.

Part of him had hoped that his first night in Applewood would be spent in Daisy's bed, but he should have known she wouldn't just let him in that easily. Why would she? Hell, he was lucky she didn't deck him for not signing the divorce papers. He'd wanted to get back that connection between them, and then she'd suggested they hook up while he was in town. He couldn't have come up with a better idea himself. He'd stay in Applewood for a while, connect with his family, get Daisy out of his system and then go home to London, free from the burnout that had plagued him and ready to get to work.

His mind lingered on that kiss. The briefest, barest skim of her lips had been enough for him to want to take her over his shoulder and get her naked. That barbarian side of him was shut down, however, as she'd had some demands of her own. Sign the papers, then he could live out every one of the fantasies he'd dreamed up about her in the past three months.

He pushed himself out of bed and stretched. Before any of that, he would have to get used to these quiet mornings on Hardwell Ranch if he was going to stay long enough to reconnect with his family. Looking out the window, he could see that even though it was early, the ranch hands had started their day. He was already late.

He reached for his still-packed suitcase, and upon first glance, he knew that his most casual clothing— jeans, sweats and T-shirts that admittedly cost more than they should have—would not do on the ranch. He would have to go shopping later, but for now, he needed to get a move on. He pulled on a pair of jeans, a T-shirt and a zipped sweatshirt, then headed to the kitchen.

He poured himself a cup of coffee and took it to the porch, where he watched everyone head off in different directions. After so many years away, he couldn't believe he was back at Hardwell Ranch. As much as he loved the vibrancy of the city, there was something about the fresh air and the stillness of life on the ranch. He was going to have to find Garrett and the ranch manager, to be assigned chores. He drank from his mug. *But first, coffee.*

Willa came from the house that Garrett had built next door. "Morning," he said with a nod. She didn't respond, but instead looked at him with her arms crossed and a smirk on her face. "What's up?" he asked. It then occurred to him that Willa and Daisy were best friends. Did she know what had happened between them?

She smiled and joined him on the porch, standing in front of him, since he was seated, and glanced at him. "I can't believe you."

"Pardon?" he asked, playing dumb, even though he knew exactly what she was referencing.

"You *married* Daisy!" she exclaimed in a voice that was far too loud. "In Vegas! Months ago!"

He looked around, confirming that they were alone and that his brother was nowhere nearby. "Will you keep it down?"

"Is that why you're here? To win her back."

"No, I'm here to put in my time on the ranch. Like Elias wanted me to."

"Mmm-hmm," she said, unconvinced. "And it has nothing to do with the fact that Daisy is here.

"No, I can't see how the two things are related at all," he lied. "I wanted to come home to relax and get away from the business for a while. This being Daisy's hometown is purely a coincidence."

"If you think you're going to steal my best friend away from me…"

"I'm not going to steal your best friend away. I know that Daisy has no intention of leaving Applewood. The only business we have left is to sign the divorce papers and put it behind us."

"I don't believe you."

"What did she tell you, exactly?" he asked.

"She told me that you guys had way, way too much fun in Vegas, got married, and then she told me that you showed up at her clinic with divorce papers she'd sent you—unsigned."

He nodded. While Willa had a good rundown of the plot, her synopsis missed the fine details of their time together. "That's pretty much the story, I guess. I can't really explain it. Before leaving Vegas, we'd agreed to get it annulled, but when the papers showed up at my place, I couldn't bring myself to sign them without seeing her one more time. I kept remembering what it was like for us then—" He paused, then continued "In Vegas, I wasn't willing to let it go. The timing, and my plan to come home, just kind of worked out."

"I can't believe she's been keeping this from me for months," Willa said with an amazed laugh, shaking her head. "What's your plan here? Do you want to stay married?"

"No," he told her, his voice firmer than he felt. "We're going to get the divorce." He thought of the papers upstairs in his suitcase. He needed to sign them and pass them along. But he didn't feel any rush.

"And that's it?"

If Daisy hadn't told her friend about their arrangement, then he wasn't going to be the one to do so. "Yeah, I guess."

"You like her, don't you?"

"Of course, I do. She's funny, kind, smart. What's not to like?"

"But you *like* her, right?"

"What is this, junior high? Are you asking if I *like* like her? Or like, like, *like* her?"

"You're being evasive."

"Yeah, probably. What's your take on this?"

"What do you want from me? If this is as cut-and-dry a situation as you claim, then you sign the papers and you're done." She eyed him over her coffee mug. "But I think there's more to it than that." He shook his head, but she continued on. "You know she'll never leave Applewood, right? She's settled here. She has her business. Her friends and family. If you want her, you'll have to move here, I guess," she concluded with a shrug. "Not a chance."

He shrugged. "Applewood is nice enough for a visit, but to live?" He considered it for the briefest of moments. "Hell no. My home is in London."

"That might be your biggest stumbling block, and something you'll have to discuss with her. Daisy wants what any woman wants—love and stability—but I know she wants independence, as well. You might have to compromise on the location if you want to be with her."

He hadn't fully thought that through. For his entire life, he'd been spoiled and always got what he wanted. In England, he was well known and respected and always had a woman on his arm. In his mind, he thought briefly about a future with Daisy. That was a fantasy world. Daisy would never drop everything to go back with him. He had no intention of staying in Texas, and he wasn't going to give everything up to stay in Applewood and work as a ranch hand on his family's ranch.

"Well," he said, standing and draining his cup. "You've given me a lot to think about," he told her.

"Where are you going?"

He hooked a thumb over his shoulder. "I'm going over to the stables and do what Daisy and my grandfather told me to do—stay here, work the ranch, reconnect with my family."

Willa smiled. "I'm glad to hear that."

Wes headed for the stable, where his brother and Dylan were assigning duties. He stood near the back, and when the rest of the employees left, Garrett's gaze settled on him.

"'Bout time you got up," his brother said.

He'd chatted with Willa for longer than he'd realized. "I'm here now. Just tell me what you want me to do."

Garrett and Dylan exchanged a look, slick smiles that Wes didn't like. "Yeah," Garrett said. "We do need a hand around here. You can start by mucking out the stalls in the main stable."

"All of them?" There were dozens of horses being stabled at any given time on Hardwell Ranch, not including the training facility, where they prepared race and show horses.

"Yeah, for a start," Dylan said. "And we've got to get a start on cleaning out the hay silo."

Wes internally cringed. He wasn't afraid of a little hard work, but it sounded like his brother and Dylan were cooking up a list of unpleasant chores for him. His punishment for being *posh*, no doubt. He certainly wasn't looking forward to mucking horse stalls, or the hot, sweaty work involved in cleaning the silo. He could already feel the hay and dust sticking to his soon-to-be sweaty skin. It wouldn't be fun, but Wes was done looking like the weak city boy they all thought him to be. "Sounds good to me," he said with a firm nod. He grasped a pitchfork from where it was resting against the nearby wall. "Lead the way."

Five

Despite the sun high in the sky, the early spring air held a slight chill, and Daisy was grateful for the thick flannel shirt she'd pulled on over her work clothes when she parked her car at the Hardwell Ranch. Today's visit was to check out a small herd of longhorn cattle that Garrett had brought in and had absolutely nothing to do with the fact that Wes was in town.

She finished up, and Garrett finally came over to her, after giving her space to do her work. "How's everything look?" Garrett asked. "I took a cursory glance and they all seemed strong and healthy. But I definitely needed an expert opinion."

"As far as I can tell they all look great. Beautiful creatures, really. Quarantine them before you send them out to pasture, and I'll come check on them again in a week," she told Garrett.

"Thanks," he said.

"No problem. I'd better get back to the clinic."

Out of the corner of her eye, she saw Wes approach them. He looked tired, like he'd been worked to the bone all day. He turned to his brother. "Stalls are clean."

Garrett widened his eyes in what Daisy could only assume was surprise. "Really?"

"Yeah, I just took a quick break to shower. It's dirty work. What else do you need done?"

"Why don't you take a break?" Garrett suggested. "I don't want you to wear yourself out on your first day."

"I don't need a break. What else can I do?"

"We're taking a run to some of the further pastures later if you want to join us."

"Yeah, sure," he said with a nod, before turning her way. "How are ya, Daisy?"

She smiled. After only a couple of days in town, he'd begun to adopt the same slow drawl as the other men in Applewood. *You could take the boy out of Texas, and all that*, she thought. "I'm good," she told him. "I just came in to check on the longhorns."

She picked up her backpack, and just like his brother usually did, Wes took it and slung it over his own shoulder. Their eyes connected, and she expected him to say something, flirting or otherwise. The brief kiss they'd shared the day before still lingered at the forefront of her mind.

"How's your day been?"

"Good. I've been busy."

"I imagine so. All you do—it's such a big job. Have you thought about bringing in any help? Another livestock vet, or anyone?"

With how long her days stretched sometimes, she'd given some thought to courting some outside vet help. She'd made several connections at the Las Vegas conferences and the clinic was doing well enough that she could entice someone with an attractive salary and benefits package. But admitting she wanted or needed the help was another thing. "Oh, you know me," she said. "I'm far too much of a control freak to let anyone else step in and take care of my animals."

"Your animals?" he asked. "All of the animals in town?"

"Of course." Whether they were technically her animals or not, she felt a certain pride of ownership over all the creatures she looked after and treated.

Garrett laughed. "Just don't work yourself to death," he warned. "I learned my lesson this summer—with a little help from Elias and Willa."

Daisy grinned. Garrett's grandfather, who had retired from the ranch a few months back, had insisted his grandson find a wife in order to inherit the ranching business. After a convoluted fake engagement with Willa, they'd finally come to their senses and decided that they should be together. She looked toward Wes…her own husband. Another phony marriage in the Hardwell family. But theirs was not phony. Whether she liked it or not, their marriage was unfortunately very real.

"Thanks for the advice," she said.

"Need a ride to your car?" Garrett asked. They were a ways from where she'd parked, at the main house. But Garrett's four-wheeler was sitting nearby.

"No thanks." She waved him off. "I like the walk. It's beautiful out here."

"Alright. I've got a meeting to get to. Send me the bill, all right?" he said, mounting the four-wheeler.

"You better believe I will. Minus the cost of the life advice, of course."

Garrett drove off, and she and Wes were left alone. "I'll walk you back," he offered.

"That's not necessary," she told him.

"It's the least I can do."

They headed off on foot. She always loved walking the Hardwell Ranch. It was busy, bustling, with people and livestock heading in every direction, but it was also quiet and serene, with flat land and rolling hills. But with Wes walking next to her, she barely noticed any of it.

They passed a couple of ranch hands hauling bales of hay off a truck. She didn't recognize them and from the way they were struggling, she assumed they were new, maybe a little green. Judging from the stack of bales, they'd been at it for quite a while.

Wes stopped walking and handed her backpack to her. "Just wait here for a minute," he said before jogging over to the young men and helping them with the last few bales. He surprised her. He was already taking to the ranch life, and she knew from experience that hauling heavy bales of hay was one of the most tiring jobs on the ranch…and one often assigned to the greener ranchers. When they were finished, he jogged back to her. When he took her knapsack again, he leaned in close and, unconsciously, she inhaled, getting a lung full of his scent—his cologne, mingled with the faint smell of sweat and fresh air—and it almost knocked her over.

"Sorry, about that," he told her. "Those guys have been working their tails off all morning."

"It was awful nice of you to help."

"Well, everyone has to work together. There's no other way to run a ranch, I'm learning. I saw your car, and I figured I'd find you up here. It's nice to see you."

"You came to look for me?"

"Yeah, we have that bit of unfinished business to attend to."

"The divorce papers?" She exhaled. "Well, I was hoping I'd run into you. Can we go somewhere private?"

"We can head to the main house," he suggested. "There shouldn't be anyone around."

"Sounds good."

When they entered the main house, she was greeted by pure rustic opulence. The place stole her breath every time. It spoke of a long family history. If the home—including the walls, the scuffed hardwood floor and the large solid wood table in the dining room—could speak, she wondered about the many stories it would have.

"I love this house."

"It's nice. We were all surprised when Elias announced he was leaving it to retire in Arizona with Cathy."

"I still can't believe it."

"Although, he apparently visits enough to make Garrett want to pull his hair out."

He pointed to the staircase. "Follow me."

"Really?" she asked. "You want me to go upstairs with you?" Upstairs—with its bed, showers, other reasonably flat surfaces… "I don't think so."

"That's where the papers are. You wanted somewhere private. There's so much activity here during the day, this might be the only option for some privacy."

"Fine." She followed him up the stairs and he opened the door to a large bedroom. She inhaled, and even after the short time he'd been home, it already smelled like him. Wes had led her to his room. He leaned against the dresser, facing her as she stood at the edge of the king-size bed.

"Where are they?" Daisy asked. She turned her head and her eyes slid over the immaculately made bed, but she had to force away her gaze and focus on Wes. But that too was proving difficult.

He opened the top drawer of the dresser and produced an envelope.

"Have you signed them?"

"Not yet."

"Wes," she admonished.

"I haven't gotten around to it," he said with a shrug and a laugh. She didn't think it was funny. "I didn't know if you'd change your mind."

"You can't be serious, Wes," she told him. "We're

not staying married. I'm not going back to England with you, and you're not staying here with me. We don't have a future."

"You're telling me that you wouldn't come to London with me?"

She shook her head in confusion and raised her eyes to the ceiling. "What have I been saying? No, it's not going to happen." Ever since high school and getting away from her parents' strict household, Daisy had made a habit of falling for the wrong kind of guy. Wes was only the latest in a series of bad decisions, and she wasn't going to let him derail her from her sensible future. "Applewood is my home. You're just so used to getting what you want that you can't imagine a woman telling you no."

He smirked and she knew that it was true. "You're my wife."

"Oh, my God, we made a drunken mistake. This isn't a marriage. And the sooner you realize that, you can return to your real life."

There was something in Wes's eyes that Daisy couldn't identify, but she turned so she wouldn't have to look at him. Had she gone too far? Her words had been harsh, but she needed him gone before he made her weak enough to throw everything away to move overseas with him. That's how dangerous he was to her. She threw the envelope on the bed. "Sign the papers, Wes."

"Fine," he said, looking at the envelope and then at her. His expression was cool and impassive. Ignoring the papers, he took several steps toward her, then pulled her to him. Pressed against his chest, she knew she was done for. There was no escaping his masculine scent and his warm, strong arms. "You know you're beautiful when you're exasperated?"

"Wes. You're the reason I'm exasperated."

His fingers blazed a trail along her spine, and she couldn't help but shiver against him. His self-satisfied chuckle told her that he didn't miss it. "I know."

He always did this to her. Every time he touched her, she melted, and every bit of strength and resolve she had puddled at her feet. He lowered his lips to hers and the effect was electric. Part of her thought she should pull away. But thankfully, his strong grip held her close.

With his lips still on hers, he walked her back until the edge of the mattress bumped her thighs, and then, instead of exercising any amount of will power, she let him lower her to the soft, yet firm mattress. He followed her down, bracing his weight on one elbow. He played with the edge of her shirt and his fingers slipped underneath. When he began pushing his fingers up her stomach, she put a hand over his, stopping his upward progress. "Wes, wait." He stilled and his eyes sought out hers.

"Do you want me to stop?" His palms flattened against her rib cage. "I will if you want me to."

Did she? The rational part of her said yes, but she couldn't vocalize it. She needed him too badly. Finally, her body and her potent desire for him took over. "Don't stop," she told him. She lifted her hand from his and traced his jaw with her index finger. "But it's just this one last time, okay?"

In response, he kissed her hard. Her arms encircled his neck, and he pulled her T-shirt over her head. He cupped one breast through the lacy material of her bra, and she arched her back to get closer to him. He made quick work of the silky material, pulling it down, then pushed her breasts toward him. He opened his mouth over one of her breasts and pulled her taut nipple between his lips. She held his head in place and moaned at his expert touch. She felt jolts of electricity between her thighs. Daisy tilted her hips upward, desperate for a climax.

He shot her a grin, then trailed kisses over her stomach, until he reached the waistband of her jeans. He unsnapped the button and took the tab of the zipper between his teeth, lowering it. Daisy watched, holding her breath...

"Hey, Wes..." It was Garrett, calling from the bottom of the staircase. "You up there? Dylan and I need to head up to the southern pasture to check on the herd. Coming with us?"

"Dammit," Wes grumbled against her stomach. "Yeah, I'll be right down," he said loudly, then pushed himself up from the bed.

Daisy raised on her forearms, watching in surprise as he straightened his clothing. One look at his jeans told her that he'd rather be on the bed with her.

"Sorry, sweetheart, there's nowhere else I'd rather be than in this bed, doing what we were just about to do, but I told Garrett I'd help out with the pasture this afternoon. Maybe one day they'll stop making me muck the stables."

With the separation came clarity. Thankfully, her head cleared. "Yeah, you should go. You don't want to get stuck with those chores for the next six months."

"Are you still sure you want out of this marriage?" he teased.

"Because you kissed me? You think you have some kind of magic lips?" *He did.* But that wasn't enough. She needed more and she knew that sticking with Wes would prove to be a mistake that would likely break her heart if she let him.

He nodded. "I hate that it worked out like this."

"Me, too." She blew out a heavy breath. "I guess this is goodbye for us."

"Why do you say that?"

"I mean, you're not going to stick around now that the papers are signed. You've got your life in England. You're obviously going to London ASAP, right?"

"What makes you think I'm leaving? I'm not going anywhere. Believe it or not, I have my reasons for staying that have absolutely nothing to do with you."

He was right. She was being self-centered thinking it was all about her. But there was no doubt that her presence was at least part of his decision to come to Applewood. "We should get downstairs," she said. "I know I started this conversation, but I can't seem to think clearly when I'm standing next to you in a bedroom."

He chuckled. "You're not the only one." They shared

a moment where their eyes connected. He cleared his throat. "I guess I'll walk you out."

She nodded. "Please do." She was relieved to have had the conversation, and they were on their way to putting the whole sordid situation behind them. She'd signed the divorce papers, and he would do the same. Whether he was staying in Applewood for the next six months or not, she would have to learn to live with that without completely losing her head.

He headed out of the room, and she followed him. Coming down the stairs, they ran into Garrett and Dylan at the bottom.

Garrett looked at Daisy. Then at Wes. Then at Daisy again. "Is everything okay?" he asked her.

"Yeah, everything is fine," she told him, not sure if she was lying or not.

"You sure?" he asked only her.

"You heard the lady," Wes told him, his voice gruff. He pulled on a plaid flannel jacket. "We're fine."

Daisy nodded. "Enjoy your ride to the southern pasture," she told them. "If you haven't been out there in a while, you'll enjoy it. It's beautiful out there. I should be going."

"I'll see you later," Garrett told her. "Send me that bill, remember?"

"It's already on your tab."

"I'll see you later, Daisy," Wes said, and she wasn't sure if it was a promise or a threat.

She nodded, turned her back on the men and headed out the door. Daisy could feel Wes's eyes on her as she walked out of the house. Even though she wanted to turn look back at him, she forced herself to stare straight ahead, get into her car and drive away.

Along with Garrett and Dylan, Wes headed to the southern pasture to check on one of the grazing herds, and to see if there was an area that would be good for the new longhorns. He hadn't been on a horse since his teenage days. But it had felt natural getting back in the saddle. It was only his first day working on the ranch. He was absolutely exhausted, but his too-brief interlude with Daisy had left him energized. He hadn't been lying to her—there was nowhere else in the world he'd rather be than in bed with her—but he was in Applewood to prove to his family that he belonged. Reconnecting with his family, especially Garrett, and recharging from his burnout were too important to mess up. The invitation to ride with his brother and Dylan was a good first step.

He looked around at the sweeping, rolling hills of the ranch, and the majestic beauty of the land—it was an incredible, healing, change of pace. He thought of Daisy, how she looked, panting and wanton beneath him; his body still ached. If he could spend his nights in bed with her—hell, that would be an added bonus.

Wes was grateful for the silence that Garrett and Dylan gave him as he worked through his thoughts—

"Mind telling me what all that was?" Garrett asked, clearly tiring of that silence. "Why was Daisy in your room?"

"And why did y'all look like you'd just had a pretty good tumble?" Dylan added, with a laugh.

He grinned and cast a glance over at Dylan. He didn't want to get into it in the presence of someone outside the family. But Dylan was also Willa's brother and Garrett's life-long best friend.

"It's nothing," he told them, and both men looked at him like they knew the statement was the equivalent of what they typically shoveled out of the stable stalls. He knew he hadn't fooled them.

"It looks like y'all have some things to talk about," Dylan said, before giving his horse a command and galloping away. Wes liked the man, but was glad to see him go for now.

On their own, Garrett turned to face him. "You can tell me that it's none of my business, but you're my brother, and I would like a no-BS answer. I've been thinking about it. There must be something else going on with your visit here. You don't need the money from the inheritance, so where does Daisy fit into this?"

Wes gently pulled the reins, and his horse came to a stop, and Garrett did the same. "A few months ago, I went to Las Vegas for a convention. After it ended, I had a couple of extra days to have some fun. I was on my way to the blackjack table, when I saw a familiar woman sitting alone at the lobby bar of my hotel."

Garrett grinned. "Now the story's getting good."

"It was Daisy," he revealed, almost needlessly, he assumed.

"And you guys hooked up," Garrett stated.

Wes laughed. "*Hooking up* would have been one hundred times simpler than what actually happened."

Garrett's eye widened. "Why? What happened?"

Wes looked off into the distance and blew out a heavy breath. "We got married."

Garrett's mouth dropped. "What? Married?"

"Yeah, after too many shots, and too many hours in my suite, we decided to get hitched. I swear, it made perfect sense at the time."

Garrett laughed. "I'm sure it did. I can't believe you didn't tell me."

"It was probably for the best that we kept it quiet. Willa knowing is probably too much."

"Willa knew. I can't believe she didn't tell me."

"Don't blame her. Daisy only told her last night." He gave his brother a knowing look. "And if you wouldn't mind keeping it all under wraps, I'd appreciate it. We both know, better than most, how gossip works in this town."

"Yeah, definitely. But I'm your brother—you know you could tell me anything."

"I know." He paused. "But you know what happened to me here in town, with the fire. I didn't want you, or anyone else, to think I was the same screwup I was."

"I wouldn't have," Garrett protested. But when Wes gave him a look, he relented. "Okay, fine. I might have judged you."

Garrett blew out a breath between his rounded lips. "You're not off the hook yet. I need more," he told him. "You're married. To Daisy. That's pretty heavy stuff." He let out a small laugh. "I thought I knew how to complicate a relationship. You're looking at the poster child for a messed-up wedding," he said, talking about his own relationship with Willa, where they'd faked being a couple so that Garrett could take over the Hardwell Ranch and the rest of the family's business interests. "So, you and Daisy—what happened then?"

"After the weekend, we kissed and walked away from each other at the airport. But I never made any arrangements for a divorce. She did, though, and sent me the papers. I brought them with me, divorce but I haven't signed them. I didn't want to put that weekend behind me yet." He paused, not sure how much he wanted to say. He didn't want to appear too vulnerable. "That weekend was the best I've felt in a while. Work was piling up. We're working on some exciting projects, so things are intense. There's a lot of pressure hitting me. But that weekend… Well, I felt good, relaxed. I felt like maybe Daisy was the difference, you know?"

"Makes sense."

"I got off the plane with divorce papers and an urge to get to know the place I came from. I've been looking for ways to reconnect with the town I ran away from when the going got tough. Although…" He stopped as a realization struck him. "I guess running is what I do. This time, I came back to where I started."

The plan was that we'll get them signed, but I'm not sure that'll be the end of it, though. At least while I'm here. Hoping we can have some sort of *arrangement*."

"Sounds interesting, but I'd be careful with Daisy. She's had some bad luck in the relationship department."

"It's not a relationship—it's an arrangement," Wes corrected.

"You sure about that? I know how quickly these things can get out of hand."

"She's out-and-out told me she isn't leaving town."

"You could always stay here."

Wes guffawed a little too loudly, and then regretted it when his brother furrowed his brow at him. "I do think I'm going to enjoy my time here...

"But?"

"But it's the same as Daisy said. My life, my work, is in England. I can't trade it all in for a life in Applewood."

"What are you going to do?"

"Hell if I know. I know that I want her," he said. "But everything else is big question mark."

"If you're telling the truth, that means she's already told you that she won't be leaving Applewood. And if you won't stay here, maybe she's right. Maybe it's time for both of you to cut and run. Just sign the papers so both of you can get on with your lives."

"My brain knows that you're both right. But I just can't let her go that easily."

He looked at his brother, and saw that Garrett was now glowering at him. "Something wrong?"

Garrett shrugged. "Daisy's the best vet we've had in town for a long time—and our only vet right now. Plus, she's my wife's best friend. So now Willa is involved, so that affects me. If whatever you guys have going on goes sideways, I don't want it to mess up my working relationship with Daisy when you go home."

Wes frowned. *Home.* And by that, Garrett meant England. Wes knew that he was being dramatic, and even though he was beginning to feel more connected to the ranch, those words were the reminder he needed that Applewood, Texas, wasn't his home, and it never would be.

In the distance, Wes saw Dylan approaching on his horse. He soon closed the distance between them.

"I thought you guys got lost or something."

"We were on our way," Garrett told him.

"No need. Everything is good out that way. I'm going to get some of the guys to bolster the drainage ditches, but it should be a fine place for the longhorns."

"Thanks for checking on that," Garrett said. "Sorry we fell behind. We can head back." He turned to Wes. "You ready?"

Wes nodded. He felt that the conversation he'd had with his brother was one of the longest, most meaningful they'd ever had, but it had ended on a cautious note. His brother's words ran through his head, urging him to tread lightly when it came to Daisy. One wrong move could topple everything he was trying to rebuild.

Six

Daisy smoothed her palms down the front of her skirt as she walked across the full church parking lot and headed for the basement door. These events were always popular for among the members of the congregation, but as the minister's daughter, after attending them all these years, she'd grown tired of them. She took a deep breath and pushed open the door.

Her mother saw her and crossed the floor. Before saying hello, she gave a Daisy a cursory up-and-down look, appraising her outfit, and frowned.

"What's wrong with it?" Daisy asked, looking down at herself.

Her mother leaned in. "It's a little short," she whispered.

Daisy looked down again. The hem of the dress hit two inches above her knee, at most. "Are you serious?"

"Daisy, how are you going to find a nice husband if you come to these functions dressed like you're going to night club?"

Daisy pressed her lips together, willing herself not to say anything. If this was how her mother believed people dressed at night clubs, she wasn't going to be the one to explain it to her mother.

Her father came up them. "Bonnie, stop pestering our daughter." He pulled Daisy into a hug. "You look lovely, dear."

"Thanks dad." She looked around the room. "Nice turnout."

Her father nodded. "Yes, it is. It's nice to have these every once in a while. It brings the community together."

"Some people treat it like a dating game show," she cast a sideways glance at her mother.

"Oh, you. I mean well, Daisy, and you know it."

"I know you do, mom."

"I just don't want you to end up some unmarried spinster."

Daisy swallowed hard. What would her mother say if she knew her only daughter had gotten drunk and took a walk down the aisle in Las Vegas? "No chance of that happening." *For better or worse,* she added silently.

"Not if you don't get to looking now," her mother added. "You're in your thirties now. You might not have much time."

Daisy rolled her eyes, while her father chuckled, clearly enjoying the back-and-forth that took place whenever Daisy was in the same room as her mother. She looked around the room, looking for an out, a way to end the conversation and then she saw it—Wes, Garrett and Willa had come into the reception room.

"Mom, dad, I have to go," she said. "I'm meeting the Hardwells here."

"Okay, say hello to Willa for us."

"I will."

As quickly as she could, Daisy crossed the room. Garrett and Willa had stopped to speak to someone, and Wes stood alone. She stopped briefly to pick up two cups of her mother's fresh-squeezed lemonade.

"Fancy meeting you here," she said, offering one of the cups.

He accepted it, smiling down at her. "Thank you, darlin'." He sipped. "That's some mighty fine lemonade." He looked her up-and-down. "You look beautiful."

"Thank you. My mother says it's too short."

He looked again. "I think I'd argue the opposite."

"I thought you might."

He drank again. "Why was your mother talking about your dress?"

"She always looks at these things as a way for me to meet my future husband. She's trying to get me married off."

"Really?"

"Yeah, unfortunately."

"Well, all we have to do is tell her the truth," he teased. "We are married." He looked around. "Where is she?" He waved over. "Mrs. Thorne," he called.

She slapped his chest. "Stop it."

"What? It'll get her off your back, won't it?"

"Can you imagine what she'd say if she found out we got married in Las Vegas?" she finished in a whisper.

"You don't think she'd like me as a son-in-law?"

"She's never going to get to find out?"

He cracked a smile. "If I didn't know better, I'd say you were embarrassed of me."

"Not of you; just of what we've done." She looked around and saw that her mother was watching them.

He was looking down at her, the corners of his eyes creasing, his lips turned up in a playful grin. "What's that look for?"

"I think you're still that same good girl you used to be."

Her breath caught in her throat, and she felt herself unconsciously lean into his space. When Wes was around, she didn't much feel like a good girl.

"Are you okay?" he asked, his voice taking on a husky quality. "You look a little flush."

"No," she told him, backing away. "I'm fine."

"Daisy," she heard her mother call out her name. Turning her head to look over her shoulder, she saw her mother waving to her from across the room. She waved back, to say that she was coming.

"I have to go," she told Wes, before turning away. His hand on her forearm stopped her. "Before you go, Daisy. For what it's worth, I don't want you to feel embarrassed about what happened between us. It happened. We had fun cutting loose, though, right?"

His eyes burned into hers with an intensity that almost killed her ability to think. Little did he know that despite the fact that they'd gotten married, the weekend they'd shared in Vegas was one of the best in her life. "We did."

He removed his hand from her arm, and she had to look down to make sure he hadn't burned her. "All right, then. Promise me that you'll remember that."

"Liza, do we have any more appointments on the books today?" Daisy asked her administrator.

"No appointments," she told her. "And the evening techs just got in. You're free to go for the evening.

"Another free night?" Daisy asked. "Whatever will I do with myself?"

"Not too late to find a hot date," Liza suggested.

Daisy thought about it, but the only image she could conjure in her mind was of Wes. She'd managed to go a period of twenty minutes without thinking about him. "That sounds—" she checked out her jeans and plaid button-down shirt and considered how long it would take her to get ready for any kind of hot date "—like a lot of work."

Liza laughed. "Please, girl, you still look great."

"Kind of you to say, although I'm pretty sure you're just sucking up to the boss."

"Speaking of which, can I have Friday off?"

Daisy laughed. "Get Tony to cover your shift and it's all yours."

Once home, Daisy opened her door and was greeted by Ozzie. Again, paws on her chest. She was opening the back door for him when her cell phone rang. Picking it up, she saw Wes's London phone number on the screen. She rolled her eyes but couldn't help the pang of exhilaration she felt.

"Hello?"

"Hello, my wife."

Despite herself, she smiled. "What do you want?"

"Are you busy?"

She opened the door for Ozzie, who bounded into the house and took up residence in front of his food dish. She scooped kibble for him, and he ate voraciously. "No. I'm just getting home. What's up?"

"I need a favor."

"What is it?"

"I'm outside," he told her. "Why not invite me in?"

She looked out the window and saw that his car was parked behind her SUV in the driveway. He was standing beside it, leaning on the door, his phone to his ear. He waved. She considered inviting him in, but she knew that with anything he said to her, the evening would end with them in bed together. And she couldn't risk it.

"Are you stalking me now?" she asked.

"No, of course not. If you won't invite me in, come out. I've got something to ask you."

"For my hand in marriage?"

He chuckled. "It's too late for that."

"That's right. Sign those papers yet?"

"Not yet. We got a little distracted yesterday, didn't we?"

She thought about the how they'd parted the day before. They'd come close to sleeping together and definitely would have, had they not been interrupted. "Alright, give me a minute." Again, she looked at her outfit. Her wavy hair was in a ponytail, and she hadn't even considered putting on makeup when she'd left for work that morning. She would need a lot more than a minute.

"You look fine," he told her, as if he'd read her mind. "Get on out here." The low rumble of his voice rolled over her, and she closed her eyes.

"Okay, fine." She disconnected the call and walked outside. He was wearing a pair of well-fitting jeans and a white T-shirt that stretched across his chest and shoulders in a way that was pleasing to the eye. " You're still in town," Daisy noted with an impressed nod. "I'm surprised."

"You know, it's only been three days," he said. "But, of course, I'm still here. I'm here for six months, remember?"

"How was work?" she asked.

He put down his phone and held out his hands. They looked red, sore and calloused. His previously manicured nails were chipped. "I had a good day but it's definitely harder on the hands than my regular work. But luckily, I don't give up that easily."

"What's up? Why are you here?"

"I need your help."

"With what?"

"None of the clothes I brought are really fit for life on a ranch. I need to get a few things. I'd like your help choosing the right clothes." He must have sensed her hesitation. "Come on. It's just an hour of your time."

"Okay, fine." So maybe she did have plans for the evening. It wasn't exactly a hot date, but as she looked over the city boy in front of her, she knew that it could be a lot of fun. "There's a place called Cowboy Style not far from here, and it's open until eight. Let's go there. Just give me ten minutes to change."

It surprised Daisy when he didn't push for an invite inside, and instead stayed in the driveway while she freshened up. It surprised her even more that he didn't bring up their last conversation—that they would hook up. While Ozzie watched her from his favorite spot on her couch, she called the teenager next door to come over to walk and play with the dog while she was out. She felt bad leaving him alone after being at work all day.

Wes was leaning against the hood of his car when she came outside. He opened the passenger side door and she slid inside. He came around the other side and got in, and as he fastened his seat belt, she took a deep breath, taking in the scent of his cologne. It had depth—dark, earthy, expensive—and it triggered her senses, and elicited memories of three months ago, the way he'd touched her, the way he'd looked at her...

"It's crazy how much Applewood has changed since I left."

His words shook her from her reverie as they drove

by a short strip mall that held a couple of restaurants, a bar and a café. She nodded. In the past decade, the town had undergone many updates and changes—new businesses, townsfolk investing their money into growth, everyone coming together to create a place where people worked together to grow, while still maintaining a small-town feel. "Ah, yes, this is the Applewood dining district. It's great."

He nodded at the line of restaurants. "Pick the nicest place—maybe we'll have to get dinner sometime."

She didn't respond. With the way that sitting so closely next to him in the car was affecting her, she wasn't sure if she could handle sitting across a table from him.

Silence filled the car until Daisy pointed ahead. "The store is around the corner here. Turn left."

He did as she instructed, and they pulled into the parking lot of the shop. When parked, Daisy opened the passenger door and got out, but Wes hesitated, his eyes fixed on the storefront. "You coming?" she asked, leaning in through the now-open passenger door. "Or are you having second thoughts?"

He sighed and opened his own door. "I'm coming."

When Wes pulled open the shop door for Daisy, letting her enter first, they were greeted with the familiar twang of country music. "Hey, y'all," the perky store clerk greeted them. "Welcome to Cowboy Style. If you need anything, I'm Mandy."

He looked around and realized just how out of his

element he was. He stopped in front of a mannequin, dressed in Western garb. A button-down plaid shirt, a cowboy hat and boots with—he shuddered—spurs. He turned away and saw that Daisy was watching him with a playful smirk on her lips. He was there to commit—to his family, to the ranch lifestyle. And commit, he would.

"Thanks, Mandy. We'll let you know," he said, as Daisy led him to a rack of shirts.

"What's the kind of vibe you're looking for?" Daisy asked as they perused the racks. "*The Good, the Bad and the Ugly*? A little John Wayne?" She paused and removed a hanger from the rack. It held a red polyester button-down shirt with black embroidered embellishment on the chest and shoulders. "*Urban Cowboy*?"

He cringed. "Not quite. You know, maybe you won't be as much help as I thought you might be."

She laughed. "Alright. What are we looking for?"

"Something I can work comfortably in. But I also need some nicer things for when I'm not working. Things that won't make me stand out like a sore thumb."

She looked him over. "Yeah, I guess the designer labels aren't going to cut it, huh?"

"We've got a great selection of Wrangler and Carhartt outfits," Mandy called, obviously eavesdropping on them.

Neither Wrangler nor Carhartt featured regularly in his wardrobe. Wes frowned, but he looked at Daisy and saw she was smiling, clearly enjoying this.

"Come on, Mr. Gucci jeans," she said, taking his hand and pulling him across the store. "Let's make a rancher out of you."

With Mandy's help, Daisy loaded Wes's arms with a wardrobe suitable for a rancher. Denim, flannel, button-down shirts. Wes grumbled as he walked into the fitting room and pulled the curtain across.

A few minutes later, he came out wearing a pair of jeans and a navy plaid button-down. "Will this work?"

"It looks good," she told him. "It's the kind of thing everyone else is wearing."

"Yeah, I can put my chew tin in this handy front pocket," he joked.

She rolled her eyes. "I don't know a single person who chews tobacco," she told him. "Whether they work on a ranch, or not. You're such a snob."

"I'm not a snob. So, these are a *yes*?"

"Those are a *yes*," she told him. He turned to go into the dressing room, and she couldn't help but notice how the denim clung to his ass and thighs. "A definite *yes*," she confirmed.

He went inside the small fitting stall and pulled the curtain. But this time, he didn't close it the whole way, and Daisy couldn't help but notice that the narrow space allowed her a view of Wes as he removed the blue flannel. His skin was tanned, the muscles of his back rippled. She'd tried to forget about him, but all she could do was remember how he looked when they were in Las Vegas. He was still the perfect specimen of masculinity that she remembered.

Without warning, he turned, and she looked away, hoping she'd been quick enough that he hadn't caught her staring. But when she looked at him, the slow up-turn of his lips told her that she'd been caught.

"What about this?" He emerged wearing a pair of black jeans and a more formal buttoned shirt.

"That would work for a night out," she told him. "If you want to kick up your boots at Longhorns." She brightened, coming up with an idea. "I know exactly what it needs. Stay right there."

She went to Mandy for the appropriate items. When she returned, she was holding a pair of dark cowboy boots and a large belt buckle.

He chuckled. "You've got to be kidding."

"It'll complete the outfit, I promise."

Surprisingly, he listened to her advice. "How about now?"

"I don't know. There's still something missing." She looked around the store and then she found it. She plucked a gray cowboy hat from the head of a nearby mannequin, and reached up, placing it on his head. She took in his entire look. "Perfect."

"You think so?" he asked, checking out his reflection in the mirror.

Daisy examined him. Wes cut a fine form in his Western gear. He certainly looked the part of a cowboy. It was a far cry from the tailored business-wear she'd known him to wear, but the result was just as devastating. The material of the shirt clung to his chest and the denim jeans highlighted some of his greatest *as-*

sets... She swallowed hard and nodded her head with a bob. "Yeah, this is absolutely how you fit in here."

He shrugged. "Okay, fine. Let's get all of this wrapped up, then."

"Oh, not so fast, cowboy," she said, stopping him. "You've got a lot more to try on yet."

An hour later, Wes passed his credit card to Mandy, who was no doubt calculating the commission in her head.

"Anything else I can get you?"

Wes looked around the store. "Yeah, maybe there's one more thing." He picked up a tan cowboy hat, in a woman's fit. "I'll get this one."

"For who?" Daisy asked.

He put it on her head. "It's for you."

Her eyes snapped to the price tag. "I can't let you do that. It isn't necessary."

"Nonsense. You've been a great help today. I couldn't have done any of this without you."

"I picked out a couple of shirts for you to try on," she insisted. "Nothing more."

"You did more than that," he told her. She hadn't just helped him shop; she'd spent her evening with him. He couldn't help but feel as if he was under a microscope around the other guys, as they snickered and made comments about him being the *city boy*. It annoyed him but gave him the drive to work harder. He'd prove himself to all of them. He'd work harder, faster and better, and he wasn't going to complain.

Mandy rang up his purchases and placed his items

in shopping bags. After gathering all the bags together, including the boxes that included both his and Daisy's new hats, they walked out of the shop. It had been an expensive trip, but with Daisy's help and experience, he knew he had everything he needed to be a rancher. Well, at least he looked like one.

"Daisy, thanks for helping me out. I had fun."

"You know, I was skeptical, but I did, too," she said, settling into the passenger seat next to him.

"What do you mean *skeptical*?"

Daisy shrugged. "Maybe that wasn't the right word to use. But I was wondering if you were going to use the evening to try to get me into bed."

"Were you hoping for that?" She couldn't deny it, but she shook her head. He laughed. "I thought you wanted a *no-commitments* thing.

"I did. But I thought it would be a replay of our last conversation. Us talking about…" She trailed off.

"Our marriage," he ventured.

"Our mistake," she corrected. "It hadn't come up the entire time. And I think that's really what we need to talk about."

"I don't think it's a mistake yet. I'm here, aren't I?"

"For how long?" she muttered without looking at him, and she sighed. "See?" she said, throwing up her hands. "We had a great time until…that topic came up."

"I'm still having a great time." For a second, he took his eyes off the road to look at her. "Okay, let's stop talking about it. But I'll point out the fact that I just bought a couple of thousand dollars of clothing that I could never get away with wearing in my normal life in England." He laid a hand on her thigh. "I'm here now."

She nodded, but he knew that she didn't buy it. "Okay. Let's stop talking about it."

"Yeah, and let's enjoy the time we have together. Today proves we can do more than have sex and argue." His body heated at the mention of sex. He shouldn't have said it, but honestly, their nights together were never far from his mind.

"You forgot 'make bad decisions.'"

He chuckled. Daisy always made him laugh. "You remember what we said about bad decisions?"

"They make the best stories, right?" she said in response. After a few more beats, she spoke again. "But I have to admit, those were some great nights, though, weren't they?" she asked, her voice wistful, as she looked out the window at the passing scenery.

"They sure were."

"No reason why we can't do it again."

Wes almost drove his car off the road. "Yeah?"

"You mentioned having a honeymoon of sorts, didn't you?"

"Yeah, I did."

"That's all it can be. No commitments," she said, crossing her arms and jutting out her chin.

"What's that?"

"We can explore whatever this *connection* is between us, but it goes no further than that."

"That's what you want?"

"Is that what you want?"

"I think I can handle that. What do you have in mind?"

Before she could answer, they arrived at her home, a charming bungalow on a quiet street. He parked the car in the driveway behind her SUV. "Here we are," he announced.

She looked up at the closed door of her house. "So we are." She paused. "Do you want to come in? For a coffee?"

He knew that she wasn't asking him in for *coffee*, but he wanted her to say the words. "I don't know." He shrugged. "It's a little late for coffee. But if you can think of another reason I should come in… We can *talk* a little more about your proposition."

She opened the passenger side door, and stepped outside. Leaning into the car, she smiled. "I don't really want to talk. But I'm sure we can think of something to pass some time."

"Love that Southern hospitality," he said, getting out of the car and following her up the walkway to the door.

When Daisy opened the door to her home, she could feel Wes right behind her. The warmth of his chest on her back. He followed her inside. Ozzie was stretched out the length of the couch sleeping. He awakened, opened one eye and looked at them, then snuffed out a hello, before closing his eyes again and returning to sleep.

"Hello to you, too," Daisy said to the now-sleeping dog. "That's Ozzie," she explained, walking over to the couch. "Excellent guard dog, lover of bacon." She laughed. "Terrence, the kid next door, must have tired him out on their walk." She ruffled his fur.

Wes nodded. "He's a beautiful dog."

"Thanks. He knows it, too." She turned to face Wes. "Enough about him, though. He always gets all the attention."

He smoothed his palms over her hips and pulled her close. "It's a damn shame you feel you're lacking attention."

"That's never quite my problem when you're around." Her arms circled his neck, and she drew him near.

"Well, that's because I can't seem to notice anything else when you're near me. Let's go upstairs."

While her heart thundered in her chest, she had a moment of clarity. They shouldn't do this. She knew that after one more night with him, she would want more and more. Wes Hardwell was habit-inducing. But when he left Applewood—and he would leave Applewood—she would be left without him and suffering from a massive case of withdrawal. Part of her knew this, but the other part of her wanted nothing more than to take him to her bed.

He sensed her hesitation, and he drew a finger across the line of her jaw. "Daisy, do you want to do this?"

Did she? Before she could delve any further into her psyche, Daisy listened to what her body was telling her, and she nodded. She wanted Wes—*needed him*—no matter what was best for either of them.

He lowered his head and placed a soft, warm kiss on her lips. His fingertips grazed her cheek, went to her chin, and he tilted her head so that her eyes met his. "I need to hear you say *yes*."

"Yes," she said, her voice a breathless whisper.

In that one word, all of the wanting, waiting and yearning that she'd held on to for the past three months came rushing in. He held her closer, pulling her tighter against his chest. His lips landed on hers, and when she parted her own, he took full advantage. Swiping her tongue against his, she tasted him.

Not leaving his kiss or embrace, she walked him to the bed, until her mattress hit her knees.

He attacked her clothes. To help him, she raised her arms, and he pulled her top over her head, as she pushed down her leggings. Meanwhile, her fingers went to the buttons on his shirt, and they worked deftly to free every one. When she fumbled, he let loose with a rough growl and ripped off his shirt. The rest of their clothes soon followed, and Wes lifted her, holding her to his chest, and then laid her on the mattress.

He kissed her mouth, then over her jaw and down her throat, pausing at her breasts. He took one nipple into his mouth and dropped to his knees. He trailed kisses over her abdomen until he found her overheated core.

With his mouth, he kissed, nipped, lapped, until she was gripping her duvet. He brought her to the height of pleasure, and she cried out. He kissed his way up her body, and she wrapped her legs around his waist.

His body against hers was oh-so-familiar, as he retrieved a condom from the pocket of his jeans and primed himself before thrusting into her, transporting her back to that glorious weekend in Las Vegas, when it was just the two of them, some champagne and a hotel suite.

"Wes," she panted, throwing her head against the pillow. He took advantage of her exposed throat to press his open mouth against it. His body was warm against her as he moved inside her, again bringing her to a sexual high. His lips, his breath, were scalding hot, singeing her skin.

Soon, she felt the pleasure build low in her core. He stayed with her, until she came, crying out her release. He soon followed suit, with a satisfied grunt against her shoulder.

They stayed there like that for several moments, before he turned onto his side and took her with him. Daisy could have stayed there all night, but after several moments, he rolled away and got to his feet. For a moment, she thought he might be leaving, and the pang of need that tightened her chest worried her. But instead, he disposed of the condom and shucked off his jeans, before returning to the bed, now naked. Daisy couldn't help but admire his naked body. He was firm and ridged in all the right places.

He caught her staring and smiled. "I'm not a piece of meat, you know. Why are you looking at me like I am?"

"That was…" She trailed off.

"Amazing."

"Just like Las Vegas."

"Not entirely like Las Vegas," he noted.

"No."

"No. In Las Vegas, I remember there being a marble two-person shower and a large soaker tub."

Closing her eyes, she recalled the night he was talking about. Their first night together in Las Vegas, they'd taken advantage of the extra-large, walk-in, marble shower in his hotel suite, indulging themselves with the luxurious amenities. "You know, I've got a pretty standard shower. It's not marble, but I'm sure we can put it to good use."

"You're goddamn right we can." With those words, he scooped her up and carried her into her en suite bathroom. He pinned to her to the wall next to the stand-up shower stall, and with one hand, turned on the water.

He kissed her, and she kissed him back. She already knew that she would never be kissed that way by another man. When they parted, she looked up at him, through the steam that filled her small bathroom. "So have you finally scratched that itch?"

He wrapped his arms around her waist and lifted her into the shower. "Not by a long shot."

Seven

A few days later, Daisy parked her car outside of Willa and Garrett's ranch house. The past two days, she'd thought about her time with Wes. The sex the night before had been amazing. Not only that, though, she'd had a lot of fun shopping with him. No matter what they were doing, she and Wes had a good time together. Their budding friendship was just as important to her as their physical connection. No matter the how much Western clothing he bought, or how many nights they spent in each other's arms, there was no way he was sticking around Applewood. And she couldn't let herself get too close to him.

She'd grown up a preacher's daughter, and she'd been a model daughter to her parents. In her veterinary training, Daisy had travelled extensively, and lived in many different cities. However, no matter where she went, who she met, when it came to men, she had what her mother referred to as "a broken picker." Jerks, elitists, chauvinists, men more concerned with getting power and taking it from others—find a prototype of a bad man, and Daisy had probably dated him. She knew that Wes, CEO and co-founder of a billion-dollar company, had to fit in at least one of those categories, just because she liked him.

She took the bottle of wine and the pie she'd picked up at the bakery and headed for the door. Before she could juggle her items to reach for the handle, Willa came out on the porch and waved to her. "You're here! Sorry the invitation came at the last minute." She spied the bottle. "Ooh, good bottle. And pie!" Her friend's voice was high, her words coming out at a rapid speed, and Daisy wondered if there was something fishy going on.

"Thanks for having me. You know I can't resist someone else doing the cooking," she said as they entered.

"You're welcome here anytime," Willa told her.

She noticed Willa had set four places at the table. "Who all is here for dinner?"

"It's a small barbecue. Nothing fancy."

"That didn't answer my question."

"Fine. It's just Garrett and me. And you. And Wes."

She should have known. She and Wes had had an incredible night together a few days ago. But she hadn't seen him since then. He'd texted her, saying that the ranch work had kept him busy. Daisy wanted that to be fine by her, but she couldn't ignore the small niggling of hurt that budded deep within her chest. Already, her fears were being realized. If she let herself fall for him, it would break her heart when he went home. She had to remove her feelings from the equation.

"Well, that's convenient."

"He lives here. No reason we can't all have dinner together."

"Did you tell Garrett about Wes and me?"

"No, of course not. How's all of that going now? Did you get the divorce?"

"We're working on it." She recalled the day she'd visited, and they'd been *distracted* before they could continue with signing the papers.

"A few nights ago, Wes went out, but strangely didn't come home until the wee hours of the morning."

"What are you…sitting in the window watching him?"

She shrugged. "It's not hard to notice the things that go on here. He was with you, wasn't he?" Daisy said nothing, but Willa still took her silence as an admission of truth. Her friend's mouth dropped open. "And I'm going to need all the details." She nudged Daisy with her elbow.

"He needed a little help shopping," Daisy replied.

"And I'd say that your trip was successful, because he got some good pieces."

She knew how good he looked in everything he tried on. He looked good in everything, actually. *He looks even better in absolutely nothing.*

"We had a lot of fun."

"I'm sure you did."

She leaned forward. "And there was one point when he didn't pull the fitting room curtain the whole way, and I got quite an eyeful."

Willa laughed. "Not your first eyeful, though." They turned the corner to the kitchen. She saw that Wes was standing by the sink, holding a beer. When she entered the kitchen, their eyes connected. He was wearing one of the outfits that she'd helped him pick out and he was looking more and more like the rancher he'd told her he'd wanted to become.

"What's so funny?" Garrett asked when he heard them giggling.

"Just girl talk," Daisy replied.

Willa busied herself with putting away the pie while Daisy opened the wine. When she twisted the screw into the cork, Wes took the bottle from her and proceeded to uncork it.

"Hi, again, Wes."

"Daisy," he said with a slow nod. "Glad you're joining us." He was already adopting the mannerisms of a Texas rancher, and his drawl was growing stronger by the hour, it seemed. Daisy swallowed hard. She was already in trouble.

Daisy watched as Wes used his very capable hands to pour them wine. He handed a glass to each of the women.

Willa looked between Daisy and Wes with a grin on her face. She was clearly enjoying the awkwardness between them, and Daisy briefly regretted telling her what had gone on between them.

Willa took charge. "Garrett, why don't we go check the grill?"

"I just checked it," her husband said.

"We'll check it again," she told him.

Garrett seemed confused for a moment, but then a peculiar look passed over his face. He shrugged and followed his wife out of the kitchen, leaving Daisy and Wes alone. He was leaning against the sink, and she was pressed against the edge of the island, leaving only a foot of charged space between them.

"Long time, no see," she said ironically, unable to form any other words. She knew he could sense her awkwardness and was enjoying it. "I like your outfit."

"Thanks for helping me pick it out, but that wasn't the most memorable part of that night."

"No, it wasn't."

"I'm sorry I haven't called or come to see you. Things have been nonstop here."

"It's fine." She tried to sound as casual as she could.

"It's not very gentlemanly of me."

"It's a good thing no one's ever accused you of being a gentleman."

He laughed. "You have a point there. But it won't happen again."

"You don't have to make any promises to me. It's a casual thing. Why don't we agree that it's an I'll-see-you-when-I-see-you type thing? No need for all of these rules. It's just casual." She croaked out the last word, not feeling very casual at all, as she stood in front of him.

He leaned in. "Daisy, this is anything but casual.

And you know that. Try as either of us might, there will always be this tension between us. Like we're one breath away from ripping each other's clothes off. And plus, you're the one who keeps looking at me that way."

"Looking at you what way?"

"Kind of like you are now," he told her. "In a way that tells me that if Willa and Garrett weren't just outside, you wouldn't stop me if I lifted you up on the counter and took you right here."

She couldn't dispute that. She sighed. "This is already getting out of control, isn't it?"

"It might be." He gave her a lopsided grin. He took a step closer to her, took her wineglass from her fingers and pulled her closer to him. She was now pressed against his chest and his hands grasped her waist. She looked at him and saw the same heat that she was feeling build inside of her reflected in his eyes. Even though she knew they were in Willa's kitchen, and that she or Garrett could enter any second, Daisy couldn't help but press closer.

"Every waking moment since the last time I saw you, I've missed how you feel pressed against me," he murmured. His hips flexed lightly against her, and she could feel just how much he'd missed it. She hummed in response. His closeness triggered memories within her. Images of them—kissing, touching, smooth skin, strong muscles, lips on skin, fingernails raking tanned flesh—flashed in the forefront of her mind. Desire curled its way from her belly; she could feel it in her toes, her fingertips. Her hair stood on end from his nearness. Daisy's peripheral vision became foggy and just the two of them existed.

Just like always, he held her under some kind of spell, and no matter how much she'd managed to resist him and had tried to forget the heat between them over the last two days, she couldn't resist him. She was helpless. *Hopeless.* He lowered his head, and his lips brushed against hers. She'd had a taste of him, and now she wanted more. She lifted her lips to his and wrapped her arms around his neck, pulling him closer.

"Hey, y'all, steaks are done," Garrett announced, coming into the kitchen.

Daisy and Wes parted quickly as Willa and Garrett entered the kitchen, carrying platters of food from the barbecue. Garrett stopped at the door and narrowed his eyes. Had he seen them kissing? If he hadn't, she knew that he must have had some idea that he'd walked in on a private moment between them.

Wes lifted his beer and drank most of it. "Looks great," he said, taking one of the plates from Willa. "Let's eat."

Willa watched her closely, as if she had every idea of what they'd almost walked in on, but she thankfully remained silent. Which was good because Daisy wasn't sure she could respond in any coherent way. Without any sort of response, both Garrett and Willa followed him out of the kitchen, but Daisy was frozen in place. She felt the way she had in Vegas. When he'd completely intoxicated her, taken her over, stripped her of her senses. And one small kiss had been enough to want him to take her in the middle of her best friend's kitchen. She picked up her wine and drank it, then poured another glass for herself.

She could hear the three of them in the dining room, talking and laughing. Wes was acting like the kiss hadn't affected him. At least, not as strongly as it did her. Perhaps Wes was a better actor than she was. Daisy took another drink. When it came to Wes, she'd attempted to be strong, to stand her ground. But all it took was one kiss to fog her mind with desire.

Despite his insistence that he'd come to Applewood to work the ranch, she knew that part of the reason for his visit was to convince her to go to London with him. She told him she wouldn't, but a part of her knew that he was right—Wes could probably make her to do anything.

With everyone at the table, Wes was seated across from Daisy. He could still feel his heart racing from his encounter with her in the kitchen. She always managed to make his heart race. Hell, even just thinking about being with her made his body temperature rise substantially higher than that of the desert where they'd been married. He looked at Garrett, who was watching him, and Willa, who was watching Daisy, with an amused smile. She certainly had planned one messed-up family dinner.

"It's been a few days now, Wes," Daisy began. "How are you finding ranch life so far? Are you tired yet?"

Physically, he was exhausted, but he looked across the table at Daisy and his energy surged just thinking about the things he would have done to her in that kitchen. But he played it off. "I'm beat. It's definitely the most physically demanding job I've ever had."

"Yeah, I'll bet."

"It's a little tougher on the hands than my regular job," he responded. He put down his beer and held out his hands. Daisy's gaze dropped to his digits. He didn't need to be a mind reader to know exactly what she was thinking about. Just as well as Daisy could, Wes could imagine his hands on her body, gliding over her unbelievably soft skin, over every plane and curve of her body. The way she would giggle or moan in response, depending on where he touched her. He felt himself grow hard under the table. He realized he hadn't spoken in a while, so he took a big mouthful of beer, while Garrett handed him the platter that held the steaks.

"It looks like they're really putting you to work," Willa noted. "You've already cleaned out the grain silo. That isn't an easy job."

"In addition to mucking out the stables," Wes added.

Willa looked to Garrett. "You're seriously not giving your brother all of those kinds of jobs."

"Everyone has to do their share," Garrett said, defending himself.

"When's the last time you mucked a stable?" Daisy teased.

"Quiet, you." Garrett mock glared.

"The work is actually a lot more rewarding than I could have imagined." Wes sounded rueful.

"Yeah, for a change you're out of your cushy bubble and seeing what real life is like."

The positivity died in an instant. "What the hell kind of dig was that?"

"It wasn't a dig," Garrett said. "Just a comment. You left here the minute you could, barely ever setting foot on the land in the past decade."

Wes rolled his eyes. "Sorry I didn't sweat my ass off here with you, when I had other things to do." Wes hated the way this conversation was going. He'd resented being exiled to the ranch in his teenage years. He'd gotten up to no good, smoking behind the barn with Maverick Kane, the grandson of Elias's sworn enemy, chasing girls and just generally loafing. They were things that might be considered typical teenage stuff, but not in Applewood; not when he'd been a Hardwell. He'd been expected to work hard and show loyalty to the family, and when he didn't, it created problems.

As an adult, Wes had made his own choices. It was why he'd thrown himself into his business. It had even caused his burnout by wanting to prove himself right for leaving Applewood. Clearly, though, it hadn't been enough. He wished he hadn't brought it up. This conversation would serve only to dredge up terrible memories.

"Yeah, I know the things you got up to in high school," Garrett mumbled.

Wes set aside his fork and looked at his brother. "You know, I don't need this."

Garrett held out his hands. "Man, I'm razzing you. Relax. You're too uptight. I remember when you used to be a lot more fun."

"Guys," Willa said. "Enough. We have company," she said, gesturing to Daisy.

"Oh, don't mind me," she said, holding up her hands. "What's a family dinner without an argument?"

"Anyway, I'm just saying, around here, everyone does their share of the work," Garrett defended himself, leaving Wes still wondering if his brother was just having a bit of fun, or being a jerk.

"Willa, how're the renovations going at the inn?" Daisy asked, masterfully changing the topic to the old mansion that Willa and Garrett had bought a few months ago. The property had long ago belonged to Willa's family, and it was the only link she and her brother, Dylan, had to their past. She had been working hard to renovate the building and turn it into an inn. She still had a ways to go, but it would someday soon house beautiful accommodations and an event space.

Everyone listened as Willa talked about her project, but Wes clocked Garrett's words as the insults that they were. They raised his hackles and he wondered if maybe he'd made a mistake thinking he could reconnect with his brother on this visit.

Uptight. He was now the complete opposite of the rebellious young man he'd been in high school. That was what the family always said about him. But now he was *too* uptight. No matter what, he was never good enough for them.

When Willa was done talking about her inn, the room was silent, neither of the men offering any conversation.

"Sorry, Daisy." Willa shook her head at the two brothers, who were carefully ignoring each other.

"Don't worry about me," Daisy said. "I love a bit of family drama over dinner."

"Well, you're basically already family," Willa said. Wes's gaze whipped to his sister-in-law, and he watched as Garrett looked to Wes and then Willa. He could tell that Daisy had kicked her under the table. He looked at Garrett, who was still eating his steak, unaware of the drama occurring around them.

"Well, maybe that's why I came home, brother. To unwind a little. Take on some kinds of different work. To get in touch with my family and history." *And my wife*, he added silently to himself. "Elias wanted me to come home, so I did."

The table grew quiet, and Wes knew that he and Garrett had ruined dinner by making things tense with their bickering. But Wes found the silence preferable to the conversation that Garrett started next. "So that's the only reason you came home?" he asked with a sly grin on her face. "There was nothing else that brought you all the way from London?"

He glared at his brother, knowing that he was making his life difficult by teasing at spilling the secret of his relationship with Daisy. Willa and Daisy both looked at Garrett, clearly wondering what he knew, and Garrett looked at his own wife, wondering the same thing.

"I don't know, Garrett," he said. "I think that maybe the past few months have taught me to reevaluate my life. It was time for a change, and I think it's a good time to reconnect with this place."

Garrett drank from his beer, and then held the bottle aloft to him. "No matter what just happened here, forget about that. We're family. We're glad to have you on the ranch," Garrett said. "For no matter how long your stay is, and no matter what our history."

"Thank you, Garrett." He didn't want to reveal exactly how much that meant to him. "I feel it's definitely been a long time coming. I'm glad to be here, and I appreciate you welcoming me and teaching me what needs to be done around here."

Will a clapped her hands together once. "Well, now that that this is done, who wants desert?

When the dinner dishes were cleared, Wes and Garrett retired to the rec room to for an after-dinner drink, while Willa and Daisy stayed in the kitchen. They sat at the large marble-topped island, drinking coffee and eating pie.

Willa speared a piece of pie and popped it into her mouth. "Tell me about what we almost walked in on earlier," she said.

Daisy sighed and put her head in her hands. "This is such a disaster."

"Tell me."

"We're going through with the divorce, of course, but…" She paused, thinking about the as-yet unsigned divorce papers. "But we've agreed to still…hook up, casually. It's more about scratching an itch that we've both been feeling since Vegas."

"But?"

"But I feel like I'm already falling for the guy."

"What's wrong with that?"

"We've been through this—the geography, our priorities are different. I don't want that kind of relationship. I need someone who's one hundred percent in."

"Yeah, of course."

Daisy dropped her forehead to the tabletop. "What am I going to do?"

"What do you want to do?"

"I want to ask you and Garrett to leave your own home so I can mount him in your living room."

"Then why don't you?"

"Maybe suggesting a casual relationship wasn't the right idea. I can't waste any more of my time on a future that won't pan out."

"Why are you so sure that it won't work out?"

"It won't."

"But do you like Wes?"

"Yes, of course."

"Well, it's the twenty-first century. You can do long distance."

"I'm getting too old to have an internet boyfriend. We made a mistake. A quickie Vegas wedding isn't something I want. And what happens if we ignore our differences until it's too late? I know that if I let myself fall any deeper for him, he'll break my heart when he goes back to London."

"Well, I guess you know what you have to do," Willa said, her voice low.

"Yeah." Daisy knew that things couldn't continue

the way they were. In order to protect herself, she had to end things with Wes, cut it off entirely and get him out of her life. She picked up her purse from the chair, where she'd slung it earlier.

Wes walked into the kitchen, carrying a couple of empty beer bottles. Daisy saw that as a sign that she should leave while she still could. Before Wes had a chance to affect her in the way he normally did. "I should be going."

"So soon?" Willa asked.

"Yeah, sorry," she said, not looking up. "I've got an early morning."

"Why don't I walk you out?" Wes asked.

"No thanks," she said. "I'm good. Daisy, I'll call you tomorrow," she said before escaping from the kitchen. Though she wouldn't be leaving the memories behind her.

Eight

Daisy's strange exit from the house was still on Wes's mind two days later. It was a rare April scorcher on the ranch—according to Wes, who still hadn't become acclimated to the temperature difference from London, that is. Using a bandana, he wiped the sweat from the back of his neck. Again, he thought about Daisy, and how she hadn't answered any of his calls or responded to his texts.

He, Garrett and Dylan had taken another ride to the southern pasture to check on the longhorn herd that had been brought out there.

"It's a hot one," Garrett noted. "The longhorns seem comfortable enough. Though I'm getting pretty thirsty out here. And speaking of Longhorns…" Wes knew that Garrett was referencing the bar in town, and not the herd. "Why don't we head out to the bar tonight? Willa and Daisy are hanging out together, so I'm free."

"Have any plans tonight?" Dylan asked Wes.

"Are you kidding me? Of course, I don't have plans." Especially since Daisy wasn't talking to him, for whatever reason. The invite had been a long time coming from his brother. Even when they were kids, they'd gravitated to different groups. Garrett and Noah both spent time on the ranch, and hung out with like-minded kids, while Wes had taken a different path. As an adult, he regretted that he hadn't been closer to his brothers. "That sounds great. I could really use a night to relax."

Dylan laughed. "Yeah, you've got to check out that Applewood nightlife."

He'd gone to Longhorns a couple of times on his infrequent visits to Applewood. He could picture the dark, loud country bar. Applewood might be home to some of the richest ranchers in the country, but the popular spot to be was a dive country bar. "They still line dancing over there?" he asked.

"Why? Did you forget how?" Dylan asked.

In response, Wes flipped off his brother's friend, but he still smiled. "I guess I can find a video on YouTube as a refresher."

"Don't worry about it," Garrett said. "You know how it goes there—the same thing it's always been. Kickin' back, beer drinkin'."

"Boot scootin'?"

Garrett nodded. "Same old rodeo."

"I'm glad you're going. I need another single guy.

Since this one got married—" Dylan hooked a thumb at Garrett "—I'm in need of a wingman."

Wes grinned. Little did Dylan know that Wes was also married. "Been a while since I've been a wingman, but I'll do what I can. Sounds like a good time," Wes said. "I'm in." They started in the direction of the ranch, but Wes hung back. "You know, I'm going for a bit of a ride before I head in."

"Want anyone to come with you?" Dylan asked.

"No." Wes waved him off. "I'm good. I'll see you at the main house."

Riding gave him quiet time to think—about his business, his family, his obligations to Elias. Daisy. His thoughts always circled around to her. The divorce papers were still sitting on top of the dresser in his bedroom. He should sign them. But he couldn't bring himself to do it. If he signed them, there was no reason why she wouldn't waltz out of his life just like she did after that barbecue. He blew out a frustrated breath. Whenever they were in the same room, they couldn't keep their hands off each other. It definitely complicated things. He should learn to behave himself, give her the divorce she wanted and go back to England, even if it meant bailing on the ranch and his relationship with his family.

But there was no chance of him doing any of that. Not yet.

Instead of riding over the Hardwell ranch land, he opted instead to head outside the ranch's boundaries. He traveled the gravel driveway down to the main road. He chose a direction and randomly headed eastbound.

He rode for several minutes, until he came to the fence of the neighboring ranch—the Kane Ranch.

The rivalry between his own grandfather and Corwin Kane went back decades. Wes was never quite sure what had happened between the two men—as far as he understood, they had once been close friends and partners, but the business had come between them and now the bad blood between the families ran as thick as the oil that Kane had found on his land.

There was someone at the end of the Kanes's driveway, a man on a horse. His hat was pulled low, and the brim obscured most of his face. He had to get close before he realized who he was looking at. It was Maverick Kane, Corwin's grandson, and an old friend from Wes's days as a hellion.

"Well, if it isn't the old devil, himself," Maverick said in greeting.

Wes stopped his horse. "Nice to see you, Mav. How are things?"

"Can't complain. I just took over this place from my grandfather. I hear your brother did the same."

"Yeah, the old man finally retired. I'm sorry to hear about your grandfather." Wes had gotten word that old man Kane had passed away a few months before.

"Thank you. He should have gone sooner, but the old bastard was more stubborn than a mule," he said with a laugh. Wes joined him, thinking about the hard Kane patriarch. He'd had a reputation in town of being hard to deal with, impossible to reason with. "I moved here to take the place over. So, what brings you to Texas? I never thought I'd see the day."

"It was time to come home," Wes told him, settling on the vague answer he gave everyone else.

"Make up for past deeds, huh?" Maverick asked him.

It surprised Wes that Maverick knew exactly what his goal in Applewood was. "Yeah, something like that."

Maverick nodded. "Yeah, I'm on a little goodwill mission myself here. That kind of stuff follows you in a place like this."

"Yeah, that's what I was afraid of."

"We used to have some wild times here, didn't we?" Maverick cracked a smile.

"We really did. It was definitely time to grow up when we did."

"Yeah, that fire changed a lot of things. It could have been so much worse."

Wes sobered and nodded. Their careless act of smoking and discarding their still-lit butts in a pile of dry hay had almost cost both of their family ranches. Wes had been a rebellious kid, and the most rebellious thing he did was become friends with Maverick.

"Listen, I've got to get to work. Updating this place is like having four full-time jobs."

"I'll leave you to it, then. Nice seeing you."

"Why don't we get together some night? We'll have a couple of beers, catch up, trade some old war stories."

"Yeah, I'd like that."

"Why don't we meet at Longhorns tonight?"

Wes smiled. Despite what his family thought of the Kane family, Maverick always had always accepted him. "Alright. I'll see you there."

Nine

As predicted, Longhorns hadn't changed much in the past several years. The music was loud, blaring out country hits from the 90s, and the crowd was raucous. Everyone was having a good time—drinking, dancing, unwinding after a long week on their respective ranches.

"There's a table," Wes said, pointing to an empty booth across the floor. A server had just finished cleaning it and they quickly took up residence.

"What can I get you fellas?" the waitress asked, obviously running her eyes over each of them.

They each ordered a beer, and when the waitress was gone, they quietly scoped out the place.

Garrett picked up his phone and read the screen. "Willa just messaged me. She's coming by here soon.

They're on the way." Garrett turned to him. "Daisy's coming with her. It's a girl's night," he said with a pointed look at him.

In Wes's experience, a girls' night would take place in place separate from their men, but Applewood was short on social venues. "Well, I hope they have a fun night together," Wes said, without meaning it.

"I'm sure you do." Wes knew that Garrett was playing with him. Maybe this wouldn't be the fun, relaxing night he'd envisioned.

"I'm going to go get a beer," Wes said, pushing himself from the table.

"We just ordered beer," Dylan reminded him as the server approached them, three bottles balancing on her tray. She put the beers on the table in front of them.

Wes picked up one of the bottles by the neck and drank from it. "Well, I'm going to do a lap around. See if I recognize anyone." He'd made plans to see Maverick tonight, but Wes knew he was going to look for Daisy.

Garrett shrugged. "You do you, man."

Wes stood and walked around the bar, checking out the patrons. There were many he didn't recognize. A lot had changed since he had spent any time in Applewood as a teenager. He saw Maverick talking to a woman at a high-top table. He waved and moved on. He didn't see Daisy, and he couldn't help but feel disappointment.

"Well, if it isn't Wes Hardwell."

Wes heard the voice behind him, then turned his head and smiled when he saw some of his old friends,

Kyle and Darrin. They'd also run around with him and Mav, chasing girls and causing trouble.

"Hey, fellas," he said, shaking both of their hands. "How's it going?"

"Just fine," Darrin responded. "In fact, I opened a bookstore on Main Street."

"And I've been with the fire department for a few years now," Kyle said.

"That's great news. I had no idea either of you stuck around. We were all pretty set on getting out of here the minute we could."

Darrin laughed. "And you're the only one who did."

"Well, I left for a hot second," Kyle said. "Darrin here stuck around. But you know, it's hard to stay away."

Wes nodded. Up until a couple of weeks ago, he hadn't thought that—but now, he thought there might be something to that. Out of the corner of his eye, he saw Daisy and Willa enter the bar. Maybe it was Daisy who made him feel that way, but maybe there was something about the small town that had him seeing it in a different, more positive light. "Yeah," he said. "I can definitely see that."

"How long have you been back in town?" Kyle asked.

"A little over a week. Just long enough to get my footing."

"It's been a long time since you've spent any time in these parts."

"Yeah," he admitted. "The last time I was here was for my brother's wedding."

"What brings you back?"

He hesitated, and across the bar, his eye caught Daisy's. "I've got some family matters to take care of." They must have thankfully taken the hint that he didn't want to get into what those specific *family matters* were. "I figured it was time. At least for a little while."

"Sounds intriguing," Darrin said, taking a drink from his glass.

"It's definitely something to get into at another time."

"I can understand that," Kyle agreed. "Why don't we all get together sometime. We can really catch up."

Wes smiled. He hadn't seen it coming, but it was nice to see some of his former friends. "Yeah, that sounds fun."

"I hear you're working on the ranch?" Darrin asked.

He nodded. "I've been working with Garrett, doing some odd jobs on the ranch."

"Rebuilding those old barns that we burned?" he asked with an embarrassed laugh. "Man, we raised a lot of hell back in those days, along with Maverick."

"Who is still raising hell, I hear," Kyle added.

Wes didn't think any of what had happened in the past was quite as funny as his old friends did. They'd screwed around quite a bit back in the day. But the day of the fire was one of the worst days of his life. Every other thing he'd done up until that minute had just run off his back like water, but the disappointment on the faces of his parents and grandfather had been enough to make him tuck his tail and get the hell out of town. That was one of the reasons that no one took him seriously here. He'd grown up as a rebel in Applewood, and that was even before the fire he'd accidentally started on the ranch. No one had been injured, nor had any of the animals, but he knew that he would still have the reputation of bad seed. The one with bad intentions. He tried to laugh it off. "Those have long been rebuilt. But thanks for your concern."

"Remember all the crap we used to get up to as kids?" Kyle asked.

Wes nodded. He sure did remember those days. Skipping school, bailing on ranch work, drinking and smoking with his friends under the bleachers at the high school football field. He'd bought a motorcycle; a helmet replaced his cowboy hat and completed the bad ass look with a well-worn leather jacket. All those things had made the town wary, but the negative attention from the fire had been enough to turn the people of Applewood against him. No amount of goodwill based on his last name had been enough to reverse it. The name Wes Hardwell was as good as dirt in Applewood. So, he'd done what any cocky eighteen-year-old boy would do when sulky and challenged by authority—he got the hell out of town, and never looked back.

His attention again snagged on Daisy across the bar. *Until now.*

"What have you been up to all these years?" Darrin asked.

Wes was enjoying talking to his old friends, but all he wanted to do was cut the conversation short and jog across the bar to Daisy. Whenever she was in the room, his attention was immediately on her. But he turned his attention to the conversation. "You know how it goes. I left Applewood; I went to college in England, started a business and stayed there." He looked past them again and saw Daisy and Willa standing next to a high-top table. "It was great running into you guys. We should get together again soon." They shook hands and made plans to meet later.

Wes moved on and it only took a few seconds before he was making his way across the floor. Toward Daisy.

"I'm glad you could come out tonight," Willa said to Daisy as they looked around the busy bar. It was pretty much the only place in town to have fun on a Friday night, even though the decor, music and clientele hadn't changed much since 1995.

"Thanks, I haven't had much free time in the past little while," she admitted. She'd been working so many hours at the clinic; she was even putting serious thought into recruiting a partner.

Glancing around the room, her gaze stopped on Wes, who was talking to two other men. He drew her attention like no other man ever had. With her eyes on Wes, she and Willa made their way to the bar and the cute bartender came right to them. They both ordered vodka and soda and took up residence at a high-top table.

"So, I see where your eyes went. You want to talk about the fact you're still married to my brother-in-law?"

"Don't remind me. He hasn't signed the papers."

"He's stubborn."

"Is he ever. It's too bad, though. He's hot, funny, we have fun."

"Where exactly is the problem, then?"

Daisy sighed. "Nothing else about him or this situation fits into the list." She picked up her phone and opened the notes app, then showed it to her friend.

"What is that?" Willa asked.

"It's my list."

"What kind of list?"

"I spent so much of my twenties bouncing around and coming back here to Applewood after college, and opening the clinic is the most stability I've ever had in my life. I made a list of everything else I want."

"Okay, tell me what you want."

"I want to be married."

"We'll, you're already married, so you can cross that one off."

"Very funny. But you know how traditional I am. I want the big family wedding. Not just some quick drunken Vegas romp."

"Noted. What else?"

"I wouldn't mind a couple of kids. Learning how to ride, spending time in nature. They could never do any of those things in the city"

"A city like London, you mean." Daisy didn't respond. "Okay, fine, the mythical guy on this list. Tell me about him.

"Hmm. He's sexy, rugged, can absolutely bowl me over with just a kiss." She stopped and exhaled heavily.

"What is it?"

"Wes fits that best," she admitted.

"So why are you looking for a divorce? Why not pursue a real relationship with him? Make it make sense."

Daisy gestured to the crowded bar. "Look around. You can't throw a rock without hitting a good-looking guy in this town, one who's settled here and wants to stay. And that's the thing. You know as well as I do that Wes won't be in town long. Sure, he might be here for six months, at most. As much as I like him, he can't give me what I need—romance, stability, the country life I want for me and my family. That's why I need him to sign the papers and get out of my life before I do something stupid like fall for him. He reminds me of what I desire, and that's not what I need."

Daisy saw Garrett come up behind Willa and hug his wife from behind. Speaking of a man a woman needed. She was happy that Willa had found a man who was so perfectly matched for her. She looked at their closeness, and it was something she wanted for herself.

"Hey," Willa said, turning in his arms. They kissed.

Daisy looked away to give them a little privacy, but instead her gaze latched on to Wes. He turned his head and they locked eyes, making her wonder if he could feel her thinking about him. She'd felt his presence the minute she'd walked into the bar. The connection between them was tough to ignore.

"Thanks for messaging," Garrett said. "I didn't realize you guys were coming out here tonight, too. I just wanted to say hi." He turned to Daisy, momentarily forcing her attention away from Wes. "I'll be getting out of here soon. I don't want to interfere in your girls' night."

"Yeah, you'd better get out of here. Girls only," Willa teased.

Daisy watched Wes leave the group he'd been speaking with, and knew he was headed straight for her.

Not wanting to give Garrett any more fodder for teasing, she stepped away from the table. "You guys get five minutes," she warned. "Make out all you want. I'll be back," she told them, then headed outside. One quick but seductive glance over her shoulder told her that Wes was following closely. She knew they should stay away from each other, and she reminded herself that they didn't have any kind of a future. But when she laid eyes on him, none of that seemed to matter. When it came to Wes, nothing mattered to Daisy but getting her hands on him.

Outside, there was a bit of a chill in the night air, and Daisy wished she'd remembered to bring a jacket. She folded her arms across her chest as she made her way to an empty table in the far corner of the patio.

"It's cold out here," he said behind her. She didn't turn to face him, not even when he put his jacket over her shoulders. She inhaled, and took in the faint notes of his cologne, and a scent that was purely him.

"Hi, Wes," she said, watching him over her shoulder.

He turned and smiled. "Hello again, Daisy."

"You somehow keep turning up," she noted playfully.

"What can I say—it's a small town."

"That might be true, but you followed me out here, didn't you?"

"I can't argue with that. Any sane man would follow a woman like you anywhere, Daisy."

Even the way he said her name made her heart stutter. But several breaths stilled it to a normal rhythm. "We need to talk," she told him.

"You always say that."

"It's always true."

"We could have talked a few nights ago, but you ran out after the barbecue like you'd been asked to pay the bill."

"Let's go over here." She gestured to a dark, empty area away from the building. "You know how people talk. I don't think we need an audience."

He pointed to a more private spot near the side of the building. "Let's go over here."

The place where they stood was lit solely by the yellow glow of the bulbs that hung over the patio, and because they were farther away, the light cast a golden glow that slanted across the bottom half of his face and highlighted his square jaw and full lips, which turned up in a grin.

"We made a mistake…" she said, trailing off.

"In Las Vegas."

"No, not just then." She shook her head. "Man, all we seem to do is screw up massively."

"That's one way to look at it."

"The mistake we made was deciding to keep seeing each other casually."

"I don't see it that way."

"Of course, you don't."

"I think that agreement proves that we still have a pretty powerful connection."

"It's only physical."

"I still fail to see the problem."

"And that's the problem. I need more than that." He stepped closer to her, near enough for her to feel the heat from his body. She pulled his coat tighter around her shoulders so that he was surrounding her completely. "You complicate my life," she revealed, not even realizing that was what she was going to say.

It also clearly wasn't the response he'd been expecting, and he tilted his head to the side. "What do you mean?"

She shook her head, trying to piece together the words and put them in the proper sequence. "My life is here in Applewood. I have a home here, friends, family, my dog, my practice. I never questioned that or felt any different—this is where I belong. And then you ride in here, say some nice words, touch me like you do, and you make me question that. As much as I know that we need to part ways and get on with our lives, I take one look at you, and I don't want to." Daisy exhaled heavily. Holding on to all of that had been a burden, and letting it go made her feel much lighter.

Wes quietly watched her for a while and, unable to handle the scrutiny, she looked away from him. Putting his fingers to her chin, he drew her attention back to him. "Thank you for sharing that. And I'm not here to make you do anything you don't want to do. I was having some fun. But if it means that much to have it all squared away, I'll sign the papers, and get them to you tomorrow."

"Thank you."

"But I'm still going to be here. I still agreed to stay here for six months. I'm not going anywhere."

"I know."

"And I can't promise I'll be able to stay away from you."

She sighed, but that fact didn't make her unhappy. "I know that, too."

Daisy closed her eyes. Despite everything she'd told him, with Wes in front of her, his fingers on her chin, everything he said was pretty darn tempting.

"Let's start over," he told her.

"Start over?"

"We can put this whole mistake behind us and do it all over."

"Nothing's changed, though. What kind of future will we have together?"

"We can have any sort of future we want."

"You know that my life is here," she told him.

"And mine is in England. But why don't we worry about that later?" He drew her near, and she felt herself melt against his chest. His lips lowered to hers. He kissed her gently, stealing her breath from her lungs.

His kiss was full of fire and strength. He pinned her against the side of the truck as his tongue explored her mouth, entwining with her own.

"I haven't been able to stop thinking about you," he confessed.

"Me neither," she told him, and they kissed again.

Each kiss between them got more frantic, more desperate than the last. "Wes," she whispered, and she knew that if she wasn't careful, she would be gone.

"What?"

His lips found an oh-so-sensitive spot on her throat, and Daisy hummed in satisfaction. She almost forgot about her friend and their plans. But then she found the resolve to not let herself be completely taken outside of Longhorns. She put her hands on his chest and regretfully pushed him lightly. "Not right now. We can't do this here."

"You're probably right. Let's go."

"I should go find Willa and let her know I'm leaving. She's by herself."

"Garrett's inside, she'll be fine." He took her hand and led her to his rental car. "You can text her on the way."

Ten

The interior of the car on the short drive to Daisy's was fraught with tension. Daisy felt herself all but vibrate with need, and her fingers shook as she texted Willa.

Something came up, she wrote, intentionally vague. I had to take off.

The response came less than a minute later. I saw Wes follow you outside. I can only guess what came up. ;-)

Daisy laughed to herself and put her phone away, just as Wes pulled into her driveway, parking his car behind her own.

They walked inside, and Ozzie, feeling more energetic than he had the last time Wes had come over, greeted them at the door. He jumped on Wes's chest, and he laughed and scratched him behind his ears.

"Sorry about that. He knows he isn't allowed to jump."

"I don't mind."

Daisy gave Ozzie a bone and the dog promptly ignored them. "Now that he's occupied…" She turned to Wes, and wrapped her arms around his neck, pulling him close for a kiss.

Wes didn't need to be told twice. He turned his attention to Daisy's mouth. Her lips were red and full, and she lasted like heaven. He pulled her closer to him. As his mouth took hers, he felt her smoothness against the roughness of his jaw, and he hoped he wasn't scratching her delicate skin.

Putting both of his hands on Daisy's hips, he lifted her, and she wrapped her legs tightly around his waist. Pinning her to the wall with his upper body, Wes ran his hands over her thighs. Her short skirt shifted up her thighs, exposing the bare skin, which was softer than he'd remembered. Every time with Daisy felt like the first time.

He smoothed his hands up her thighs and when he trailed a couple of fingers to her center, he discovered her ready for him. He damn near swallowed his tongue with need for her. He didn't care if they were married, annulled, friends with benefits; all he knew was that he wanted her and there was nothing that would stop him from having her.

At his touch, Daisy gave a small cry and tossed her head against the wall. The muscles of her thighs quivered and tightened around him, gripping his waist like a vise as he touched her. He watched her react to his touch, and he loved how responsive she was.

He reached into his pocket for the condom he'd put there before leaving the house. He lowered his zipper, and in record time, he rolled the condom over his length and pushed into her. Wes raised Daisy against the wall and thrust in and out.

Daisy gasped. Her quick intake of breath was raspy and loud in his ear. The feeling of Daisy was so great, so intense and hot, *every time*, that he dropped his head and groaned into the crook of her neck. Then he pulled his hips away, withdrawing himself and then sliding into her, filling her again. Whether he wanted to admit it or not, Daisy did something to him. He'd never experienced any pleasure greater than being with her, and he didn't know what exactly he would do when it was time for him to leave Applewood and go home.

Wes could feel the pleasure rising low in his stomach as he pumped in and out of her, and the heat of his oncoming orgasm could be felt radiating through his limbs. He knew he would soon come, but it also felt like he could go on with her forever. He felt her clench around him, signaling her oncoming climax, and it was enough for Wes. Daisy cried out, and he ground himself against her, finishing as well with a hoarse shout.

Breathing heavily, Wes rested his forehead against Daisy's shoulder, which was also heaving. Wes heard a sharp whine, and quickly rose his head, thinking he'd hurt Daisy. But when he looked down, he saw Ozzie staring at them. His bone laying at their feet, and the dog demanded attention.

"Was he there the whole time?" he asked, lowering Daisy to the floor while he tossed the condom in the trash and adjusted his clothes.

Daisy laughed. "Yeah, probably. Is that a mood killer?"

"Not for me," he told her, before pulling her over her shoulder and heading upstairs.

Eleven

It was just daylight when Wes climbed the stairs to his bedroom in the main house of Hardwell Ranch. It was Saturday, and even though work on the ranch never stopped, he could take a day away from the duties, but the workaholic within him tried to tell him otherwise. However, he couldn't feel bad spending the night with Daisy. In his room, he found his discarded cell phone on top of the dresser and, seeing it needed charging, plugged it in.

He headed for the bathroom and turned on the water. Stepping underneath the spray, he grimaced at the sting of the hot water. His night with Daisy had been incredible, like every time they came together. He remembered why he'd asked her to marry him after only one night those months ago.

She'd taken over his rational thoughts, made him lose control. If he was smart, he would cut and run, get out of town before she asked him to stay forever, because he surely would if she asked. She'd explained to him what she wanted—a commitment, and a man who would settle here, one who wasn't going to leave town… Which was exactly what he was planning on doing once his six months were up. Although, small-town life had become more appealing to him.

He turned off the water and wrapped a towel around his waist. In his bedroom, he powered on the phone and saw several text messages from his partner, Bryant, telling him to call him back.

Wes rang him.

"About time you called me."

"Sorry, I didn't realize you needed me to check in."

"Mate, you've been in Texas for a little over a week, and we've spoken, what, one time?"

"Yeah, I'm sorry I haven't returned your calls. I've been busy."

"Yeah, me, too. I'm keeping everything afloat out here, while you're living out your cowboy fantasies."

"Is there a reason you were calling me all night?"

"Yes, while you're gallivanting around on horseback, I've been talking to some people."

That piqued Wes's interest. "Which people?"

"Remember the meetings we had with TotalCom before you left for the dude ranch?"

Wes rolled his eyes at the slight, but he knew of the meetings they'd had with the communications giant. "Yeah, of course."

"Well, we are *this close*—" Wes pictured Bryant holding his thumb and forefinger close together "—to forming a partnership with them to launch a new social-media platform."

That stopped Wes. "Are you being serious right now?"

"As serious as a heart attack. You need to get over here. You know how old school their CEO is. He's in London now and wants a meeting."

"I can jump on Skype."

"No Skype. It needs to be in both of us in the same room so we can talk this thing over."

"When?"

"Today." Wes heard Bryant let out a heavy breath on the other end, as if he expected Wes's reluctance. "Listen, Wes, if we're doing this, I need you here. Maybe not full-time, but at least most of the time. I know you said you'd be in Texas for six months, and while I agreed to cover for you, given this shot we have with TotalCom, we might need to revisit that."

"I'm not going to bail on this. It's too big."

"All right. Get your ass back here and we'll get it sorted."

"Sure thing," he said, hanging up the phone. He knew that he had to return to London, but he was already dreading the thought of leaving Daisy.

Wes thought about his promises to Daisy. He was supposed to be cooking dinner for her tonight. But if he was smart, he had to get his ass to London, and make the moves to the biggest business deal of his career. It would mean everything to them—money, prestige—

and it would put Intel-Matrix Communications on top of the tech world. He couldn't pass up the opportunity, and Daisy would surely understand.

Right?

Daisy was seated at her kitchen table, drinking her coffee, when she saw Wes's car pull into her driveway. She smiled, reminiscing about the night they'd spent together, and thinking ahead to tonight, when he would cook her dinner.

He jogged up the walk and she met him at the door. "Hey, what's up? I didn't expect to see you until tonight." She took in the frown on his face. "What's wrong? Is everything okay?"

"Yeah, it's fine," he said. "It's about dinner tonight."

"What is it?"

"I'm just going to say it—I need to go to London today."

That took her aback, but she tried to cover her disappointment. "Oh."

He put up his hands. "It's only going to be for a couple of days. My partner and I have an amazing opportunity. There are some meetings I need to attend."

"It's okay."

"You're upset."

"No, I'm not upset," she lied. "If you need to go, you should go." He'd said that he was only going to be gone for a couple of days, just like he'd said. But it made her realize that anything they had wouldn't be permanent.

He reached out and cupped her upper arm with hand. "I'm coming back,"

"If you say so," she said with a shrug.

"Don't do this, Daisy. It's a business trip."

"It's not a business trip when you're going to the city where your business is located."

"Tell me what you want me to do."

"I want you to do what you need to do," she told him, taking a step into her house. "You said this was an opportunity. I want you to go. I don't want to be the reason you have to stay. Why don't you call me if you come back?"

He exhaled. "*When*, Daisy."

"What?"

"You said *if I come back*. I'm coming back."

"Well, then, give me a call when you do."

He sighed. "I had an amazing time with you last night," he said.

Despite her best effort, her smile was sad. "I did, too."

"And I meant every word I said."

"About?"

"About us starting over. We can still do that. I need some time to deal with these business matters. We can still try that, right?"

She nodded. "Of course."

He put his hand on her waist and drew her nearer. "I promise, I'll cook you dinner when I get back."

With his arms around her, she was able to forget how she felt about him leaving. "Okay, fine."

He kissed her and she almost collapsed against him. But he pulled back. "I have to get to the airport."

She nodded. "Have a safe flight."

"I'll call you when I get there."

"Yeah, text me when you get home." She hadn't meant to say it, but she was sad, annoyed, irritated at herself letting herself believe—ever so briefly—that they could have something.

"Sure."

He turned and walked away from her. She closed the door, knowing that everything she'd feared had happened. She'd fallen for him, and even though she knew he'd return, she felt like it wouldn't be for long.

Twelve

When Wes opened the door to his condo, it was a familiar comfort to him. As much as he'd grown to like living at the ranch and Applewood, he couldn't help the way that that London still felt like home to him. And that reminded him of Daisy…and how settled she was in Applewood. This would never be her home. But all he could do was what he'd said to her the night before—take it one day at a time. And today, he had to focus on the partnership that could potentially make him a billionaire.

He'd been working non-stop leading up to his trip to Applewood and hadn't spent much time there in the days and weeks before. He walked farther inside, but when he opened the fridge door, he regretted not arranging for a housekeeper to give the place a cleaning, when he smelled the weeks-old take-out boxes he'd accidentally left behind. He quickly disposed of the leftovers.

He picked up his phone and sent a text to Daisy, telling her that he'd arrived at his condo safely. He thought briefly about calling. He would love to hear her voice. He'd hated the look on her face, the sound of disappointment in her voice when he said he was leaving, after just spending the night with her. Her response was cordial, telling him to text when he got home, but he could almost hear her emphasis on the word *home*. He knew that she was disappointed in him.

He had to put it aside for now and focus on the deal with TotalCom, and make it happen. He dialed Bryant's number and waited for his friend to answer the phone.

He did after two rings. "You'd better be calling from your flat," he warned.

"You know I am."

"Great. Now that you're done with your dalliance in Texas, we can get down to business." Clearly, Bryant didn't know the extent of his trip to Texas, and his reasons for going back—to collect his wife.

"Do you want to grab a bite, or something?" he asked, not ready to get into what he'd been doing on his time away.

"Sure. I could eat."

"How about the Black Sheep?" Wes asked, suggesting a nearby pub they'd often frequented.

"Sounds good to me. See you there."

* * *

An hour later, Wes was sliding into a booth at one of his favorite pubs. It was a dark, raucous dive bar that he and Bryant had frequented while in university. They'd wallowed in the lows and celebrated the highs in their college and professional years. They'd even drawn up their plans for their communications technology company on a Black Sheep-branded napkin that was framed and mounted on wall in the lobby of their offices.

When the server came, he ordered a couple of beers. While he and Bryant had moved on to high-end whiskey and bourbon over the past decade, every visit to the pub required several rounds of beer.

"Well, if it isn't 'the Man with No Name,'" Bryant said with a laugh, referencing the Clint Eastwood character from the popular spaghetti westerns. "With the way you were before you left, the burnout, and all, I honestly didn't think you'd return."

"I told you I'd be back."

Bryant slid into the booth. "How's everything at the O.K. Corral?"

Wes shrugged and slid the second beer bottle across the table to him. "Not as many shootouts as you'd been led to believe."

"That's a disappointment."

"You know, if I didn't know any better, I'd say that you have no idea what actual ranches are like."

"Maybe I'll have to pay a visit sometime. Maybe you can show me the ropes."

Wes laughed, knowing that Bryant would have

no idea of how to cope with life on a working ranch. "You're welcome anytime."

"So, you're here now?"

"For a couple of days," he said.

"Oh."

"I know I need to be here," Wes said carefully. "But there are things I need to take care of in Applewood."

"Is this still about the inheritance from your grandfather?"

"It was never about the money. There's a bit more."

Bryant blew out a breath. Wes was sure that from a gambling problem to alcoholism, every worst-case scenario was running through his friend's mind. "All right, give it to me."

"Remember my trip to Vegas for the tech conference? About three months ago."

"Yeah, of course." Bryant frowned. "What happened there?"

"I got married."

"You did what?"

"To a woman from Applewood." He told her the story of meeting Daisy in Vegas. How good it had been to see a familiar face. "We had one drink too many and we ended up at a twenty-four-hour chapel. She sent divorce papers, and I couldn't sign them."

Bryant didn't say anything for a while. He drank from his bottle. "Are you serious?"

"As a heart attack."

"Are you and this woman in a relationship?"

"I don't know what's happening. I think I'd like to

try. We got together as a honeymoon of sorts. She's been taking up too much space in my mind."

Bryant nodded. "Where does that leave us? We're on the cusp of a partnership that could put us on easy street for the rest of our lives."

"It's the twenty-first century. I can do work from anywhere in the world."

"It helps to have us in the same city, though."

"I know."

"I hope the news of this divorce doesn't get out," he said. "We're both going to be under TotalCom's microscope. You know the people behind some of these companies. They're skittish, especially when there are billions of dollars at stake. Something like this could be interpreted as you hiding a wife, or not able to maintain control, especially with alcohol involved. I hope it doesn't put the kibosh on the deal."

Wes hadn't thought about that. It was best to keep his reputation clean and not have any complications when it came to TotalCom investigators, who would be looking into their lives. "It won't interfere with anything," he told him. "It was one night. You know I don't have an impulse control or drinking problem. I'm going to sign the papers and get it settled away the minute I get home."

"Make sure you do, because if you sign this deal and you're still married. Your wealth becomes her wealth."

"I know all that."

Bryant sat back and crossed him arms. "Unless you want to be with her. Are you going to travel back and forth? Or pack everything you own and move to Texas permanently?"

Wes blew out a heavy breath. "I don't know. I know I want Daisy. But I know I can't leave our partnership here. Living and working in different countries wouldn't be good for us." Even though there were many telecommuting options for them to work together, Wes and Bryant knew that they did their best work in the same room—in direct communication, bouncing ideas off one another. With the new partnership with a tech giant on the horizon, Wes just couldn't see them having success if they weren't in the same city.

"I want you to do what's best for you," Bryant said. "But this partnership is going to be tough to pull off with you on a ranch in small-town Texas."

Wes knew that. Bryant wasn't telling him anything he hadn't already thought about. "You're telling me," he admitted. "I want two very different things—different lives—but I don't know how to go about having both of them."

Thirteen

Daisy was at her desk, signing off on the day's patient files, when she was startled by a knock. It was late in the day and because they didn't have any overnight patients, most of the staff had gone home already.

"Come in," she called.

When the door opened, she saw it was Wes. He'd been in England for a few days. He'd called once, texted three times. Not like she'd been counting, or anything.

"Wes, hi." She tried to cover her shock by acting casual. "What brings you by?"

Instead of answering, he leaned against the doorframe and folded his arms, the movement stretching the material of his shirt over his arms. "Mind if I come in?"

Her eyes dropped to the envelope in his hand. She knew what it was—the divorce papers. "Yeah, sure."

"Everything okay?" he asked. "You don't look especially thrilled to see me."

"I've had a long day." She said nothing of how she'd stayed awake the night before, thinking about Wes.

"You sure that's it?"

She nodded. "How was your trip home?"

"Good. We laid some fantastic groundwork for a huge deal."

"I'm glad you were able to get back to your real life and business in London."

"Daisy, please stop talking."

There was a potent silence between them.

"Why are you here?"

"I just got back an hour ago. I wanted to see you."

"Why?"

"Because I missed you. We barely spoke when I was away. I didn't like that."

She had no idea what to say, because…sure, they hadn't spoken much while he was gone, but it was as much her fault. She hadn't exactly reached out to him—no matter how much she might have wanted to. She just couldn't bring herself to do it. "What's in the envelope?" she asked, already knowing what it was.

He dropped the envelope on the desk. "The divorce papers. I signed them. I'm sorry it took me so long to get them to you."

She took the envelope and put it in the top drawer of her desk. She couldn't explain the feelings she had. She'd wanted him to sign the papers, true. While in his arms, it was easy to imagine that they could be together, but it was easy to forget that he lived in another country, across an entire ocean, and that nothing was permanent. But since his impromptu trip to England, she couldn't help but be reminded that it was all an illusion. "Thank you. I'll bring it to my lawyer and take care of the rest."

"Thanks. Because you can't trust me to get it finalized?" he smiled, showing he was teasing, but she wasn't in the mood for it.

"I guess that's it—we're divorced now."

"Yeah, I guess so. We can put it all behind us now and move on with our lives."

"I can't help but feel a weirdness between us," he noted. "What's going on?"

"Nothing's going on. What makes you say that?"

"You don't look exactly thrilled to see me. I thought we left things in a pretty good place, didn't we? You wanted me to sign the papers. I finally did that. If that's what this is about, tell me."

"No. Thank you for signing them." She wasn't sure how to process what she was feeling. Getting their mistake of a marriage annulled was the best way to move forward, but she couldn't help but feel it was sealing their fate. Again, the chorus ran through her head—*he isn't here for long, and you're going to end up heart-broken and alone.*

Daisy dismissed the thoughts and looked at the man in front of her. He was the man who could make her feel like no other. His touch was enough to make her want to upend her life and follow him wherever he went. She had to keep reminding herself that he couldn't give her what she wanted, the stability she craved.

"I don't know, Wes. We had a good time together before you left, but it's all just a precursor of things to come. Pretty soon you're going to get bored with this life. A couple of trips back and forth to London, to remind you of your regular life. One of these days, you'll end up staying there."

"It's the twenty-first century—you know that I can travel a few hours and be in another country, that doesn't mean I can't be with you. Sure, London was comfortable. It was nice seeing my friends, getting back into my business. But the whole time, I wanted you by my side."

"That's the thing, Wes. That isn't the life I want. I've already explained that to you."

"What about starting over?"

"That was a mistake."

"I don't think so," he said. He pulled the chair closer to his side of the desk and rested his elbows on it. He looked at her, his green eyes staring straight into her face. She looked away to avoid his scrutiny.

But he didn't waver. "Do you have plans tonight?" he asked.

"No, I don't."

"I haven't forgotten that I still owe you a dinner."

"You don't have to do that."

"I know I don't have to, but I want to." He stood. "Tonight," he said. "Come over and I'll pay what's due."

God help her, Daisy almost said yes. But she still

had some pride. She didn't have dinner plans, but she didn't want to just obey. "I can't tonight." He frowned. "What, did you think you would just roll back into town, and I'd drop everything because you told me to?"

"I didn't think that. I'm sorry if that's how I made it seem." He crossed his arms. "How about tomorrow night? Do you have plans tomorrow?" he said.

She looked him over, purposefully making him wait. Daisy knew she should refuse again, but she was only human, after all. "Fine," she said. "Tomorrow works for me."

He smiled at her, showing a row of straight, white teeth. "Great. See you at eight."

That evening, when Wes walked out onto the pool deck, he was looking forward to a peaceful night. A couple of beers, the hot tub and a game on the projector screen he'd set up were all he needed. He reached into the small fridge that had been built into the outdoor cooking station, grabbed a cold beer and sprawled on a chaise. He'd had fun seeing his friends and it felt good getting back to work, and moving on to big things in London, but he'd found a pretty perfect slice of heaven in Applewood.

"I like what you've done with the place," Garrett said from behind him.

Wes startled, not having heard him come in. He turned his head and saw that Willa was with him. "Thanks," he said. "I don't think Elias would care for the changes."

Willa helped herself to a beer as well and handed

another to Garrett. "What's not to like?" she asked, as she and Garrett also settled onto the plush outdoor furniture. "How was your trip home?" Garrett asked.

"Good," Wes said simply. Even though he and Bryant were working on a huge deal, they were keeping it quiet. "There were a couple of things I had to take care of with Bryant. It was good to go there for a while."

"And you came back here," Garrett noted.

Wes held up his hands. "Why is everyone so surprised by that?"

"Can you blame anybody for thinking that? Staying away from here is pretty much what you do." Garrett was smiling, but Wes bristled at the words. It was the screw that Garrett kept twisting.

"Who else was surprised?" Willa asked.

"You know who. Daisy. I showed up at her door and she was good and shocked."

"I'm actually kind of shocked that she isn't here tonight."

"Naw," he said with a shrug. "I invited her, but she said she couldn't. Although I'm sure she was just giving me a hard time."

Willa laughed. "Yeah, probably. I was just talking to her, and she's curled up at home watching episodes of *Seinfeld*."

Wes laughed. It wasn't often that women rejected him, but Daisy was different. "That's what I get for springing plans on her, I guess."

Garrett drank from his beer. "No luck winning over Daisy?"

He thought about the night he and Daisy had spent

together after they'd left Longhorns, before his im-promptu trip to England. He didn't want to go into too much detail. "Well, I thought we were on track, but not so much anymore. She's pissed at me."

"Why? Because you slept together, talked about starting fresh and then you took off with no notice?" Willa asked, with a withering look, one eyebrow raised.

"So, you talked to her."

"Of course, I did. She's my best friend. Tell me any of that was wrong."

The thing was...she was absolutely right. "Any tips to win her over?"

She shook her head. "I don't know, Wes."

"Come on, Willa. She's your best friend. You have to know something I can do."

Willa sighed. "She'll kill me if she knew I was talk-ing to you about her. But what Daisy wants is stability. She wants to be romanced. But most of all, she's look-ing for a simple, small-town life with marriage, kids, the whole shebang. Can you give her that?"

"No. I can't give her that."

"And then you went home to London, with no no-tice. You think it didn't hit home to her that you're going to be based there. That's no good to her. It isn't the life she wants."

At his core, Wes knew all that, and he should have known they wouldn't be able to make it work. He still didn't know how he expected to work. All he knew was that he wanted her in his life. He would have to make some sort of compromise. "She wants romance, does she?"

"At least! Like every woman. Believe it or not, we sometimes want more than drunken Las Vegas weddings and sex in a shower."

Wes heard Garrett choke on his beer but ignored him. "You ladies really do share everything."

"We're best friends—of course, we do. But, yes, romance. And not only that. If you want to prove to her that you can commit to her, you have to commit to this town. She loves Applewood, and if you can prove you're part of the community, it might help her come around."

He thought about everything Willa had just said. Romance and commitment—to her and to Applewood. Honestly, one of those was far more palatable than the other. But that was why he'd returned home, wasn't it?

"Think you can handle that?" she asked him, after he'd been silent for some time.

Wes nodded. "Yeah. I know a good place to start."

Fourteen

Daisy parked her vehicle outside the main house of the ranch. The main house was massive, constructed mostly by hand, and once used to house the large family over several generations of Hardwells. She looked up at the house—two stories, featuring a high peaked roof and walls of windows. The lights inside were on and cast a golden glow over the driveway and parking area. She couldn't see Wes inside—he was likely in the kitchen, which wasn't visible from where she was standing.

She held the box of cannoli she'd picked up at the new bakery on Main Street and walked up the five stairs to the porch that wrapped around the entire house. She had grown up in a humble, middle-class home, and this ranch house served to remind reminded her of the differences between she and Wes, and what they both wanted. She was content with a simple, small-town life, while he came from an extremely upper-class family and had lived a life filled with the finer things. Add that to the list of their incompatibilities.

As Daisy stood in front to the door and took a deep breath, she knew exactly how this evening would play out. They'd eat and no doubt end up in bed together. And depending on the hour, she had different feelings about that outcome. But still, the indecision hadn't stopped her from indulging herself, doing her hair and makeup—not something she did every day. And buying new—and very expensive—lingerie, going to a waxing appointment and covering her early morning appointments for tomorrow. She'd put off his invitation the night before to keep her distance and teach him a lesson, but it had also given her an extra day to make such arrangements.

She fluffed one of the waves in her hair, and knowing that she was probably making a mistake, she knocked on the door. She exhaled roughly. They should be staying away from one another, not starting over, but Wes made a convincing argument just by looking at her, just by touching her. Just by putting his lips on hers.

The door opened and Wes stood on the other side. He'd foregone his new style of ranch wear for a fitted black button-down shirt and dark jeans. "Hey," he said, with the smile that almost knocked her over. "Come on in."

"Mr. Gucci Jeans is back," she said, shaking off her

plaid jacket. He took it, and she glanced at her own outfit of black leggings and a T-shirt. She'd thought of wearing something a little nicer, but despite the amount of preparation that had gone into planning the night, she didn't want to *look* like she'd tried too hard. "I feel underdressed," she commented.

He didn't hesitate. "You look beautiful," he told her, dropping a quick kiss on her lips, as he took the box from her hands.

"What's this?"

"Oh, I forgot. I brought dessert."

"You didn't have to bring anything."

"Come on, I was raised better than that."

He peeked inside the box. "Looks great. I've got to get to the kitchen."

She followed him into the kitchen, and he handed her a glass of red wine as she took a seat on a cushioned barstool that had been pushed up to the island.

The granite countertop was neat and contained salad fixings. In the kitchen, Wes seemed to be completely at ease as he moved about, tending to pots, checking on the cooking rack in the oven, all the while multitasking, prepping and cleaning as he went. The aroma spread throughout the house and Daisy inhaled. Honestly, she'd partly expected him to call in a caterer. She was pleasantly surprised. There was something irresistible about a man who knew his way around a kitchen. "It smells amazing in here, Wes."

"Thanks," he said, stirring his béarnaise sauce in the pot on the stove. "I hope you like rib eye."

She'd skipped lunch and her mouth was just about watering. "I do. What else is on the menu?"

He washed his hands and dried them on a nearby towel, then turned to face her. Leaning against the counter, he picked up his own glass of wine. "It's nothing fancy. Salad, roasted potatoes, garlic bread with cheese."

She nodded, impressed. "It doesn't need to be fancy to be delectable. I'm just a plain girl with a simple palate."

He stopped and turned to her, and his eyes gave off more heat than his stovetop. "There's nothing plain about you," he told her.

The intensity of his stare made her look at her wine, and she took another sip, careful not to overindulge before she had a chance to eat anything. "Looking at you, you probably didn't get much food like that."

He turned playful again. "Let's say that before coming home, I hadn't had a carb in seven years."

Daisy laughed. "You know, the world is such a crazy place these days, I'm not sure I'd be able to stick to a diet that doesn't let me indulge in my favorite things. Life's too short, you know?"

He was watching her, and she looked away, and finished her wine. "You're right," he said. "Life is far too short to not go for what you want." She didn't have a chance to respond before he pressed a kiss to her lips. There was no time to react, or kiss him, before he broke the connection and moved away quickly. "Sorry. I just had to do that." He walked briskly to the back patio where the grill was located and busied himself with the meat and plated two amazing-looking pieces of meat, covered with what looked like rosemary and some other spices.

"No need to apologize. I'm going to be honest. I didn't know you could cook."

He shrugged. "I dabble. It helps me relax." Noticing her glass was empty, he poured her a little more.

"You're doing more than dabbling. Tech genius, rancher, master chef." She raised her glass in a toast and said, "Impressive."

"I've got a lot of talents you know nothing about," he said with a chuckle and a wink.

Before she could stop herself, Daisy felt the words slip past her wine-loosened tongue. "Feel like I've seen a bunch of them, but I can't wait to see the rest."

"Anytime. All you have to do is ask."

"That sounds good."

"Don't worry, it will be."

She knew that they were no longer talking about cooking. He had talents and he wasn't shy about showing them off. "Is that a promise or a threat?"

Separated by the kitchen island, their eyes were locked on each other. The oven timer went off, breaking the moment and he backed, taking a pan of roasted baby potatoes from the bottom rack of the oven.

He brought the plates to the table and, picking up their wineglasses, she followed. It felt like a hopelessly domestic scene that she craved. Maybe for one more night, she could put aside her reservations and enjoy herself. They could worry about the rest in the morning.

* * *

"That was amazing," Daisy told him, sitting back and patting her stomach. It wasn't elegant, ut Wes didn't care. He liked Daisy's realness. She didn't pick at her food or push it across her plate. Just like him—she'd cleared hers. She looked up at him and gave him a needlessly embarrassed smile. "I'm not very lady-like, I guess."

"You're perfect," he assured her. "I'm glad you liked it. Room for dessert?"

"Are you just being suggestible or are you still hungry?"

"I was mostly being suggestible. There is always time for dessert later."

"Later?"

"Later," he promised, laying his hand over hers.

Her eyes connected with his for a few moments before she looked away, breaking the moment. That was something that he realized she did when the feelings became too much. "So, what now?" she asked, breaking away from the intense connection they shared. "Do we go over the terms of our divorce? Can I get this house?" she joked.

"We had a divorce," he reminded her.

"Right. But in all seriousness, I love this house. I don't know why Elias and Cathy moved to Arizona when they have all of this here. With Garrett and Willa in their house next door, it's unfathomable that no one lives in this one anymore."

"Except for me," Wes pointed out. "And Noah, on his infrequent visits." When Wes had first arrived, he'd felt out of place there, but the longer he stayed in the main house, the more he was beginning to make it his own.

She shrugged "Yeah, but how long will you actually be living here? Six months? Then the place will be empty again."

He couldn't give her a definite answer. "It's back to that again."

"Yeah, I guess so. We have to be realistic," she told him.

He took her hand again and stroked his thumb over her palm. "I am. What's real is that spark between us whenever we look at each other." She said nothing, and Wes didn't want to push the issue in case it caused her to run. "Why don't talk it out in the hot tub?" he suggested. He had no intention of talking. Talking just made them go in circles. In bed was where they connected—and there was no doubt, no question, about that.

She hummed and shook her head. "I didn't bring a bathing suit."

He grinned and raised an eyebrow. "That's even better." Still holding on to her hand, he stood. "Come on."

He led her out to the patio, where the hot tub was already bubbling in the chill air. He'd set out a bucket that held a bottle of champagne. Much of the ice had melted, but judging by the condensation on the bucket, it was still plenty cold. He plucked the dripping bottle from the water and efficiently and quietly popped the cork. He returned the bottle to the bucket.

The rolling hills and trees surrounding the patio of

the main house provided them with complete privacy. Starting with the top button, he undid his shirt and then shrugged it off. He tossed it onto the nearby chaise and saw that Daisy was watching him. He smiled. "You've seen me without my shirt before," he reminded her, secure in the knowledge that even if they were on different pages about the state of their future, he was happy that he could still affect her physically.

"Right," she said, shaking her head. "Sorry."

"No need to apologi—" Before he finished his sentence, she pulled her long shirt over her head and exposed her generously curved body. Her substantial breasts were covered with a small slip of black lace, through which he saw the shadow of her nipples, and his entire body tightened in response.

Before he embarrassed himself, Wes quickly shucked his pants, leaving his briefs on, and then slid into the water. The water was hot, and after a long day at the ranch, it was exactly what he needed. To share the night and a bottle of good champagne with a beautiful woman was all the better. He tried not to stare as she pushed her leggings over her thighs and kicked them off her feet. Apparently, her bra was part of a matching set, and a nice one at that.

She joined him, getting in on the opposite side of the hot tub. "Wow," she said, her voice soft. "This is quite a way to unwind after a long day."

"I know a couple of other ways," he suggested, pouring two glasses of champagne and handing her one.

"Of course, you do."

Wes drank from his flute. "You said you didn't have a bathing suit, but what you're wearing is just fine."

She laughed, then took a sip of champagne herself. "I went to a lingerie boutique in High Pine this afternoon. I can't believe I spent so much money on something I'm wearing in a hot tub."

"Don't mind me," he suggested. "Feel free to take it off."

She splashed a small wave of water in his direction. "You're terrible."

"One way or another, it's coming off. Whether that's sooner or later…it's entirely up to you."

The mood turned serious between them. Daisy knew that Wes was right. There was only one way that the evening was going to end, and she'd known it all along. Wes's eyes were on her mouth as she took her bottom lip between her teeth, thinking about what he'd said. "You're right," she said. She took another sip of champagne and placed her glass on the deck. She licked the remnants of the champagne from her top lip. "Maybe I should take it off."

On her knees, she crossed the short distance of the hot tub, getting closer to him, and despite the screaming in her head telling her it wasn't a good idea, she couldn't ignore the thrumming between her thighs, as desire took hold of her body.

"That might be the safest bet," he said, his voice low.

"I think so, too." She reached behind her to the unhook the now definitely ruined bra.

"Need a little help with that?" he asked.

"No. I got it," she told him, unhooking the bra and tossing it off to the side. It landed on the teak deck. She noticed the way his body stiffened, and she laughed. He'd given her a hard time about being distracted by him undressing, but she loved that he was in the same boat as her. Her temperature worked its way higher, and she knew that it had nothing to do with the heat of the water.

The arm stretched along the lip of the hot tub closed over her shoulders and he pulled her closer. "Daisy." His voice was a low growl, his fingers curling over her shoulder. She went to him willingly, pressing against his side. She placed a palm on his pec, tracing little lines over his skin with her fingertips, smiling at the way his muscles tensed and twitched under her touch as she scraped her nails over his body. Her hands dipped lower, over the tense ridges of his abdominal muscles. She played with the thin layer of hair that covered him, and the trail that dropped below the waistband of his briefs. When her fingers ventured lower, to his lap, she found that he was already ready for her. She brushed her hand against him and was rewarded with a husky groan torn from his lips.

In one quick movement, he grasped her by the waist and then deposited her onto his lap so that she was straddling him, and his large palms flattened and smoothed against her back, pulling her closer so that her bare breasts pressed against his chest. The short hairs tickled her skin.

He kissed her hard, and she parted her lips for him. As always, his kiss lit something deep within her. Desire and desperation compelled Daisy to get even closer to him, and she wrapped her arms around his neck and ground herself against his length.

Wes pulled his mouth away from hers, and his lips blazed a hot trail over her jaw and down her throat. As his lips skimmed her electrified skin, she let out a sigh that turned into a shocked cry when his teeth sank lightly into the skin of her shoulder.

Wes dipped his fingers underneath the lacy waistline of her thong, lowering it, but then he ripped the delicate material. "Hey!" she protested against his lips.

"Don't worry about it."

Daisy was now naked against his body, and even though the night was dark, the exterior lights would have illuminated their bodies. "Wait."

He stopped kissing her long enough look up at her. "What's wrong?" he asked.

"Can anyone see us out here?" she asked, looking around into the darkness.

"No. Don't worry about that," he told her. "We're perfectly secluded from any prying eyes." He smoothed his hands over her breasts, playing and squeezing, as she arched against him, bringing her nipples close to his mouth. He closed his lips over one bud, while he played with the other with his fingers, which caused a jolt of electricity to fire through her.

Wes brought his hands down her spine, under the surface of the water, and they dipped to her behind. He pulled her closer, and without warning, he stood. She wrapped her legs around his hips.

With his lips locked on hers, and her thighs around

his waist, he walked inside the house. She hadn't noticed before, but he'd a lit a fire in the large stone fireplace. "I'd meant to take you upstairs to my room," he said in her ear, his voice a rumble. "But I don't think I can make it that far." He laid her on the rug in front of the fireplace.

"This will do," she assured him. It didn't matter where they ended up—if it ended with her body against Wes's, that's all that mattered to her.

"I was hoping you'd say that." He leaned over her, kissed her again. In the light of the fire, his damp skin was a golden color, and she pulled him closer. Wes ran his hand up her thigh, and when he touched her in just the right way, she nearly exploded.

"Do it," she pleaded, needing him in that moment. "We have all night." Even when the voice of doubt knocked on the inside of her brain, she reminded herself that they had tonight…even if they didn't have a future together.

"That we do," he agreed. He pushed away from her for a moment to reach into the pocket of his pants. He withdrew a condom, rolled it over himself as he positioned himself between her knees and entered her in one quick thrust.

She cried out as he filled her, and she scratched her fingernails across his back. Their hips met with every thrust. And their moans mingled together in the silence of the empty house. Soon, Daisy felt the rise of her pleasure low in her core, and she gripped him tightly, allowing him to bring her to full orgasm. She arched against him, and he held her tightly, before he groaned his release against her shoulder.

Daisy shivered against him, her wet skin and hair chilling her. Wes pulled a throw and a couple of pillows from the nearby leather armchair and covered them with it. She snuggled against his chest. She could still feel his heartbeat against her, and it matched her own.

"Maybe we should go upstairs," he suggested.

She shook her head. "No, this feels right." In response, his arms tightened around her, and he placed a kiss on top of her head.

"I'd like to agree with you, but tell that to my back," he said with a chuckle. "I've got a better idea. You wait here."

He slid from under the blanket and, naked, he headed up the stairs. She could pull her eyes away from the rippling muscles of his back and his round behind.

When he disappeared around the corner at the top of the stairs, she rolled over and stared at the high ceiling. She'd known she would end up sleeping with Wes again, even though she knew it would prolong things with him and continue to complicate her life. But as she curled up under the sheepskin rug in front of the fireplace, she didn't want to worry about anything like that for the rest of the night.

Wes descended the stairs wearing a white robe and holding another over his arm. "Here you are," he said, handing it to her. "As reluctant as I am to have you put something on, I don't want you to get chilly."

She pulled the robe over her body and tied it. It was thick, soft, the fluffiest thing she'd ever put on her body. The robe was white and embroidered with the Hardwell Ranch logo in green thread. She pulled the thick collar around her neck. "Where are we going?"

"Back outside."

"I think we both know what's going to happen if we go out to that hot tub."

"I've got a better idea."

They went outside and Wes picked up the blanket from the floor. "Have a seat," he said, pointing to the double chaise. Using a remote, he turned on the firepit and picked up their discarded champagne glasses and bottle.

Daisy covered up with the blanket and spread it over both of them. The night air was chilled, but when they cuddled together, their body heat was more than enough to make up for it.

Daisy looked at the clear night sky and took in the near silence of the dark night.

"God, this is amazing," Daisy said beside him. "So, this is the good life."

Wes pulled Daisy closer, aware that at any moment, she could sit up and leave again. And tomorrow morning, she would do just that. At least for the moment, she was his. As he'd learned, any instance of closeness was short-lived. "It sure is."

"Willa told me once that she and Garrett spend a lot of time stargazing. It's something special for them," Daisy said. "I get it now. This is nice."

"I get it now, too. I never really paid attention. And

living in the city doesn't really give me a chance to watch the stars."

"That's too bad."

"I'm glad I'm seeing them now." She said nothing, and Wes ran his hand and down her back, cursing the thick layer of terry cloth that stood between his fingers and her smooth skin. "What do you want out of life, Daisy?"

She waited a bit to answer, as if searching for her reply. "It's not too complicated. I want what a lot of women want," she said. "As much as I try to put out there the image of a modern, independent woman—and I am that—I want to get married, have a family. I spent so much time traveling when I was in school. I had different rotations and placements, all over the world, and I have so many amazing experiences because of that opportunity. I know I'm lucky. But I'm just so ready to settle down and start the next part of my life. Marriage, kids, the picket fence, the whole nine yards. It sounds old-fashioned, but that's what I want."

He nodded. "That sounds great." Then he chuckled. "You know what's funny?" he asked. "We have a lot of the same goals here."

She tilted up her head to look at him. "Do we?" There was a skeptical edge to her voice.

"Yeah. You just admitted that we both *want* to be married. And up until I signed those papers a couple of days ago, we were." A realization dawned on him. "Ah. It's me, right? I'm not marriage material."

She sighed. "You're sexy, rich, funny, kind and you work hard. You are absolutely marriage material."

"Just not for you."

"No. I don't believe you can give me the future I want."

"Okay, that stung."

"I'm sorry. I don't want to hurt you. I'm just being honest."

"No, it's fine. I want you to be honest," he told her.

She twisted out of his arms and sat on the chaise, facing him as she crossed her legs. "Wes, I really like you, and we are compatible—sexually, that is—but this isn't long-term. I'm in my thirties, I've established my own practice. That's what I need. I need long-term, I need stability and I need the life I've created for myself here. I don't know if you can give that to me."

He had no defense. It always came down to that, didn't it? As much as Wes wanted to insist that he was here for the long haul, he just couldn't, and he knew that wasn't fair to her. He and Bryant were on the verge of a deal that could put them on top of the communications tech world. He needed to be with his partner. He couldn't do that in Applewood, Texas. As much as he wanted to believe he could be content with small-town life, it wasn't true. While he enjoyed his time here, he missed the restaurants, the nightlife, people from different walks of life.

Once he finished his term on the ranch, the only thing keeping him in Applewood would be Daisy. He'd thought it might be enough, if she hadn't already decided that it wasn't.

But then she turned it on him. She reached for their

neglected glasses of champagne. "What do you want out of life?"

"I want to be happy," he revealed. "And, you know, maybe I do want a family, and stability—all of that good stuff that you want."

"Do you?"

He shrugged. "Kids have never been on my radar. But the more I think about it, the more attractive it feels." He paused, knowing he wouldn't be able to come back from the words he was about to say. "But I don't know if Applewood is home for me."

She nodded, as if accepting the words, he was saying. "I know. That's what I was afraid of."

They shared a silence as they sipped their champagne, their eyes connecting over the rims of their glasses. Wes didn't want to leave the conversation on such a serious note. He wanted to get back to the nice time they'd been having. "You know," he said, "I never planned to get married, but I have to say, I picked a good woman to be my first wife."

She laughed. "I think you meant that the tequila picked."

He hummed and nodded. "Yes, definitely. The tequila played a very important part. Also, the hot roulette wheel put me in the marrying mood. Although, if I'm being honest, I like to say that fate played a bigger hand than the blackjack dealer." He finished his champagne and noticed that her glass was also empty. He filled them both again.

She shivered, and he pulled her to him, so they were both once again lying on the chaise. "You cold?"

"A little. The fire is nice, though."

"I'm glad you're here," he whispered against the top of her head."

"I'm glad, too. Despite our last conversation, I'm having a really good time."

Unable to stop himself, he decided to prod at the issue a little more. "You know, if you agree to marry me, then every night could be like this. Hell, we could even get that white picket fence you want."

Even if Wes couldn't see it, he could virtually hear her eye roll. "I don't know if your big-city condo association will approve of a white picket fence, though."

"Ah, we call them flats, though. But maybe we can convince them," he said, not fighting it. "Or buy them off."

She didn't say anything for a bit. "What exactly made you sit with me at that hotel bar?"

Wes's mind flashed to that night in the lobby of his hotel. "Mainly, I was thinking about coming to the ranch, and how I was going to balance that and my work in London. I was stressed about how I would be received by the people here, and my family. I was feeling kind of nostalgic, and then I saw you. You were a beautiful, familiar face and reminded me of home."

"Why would you want to be reminded of home? You never spent much time here."

"I was in a pretty bad place when I was in Vegas. I was on the cusp of a massive burnout caused by work, and it only got worse after I returned to London. You were a tie to the past, a simpler time. You might not know it, but I often thought about you."

"Really?"

"Of course, you were the gorgeous good girl, and I was the town rebel. Even then you were too good for me. But that night in Las Vegas, you were stunning, sexy, and I wanted to get to know you again."

"I think you were right. It felt like fate a little, didn't it?" she asked. "Both of us were there at the right place, the right time. Just when we needed each other's company."

"Absolutely. You took the words out of my mouth. I just wish we could figure this out."

"You don't give up, do you?"

"I don't want to lose this connection. You have to admit that whenever we touch, there's electricity, right? I've never had that before. When was the last time you've had that with another man?"

She shifted so that she was on top of him, her thighs straddling his waist. Wes gripped her thighs and slid them upward under the robe. "I haven't. But you're right. We have a truckload of sexual chemistry." He smoothed his palms around the back and gripped her firm ass. "We agreed to keep this casual, remember? We keep having sex, but not letting ourselves get too deep."

Wes grasped Daisy's waist and flipped her so that she was now lying underneath him. "I can do deep." And he proceeded to show her.

Fifteen

"Thanks for inviting me to lunch, guys, I really appreciate it," Wes said to Maverick, Kyle and Darrin. They'd joined him in the booth at Patsy's, the longest-serving diner in Applewood. While the population in Applewood trended wealthy, the greasy spoon's high-quality food was a favorite among the townsfolk. "It's been a while since I've been here."

"No visit to Applewood is complete without a trip to Patsy's," Kyle said.

"What have you been doing to keep yourself busy?" Darrin asked.

Wes thought of the nights he'd spent with Daisy. But he wasn't going to share those details. Since a week ago, when they'd agreed to keep sleeping together, but not taking it any further than that, they'd spent every night together. "The ranch work keeps me pretty busy. Garrett and Dylan make sure I've got plenty to do."

"Wes Hardwell." He heard the voice next to the table and looked up to see one of the town's elders, Isiah Adams, standing next to their table. His family had been among the town's settlers and of the first to ranch the land. Wes remembered that the man's opinion meant a lot to Applewood's decision makers. "I heard you were back."

Wes bristled at the tone. He normally wouldn't let anyone get away with speaking to him like that. But he knew that it wouldn't help him to challenge the old man. He nodded. "Yes, sir, I am."

"Not for long, I hope." Why was everyone so concerned about how long he would be in Applewood?

"As long as I need to be."

"So, you're here for the money then. Your share of the family ranch."

Wes resented the other man's interest in his life, but he tried his best to stay civil. "I came to visit my family."

Isiah didn't seem to care for that answer, so he turned his attention to Wes's old friends. "Back with the old crowd, I see. I trust you're on your best behavior this time, Wes."

The fact that Wes's wild antics had been years ago was lost on the long-time resident, who no doubt remembered the tales. Wes was in his hometown on a redemption trip, so instead of a making a smart remark to the most powerful man in town, he agreed. "Yes, sir, I am."

"It's good to hear that," he said,

"Can I help you with anything?" he asked Isiah, when the man didn't make any movement to leave.

"I hope you're not here to cause any trouble. I remember what you all used to be like."

And now he was targeting Mav, Darrin and Kyle? "With all due respect," Wes began, meaning absolutely no respect, "we all were a little wild in our youth, but I know that we've done a lot of growing in the past few years. Darrin is a business owner here, and Kyle a member of the fire department. And in the years since I've lived here, I've become extremely successful, and have contributed to society."

"If you're so successful, then why are you here to collect your grandfather's living inheritance like the rest of your family. You're here to collect a check."

Wes was done. He stood from the table and faced the older man. "I'll have you know that my reappearance in town has nothing with my grandfather's money. And it's absolutely none of your business."

The older man huffed, indignant that anyone would dare speak to him like that, but he held firm and jutted out his chin. "I'll be keeping my eyes on you, young man," he said, before turning on his heel and walking out of the room.

Wes returned to his seat and picked up his beer.

"Well, that was a friendly visit," Kyle muttered.

"Quite the welcome home," he said. "Is that a common occurrence? Does he normally get on your ass like that?"

"Not since I joined the fire department," Kyle said. "They all pretty much leave me alone."

Maverick laughed. "It took a lot of donations and service to the community to be taken as anything more than the town screwup."

Wes drank his beer. He'd left town and left his friends holding the bag for what they'd done. But Darrin and Kyle had gained respect. Maverick had made amends. "There needs to be a way to get the town on my side."

"What do you mean?"

"How did you get people here to take you seriously? To forget about your past?"

"Is that what you're her looking for?" Kyle asked. "Some kind of redemption from the fire?"

"That's part of it. It never sat right with me the way I just ran. I shouldn't have done it. I want to make amends for all the crap we used to pull."

"It wasn't easy. I mean, hell, your own brother still won't give me the time of day," he said with a shrug.

Wes thought about the feud between his own family and Maverick's. It went back to their grandfathers, men who had once been partners, but had turned into enemies. Part of his teenage rebellion had included befriending the grandson of his grandfather's sworn enemy. "Sorry about that," he told him with a frown.

Maverick shrugged. "At this point, it is what it is. But for the rest of the town, you can do it. Money's probably the easiest way to do it—just make some high-profile donations. But most importantly, you need to endear yourself to the townsfolk. Maybe you could plan some town event, a fundraiser—do some things to help the town."

"Hell, the fire hall could use a new engine. We're about to start fundraising for it." In a town like Applewood, "fundraising" meant asking which millionaire would like to write the check, but still came along with expensive benefit dinners and galas.

Wes thought about his options. It was a two-pronged idea—if he endeared himself to the town, it might be a way to win over Daisy. If she saw him working with the people in town, then perhaps it would help her realize that he had connections to Applewood that he wouldn't abandon, even if he stayed in London.

Sitting in front of the mayor, who happened to be Willa's ex-fiancé, Thomas Albright, and the fire chief, Michael Elliott, Wes felt his nerves building. He wiped his sweaty palms on his denim-clad thighs. It was ridiculous. Wes had sat in boardrooms with some of the most powerful people in the world. It made no sense to him why ae mayor and fire chief in small-town Texas made his blood pressure rise.

"What are we all doing here?" the mayor asked, clearly impatient to be seated across the table from a Hardwell.

"Gentleman, let me begin by saying, I know I haven't always been the most welcome citizen in Applewood. I have a history with this town. But I want to make amends for everything I've done wrong. I've heard that the fire department is looking to fundraise for a new truck."

"Yes, that's right," Chief Elliott confirmed. "We also need some renovations at the fire house."

"I would like to help with that."

. "How would you like to help?"

"I'd like to buy the truck, but I would also like to include the rest of the town. Summer is coming up around the corner. It's an important time of I'd like to plan a fundraiser and silent auction. I'll personally cover all costs and all proceeds will go to the fire department."

Wes could tell that both men were interested in his proposal, but only the mayor didn't want to admit it. He watched as Thomas shifted uncomfortably in his chair. But Wes ignored him. "So how about it, Chief Elliott? Would you be interested in us helping raise the funds you need?"

"I love that idea. I appreciate you thinking about us, and I don't really care about what your motives are. We need a new truck and to upgrade our facilities. An event would be the perfect thing to bring people together for the summer festival. Mayor?" He turned to Thomas.

Thomas grunted, clearly not happy that Wes and the chief had come to an agreement without him. "Yes," he said finally. "If you're both in agreement, you can see to the details."

Wes stood and shook each of their hands. The fundraiser was on, and now he had to work on planning it. Luckily, he knew one of the best event coordinators in town.

Sixteen

Daisy lifted her paint roller from the tray, then applied the light gray paint with the sponge. She looked around at the work that had already been accomplished in the few months that Willa had owned the century-old mansion. Her plans to turn it into an inn were coming along ahead of schedule. "Willa, I can't believe how far this place has come in such a short time."

"Yeah, it's amazing the things you can get done when you have enough money. Plus, you and every hand at Hardwell Ranch looking to chip in with the renovations."

"I'm happy to do so," Daisy said. Helping Willa kept her busy, but she was happy for the distraction. Anything that kept her from thinking about what was happening between her and Wes was all the better.

"I appreciate it," Willa said. "But don't feel like you have to be here helping me all the time."

"I don't feel that way. Whatever keeps my mind off Wes."

"What? What's happening with Wes?"

"Girl, I don't even know where to start."

"What now? I thought the divorce papers were signed."

"The papers have long been signed, and they're being processed as we speak. But that hasn't stopped him from staying at my place almost every night."

"It sounds like you're a married couple."

"Nope." She shook her head. "We're not a real couple. There's no commitment, no future. That way, we'll be able to cut ties when he has to go back to England." Willa gave her a funny look. "What?"

"What's so impossible about you guys being together? You have chemistry, you got married once—why not see what can happen between you?"

"You sound like your brother-in-law," she told her. "I've gone over it every way in my head. It's not going to work. I don't want long distance—he won't move here permanently and I'm certain that I won't be leaving. So, it is what it is."

A knock on the front door startled them both. "Are you expecting anyone?" Daisy asked.

"No."

"Anybody here?" It was Wes calling from the foyer. Daisy's mouth dropped—she was unsure if Wes had heard them talking about him.

"In the dining room," Willa called.

Wes entered the room that would soon be the dining room, looking around. "Wow, Willa, this place is really coming along." His eyes landed on Daisy and his eyes rounded, as if he had just realized she was there. "Hey, Daisy."

She smiled. "Hi." Their greeting was amicable, but like always, a snap of sexual tension crackled between them.

"Is this a bad time?"

"No, we were taking a break," Willa said, even though they'd been talking and had barely painted anything all afternoon. "What brings you by?"

"I need your help."

"With what?"

"I had an idea, but I might need you to pull it off, as an event coordinator."

Up until recently, Willa had worked as one of the best wedding planners in the area. But now she spent her days with paint swatches and tape measures.

"What's on your mind? A second wedding to Daisy?" she teased. Wes groaned and Daisy threw a rag at her. She dodged it with a laugh. "Oh, lighten up, you two. Is this one—" she hooked a thumb at Daisy "—not falling for your charms yet?"

"Go to hell, Willa," Daisy said with a laugh, at the same time that Wes said, "I don't think so."

Daisy thought back to the night before, and the nights they'd spent together since he'd come home. The things they'd done in her shower, in her bed, in her kitchen, over every surface of each of their houses… She pictured what a second wedding for them might look like. How tempting it might be to meet him at the end of the aisle once more. Maybe she'd remember the vows this time.

"Okay, Wes, what is your idea?"

"I want to plan an event. A fundraiser for the fire department." As he detailed the event he had in mind, Daisy watched him with admiration. He'd gone from never wanting to be around, to wanting to do something for the people who lived here. Given his past in the town, and the trouble he'd caused as a wayward teen, and how bad it truly could have gotten, the fire department would be the perfect place to help rehab his reputation. With him doing this, it showed that he was looking to form a commitment to the town, and by extension, in some strange way, to Daisy.

"The inn is keeping me pretty busy, but I've got some free time in the coming weeks," Willa said. "I would be glad to help you with it."

"Yeah, me, too," Daisy said.

"Thanks, ladies."

"I know where you're coming from, Willa said. You aren't the only one who's working to build a positive reputation around here."

Wes knew that Willa had also faced an uphill battle with the people in the town of Applewood after her own ill-fated first wedding to the town's mayor, where she'd left the man at the altar. "I really do appreciate it. I'm not sure I know where to start."

She smiled. "Well, I guess you do need me. Let's get together tomorrow evening and we can go over some of your ideas."

"Sounds good. But for now, I should get back to the ranch." He raised his hand to Daisy. "I'll see you later."

She didn't miss his intention. He'd invited her over to his place tonight. She raised her own hand. "Sure thing." She was glad he played it cool with her in front of Willa, but even though she had been the one to suggest they keep things casual between them, the simple, informal way he'd greeted her and said goodbye struck her the wrong way.

When he was gone, Willa turned her attention to Daisy. "What are you guys doing later?"

. "Oh, nothing," she said, waving off her friend. "It was just a way that people say goodbye." Willa raised an eyebrow, clearly skeptical.

But Daisy wasn't interested in an interrogation, and she picked up her paint roller again. "We should get this room done before it's too late, right?"

Seventeen

The sun had gone down and after the work was done for the day, Wes and Garrett were sharing a quiet moment in what used to be Elias's study. It had become their evening ritual—after work, they would both go in there, share a drink and quiet conversation. With the exception of his time with Daisy, it had quickly become his favorite time of day.

Wes's cell phone vibrated in his pocket. He pulled it out and saw several messages from Bryant. It had been a while since he'd been in touch. But his entire body ached from the day's work, and he was too mentally exhausted to talk to him at the moment.

On top of the physical labor, he also had to start planning the fundraiser. Thankfully, Willa and Daisy were on board to help with that. Wes was going to need all the help he could get. His phone buzzed once more. Bryant again, most likely. He'd have to call him back as soon as possible. When his phone unlocked, he saw that were several messages from Bryant, but the most recent was from Daisy, and it stole his attention from everything else. It was a picture of herself and Ozzie. The dog was cute, of course, but his eyes drifted to Daisy, casual with her hair down and wearing a loose-fitting red-and-black plaid shirt, with several buttons undone. And while the picture itself was wholesome in nature, it was scandalous in a way he appreciated.

Garrett, who had gone to the bar, approached him, handing him a glass that held a couple of fingers of a golden-colored liquid. "Scotch?" he asked.

Wes quickly set aside his phone. "Only if it's Elias's best stuff."

"Oh, you know it is. I hid the bottle before he packed up and moved."

The brothers sipped quietly. His thoughts drifted to the fundraiser and how he was going to make it happen, and if that was a success, what other events he could host. And there he went, accidentally planning on staying later than he'd had any intention. He needed to return to London eventually. He knew it; Daisy knew it. But for right now, Wes was perfectly at ease. He bit back a yawn as he eased back into his chair.

"You tired?" Garrett asked.

"I reckon I should cancel my gym membership."

"Yeah, not much need for it when you're ranching." Garrett took a sip of his drink. "I wanted to tell you that you're doing a really good job."

Wes grinned at his brother. "I appreciate that. Even the more menial tasks are a lot more rewarding than I could have imagined."

They heard the front door open, and Wes thought, briefly, that it might be Daisy, but instead was even more surprised to his grandfather. Elias appeared in the doorway of the study.

"Is that my Scotch?" he asked, instead of a typical greeting.

Both Wes and Garrett stood and hugged their grandfather.

"What are you doing here?" Garrett asked. "I didn't expect you to leave Arizona until the New Year."

"Well, seeing as how Wes is here, I wanted to see what you boys were doing to keep busy."

"Oh, there's lot of keeping busy," Wes assured his grandfather, taking it upon himself to pour his grandfather a drink.

Elias sat and accepted the glass. He watched Wes carefully. "So, what are you doing now? I know you don't need the money that would come with your shares."

Wes shook his head. "It was never about the money," he told his grandfather. "It was more about redeeming myself for who I was as a kid. I decided that I needed some time away to clear my head."

"And you came her to get that clarity by mucking out stalls?"

From his spot the opposite couch, Garrett snickered. "And that's not the only reason he came back."

Wes sent his brother a stern look of warning, willing Garrett to shut the hell up.

Elias looked between them. "What else is there?"

"There's a woman involved," Garrett teased.

"Oh, really?" Elias asked, interested. The gleam in his eye told Wes that his grandfather was looking for all the juicy gossip.

"Okay, fine. A few months ago, I went to Las Vegas for a convention. I was having a great time—made some great connections—but I had some fun, drinking, gambling, winning. But something happened."

"Oh, God, did you get someone pregnant?"

"No, not that. But through a stroke of fate, Daisy Thorne was at the same hotel. She was there for her own conference. We ended up drinking too much, and somewhere along the way, we decided that we may as well get married."

Elias took a moment to digest the information. "Oh, Christ. Between the two of you, can you possibly manage to have one normal marriage?"

Wes looked at Garrett, who was just as amused. Not long ago, he and Willa had been engaged in a fake relationship so Garrett would be able to win control of the ranch. "Nothing wrong with my marriage," Garrett said.

"And I'm no longer married. The divorce papers were signed already."

"That's too bad," Elias said. "I like Daisy."

"Me, too. But it wouldn't have worked out between us."

"And why's that?"

"How much time do you have?" He laid out for his grandfather the differences between them.

"Your visit home is temporary then?"

"Yes. Maybe. I mean, my company is in England."

Elias snorted. "It's the twenty-first century—I don't know if you know about the internet. You can video-call."

Wes and Garrett both laughed. Their grandfather, who still complained about having an email address, was one to lecture him, the tech CEO, on the existence of the internet. "Yeah, I know about the internet. But she doesn't want distance, and she doesn't want to move."

"And you, Wes, what do you want?"

Wes drank his Scotch, contemplating his answer, and then looked at his grandfather. "I want Daisy."

"How are you going to make that happen?"

He thought it over. "I have to move here. I have to do that for her. But I don't see how it's possible."

His cell phone vibrated in his hand, jolting him. He looked down and saw that it was another image from Daisy. This time both Ozzie and the flannel shirt were missing. In response, his heart stuttered in his chest, and he could feel the majority of his blood head south.

As casually as he could muster, Wes stood from his chair and slid the black hat onto his head. "This has been a nice family moment. But I've got to run out. I've got some things to attend to. Elias, it's been nice seeing you."

"You going to see Daisy?" Garrett asked, bringing his glass to his knowing grin.

Wes tipped the brim of his hat to his brother. "You know a gentleman doesn't kiss and tell."

Wes headed outside and, having returned his luxury rental car weeks ago, jumped behind the wheel of the ranch truck and headed down the long driveway to the main road.

He made quick work of the drive to Daisy's home. With every day that passed, the more he saw her, the harder it got to spend time apart. If he didn't hear from her, he grew antsy, she consumed his thoughts, making it harder to focus on anything but seeing her again.

He pulled into her driveway, and she was just getting there herself. He shut off the engine, and after several long strides, met her.

"That was quick," she said.

"I was in the neighborhood."

"Is that a new hat?" she asked.

"It is. Get in the house."

"Don't need to tell me twice," she said, then turned and bounced up the three stairs to her door. He was hot on her heels.

Inside, Ozzie greeted them, but Daisy quickly put him outside for his evening romp in the yard. With the dog occupied, they wordlessly made their way to her bedroom, where he grabbed her wrist, stopping her, and he held her to the wall. His lips crashed down on hers and he felt the tension, his need, for her grow, instead of becoming sated. With every kiss, every touch, every caress of her breath, he needed more.

* * *

Like every time, Daisy's knees nearly buckled when his lips touched hers. Like every one of their kisses before it, it led to more. He lifted her and brought her to the bed. Laying her down, he followed and was pressing against her. He took her mouth again in another kiss. Her hands made their way underneath the hem of his T-shirt. She felt him shudder as she ran her fingertips along the ridges of his abdominal muscles, her touch tickling him lightly. She pushed his shirt up and over his head.

He deepened the kiss, and she felt him about take the air from her body. She might drown in his kiss, but she didn't care. *What a way to go.* She was still dressed, but he broke away to made quick work of her top, pushing it over her head, and then unsnapped her bra. They were skin-on-skin, and he cupped her breasts with his hands, before he kissed his way down her throat, over her chest.

Wes kissed his way to her nipple, where he sucked and nipped at her. Daisy arched, pushing closer against him, as he used his lips and fingers on her nipples, plucking pleasure from deep within her core. He then kissed his way along her midline, detouring only to dip his tongue into her belly button before he reached his destination. He hooked his fingers into the waistband of her pants and pulled down her scrub pants and panties, leaving her naked, as he settled between her parted thighs, his mouth finding her magic spot.

Wes opened his mouth over her, and she eagerly pushed her hips against him. Using his mouth and fingers, he touched her deeply, hitting just the right spot. It almost shocked her how quickly he was able to bring her to the highest of heights every single time. In such a short time, he'd learned every part of her body. Her heart. Her mind.

Wes kissed his way up her body. He kicked off his boots and jeans, and then settled between her thighs again, and pushed inside her. His thrusts were long, slow, and she savored every one of them. Their moans filled the quiet of her bedroom, mingling into air into a crescendo, before Daisy cried out, pushing into Wes's bare chest as he plunged into her one final time, growling out his completed satisfaction in her ear. "I love you, Daisy."

At first, she hadn't been sure she'd heard him right, but when she looked into the depths of his eyes, she could read his thoughts exactly. She couldn't believe what she was about to say. "I love you, too."

His head dropped to her shoulder, and his lips grazed the bare skin of her shoulder. Her skin was electrified, and he lit her nerve endings on fire. He chuckled against the hollow of her throat. She squirmed involuntarily with the feeling, and giggled, as his mouth tickled her skin.

He raised his head and stared at her. His smile was wide and satisfied. His hair fell over his forehead and Willa pushed it aside. He kissed her again, his tongue snaking into her mouth quickly, before retreating, and he scooped her into his arms, pulling her across his chest.

She twirled a finger in the curly hair on his chest,

and then flattened her palms over his sternum. Resting her chin on her hands, she smiled at him. "That was great."

"You're telling me," he replied, trailing his fingers along her spine, causing her to shiver. He pulled a blanket over them, and they lay together for a minute, in complete, comfortable silence.

Everything about Wes felt comfortable; it felt right. After years of choosing the wrong men, but Wes wasn't like any of them. If she hadn't already convinced herself that they weren't long-term, she could see building a life with him. Lying with him naked on her bed was the perfect way to end a day.

"This is nice," she told him, finally speaking using her finger to draw patterns in his dark chest hair.

His arm tightened around her. "It sure is."

She smoothed her hand over his arm, and she smiled sadly.

"What's wrong?"

"This has been a lot of fun."

"And that's got you looking so low over there, despite the good lovin'?"

She smiled. "It would be so easy to fall into an easy thing with you."

"Sure."

"But still, what happens later?" she asked, pushing herself up on her elbow.

"It doesn't matter. You can ask that all you want, but there's no indication of what the future holds, or how it's going to work out."

"You're right. But I don't know if that's enough for me."

"I know that, but that's as good as we've got."

"You say it like that's so simple."

"It is." He reached for her waist and pulled her up so that she was lying on top of him. "It can be."

"It's a good start. But if you're just looking to fly on out of here when you get tired of the ranch life, then what good are you to me?" He said nothing for a beat, and she feared she made a mistake. "I'm sorry if that sounds harsh."

He cupped her cheek, and she couldn't help but lean into his palm. "No, it's fine," he told her. "Never be sorry for how you feel. I can't promise I'll be here forever. But I'm not going anywhere any time soon. How do you know I can't give you that?"

"I guess you'll have to show me."

Neither said anything as they watched each other. They were quiet again, and the only sounds were their slowing breaths, but then the ring of his cell phone filled the air. "You'd better get that," Daisy told him.

"Yeah." Naked, he pushed himself out of bed, and saw that it was Bryant. "Hey."

"About time you answered your phone." Judging by the edge in his voice, Bryant was obviously pissed off about something.

"What's up?"

"What's up is that you've been missing in action for the past two scheduled meetings with TotalCom."

Wes closed his eyes. With how busy he'd been on the ranch, planning the fundraiser and his nights spent with Daisy, he hadn't had much time to focus on his actual business. Out of sight, out of mind. He only had himself to blame. "Dammit," he muttered. "I'm sorry. There's no excuse. I've just been so busy here."

Bryant sighed. "When you told me you were going to Texas, I thought you were still going to be connected to operations."

"Neither of us expected something this big to happen."

"No. But I need to be honest. There has been talk that TotalCom is wondering why you aren't more accessible. If they believe there's a problem in our partnership, they could pull the plug."

There was a clause in the agreement between the two parties that it could happen. "Is there a problem with our partnership?"

Bryant was quiet for a moment, and Wes could picture him weighing his options, carefully choosing his next words. "No," he said finally. "We need you here. Once this deal is signed off, things will be fine."

He cautioned a glimpse at Daisy. Even though she was trying to busy herself with the book on his nightstand, he knew that she was paying close attention to his side of the conversation. Her eyes rose to meet his, and he looked away. "I'll check flights home in the morning."

He watched as Daisy got out of his bed and pulled on her jeans and long-sleeve T-shirt. After saying goodbye to Bryant, he disconnected the called.

"You have to leave again, right?"

"I need to go to London for a little while."

"Yeah, that's fine." She held up her hands. "You don't need permission from me."

"I'm not asking for permission. But I want to know you're okay with it."

"What choice do I have?" She paused. "What about the fundraiser?"

"Willa is helping me with it. I can still be just as involved from afar."

"Oh, yeah. Of course," she said, her voice tinged with sarcasm. "I understand that you have work to do in London. You have a lot of responsibility. But you can't uproot from the commitments you've made here."

"I'll be back for the fundraiser." She scoffed. "Daisy, what do you want from me? I've been here for a couple of months now, and every day you remind me that I'm not long in Applewood."

"Self-fulfilling prophecy, I guess."

"That isn't fair."

"What's not fair? You came here and told me you didn't want to sign the divorce papers, and that you want a life with me. Then we sleep together. Then you leave and sign the papers while you're away. Then you tell me you want to start over. And now this, you're leaving again."

"You know, just because I'm going home, it doesn't mean that we still can't be together. Long distance—"

She put up a hand. "Just stop. You said everything I needed to hear. You can't even keep your company going through long distance. How do you think that'll work with a relationship? Pretty soon it would be 'sorry

I missed your call, it's late here, I'm tired, I've got a bad connection…'"

He had no response to that. He'd already almost blown the largest business deal of his career because of long distance; he knew that it would only be a matter of time before he also let Daisy fall to the wayside. And she didn't deserve that. But he couldn't let her go. "I'm coming back."

"When?" She put up her hand. "And before you answer that question, realize that I don't care when you're returning. I'm only asking because it proves what I've been saying all along. Your life is in London, and not here."

"Okay, fine. You're right, you know. You were right all along. Does that make you feel good about any of this?" Wes was agitated, annoyed at himself for missing the most important meetings of his life, and mad at himself for upsetting Daisy.

"No. None of this makes me feel better. The one consolation I have is that I was right. I didn't let myself fall for you. I just knew that when you left, it would break my heart."

Her lips might be saying that she hadn't fallen for him, but the way her eyes shimmered told him otherwise. He couldn't blame her. He'd felt the same way, and he couldn't help but blame himself.

Eighteen

Wes's suitcase sat on the bed, and he was packing the denim jeans and plaid flannel shirts he'd bought while in Texas. He knew he wouldn't have much use for them in London, but part of him didn't want to leave them behind.

"So, you're leaving." He hadn't heard Garrett come up the stairs and enter his room.

"Yeah. For now, at least. Bryant needs me over there. We're working on a huge deal right now to partner with a social-media giant, and it's too hard to manage that from here."

"You'd think you'd figure out a way, you know, since you specialize in technology for communicating."

Wes laughed. "Yeah, you're right. But if I don't leave now, then I might never. I could easily stay here. With

Daisy, the family, everything. But professionally, I'm on the cusp of something huge."

"You have money."

"It's not just the money. This deal will put me right up there—Jobs, Gates, Zuckerberg."

"Hardwell."

Wes nodded. "It's what I've worked for my entire career. And I was too close to just give it all up. I need to do some work before I trash my entire career."

"And what about Daisy?"

He shrugged. He pictured the look on her face when he'd told her he was going back, and he tried to banish it from his mind. "She seemed to know better than I did that this was going to happen. What can I say? She was right."

"So, you're just giving up?"

"What's the point in staying?"

"Wow. Hurtful."

"I'm sorry," Wes said. "I didn't mean it like that. But I have to get back to London. If I can't be with her, I need to surround myself in my work."

"Fair enough," Garrett said. "I got something for you. It's stupid, but I thought you might like it for the fundraiser. I got this for you. I missed your birthday, for probably the last five years. And it looks like you won't be here for your next one. So, you might as well open it now." He went into the hall and picked up a large, wrapped gift box that he'd left outside the door, then gave it to Wes.

"What's this?"

"Just open it." Wes opened the box and when he

cleared the top and the paper aside, what he saw made his chest clench. It was a black Stetson. He pulled it out. "You didn't have to do this," he told his brother. He turned it over and saw the logo for Hardwell Ranch, embroidered in red and gold thread on the inner lining.

"The embroidery is the same on mine and Elias's."

"Thank you," he said.

"You know, you came here, believing that you didn't fit in. But you do. You're always going to be a part of this family, this town."

"I don't know what to say. I really appreciate it. I'm glad we got to have this time together."

"Me, too."

For the first time he remembered in a long time, Wes and his brother embraced. Not one of those one-armed things, but a full hug. And when they knew they were approaching too much sappiness, they broke apart.

Garrett cleared his throat. "That's not everything," he told him, handing him an envelope.

"What is this?"

"You worked hard," his brother said. "I talked to Elias, and while you may not have been here for six months, it was more like one month, you did the work. He thinks you're entitled to your money and a share of the ranch. And so do I."

Wes looked at the check. He hadn't wanted or expected the money. Hell, his trip home wasn't even about the shares in the family business. "This is too much. It's not why I came here."

"I know, but you did it, anyway. You earned it."

"Thanks." He slipped the check into his wallet, The

money was a nice bonus, but as he thought of Daisy, he could have burst into tears. He could never go back to their dinners together, the nights with her in his bed. The decision to return home would forever alter his life, and he wondered what it would cost him.

Nineteen

Daisy was seated in a booth at Patsy's as Willa joined her. She was already sipping on a glass of red wine, and her and Willa's regular orders were already being prepared.

"Hey," Willa said, sliding into the booth. "Sorry I'm late."

"Don't worry about it. I'm only just getting here myself. I was a little later getting away from my last house visit."

Willa nodded. "Garrett and I just dropped Wes off at the airport in Austin."

"I hope he has a safe flight."

"That's all you have to say about it?"

"What else am I supposed to say?"

"Oh, I don't know," Daisy said. "Something about how you're bummed that Wes is in London."

Daisy shook her head. "I was a realist from the start. Even if he didn't know it."

Willa clearly saw through her. "Cut the BS, girl. How are you feeling?"

"I'm fine."

Willa clearly wasn't convinced. "The truth, though?"

Daisy sighed. "I knew that it would never be forever with him. From day one, I knew that letting myself get too involved was a mistake. I was stupid. He was always going to live in London. After he signed the divorce papers and suggested we start over, I just let myself believe it could be different."

"You weren't stupid," Willa assured her. "He was convincing as hell."

"I didn't take much convincing," she muttered into her wineglass. All it took was Wes showing up in her town, one or two smoldering looks and a touch for him to wind up in her bed.

"Don't be so hard on yourself. You've still got your list, right?" Willa said, trying to lighten the mood with a joke.

Daisy laughed sadly, thinking about the list she'd made on her phone, of the future she wasn't even sure she wanted anymore. "Yeah, I do."

"But really, though. Is it that hard to carry on a long-distance relationship? It is the twenty-first century, after all."

"Long distance is not what I want. You've seen my list. I want someone who can start a life with me here.

I don't want to have to coordinate time zones, work around schedules, show my boobs over video chat," she said, finishing with a laugh. "It's just not the same as having a man in your life. In the flesh."

"I can understand that. I know that you'll find everything you want, and you won't have to compromise your dreams."

Daisy smiled, but she couldn't put too much enthusiasm behind it. She talked a big game, and for a while, even though she knew it wasn't meant to be, it had felt like Wes was it for her. But when reality came knocking, she'd been forced to answer the door and let it in. Wes was leaving, and he'd shown her that while he may visit, he was never coming home for an extended period of time. She'd known it all along, but she was now certain that whatever her future held, it didn't include Wes Hardwell.

While Daisy was consumed by her own melancholy, their meals arrived. "Can we move on?" she asked, picking up her chicken burger. "What's happening with the fundraiser Wes proposed?"

"It's happening, whether he's here, or not," Willa confirmed. "He gave me control over credit card, so it's going to be an amazing event, even if he isn't here to see it."

"Need any help with anything?"

"I think it's under control. You just need to show up on May 17th in a fabulous dress and have a great time."

"Top-shelf open bar?"

"It's all on Wes. Of course, it is."

"Well, I'm in."

Twenty

"Well, ladies and gentlemen, I think we have reached a deal." Otis Easton, the CEO of TotalCom, looked around the boardroom at everyone who'd assembled, including Wes and Bryant, and other key members of their team, and their counterparts at TotalCom. "The papers will all be ready to be signed in the morning, and we can announce the partnership tomorrow after the North American markets open."

Bryant slapped Wes on the shoulder, and the partners exchanged broad smiles. "We did it," Bryant said, before standing to shake the hands of the rest of the people in the room. The deal had been finalized, and they were now partnering with one of the biggest technology companies in the world for their new social-media venture.

Despite the high energy in the room, Wes found himself distracted by the large windows that overlooked the city. The windows of the neighboring buildings twinkled in the darkness of the night. Instead of a deep indigo night sky, the lights made the sky a light violet. Instead of the lights of the city, he found himself missing the stars, which were bright in Applewood. He missed the pace of Applewood, the neighbors, his family. He missed the horses and livestock. He missed working with his hands, putting in the physical work to meet the demands of the ranch, the teamwork with the other ranchers.

Bryant handed him a champagne flute. He'd been too distracted to notice that they'd opened the bottle. This was everything he and Bryant had worked for. Why wasn't he as excited as everyone else? He was missing something, and he knew exactly what it was.

"Everything okay? You're looking more morose than usual."

"Yeah, I'm fine. Just doing some thinking."

"About what? What you're going to do with your pockets full of cash?"

"Yeah, really." He laughed, but he felt none of his usual enthusiasm behind it.

"Okay, what's going on?"

"I don't know," Wes admitted with a shrug. "This city, this whole country, has always felt like home. But the past few months that I've spent in Applewood—it really gave me the actual feeling of home."

Before they could discuss it any further, Otis approached him, with his hand extended, and Wes shook it. "This is going to be good for everyone." Wes smiled—he had to put on a happy, positive face, lest he spook Otis out of the deal.

"We're both very excited."

"Only good things to come for all of us," Bryant said, joining them.

"Now all that's left is the announcement party," Otis said. "We'll invite press from all over the world, celebrities, athletes. It'll be great."

"I like the sound of that," Bryant agreed, rubbing his hands together, ready to get down to business. Too bad Wes didn't share his enthusiasm. It was strange. He'd been in London for a few weeks. He was on track with work, and they had just signed off on the biggest deal of their careers. But he still wasn't happy.

He didn't care about any of the celebrities that would come to their party. He was only interested in the upcoming fundraising gala in Applewood. He already had his ticket bought. It would be a short turnaround. He would only have less than twenty-four hours in Texas, but it would be enough. He only wanted to see Daisy.

"When are you thinking for the announcement party?" Bryant asked.

"We can pull it together pretty quickly," Otis responded. "So then we can roll right along into the work this summer. How about May 17th?"

"May 17th?" Wes asked, those being the only words he'd processed.

"Yeah, is that an issue?"

Bryant quickly spoke over him. "No, there's no issue. Can't wait, it's going to be an awesome party.

Would you excuse us for a moment?" Bryant led Wes out of the boardroom, and away from the congratulatory words. When they were alone in the empty hallway, Bryant turned to face him. "What the hell is going on with you?"

"Nothing."

"You could at least pretend to be happy about the billion-dollar partnership we just entered. This is what we've worked so hard for."

"I am happy about it."

Bryant crossed his arms and looked at him. Wes knew that he had dropped the ball. He'd disappointed his partner. "You've been in a funk since you returned from the States. What happened? Do you miss your family? Is it that woman? The one you married?"

He thought about brushing it off, but he couldn't. "You're right," Wes admitted. "It's Daisy."

His thoughts returned to Daisy, him planning his trip back and with her walking out of his room in the middle of the night.

"Fly her out her, mate. Take her to Paris, or Bali, or anywhere you want to. Rekindle that romance."

He shook his head. "No, she won't see me. She probably hates my guts. But that's not all. I had planned to go home for a period. There's a fundraising gala. It was my idea, as a way to redeem myself to the townsfolk."

"Okay."

"I was going to go home for it. It's important." He paused. "It's on the same night."

Bryant shrugged. "It's too bad you're going to miss it, I guess." Bryant's eyes widened as he realized what

Wes's silence implied. "Oh, come on, man. You're not going to miss it, are you?"

Then it came to Wes. He didn't need the money that came with the business. He didn't need to live thousands of miles away, on a different continent, then his family. He was his own man, and he didn't need the approval of the people of Applewood. He could live happily on the ranch, or with Daisy, if he wanted. "No, I'm not going to miss it."

"You can't miss the party," Bryant told him. "What will Otis think?"

He shook his head. "I spent too much of my life worrying about what people thought and how I was perceived."

"The deal with TotalCom, though."

"I'm out," Wes told him.

"Wes."

"I'm going home to Applewood. You don't need me. You know the work and you have the rest of the team behind you. You don't need me. Hell, you arranged this deal while I was in America. Just see it this way—now you'll get more money and glory for yourself, and I'll always be available for you to pick my brain if you need it."

"I won't," Bryant responded. Wes knew his friend was joking.

"Jerk." He paused. "I'm so sorry, but I'm not signing. You have to do it without me."

"If this is something you need to do, then I can't argue with that." He held out his hand. "It was nice working with you."

Wes shook his former partner's hand. "It was. We were a good team."

"One of the best."

"But now I have to go."

"Maybe I'll come visit sometime. You can teach me how to be a cowboy."

Wes laughed, picturing Bryant, in his six-thousand-dollar suit, on the back of a horse. "Yeah, anytime."

"I'd better get back in there," Bryant said.

"I'll see you," Wes told him. "Best of luck with it all."

"You too, friend," he replied. "Although I think you're going to need it more than I will."

Wes watched his friend walk away, taking leadership of the company he'd helped build with him. He took a deep breath. He knew he had made the right decision; his future wasn't in London. His future was in Applewood, Texas. His home was with Daisy.

If she'd have him.

Twenty-One

Alone, Daisy walked into event space that Willa had arranged for the fundraising gala. It was the ballroom in one of Applewood's few hotels, and had been appointed elegantly with golden up-lighting and luxurious swagged fabric on the ceiling and walls. It was a full house. The town's richest and most influential citizens were in attendance, and from a quick look at the bidding table, they were already bidding large numbers on the prizes Willa had arranged. It was a stunning affair and with Wes's credit card, she'd made it perfect.

Without Wes there, she could feel the finality of the situation. They were done. No matter how ill-conceived, chaotic and lust-and-alcohol-fueled their coupling had been, it had been fun. And no matter how annoyed she might be at him, she missed Wes.

"How do you like it?" Willa asked, coming to stand beside her. She turned and took in their surroundings. "I think it turned out pretty well."

"You did an amazing job, Willa. This is phenomenal. And judging by the number of tickets sold and the bids that are already in, the fire department is on their way to getting that new truck."

"I know," she said, beaming. "It's such a great cause. Wes had a great idea."

"Yeah, he sure did," Daisy said, hiding her frown behind her wineglass.

"I'm sorry. I shouldn't have brought him up."

"No," Daisy said, putting a comforting hand on her friend's shoulder. "Don't worry about it. Of course, you're allowed to bring him up. He's your brother-in-law. I'm fine. Don't worry about me."

Willa frowned. "Then what's wrong?"

She sighed. "I miss him more than I want to."

"Of course, you do. You're in love with him."

Yes. "No, I'm not."

"I don't believe you."

"Okay, fine. Maybe I *do* love him," she admitted. "But that doesn't matter. He's in England and won't be coming back anytime soon." Even though she knew that she'd sent him away, she had no place in his world—just like he had no place in hers. Her feelings hadn't mattered when reality came knocking. She would have to move on and forget about him.

"Has he contacted you since he left?"

"Yeah, we've sent a couple of texts. But that's it. They're working on some big partnership deal that he can't talk about. But that's what I said would happen. His work is what's most important to him. He even left the ranch because he needed to be in London. His company will always be his priority. There is no way we can maintain any sort of long-distance relationship like that."

"And you don't think he's coming back?"

Daisy scoffed. "If he does, it won't be to see me."

"You don't know that."

"We didn't exactly end on good terms," she explained. "We had a pretty big fight."

"And how do you feel about it?"

"I feel horrible. But it needed to end before either of us became any more invested. A bit of hurt now is better than full-on devastation later." She paused. "But I do miss him. He brought out something in me that I haven't been able to feel in years."

"How do you know it's over?" Willa asked, looking over Daisy's shoulder.

"It just is."

"I wouldn't be so sure about that." She tilted her chin. "Look behind you."

Daisy turned her head to see Wes entering the ballroom. His black suit was immaculately tailored and paired with a crisp white shirt and black tie. The look was completed with a black Stetson that sat upon his head. He cut quite a figure in the room, standing out almost immediately, people stopping him to shake his hand. He looked up and their eyes connected. He excused himself from the group and headed in her direction.

He looked her over with obvious appreciation. The form-fitting red dress she'd selected had the intended effect. "Daisy, I don't want the first thing I say about you to be related to your appearance, but you look absolutely stunning."

"You don't look so bad yourself," she told him. "What are you doing here? I didn't think you'd be back for a while."

"I wasn't supposed to. But I wanted to get my move finished before all of the work coming this spring."

That comment stopped her. "Your move? You've got another place in London? What does that have to do with coming back to Texas."

He chuckled. "You're so determined to see the worst. I've moved home. I'll be living in Applewood."

"Oh, really?" Her heartbeat increased. She thought back to their fight. Even if he was living home, she doubted he would want anything else to do with her. "What about London? What about how difficult you found it running your company so far from your partner? What about the big deal you were working on?"

"Well, we secured the partnership."

"That's great."

"And then I left."

"What do you mean?"

"I spoke to Bryant, I told him that wasn't the life I wanted anymore. I stepped away from it all, and I moved home."

She smiled.

"What was that for?" he asked.

"You called Applewood home."

"It is home," he told her, taking her hands in his. "What I realized when I returned to London is that it wasn't my home anymore. I had everything I could have ever wanted there. But it wasn't enough. I walked away from it. I missed you, I missed your snark and your sass. I missed your hair, the way you hand feels in mine..." His words drifted off. "I'd better get to my point, before I lose myself."

"What is your point, exactly?"

"There's some of that snark and sass. I never had much of a concept of home. As a kid, I never felt I fit in here, or with my family. But being with you, I never doubted if I belonged. 'Home,' Daisy, is wherever you are."

She was stunned into silence. The party continued around them, but she couldn't see or hear anything but Wes.

"I love you, Daisy. And I know it's not the first time I say that to you, and if you let me, I guarantee it won't be the last."

She raised her hand to his firm jaw, and even though he was clean-shaven, his cheek rasped against her palm. "Wes, I don't want to be the reason you stay here. I don't want you stay or feel trapped or feel like you missed out on an incredible career. I don't want you to come to resent me someday."

"I would never resent you. Or feel trapped by you. How could I feel trapped here? Especially if I'm with you. I've thought about this, and I know what I want— a life here with you. I want you to move in with me on the ranch. There's more than enough room for all of us. There's room for Ozzie to run around. I've had business success, fortune, but that's not what I want anymore. I want the things you told me you wanted, marriage, kids. We can hang a tire swing on one of the trees. Hell, we've already got that white picket fence you wanted so much around the place. I don't care. I want my life here. I want our life here."

A tear dropped from her eye. "Wes," she said, the word more of a breathless whisper.

"Are you okay? Did I upset you?"

"No. Not at all. I'm happy. This is perfect. All of that sounds perfect."

"But that's not all."

"What else could there be?"

He pulled a square box from his pocket. "I have something else for you."

"Wes."

He took her hand and, ignoring the rest of the partygoers, he dropped to his knee in front of her. "I want to marry you, Daisy. But for real this time. Without the tequila, the flashing lights, the bells of the slot machines. No officiant dressed in an Elvis jumpsuit."

Daisy looked around to see that some people had turned their attention to the quiet spectacle that Wes was creating, but she didn't care. She turned her attention to him. "I liked Elvis, though."

He laughed. "Okay, maybe we can find another Elvis. But the point is, I want a real wedding with you. With our friends and family, flowers, the whole nine yards. What do you say? Will you marry me?"

Daisy dropped to her knees as well. "I will," she told

him. "I'll marry you." He slid the ring on her finger and kissed her. "Maybe we could find an Elvis impersonator in Applewood."

His chuckle vibrated through her as he held her close. "Anything you want."

* * * * *

Katie Frey has spent the better part of her adult life in pursuit of her own happily-ever-after. Said pursuit involved international travel and a few red herrings before she moved from Canada to Switzerland to marry her own mountain man.

She is a member of a tight-knit critique group and an avid writer. *Fake Dating, Twin Style* is her third novel for Harlequin Desire. She wrote the bulk of the book in a local coffee shop... Any excuse to stay near the fresh croissants!

You can join her newsletter here, bit.ly/3COLHoP, and visit her author website here, www.romanceinthealps.com.

Books by Katie Frey

Harlequin Desire

Hartmann Heirs

Montana Legacy
How to Catch a Cowboy
Fake Dating, Twin Style

Visit the Author Profile page
at Harlequin.com for more titles.

You can also find Katie Frey on Facebook, along
with other Harlequin Desire authors,
at Facebook.com/HarlequinDesireAuthors.

Dear Reader,

When you first start writing, common advice is to write what you know. That advice echoed as I sat down to write Amelia's story.

I'm not divorced, but I can relate to leaving bad relationships (and the havoc this can wreak on how we see ourselves). For this installment of Hartmann Heirs, I wanted to feature a heroine who builds *herself* back up after a bad marriage tears her down. Amelia has spent her life trying to make all the right choices and pleasing everyone, but an ugly divorce and her position running the failing hospitality division of her family's estate leave her wanting to prove herself. She can't fail again! But who could be worthy of our heroine?

Enter dreamy (and steamy) Antone Williams, a retired NFL player/do-gooder looking to launch a new brand of whiskey and seeking the right partner to make it happen.

Amelia and Antone both carry a lot of baggage, but a common goal brings them together, and quickly they discover that sometimes an extra set of hands can lighten any load. I was really excited to write about guarded characters, each with their own secrets, overcoming trauma and taking responsibility for their own happiness, even when it seems impossible and out of reach. And...a twin switcheroo. Because who doesn't like a good old hidden identity!

I can't wait for you to read it.

Bisous from the Alps,

Katie

PS: Please say hi on Instagram, @romanceinthealps; Goodreads/BookBub, katie_frey; or, more embarrassingly, TikTok, @romanceinthealps, or, for the juicy stuff, join my newsletter here, bit.ly/3COLHoP.

FAKE DATING,
TWIN STYLE

Katie Frey

This book is dedicated to
Ellie Biondo and Antoine Robert.
You both know why.

Let's drink some more wine and
keep dreaming up sexy Westerns.

One

Bad Days Were Made of These

Subject: Notice of Litigation

Dear Amelia Hartmann,
Please consider this letter a formal notice of service regarding the alimony and spousal maintenance request in the case of Amelia Hartmann vs. Scott Altman.

Pursuant to the Divorce Act, Mr. Altman is seeking a lump-sum payment in lieu of ongoing spousal maintenance. While we regret the necessity of legal action in this matter, please consider this demand letter as binding notice and service of process in the state of Montana.

Blah, blah, blah.

Amelia Hartmann scanned the letter for the millionth time. She bit the inside of her cheek and willed herself to stay calm. She needed to focus on the silver lining: at least the divorce process was moving forward.

"While we regret the necessity of legal action...*pfft*." Amelia, more commonly Mia to friends, read the last leg of the letter aloud, hands shaking. "Yes. I'm sure he's just howling with regret."

Of all the days to receive a demand letter, this Monday was shaping up to be one for the books. Amelia shook the letter toward her new lawyer, PJ Banks, regretting only for a moment her inability to trust this scandal with the family attorney, Saul Kellerman.

No, that would be impossible. The minute Saul sniffed a scandal, the impending lawsuit would be elevated to her mother, or worse, her big brother Nick, the poster child for responsible decisions. Then, before she could turn around, everyone would be involved in her personal business with helpful opinions—or worse, advice.

Saul had started her divorce process eleven months ago, but when progress stalled, she'd decided to switch tack. She'd asked Saul to draft up a standard divorce agreement and advised that she'd handle getting it signed herself. Anything to get out of the family rumor mill. Alas, the process was proving harder than she thought, Especially without a lawyer. When she bumped into PJ, the coincidence had felt like a godsend.

The last thing she wanted was Nick, the oldest Hartmann sibling and current CEO of Hartmann Enterprises, sighing in reproach and cracking the family checkbook to make her "divorce problem" go away. Disclosing her intentions to divorce had been embarrassment enough. A media-worthy public lawsuit to negotiate spousal support? For her unemployed deadbeat ex-husband? All this *after* she'd announced her divorce as a *fait accompli* to the family, inferring that her divorce was signed, sealed and delivered, when it was anything but? *No.* She had to keep this matter private for as long as possible. PJ was her only chance to save face, even if it was looking like that chance was getting more expensive by the demand letter…

Ironically, PJ Banks, attorney-at-law, had found her, so there was every chance this matter could resolve quickly with no one the wiser. Amelia had rubbed elbows with him at a black-tie Harvard Alumni event only two weeks prior, accepting his business card with butterflies in her stomach. He was six foot two and looked the part of James Bond—slick and devilishly attractive. When they'd met, she'd wondered if he was a little too slick and a little too charming, but when she called him, he remembered her. Anyway, maybe *too slick* wasn't a bad quality in legal representation.

Amelia curled her fingers into a fist, letting her nails bite into the flesh of her palm. She had to be the epitome of insane, continually exhibiting the same pathetic actions, expecting a different result. Thinking she might impress her family instead of disappointing them? It was time to close the door on her girlish fantasies and focus instead on the fantasy in front of her: PJ Banks.

"Don't worry, Ms. Hartmann, all demand letters read the same. They need to come out of the gate strong, or we're less likely to settle." PJ spun on the leather chair, unruffled.

"Please, call me Amelia," she corrected, wishing she hadn't needed to ask. This was feeling all too professional. All too *legal*.

"Word on the block is your friends call you Mia." PJ raised an eyebrow at her from across the executive desk.

That's better. She preferred the flirting to the cool professionalism, if only when it came to cute attorneys. "Right, but I wouldn't exactly say we're friends just yet." *Best keep him on his toes; all these Ivy boys were the same.*

"I get it, I get it." He shook the letter in her direction, letting his gaze linger a little too long. "Don't worry about it for a minute, pretty lady, we'll get this sorted before we get too friendly."

"The hell we will. I'm not about to settle anything." Amelia surprised herself with the ferocity of her answer, hoping for a minute that she didn't scare him with her vehemence. But she was more than a pretty lady, and somehow, the moniker felt demeaning. "I'm not responsible for what Scott does anymore," she said, softening her initial outburst with a half smile. "We're divorced. I mean, he agreed. He can't just change his mind a few months later."

She pressed her hands into her thighs, smoothing

the pencil skirt. She'd been young when she'd married Scott, too easily affected by his dimple and blatant confidence. The romance had burned hot, then burned out. It was hard to be in love with someone when their true colors were so…at odds with your own. Yes, twenty-two was too young to be married, but given the circumstances, twenty-nine felt a little late to get divorced.

Finally remembering her manners, she asked, "Can I get you some water?" PJ didn't have an office in Bozeman; his firm worked out of a headquarters in New York City. He'd flown in at the last minute at her insistence. But his lack of a local office was hardly a hurdle—the Hartmanns owned more than enough real estate in Bozeman. Heck, they owned a lot of real estate everywhere. It was one of the benefits of being a property magnate. But she'd wanted to keep things quiet, so they'd met in a hotel. Now they discussed her private affairs in a conference room. She'd called a few references, clients his secretary had offered up. The reviews were not raves, but were certainly strong, especially as he had no connection to her family, apart from being a Harvard alumnus. *Besides, who raved about their lawyer?*

"Sparkling, but don't worry, I'll get it," PJ answered. "It's always fun trying to find the mini fridges. Amazing how these commercial designers managed to hide them in cabinets and bookcases." PJ returned with two glasses of sparkling water. He slid a coaster across the desk in her direction and issued her a frat-boy smile.

It was hard not to feel disappointed by this lawsuit. Perhaps it was naive, but she was shocked that the man she'd once loved was now after her money and in such an overt and crude manner. Amelia tapped her thigh seven times as she sat, finding comfort in the habit. She'd gotten very good at hiding her tics, but ever since she'd been a teenager she'd twitched whenever she'd faced pressure and stress.

"Right, of course." *Tap, tap, tap, tap, tap, tap, tap.*

"Listen, the Altman family doesn't have a lot to lose. The fact that he was cut off before you were married—"

"—he never told me that." She'd always thought he'd been cut off after they'd eloped. To think Scott had let her feel responsible for his destitution… Now it was evident that it had all been part of his ploy to use her financially. One she'd totally fallen for. Hook, line and sinker.

"Hearsay." He corrected. "The fact that he was in a vastly different financial position than you at the time of your marriage, and, subsequently, the time of your divorce, puts him in a strong position to negotiate now for ongoing spousal support."

"We have a prenup, and no kids. And he's perfectly capable of working—this request for spousal support is a farce," Mia offered weakly, hating herself for being relieved that Nick and Saul had gotten involved in her affairs seven years ago, insisting on the fated prenup.

"Miss Hartmann. Amelia. I think you need to consider the facts. Legal battles are expensive and long. Bottom line, it might be cheaper to pay this problem away, and I think your husband knows that." PJ smiled.

"Ex-husband. And you're telling me a divorce might

cost me a lot more than a five-hundred-thousand-dollar settlement? What if he turns around to sue for a million? I'm surprised he forgot the pain, suffering, emotional duress and all that in his demand... I've already told my family I'm divorced. I don't want them to know it isn't finalized."

Her head sank momentarily into her hands. "This is just *so* embarrassing." She picked up the demand letter and waved it at PJ. "This letter reads like a ransom note more than a lawsuit." Her voice shook. She didn't want to say aloud the fact that the pain, suffering and emotional duress for the past five years had all been hers.

"It's a small-time settlement, Amelia, considering your trust. I can assure you these types of letters are run-of-the-mill. He's just priming his ability to negotiate. Focus on the bright side. This won't set you back much, even after my fee." He laughed.

PJ's silky optimism was reassuring. He wouldn't be making jokes if this wasn't a laughing matter...

"There is no bright side." She picked up the glass and raised it to her mouth, then placed it back on the side table with enough momentum to cause some of the water to slosh over the rim.

There had to be another way. *If she could prove he'd misrepresented his finances and that he'd been cut off before their marriage, she could perhaps negotiate an annulment in lieu of divorce. Which would void the demand for spousal support.*

Or...if he could engage in some sort of unlawful behavior, not exactly a stretch for Scott, and she could prove it... She would be free. .

PJ cleared his throat. "I'm your lawyer, I work for you. But because I'm a lawyer, I do need to give you my advice, which, based on my experience, is that it's always cheaper to settle. It doesn't need to be painful."

Amelia shook her head. "The last thing the Hartmanns need is a domino effect of settlement requests. We won't settle."

Eyeing the water, she picked it up and took a sip, replacing the glass on the leather coaster before making her way out of the conference room.

And as for her? There was only one thing she wanted: to put all this behind her. But she was awake in this nightmare.

It was not a good time to be Amelia Hartmann.

Do not cry.

Amelia squeezed her eyes shut and willed herself not to tear up. It was a mild fender bender, hardly a matter of life and death.

Apart from the fact that it was.

Because this was her fourth car accident in as many months, she was gonna lose her license.

Was it six points for speeding and then another two for the crash?

She pressed her eyes shut and tried to remember the last lecture she'd had to sit through at the DMV, only three weeks prior. Her memory was unaided by the fact that she'd done her best to block out every element of the humiliating experience, but she was pretty sure the incident included a menacing threat involving a revoked license. This was what she got for thinking her Monday was at an all-time low.

Her predicament was made worse by the fact that this accident wasn't even her fault. The Lexus ahead had braked out of nowhere. It was hardly her responsibility to have laser-like reflexes to avoid ramming an *irresponsible* driver. The offending motorist needed to follow the rules of the road.

Technically, though, it was her fault. She *should* have stopped.

The last thing she wanted was to end up with a nosy chauffeur like Nick's. How many times had she and Evie, her twin, mocked him for his penchant for personal drivers? And now, if she lost her license, she'd find herself in the same pickle, driven around in one of the family's limos, with a suited driver jumping out to open her door for her every time she craved a Starbucks? *No. Not possible.* Hadn't her divorce provided enough fodder for comedic relief? For once, it would be nice not to be the punch line of every joke at a family dinner. Or board meeting.

For identical twins, she and Evie couldn't be more different, with her sister leading a charmed life as a Hollywood starlet while Amelia headed up the struggling hospitality arm of the family's illustrious estate. As far as the family was concerned, Evie could walk on water, but when it came to actual responsibility, Evie was forever leaving Amelia holding the ball. And while Amelia considered Evie a *well-meaning* walking disaster, her twin hadn't had so much as a ticket for jaywalking. Although her ticketless state was likely due more to her ability to flirt with authority figures than to having been born under a lucky star.

Amelia bit the inside of her cheek. If they were twins, wouldn't they both have been born under the same lucky star? One glance at the cop who had witnessed her latest fender bender and she knew better.

The cop, uniform buttons protesting heavily against the too-tight shirt, walked toward her, indulging in the slow saunter of a man who knew he was in the right.

Yep. She was going to get a ticket, and when the cop saw "Hartmann" on her license, he'd fall into one of two camps: a fan of her family, or, worst case, not.

Groping at the foot of the passenger seat, she reached for her purse, but to her surprise, her hand slipped across the cool pleather of Evie's clutch.

What were the chances of her twin's ID being in the forgotten purse?

Her chest tightened as she flipped the bag open, quickly scanning its contents.

There it was. Her twin's license. Her *identical* twin's license.

Her twin, the one with the squeaky-clean record, had left her ID in Mia's car.

Again.

"License and registration, ma'am." The cop extended a hand, decidedly landing him in the "not a fan" camp of law enforcement.

It seemed like a good idea to pass him Evie's ID, but the moment the cop headed toward the Lexus with it in hand, Amelia regretted the deception. If Evie were to find out, she'd just as likely find the trick hilarious than be mad, but hilarity aside, Mia was acutely aware that she had committed a felony.

Lying to a cop was a felony, right?

Amelia pushed her hair off her face and rooted through the rest of Evie's bag, as much to distract herself as anything else. Inside was a tube of Ruby Woo lipstick in fire-engine red. Twisting the tube, she applied the lipstick-like armor and prepared to sink into her lie. If she was going to play the part of Evie Hartmann, she needed to be as confident as possible.

Amelia watched as the cop leaned toward the window of the damaged Lexus, then choked back a surprise as the cop took off his aviators. The policeman handed a notepad to the driver, awkwardly offered up his pen, then, much to her shock, turned his back to the window and took a selfie with the driver.

Of all the infernal happenings. Had she hit an Instagram influencer? No. What kind of influencer would impress a cop?

The cop was nodding and shaking his head, waving away the driver. Then she watched in horror as the cop handed over *her sister's ID to the man behind the wheel of the Lexus.*

She reached for the Perrier in the driver's-side cup holder. Selfies? Really? Perhaps she'd been responsible for the fender bender, but that was hardly as illegal as sharing her personal info with the driver of another car? Okay, her sister's personal info. Still, she was going to have a word with this cop. With his boss. With his boss's boss. Nick had the Commissioner of Labor and Industry on speed dial, and as loath as she was to involve her big brother in this incident, she didn't suffer fools easily. If the cop wasn't impressed with the Hartmann name, it wouldn't take long to flex it enough for the desired effect.

Then a chill set in. She couldn't involve her brother. Not without admitting she had passed Evie's ID as her own. Not without admitting her wrongdoing.

Amelia focused on the car in front of her, willing herself to see through the glossy black metal for a glimpse of the unknown driver. Then the door of the Lexus opened, and she watched as the most beautiful man she'd ever seen in real life stepped out of the car.

She reached again for the water and hastily gulped another sip. For a quick moment, she was grateful for Evie's lipstick and wondered if there was any perfume in the purse.

Attention back on her sister's clutch, Amelia smiled. Evie was dependable for one thing: her love of *Dior J'adore*. Pulling the thin travel tube of perfume from the bag, she grinned and attempted to spritz some of it nonchalantly.

The atomizer was stuck. She watched as Mr. Handsome took a few confident steps toward her and she manically pressed on it again. Still stuck. Again, she insisted, pushing the perfume vial closer to her top. Then her thumb slipped and an unexplainable reflex made her robotically repeat the motion.

Instantly, the car interior filled with the too-sweet smell of her sister. But it was *too much*. Because of course it was. Amelia was hardly a starlet who'd managed to indulge in a discreet dose of fragrance; instead, her sweaty hand had slipped, producing three shots of *J'adore* in a highly concentrated wet blotch on the front of her silk top. She frowned into the rearview mirror. It looked like she was lactating. Because she wasn't Evie, she was clumsy Mia, the almost-divorcée that could never *ever* manage to look good for a first meet with the impossibly gorgeous driver of the car she'd just hit.

Said driver was tall, his shadow casting ten feet of shade, but it was more than his hulking form that caused her to lose her breath. He was achingly familiar. Like a movie star, but not from any movie she'd seen. But she had seen him before, of that she was sure. Indulging in another quick look at herself in the rearview mirror, she loosed the button of her blouse and flipped back the collar. *Was it better to show off a wet splotch or a bit of skin? Skin, surely.*

Before she could put much thought into the question, Handsome was at her window, offering her ID back to her.

"Evie Hartmann. Nice to meet you." His voice was low and warm, radiating the scratchy timbre of a man who indeed found it nice to meet her. For a minute, she debated whether or not to open the window, desperate to shield him from her perfume overdose.

Lowering the window a fraction of an inch, Amelia accepted the ID and looked through the window up at warm chocolate eyes.

"I'm really sorry about the accident. I mean, you stopped out of nowhere, and I wasn't expecting—"

She was silenced as he waved his hands at her to

stop. He gestured at her to lower the window a little farther.

Amelia took in a deep breath and pressed her eyes shut against the sting of sweetness that hung in the air of her vehicle. Instead of opening the window, she pushed open the car door, managing to get out while minimizing the escape of perfume fumes.

"I'm really sorry, I didn't mean to hit you." Amazingly, she managed to sound breathy and more like Evie than she'd dared to hope.

"I'd like to believe that's true." The man smiled. Standing only a few feet away from her, he was even more impressive in close proximity. Clearly, he had no issues with dysfunctional atomizers: his scent was innately masculine, like spice and cloves and rain all mixed together in the most intoxicating packaging she'd ever smelled.

African American, fit as hell and dressed for business, the man with beautiful shoulders flashed a sure smile at her. The black T-shirt he wore clung to his muscled chest, the thin cotton doing little to disguise the ridges beneath it. The man had the body of a professional athlete or MMA fighter. A maroon blazer dressed up the shirt and matched his bordeaux slacks. He was the opposite of trying too hard. Amelia willed herself not to fling her hair and issue a shrill laugh, and instead pasted on a stiff smile. "Really. I don't even know how it happened. I guess I wasn't expecting you to brake so suddenly."

The man's relaxed expression tightened, and immediately Mia regretted the statement. She had a nasty habit of getting defensive, but being eleven months into a shitty divorce process that threatened to drag even longer would do that to the best of people.

"It doesn't really matter how we got here. I just want to keep this out of the press."

Out of the press? Who was this guy?

"Well, it's nice to meet you. I'm, er, Evie Hartmann." Her voice caught, then she pressed her shoulders back. Hartmann. She was a Hartmann. "And I'd also like to keep this out of the press."

He might not be from around here, but everyone knew the Hartmanns. He'd have to live under a rock not to know her family.

"Antone. I'm Antone Williams."

Then reality hit her. The Antone Williams? Wide receiver for the Texas Horns and the most decorated player in the NFL since Jerry Rice? That was why he looked familiar.

If only she really *were* Evie, and could think of something clever to say on the fly.

"Nice to meet you," she managed instead of something brilliant or witty. *At least he didn't appear woozy from the haze of J'adore surrounding them...*

"I'd say. Quite fortuitous, if I'm being honest."

It was an odd answer. "Fortuitous? Sure, I mean, yeah, it's downright lucky that I hit your car. Nothing better than being late for Monday meetings."

"Sorry to have kept you," he replied a little coolly.

This man could go from hot to not in a matter of seconds. Amelia shifted her weight from one stilettoed foot to another. "I mean, I hope you're not worried, I will, of course, cover all the damages."

Again, the athlete waved her away. "Honestly, its just a few scratches. I'm mostly concerned about keeping this out of the press. The cop agreed not to press charges for reckless endangerment, assuming I agreed not to pursue things."

"Reckless endangerment?" she managed to repeat. It could have been worse than losing her license; maybe she would have faced a criminal charge. *Or Evie would have...*

"There's some road work, which means the speed limit during working hours is only twenty miles per hour. I guess you were doing forty when you rear-ended me, and were speeding in a school zone..." His tone took on a disapproving affectation, and as he ticked her offences off on strong fingers, she couldn't help but bristle in response.

"The construction work, and the school zone, for that matter, are hardly well marked... I mean, I'm sure my lawyer would have a field day with this." Her voice cracked despite the false bravado. *How had she missed this? Had she been so lost in thought about Scott?*

"I signed an autograph for the cop and allowed him a selfie. I don't think this has to go any farther than that." Antone smiled, and once more, despite herself, she felt disarmed. Maybe it was the perfectly groomed beard, closely trimmed to a dimpled cheek and cleft chin, or maybe it was the sparkling eyes and barbered hair.

Or the fact that he smelled like the best part of everything male and was leaning only inches from her.

Once again, her mouth felt curiously dry, and she busied her hands in her hair, tucking wisps behind her ears. "Well, er, thanks for that." She did her best to wrestle up a smile, trying once again to channel Evie's flirty energy, something she hadn't managed much of on her own account since her recent almost-divorce.

"I didn't do it for free." He winked at her. "There's a catch."

Of course. Her heart sunk.

There was always a catch, and it was rarely her.

Two

When Opportunity Knocks

Antone Williams smiled again, eyeing the brunette as she shifted from foot to foot. Of all the people to rear-end him, Joanna's favorite actress was the last person he'd been expecting at the wheel. To think, only that morning, his best friend's wife had prattled on for twenty minutes about her latest rom-com obsession, and here she was: the lead actress, Evie Hartmann, the starlet herself, in the flesh. Sure, running into a Hartmann in Montana wasn't exactly against all odds— they were the most influential family in the state, not to mention one of its largest employers, *at least for the moment*. But catching Evie between films was lucky indeed. He hadn't sorted a birthday present for Joanna, and now he had leverage for the gift to end all gifts, not to mention a female with enough local celebrity to be of great help to his launch, should she be so inclined.

He frowned a moment. He figured she'd be of great help whether she was inclined or not; it was likely she'd want to keep this accident out of the press as much as he did.

When he'd seen the flash of brunette on the driver's license the cop had wielded, his curiosity had been piqued. It wasn't a secret: he had a thing for brunettes. But when he'd seen the name on the license, he'd agreed to break a cardinal rule and indulge the officer with a selfie in return for the privilege of returning the ID to Miss Hartmann herself. It was a price he'd happily pay again as he watched the wide-eyed woman smile up at him.

"You're not what I expected," he started, smiling at the starlet as she squirmed before him. Perhaps dropping the threat of a misdemeanor had been a little childish, but he wanted her to feel indebted to him. It would make the ask a little easier.

"And what were you expecting?" She smiled at him, batting her eyes with a little too much calculation for Antone's taste. He frowned.

"Why don't we go take a look at the damage first, then we can make a game plan." *Game plan*. He was still talking like a wide receiver, and he needed to make the transition to businessman. It was the next step, and a critical one at that. He needed to keep his head in the end game, sports metaphors notwithstanding.

Evie Hartmann was taller than he expected, at least

five foot ten, although three inches could be accounted for by the Manolo Blahniks. Not that her stature mattered much; he reckoned he could still bench-press her with one hand. Beside his six-foot-four frame, she was startlingly small despite her height, although she boasted curves in all the right places. Her power suit had him wondering if she had some sort of meeting with an agent or producer, since she hardly looked the part of a fashion victim. But he had to admit, the unbuttoned top was a delicious combination of prim, proper and sexy all wrapped up in one tantalizing morsel.

Evie made a beeline for his bumper, and he allowed himself a brief moment to watch her walk away. It was a selling point for pencil skirts, the way they hugged and highlighted the best part of a woman's body.

Ignoring the tightening that resulted from his blatant appreciation for Evie's unexpected fashion decisions, he followed her footsteps, frowning at her assessment.

"I'd say this is a pretty easy fix. I mean, I've seen a lot worse," she stammered, looking everywhere but at him.

Hell. That wouldn't work. He needed her to feel in his debt.

"Didn't realize you were a mechanic."

"Didn't realize you were so glib," she said, mimicking his tone, then blanched.

"It'll be inconvenient to lose my car to a garage. I'm in town on business. Time-sensitive business." Best not to address the razor-sharp wit of Miss. Hartmann. She could be useful. She could be just what he needed, in more ways than one.

"Look. I'll figure out the damages and sort this out, but I'm going to need something in return."

She reached for her purse and pulled out a large pair of sunglasses, quickly shading her hazel eyes. "Now, wait—"

"It's not about the costs. I was thinking, maybe you'd come as my date to a birthday party?" Antone had cut her off to avoid interrogation.

She looked stunned. And maybe a little annoyed.

Antone had asked out lots of women. Usually, it was as easy as breathing, but something about this particular woman standing under the ten o'clock Montana sun felt different. Something about Evie Hartmann was unexpected.

Maybe it was the way she fell back on her left leg, letting her hip jut forward as she teetered from foot to foot. Maybe it was the way she pushed back the hair from her face instead of the typical hair shake he so often encountered from the would-be femme fatales he tended to meet. Maybe it was her nervous laugh. He didn't know. He found it all far too appealing, and he was all too aware of the fact that he hadn't found anyone appealing for as long as he could remember.

"Are you asking me out?" The question was just loud enough to be heard, and it provoked a laugh.

"I guess I am. My best friend's wife is a huge fan, and if I managed to bring one of her favorite actresses to her birthday party, well, let's just say I'd be assuring myself more invitations to home-cooked meals than I deserve."

"So, this is for the home-cooked meals? That makes

sense, my brothers are the same, hollow legs the lot of them." She half smiled.

No, it wasn't only about home-cooked meals, but she didn't need to know that. Yet.

He took a step toward her, and he couldn't help but be aware of her. The prim posture betrayed by tempting curves, the sun-kissed strands of her hair lifted by the breeze, the way she sm—okay, perhaps the perfume was a bit much. But still. "How long are you in Montana? Between films, I'm guessing?" He grinned, unable to stop himself.

She hesitated, then shook her head. "I'm not sure. A while."

"Me too. The party is tomorrow night. I'll text you the details?" He held his phone forward and watched as she accepted it.

She hesitated before adding her number. "Where is this party?"

"My place. Springhill." He felt his chest tighten as he said it aloud. Big Sky, 12,000 acres on the outskirts of town, in the most expensive zip code in Bozeman. She'd know it because the Hartmanns lived there too. "I'm renovating, so the barbecue is outdoors. It was a hell of a push to get my place party-ready, but at least the landscaping is done. You might have to pee in a port-a-potty, though…" He shoved his hands in his pockets and tried his best not to frown. He wasn't kidding about the port-a-potty. "Renovations are the worst, and mine is even more disastrous than I'd thought possible."

"Barbecue," she repeated, shifting again and holding eye contact with an unnerving precision.

Not only would he be popular with Joanna, but Evie would draw focus to his impending career move—becoming the owner of America's next great whiskey distillery—and get him some publicity; it was the least she could do after scraping up his Lexus.

"You're not going to pull a no-show on me." He frowned again. "I also have, er, Garth's number." He nodded toward the parked police car, and Evie followed suit, blanching as the cop waved through the windshield.

"I wouldn't dream of it." She smiled.

"Right, until tomorrow, then. Around seven."

"Until tomorrow," she answered.

Evie spun on her heels and Antone watched as she stepped away, her curvy backside swaying with each step. She was even more alluring in person than on screen.

The tightening in his body aside, setting the date had felt transactional, but he was pleased she'd agreed. Sure, he hadn't exactly given her much room to refuse, but he knew that Evie Hartmann wasn't the type of woman to accept an invitation she wasn't interested in. If she was down for his invitation, she *might* be interested in his freshly formed plan.

Antone Williams. Her computer didn't have to think too hard to release dozens of pages of search results, and said search results were impressive. Amelia sipped her tepid latte and scrolled through the blue hyperlinks, hovering over a few current news links before diving into a *GQ* article on his career highlights.

MVP. Record-breaking yards. Interviews from former coaches and teammates, but it never got too personal. Unlike for many athletes, dig as she might, she didn't find any photos documenting bleary, wild, boys' nights on the town or police reports for drunk driving or casual drug busts. Scanning another article, she pursed her lips, remembering the facility with which he'd talked his way out of an incident report for their earlier traffic accident. Indeed, just because there wasn't any dirt available on the internet, it didn't mean there wasn't dirt to be found.

If she'd learned anything from her disastrous marriage with Scott, it was to not assume all people were what they seemed. That, and that men were capable of the most despicable things imaginable. She scrolled through more links, sure that if she looked hard enough, she'd find something shady.

Ten years as a star wide receiver would pretty much guarantee some slipups, but what Mia hadn't expected to see was the numerous photo ops with different charities. The man was a prolific donor to various causes and had, early in his career, given away the bulk of his signing bonus to fund scholarships for foster children. For a moment, she considered buying the latest "Baby, It's Cold Outside" charity calendar, in which he and several of his friends had stripped down for a frisky photo spread. It had reportedly sold out in four print runs. Perhaps because December featured a particularly attractive wide receiver. There was a copy available on eBay, including one signed by the models, selling for $600. So she oogled. All in the name of research...

Taking a sip of her latte, she licked the foam from the rim of her cup. She'd added cinnamon to the latte, and the spicy smell reminded her of the moment she had first gotten out of the car. She closed her eyes to savor it.

"If the latte is really that good, next time you can get me one, too..."

She was pulled from her reverie by the perky voice of her assistant, an eager, overachieving aspiring executive with a degree in political science and a master's in hospitality. The perfect combination of skills to navigate the Hartmann estate. In six years, Elsbeth had become as crucial for the hospitality operations as Amelia herself, and she flushed, muttering an apology to her assistant.

Elsbeth had arrived with arms filled, juggling two lattes and a bag of pastries. "Sorry I'm late, and not to worry, I brought reinforcements. Hopefully, they don't disappoint after your potentially more satisfying first course!" She too, flushed, turning the corner of her desk and setting down the coffee with swift decision.

"You're not late, I mean, you haven't missed much." Amelia smiled, secretly grateful for the second coffee. It was a double coffee type of day if ever there was one.

Elsbeth whipped her head round to inspect the computer screen, taking in the full girth of Antone's impressive eight-pack before Amelia could minimize the screen. She whistled. "Didn't know you had a thing for football players"

"I don't," Amelia corrected, exiting the screen.

"Ah, I see, so it's just calendars in general that you're passionate about? Haven't known you to google a non-hospitality-related subject in, umm—" Elsbeth ticked off fingers and smiled "—since I met you?"

"Are you so quick to forget the amount of time I spent researching divorce?" And just like that, she effectively killed the mood. Bringing up Scott had that effect on any conversation, and not for the first time, she renewed her ambition to stop bringing up her ex. "Sorry. I'm in a bit of a mood. Got in a fender bender this morning on the way in."

Elsbeth had the good grace not to laugh, nor did she comment on the frequency of her boss's accidents. Instead, she rounded the desk and held out her hand, gesturing toward the keys to the left of Amelia's keyboard.

"I'll call the garage and drop your wheels over lunch."

Wordlessly, Amelia picked up the keys and passed them.

"You going to explain why you suddenly developed an interest in the NFL?" Her assistant nodded toward the monitor, still full of open windows, each featuring a different article on Antone Williams.

It made sense. Of course her internet stalking would be witnessed. Anything embarrassing in her life was *always* witnessed. "Er, Evie has a date with this guy tomorrow."

"Evie's still in town? I gotta text her." Elsbeth's

usual measured tone gave way to a high-pitched squeal of excitement. It figured that her assistant was more excited about seeing her twin.

Wasn't everyone?

"She's between projects." It was true, she wasn't sure how long Evie would be in town, but it would likely be until her agent called with another film proposition, which could be anywhere from two weeks to six months. Which made her date tomorrow concerning. The longer Evie was around, the riskier it was for Mia to masquerade as her alter ego, dating high-profile NFL players after work. She scrunched her eyebrows together and frowned, but her consternation went unnoticed by Elsbeth.

"I guess I shouldn't be surprised. Evie gets everything." Elsbeth confirmed.

"Tell me about it." Amelia minimized the articles, pulling up her email in a concerted effort to focus on her job. The most recent email in her inbox stared back at her, bold and unopened, from none other than Scott, her soon-to-be ex-husband, if things went to plan. She forwarded the email to PJ without opening it. That was the point of lawyers, wasn't it?

"Yeah, I saw that come in." Elsbeth raised an eyebrow toward the screen. It was both assuring and disquieting to receive personal emails on the work server. On the one hand, Elsbeth kept track of everything. On the other hand, Elsbeth kept track of everything.

The recent shock of her lawsuit smarted. Amelia married against the advice of her family, but maybe marrying Scott was as much about rebellion as it was love. After all, hadn't she earned the right to make her own mistakes? Especially after being little Miss Goody Two-shoes her whole life? Of course, her slimy, gold-digging ex had rectified her good-girl image. Maybe that was why her current position, which required her to revitalize the hospitality branch of Hartmann Enterprises, was so important. It was a chance to earn back her family's respect. And maybe, if she was lucky, she'd earn back a bit of respect for herself in the process.

She deleted the email without reading it. Anything Scott had to say to her, he could say to her lawyer. *Step one in a well-earned fresh start.*

"I suppose I should get to work. December will have to wait," Amelia said, *in an attempt to keep the mood light.*

"Yes, ma'am." Elsbeth nodded. "I assume you're ready for your eleven o'clock?"

Eleven o'clock? That's right. Nick.

"Yes, I'm ready when he is." It was true. She knew all the numbers by heart, but she wished they were more encouraging. She pinched her thigh, allowing her hand to tap her reassuring ticks.

Step two in Project Fresh Start: get others to respect her, starting with her family.

"I printed out the presentation. You've got the booking from the Prince, right?" Edmund, Prince of a random European country Amelia hadn't heard of, was turning out to be as high maintenance as an A list celebrity. Maybe worse.

"It firmed up this weekend. I've got it." Amelia

flipped through the bound document Elsbeth had handed over. The numbers were discreetly printed on a small graph on page seven, but they jumped out just the same. Bookings were down, long-term reservations down even further. Royal families were good for revenue, but terrible for PR, as the NDA agreements made it difficult to capitalize on the celebrity of the guests. She'd figure something out.

Step three in a new beginning: Be good at her job. Be worth her salary.

Her Scandinavian-inspired office had a sleek mantel clock on the bookcase by the door and the brass hands advertised the time: 10:55 a.m.

"I'll leave you to it." Elsbeth reached out and gave her shoulder a quick squeeze before leaving.

Amelia stared at her computer screen. Then, for lack of a better thing to do, and perhaps because she wanted the distraction, she clicked the minimized window on her desktop and ordered herself a $600 calendar.

*

As a rule, she never went to Nick's office. Maybe it was because she still thought of it as her dad's office, which was ridiculous, as her father had died eleven years prior, a few weeks before she'd turned eighteen. She had been a kid, but his death had turned her into an adult. Truth was, she didn't remember the moment it had stopped being Dad's and started becoming Nick's,

The change had happened gradually. At first, Nick only took board meetings in the penthouse. Then he'd graduated to sharing drinks with customers or prospective clients, often Japanese businessmen or prominent members of the Texan cattle community. Before long, he'd restocked the minibar with his favorite whiskey and then begun replacing the art. Gone were the abstract paintings her dad had admired; now the office was plastered in photography. His favorite subject was horses, the most recent addition a large picture of the Pryor Mountain mustangs that Jackson, her second oldest brother, was domesticating on the wild plains to the east of their property.

Amelia shifted in the tufted vintage armchair opposite the large mahogany desk her brother occupied and tried to focus on what he had to say.

"So, you see, Amelia, with reservations plummeting and the Japanese interest in our Wagyu beef operation, converting the meadow to pasture would allow us to increase the herd by forty percent with minimal clear-cutting. It's the only logical option."

Amelia was sweating and hoped her brother didn't notice.

"The only logical option," she repeated.

"Mia, there's no need to be dramatic. Besides, shouldn't you be relieved? It's not like you need to work." Nick sighed.

"Is that what you think of me?"

Wasn't that what everyone thought of her? Another rich girl living on her family's wealth, good for nothing but photo ops and galas? And let's not forget the embarrassing divorce that she couldn't even manage to finalize on her own... Couple that with the extortion she was facing...

Nick exhaled a sigh heavy with expiring patience. "I thought you'd be relieved. To be honest, we all did—"

"You all did? The whole family got together behind my back?"

Was that why Evie had come home?

"There is no need to be dramatic about it. We were worried. You haven't been yourself lately."

"Well, you'll excuse me if navigating the divorce process has left me a little less chipper."

"Precisely. Maybe you should focus on yourself for a little while, let me manage the resort, wind it into the cattle operations, and give you more time to focus on what's important to you."

Because earning her own livelihood couldn't possibly be important to her? Amelia twisted her middle finger, pulling it until she felt the satisfying pop of the knuckle. Saying nothing, she repeated the action again, watching as Nick flinched with each pop. He'd always hated when she cracked her knuckles.

"I handled things the way I needed to. My divorce was my business. For the last time, I don't want to talk about it. And as for earning a living, I'm not asking for your understanding, so don't ask me for an explanation."

Pop. Pop. She didn't shy away from looking her brother straight in the eye. *Pop.*

"This will not affect your income, if that's what you're worried about," he sighed.

She frowned. As if she'd let him go about putting her back on an allowance like she was a wayward child...

Amelia kept cracking her knuckles.

"At least, review the proposal. Converting the meadow makes a lot of sense."

"Don't pretend you would make nearly as much money turning the resort into grazing ground," she maintained eye contact.

Pop. She watched as the muscle in her brother's jaw flexed with each offending crack.

"You can't get the reservations up… I mean it's time to face the music. Our resorts are not cool anymore, that's the bottom line."

"And what if they were?" She stopped and stared down at her hands, the idea forming as quickly as the urge to stop cracking her knuckles had overcome her.

"Ha." Nick scoffed. "What? You honestly think you could make that happen? On a timeline that would appease the board?"

A board made up entirely of her relatives. Yeah. She could do that. Amelia smiled. "If I could?"

Her idea was good. Sure, she hadn't totally fleshed it out, but… the NFL was cool. And she basically was dating a guy in the NFL. *As Evie.* Evie was good at anything it was turning one date into more. And she was going to channel Evie's energy… They *were* identical twins after all. With her pride on the line, she would do a lot more for a lot less. And she would *not* allow herself to go on a Hartmann allowance any more than she'd let herself settle with Scott. She needed to get a grip on her publicand familialembarrassment.

Nick scoffed again. "How?"

Right now, all she could do was think of the coolest person she'd ever met in real life. That was how. "Antone Williams—ever heard of him?"

She watched as Nick's face lit up.

"Don't pretend like he hasn't been your number one draft pick for every fantasy football team you've had the last five years."

Her brother cracked a smile. "You're going to get him to make our resort cool?"

"We're talking about it tomorrow tonight." She stood and smiled. "On our date. Er, rather, just before his date with Evie. I'm, uh, introducing them. We're friends now."

Before Nick could answer, she turned and left his office. *Always leave them wanting more.*

The trick was to figure out how to do that with Antone Williams.

Three

Birthday Suits & Meet Cutes

"You don't need me to tell you how important this next venture is, do you?" The voice of Amy, his publicist, echoed in his head. Although he had always thrived under stress, her statement felt more like a threat than a pressure tactic. It was as different from the howling pressure of a stadium full of fans' expectations as he could imagine. The fans he could manage. Could impress. Could play. But these expectations? They were foreign and all too important.

Not only did he have his savings tied up in the distillery, GreatWhiskey, but according to his publicist, he also had only *one chance* to announce his post-NFL career and ride the tailwind of his unmatched success as a wide receiver to become a successful entrepreneur. He knew she was right. Four years from now, some college recruit would be resetting his record, and his current fame would be fast forgotten. If he wanted to leverage his achievements, and NFL friends, to generate a career that would outlive his athleticism, he had just this window of opportunity.

Squinting, he let loose the basketball he'd been spinning and watched as his haphazard toss sank the ball in a perfect arc into the small hoop at the end of Rob's driveway. He'd been staying at Rob's since the renovations started—then stopped, then started again—at his main house in Big Sky. It was a far cry from the foster home they'd both shared in the Bronx, and even he had to admit it was hard not to feel pleased at the boyhood dream now realized. They each had a home, and nice ones at that. He had money in the bank, and a chance to do some good. Twelve-year-old Antone would be proud.

Antone jerked at his back pocket buzzed. His Bluetooth earbuds announced the caller, and he muttered a quiet "damn it."

It was *her* again. Amy the pit bull, but she worked for her commission, he'd give her that. "Antone here," he answered through his teeth, the swoosh of the basketball hoop doing little to calm his nerves.

"Antone, darling, have you given any thought to Sofia?" she cooed.

His publicist was as persistent as a blood-starved mosquito. Sofia Ryan was an up-and-coming actress and had just booked her second cover of the same men's magazine he'd graced a month prior. Not just any men's magazine, but *the* men's magazine, *Sports Illustrated*. Sure, he hadn't vied for the swimsuit issue, instead preferring the article featuring his ten best plays over the past ten years, he had to agree they flew in similar circles.

Antone reached for the towel he'd draped over an old stone urn and looped it around his neck, determined to focus his attention on the insistent voice echoing through his earbuds. "No. Can't say I've given her any thought at all."

It wasn't entirely true. Hard not to think of the cover model in a swimsuit issue of *Sports Illustrated*, but still, there was something brash her. Something calculating. She was as opposite to Evie Hartmann as he could imagine.

Evie Hartmann. It wasn't the first time he'd thought of her that morning. Nor was it the first time the thought had necessitated a cold shower. He couldn't think of Evie like that. It wasn't right. He needed to focus on the distillery. Mixing business and pleasure never ended well, and if he'd learned one thing from his marriage, it was to never ever let yourself invest when you had no control of the stakes.

"Sofia is perfect for your *greatest-of-all-time* branding. GreatWhiskey needs the right woman on your arm, and she was just voted hottest woman under thirty by *Vanity Fair*. Definitely boasts an it-girl energy, and her career is on the upswing." Amy prattled on, listing the myriad of characteristics tmaking Sofia the perfect candidate for his red-carpet debut. Greatest of

All Time—GOAT—might not have been his idea for the launch, but it did tie in with the charity aspect he was eager to promote—essentially, that *even former street kids like himself* could become the greatest of all time; all it took was a lot of hard work!

"Not sure I give a damn about her career." He muttered, just loud enough to be heard.

"Well, the best publicity is free, and you and Sofia together would be front-page news," Amy pointed out. "A debut with her is the *definition* of a hot launch. You need to understand— image is critical in pulling off this launch. Image matters, Antone."

"Front-page news is not exactly what I feel like right now." His finger traced his ring absently, more from habit than anything else.

"Well, it should be." Amy reminded him.

"I know, I know." He scratched at his jaw. "I actually met a woman this afternoon. I was going to ask her if maybe she'd be interested in getting involved with the launch." It didn't matter that she wasn't on the cover of *SI*. She was attractive enough to be a cover girl and there was something about her, some ingenuity he couldn't put a finger on, but it was just what his brand needed. Evie Hartmann might be a B-list actress, but she had an energy of "greatness," and he'd felt it.

Plus, with Hartmann connections, the networking opportunities for a liquor launch were endless. The princess of the West? Heck, he'd don a cowboy hat right now and ride off into the sunset if it established his brand with free publicity and the right product placement...

"A woman?"

He could hear the eye roll through the phone.

"A celebrity. Maybe not Sofia's level, but her family is from Montana. I'm sure you can use it to spin some sort of story for the press. 'The Wild West meets the Wild Wide Receiver,' or maybe 'Cinderfella meets the Princess of the West?'"

"A celebrity from Montana?" He could hear Amy think through the phone. There weren't many, he had her there.

"Evie Hartmann."

The pregnant silence was all the encouragement he needed. The Hartmann name might not carry weight in Hollywood, but as far as media and luxury goods went, the Hartmanns were legends. Not to mention the opportunity to leverage the Hartmann connections into a distribution strategy for the hospitality industry, or their political ties, which could prove useful with the red tape involved in the liquor industry... The opportunities were vast if he played his cards right.

Another absent twist of his ring, and he swallowed the unexpected lump in his throat. *It was time to move on.* "Met her this morning, Evie's coming to Rob's party tomorrow night."

"Well, it seems you don't need my help after all."

He chuckled. "I'll always need your help, just not in finding a date."

"If you're asking if I approve—"

"I wasn't," he said, interrupting. "I wasn't asking if you approved." Bending to pick up the basketball, he bounced it on his hip as he walked toward the open garage. "You know I've always preferred to ask forgiveness afterward…" He chuckled again in an effort to soften the delivery. As aggressive as his publicist was, she was the best in the business and he'd best not forget it. But the last thing he needed was another person expecting him to ask for approval. He hadn't needed any since he'd made it on his own at fifteen, and at thirty-two, he wasn't about to start seeking it now.

A hawk's sharp cry drew his attention to the skyline. He watched as the bird of prey took an elegant nosedive into the field, and he smiled. Eat or be eaten. The hunter and the hunted. Evie Hartmann was the perfect arm candy for the launch of this venture, and with their recent accident, *she owed him*.

Whether said debt would extend to help negotiating with the Hiltons, the governor, or any of her other connections, or just led to the odd red-carpet appearance, no strings attached, Evie Hartmann owed him, and he wasn't afraid to collect. Plus, it meant the chance to see her again. Maybe break down some of her bravado, get under her skin. Ridiculously, he thought about what it might be like to touch that skin. Pushing that thought away, he chucked the basketball into an open laundry basket at the opposite end of the garage and whistled.

He had to stay focused on the task at hand. This distillery was bigger than his next career move. Too many people had believed in him over the years, but he was the first to admit he'd been lucky. Sure, he'd worked hard to be lucky, but he'd watched a lot of people work hard for a lot less. Yes, he'd given away more than half his earnings over the past ten years, but it wasn't enough. He needed something bigger. He needed to pay back his karma. And for this project? The opportunity to corral his fellow athletes to create a brand that could open up employment opportunities for the disadvantaged? It wasn't enough that he'd gotten off the streets. He needed to help others get out too. It was the least he could do, and if he managed to put some ghosts to rest simultaneously, all the better.

He twisted the ring on his finger and slipped it off, threading it through the chain around his neck. He needed to keep his head in the game. Evie Hartmann was the right woman to help him launch his brand. She was perfect, and he was going to get her to agree, one way or another. And maybe he could have some fun in the meantime.

"You did what?" Evie hooked an eyebrow in her direction. "No. You didn't." It was impossible to tell from the deadpan in her voice what her sister thought about the disclosure.

Evie. I did a thing. A twin switch. And you, or rather I, have a date with an NFL player. Antone Williams. And not only does the date have to go amazingly, but we also need to convince him to move in here and help me make this resort cool, and frankly I have no idea how I'm going to do that. And if I can get him to agree to date me, at least for the press, and Scott reads about me, pretending to be you, dating a pro athlete, he will definitely resurface. Scott has never been able to resist easy money, and if he figures out the twin switch, who knows, he might even try to bribe me for his silence.

At which point I can move for an annulment based on bribery, which is technically criminal behavior.

Oh, and also, I crashed into Antone's Lexus, a criminal code violation given the school zone. But I think he might like me, er, I mean, you. So, he isn't pressing charges. Yeah.

Amelia cleared her throat and tried again, wishing it was as easy to explain to her twin as it had been in her practice conversation in the mirror. "In order to avoid losing my license, I used the driver's license *you* forgot in my car."

Evie paced Mia's bedroom, then made a beeline for her walk-in closet. Mia followed cautiously. Evie was flipping hanger after hanger across the chrome clothing rod.

"No. No. No. No."

In an effort to judge how her twin was feeling about her eventful—fateful?—run-in with Antone, Mia took a step forward. "I'm sorry. I did it without thinking. I just didn't want to lose my license. I've had, er, well, a lot of tickets lately. I know I'm a mess right now."

Her twin only knew the CliffsNotes version of her most recent demand letter; the sting of potentially paying spousal support was too embarrassing for anyone else to hear about. The fact that her divorce was dragging out was one thing. The fact that her deadbeat ex wanted a piece of her wealth to agree to their dissolution? And that he might even have a legal right to it? It was giving her a headache. The thing was, Scott was asking for money because, bottom line, there was a decent chance her family would pay out just to avoid the bad press, and he knew it. What he hadn't counted on was her not telling her family. She pressed a hand to her temple and massaged her head with two fingers. This was a nightmare.

Evie spun and smiled at her twin. "Don't. Just don't—"

Mia blanched. It was still hard to tell if her twin was mad. Certainly, she had every right to be. She rubbed her head again, seven controlled circles of even pressure.

"—don't apologize," Evie continued, to Mia's surprise, grinning ear to ear. "This is great fun. Exactly what I needed. You can be Evie, and I'll be Mia. But I'm *not* wearing any of this. No, nope. Not happening."

Of all the reactions Mia had expected, this was hardly the one she'd figured she would face.

"I'm sorry?" She picked up the cardigan that Evie had pitched on the floor.

"I am not wearing that...thing." Evie jabbed an accusing finger toward the teal cardigan in question.

"I meant, sorry, what do you mean about you'll be Mia?" *This was all going a heck of a lot further than she'd intended.*

"Well, I can either be Mia, or I can date the NFL hottie. Actually, come to think of it, I might be getting the short end of the stick here..." Evie smiled, flipping through Mia's closet, lips pursed.

"Well, if those are your options, I gotta say, I agree with you—being you is definitely better than being me these days. But don't knock the sweater. It's cute with the right bra."

Evie laughed and shrugged. "Okay, you might have a point with the wardrobe. I mean, if he wants to date you, I'm thinking he likes the package."

She hadn't thought of it that way. Did Antone like her package? Mia felt the rush of heat color her cheeks. "I mean, we're not dating. He invited me to one party. But, I mean, I was thinking, if a bunch of athletes blew up their social media with Hartmann Homestead, imagine what that could do for us!"

"And how do you see that happening?" Evie frowned.

"Er—" Mia fiddled with the hem of her shirt "—I was thinking, maybe if he moved in here..."

Evie laughed. "You crashed into his car, but you think he might move in? What exactly were you gonna do on this date?"

"I'm just going to ask him." Mia jutted her chin forward. "That is, assuming you don't have a problem with it?" It was easier to pretend it was no big deal without the athlete standing mere inches from her, looking hotter than a Greek god incarnate. He was basically Zeus, but hotter.

"As in, move in here? To our place?" Evie's eyebrow shot up in concern. "You have a plan to convince the staff?"

The staff. The team that had run the family home since Mia could remember. Evie had a point. Mia cleared her throat. "Yeah. He needs to stay here, make it seem like he loves it, and we'll find a way to publicize things... I don't know. I'm hoping if I don't chicken out, I can just see what he says. I mean, he mentioned his place was under renovation… I just wanted to talk to you before I suggested…"

It was crazy, but she couldn't propose anything unless her twin was on board.

"You're joking. You've been Evie for less than a day and you're already doing it better. Moving in with an NFL player…" Evie balled up the cardigan and threw it at her sister. " And the staff? I mean Agnes can spot the differences between us a mile away."

Deflecting the wool garment, Mia retreated from the closet and sat on the bed. *She was indeed going to proposition an NFL player.*

"I mean, I'm just going to try and be here the least amount of time possible." Mia frowned. That was not going to work if the goal was promoting the business.

Evie grinned. "I could leave. And talk to Agnes? Maybe if I tell her I need a break, she can help cover for me—for us?"

Agnes. The housekeeper extraordinaire that had acted as a surrogate mother to the girls since their own mom went off the rails when they were eight years old. Whatever Agnes said, went. If she decreed Mia to be Evie, no one would ask any questions.

"You'd do that?" Mia turned, unsure where to look.

"I would. I can just say that I need this break. Which, by the way, is true." Evie frowned. "But I see that you need one too."

Evie circled the bed and took a seat next to her sister, her hand heavy on Mia's back. "It's a twin thing. I sense all is not well." Evie sighed. "Potential hot new roommate notwithstanding."

"Bravo, really digging deep into your sixth sense for that one, aren't ya?" Mia sniffed. It was a lot. Finalizing the divorce with an uncooperative soon-to-be ex-husband, fighting for her place in the family business, and finding herself in the process, all by pretending to be someone else? *Maybe she was just losing it.*

"You wanna tell me what this is really about?"

Mia felt the weight of her sister's hand. "Not sure I'm ready to do that," she answered honestly. That was the nice thing about being a twin. Evie was the one person she could just be herself around. *Or not.*

"Well, I'm here. For whatever you need. If it's a laugh, then, great. If it's fashion advice, then, great for you. If it's just someone to sit with, that's fine too. And if you need to escape and be me for a while, I got you. You know, if you do manage to publicly date an NFL player, it could help my career and the resort at the same time. Just let me know if you need any tips on flirting."

Evie looked unperturbed. And totally fine with the prospect of swapping bedrooms for a month. Something must be up. Mia raised an eyebrow in the direction of her altogether-too-calm sister.

"Er, and Mia? This timing kinda works for me. I actually booked a detox, a yoga retreat for two weeks of intensive hatha yoga in Washington State. I need to get into shape if I'm going to be competitive with auditions, or so my agent tells me. And I could easily turn those two weeks into a month. It's very private. And very exclusive."

"Yoga retreat?" *Something was up.*

"It's more of a fat camp." Evie frowned.

"I hardly think you need—"

"It's not a secret my bookings have dried up, and maybe fitting into the traditional Hollywood definition of beauty is more important than I'd originally thought."

Mia winced. They were identical twins, and if Evie needed camp, what did that mean for her? *No. That was a rabbit hole she couldn't fall into.*

"Stop." Evie winked. "I'm mostly going so I can hide from Mom and Nick. I booked my getaway before mom booked her cruise, but I'm so glad I did. You know, figure out what I really want. If you spend your time dating a high-profile athlete—"

"Ex-athlete…"

"Whatever. I'm sure it will do more for my career than a month of hatha yoga. So, think of my retreat as more me leaving you the space to give being Evie a spin." Evie offered up a quick air-kiss and then a wink. She pulled up her phone and dialed.

"Are you going to be able to be Mia at work, and Evie for the press?" Evie asked, eyebrow hooked in inquiry.

"I mean, yeah, I guess so. If you're okay with it…"

Evie waved her away and spoke into the phone. "I need a lift. Can you get the chopper ready for Mia?"

Mia. Her sister was booking travel as Mia. But at least she was leaving, stat.

"Thanks," Mia mouthed.

Evie nodded, but the complicit support from her twin did little to calm Mia's nerves. *What had she gotten herself into?*

Four

Birthday Girls and Birthday Suits

Anton made a mental note to send flowers to his decorator. Anyone who could turn what could only be described as a hazard zone into a girly oasis was definitely at the height of their game. When he'd offered Rob the use of this place to host a party for his wife two months ago, he hadn't expected unending delays in the renovation process. Sure, the ranch had been a dump when he bought it, but with the steady stream of bills from the contractor over the past two months, he'd expected…well, more than this.

Still, looking around the yard, he grinned. What the party planner had done with his *exterior* space was nothing short of a miracle. His garden was incredible. Nothing short of fan-damn-tastic.

"Buddy, I owe you," Rob repeated for the millionth time. He was gazing at the fairy lights strung across the pool outside. At least the *outside* of his home looked fit to be a distillery owner's chic bachelor pad.

Had he told Evie to bring a swimsuit? That woman would look fine in a bikini. Or out of one.

There were large propane patio heaters scattered all over the leveled terrace, and a faint mist rose off the lit pool, illuminated from below, adding to the mystic ambience. Joanna wanted members of the guest list to party in skimpy dresses, and who was he to refuse? So the party planners had outfitted the backyard oasis accordingly, and it didn't feel at all like October, the dropping temp notwithstanding.

"Seriously. This place is magic. Jo is gonna freak! Can't believe the *outside* looks so epic." Rob waved at the glass doors to the home and frowned.

"Brother, you don't owe me anything." It was true. Rob might not be his blood brother, but after four years in the system together and the enduring friendship thereafter, he was the closest thing to family Antone had ever known.

And if it had been Rob that ended up a pro athlete? Antone had no doubts he would've laid the world at his feet, a real "brother from another mother," as they used to say. As things stood, Rob was in a different circumstance. He had a record, and that had made finding consistent employment a little trickier. Still, the man was a hell of a chef and had built his own reputation as a food truck king in Texas. A success he'd given up without hesitation at the prospect of joining Antone as his new right-hand man in Montana.

"When we get the distillery up and running, I'm not gonna let you down," Rob promised again.

"I know you won't." Antone swallowed the ball of emotion lodged in his throat. He reached for the chain around his neck. He'd placed the wedding ring on the chain this morning, as it wasn't appropriate to wear to the party. Not anymore. Bachelor vibes were necessary for the launch. Sure, he'd been single for years, dating the odd celebrity, but always under the radar. He wasn't one to kiss and tell, and the prospect of putting his dating life out there on social media for all the world to see, per Amy's insistence? He grimaced. Reaching for the chain, he swallowed again. He'd loved his wife, but had it been worth it? To get everything you'd ever wanted, only to lose it? People were so quick to say it was better to have loved than lost, than never to have loved at all, but Antone wasn't so sure.

Yeah. Marriage, or any serious relationship, wasn't for him. It just wasn't worth it. Women falling over themselves to insist on "a future," when the only future he wanted was a hot night and *maybe* friendship? Better he focus on things he could control. Things that could last forever—like business. Or branding. Or being remembered for making a difference.

He bent and retrieved a cement mixer leaning against the wooden siding of the patio. *This should go inside. God, there was still so much to do. He kicked a nearby bucket of plaster, causing a cloud of white particles to shoot through the air.*

"Hey, take it easy there, bro," Rob said, backing up, arms akimbo.

"Hey, man, don't knock it till you've tried it." Antone shook his head, but shake as he might, he was unable to dispel the echo of Amy's pervasive threats. He needed a woman, the *"Greatest of All Time,"* on his arm, to make this launch pick up the free press that would help him get a new liquor brand on the map. He had to remember that this project was *bigger* than his own image. If he could get enough press, he could put his social agenda in the media. Letting some of the unseen people in society have value. And that? That was a legacy that could outlast any marriage. Even if it did necessitate some sort of relationship, there had to be a way he could make it work without compromising his values.

Was that really the reason he'd taken off the ring? Image? Evie's face flashed in his mind. He kicked at the bucket again, watching as a second cloud of plaster spilled onto the floor. *It didn't matter; this felt right.*

Rob kicked a chunk of dried plaster the size of a softball and watched as it soared in a clean arc across the polished granite patio.

Antone gestured toward the glittering white rocks his decorator had piled on the far side of the pool. "You gotta admit, this place sure cleaned up nice." He voiced the thought that had been running rampant in his head. *Was it okay for him to look forward to this party? To this next chapter of his life?*

"Yeah, man, it's unbelievable," Rob said, then he went quiet.

Antone continued to survey his surroundings. Coordinating with the landscape, a teak structure had been built to delineate the smaller social spaces. An outdoor lounge, poolside. To the left of the pool, a polished slate bar, protruding from a cabana that married rough-hewn field rock with polished live-edge planks, created a hunting-lodge-meets-Aspen-après-ski vibe. The effect was further enhanced by wrought iron chaise lounges draped with white sheepskins.

Somehow, the decorator had managed to keep his manly vibe, but the space was undeniably stylish. The yard was littered with large wrought-iron pedestals and candelabras, with dozens of tapered candles of varying widths ready to be lit. Glass lanterns held even more candles, and it didn't take much creativity to imagine what the place would look like when the tapers were aflame.

He was distracted by the vibrating buzz in his pant pocket. He felt the corner of his mouth turn up as he eyed the home screen and read Evie's message preview:

What did you say the dress code was?

He hadn't. The kind of parties he hated most were the type specifying dress codes.

What you were wearing yesterday was fine. *Actually, it was way better than fine.* He stared at his phone, watching as the three little dots indicated her drafting an answer.

Fine? I tend to set the bar a little higher.

He laughed. Girl. Wear a potato sack. You'll still look FINE.

He hesitated, then entered a fire emoji. He was, after all, playing with fire.

See you at seven.

Antone scratched his chin, wondering for a moment if he'd pushed a little too far with the fire emoji. It wasn't as though he'd left her much room to refuse his invitation. Then his phone pinged with the winking emoji. He looked up, smiling, only to take in the incredulity on Rob's face. "Before I forget, I got Joanna an extra present."

"You didn't need to do that, man. You're hosting, paying for the party. Epic friend. Greatest of all time, indeed, I assure you." Rob laughed.

"Yeah, well, you're gonna love this one." He didn't comment on the blatant mocking of the distillery's tagline or his hard-earned *GQ* nomination, naming him the one of the greats in the September issue.

"Haven't seen you smile like that for a while." Rob added.

From the tone, Antone couldn't tell if he was pleased or not with what he was guessing at. He nodded toward his phone.

"Just figured I got your wife a great surprise. Ran into Evie Hartmann today, or guess you could say, she ran into me." He smiled despite himself. "Anyway, she's dropping by later."

"Dropping by? Mr. Celibate finally bringing a date to a party?" Rob's eyebrows drew together and he took a step away from Antone. He walked to the edge of the pool, squatting beside the edge and peering into the water as though he could see his own reflection and hated what he saw.

Was Rob angry at Antone for moving on? After all, they had both been friends with Charlotte, his late wife.

Rob looked up, grinning. "Can't believe you're bringing a date, I'd always prided myself on being a solid wing man, and here you go, bringing your own lady to my party. Unbelievable."

"Believe it." While he still punished himself for the thoughts he'd barely admitted to, namely, replaying, on a loop, the vision of Evie's round assets framed in a black pencil skirt, he wasn't going to apologize. He hadn't done anything wrong. *Yet.* And if he and the Hartmann girl could get on the same page, there was no harm in a few hot nights together. After all, there was chemistry. He could feel the spark, hot and clear, between them.

"I thought your publicist was finding you a woman?" Rob asked quietly. Rob was one of the only people who was privy to the details of Antone's serious relationships, or, rather, his aversion to them. He and Charlotte had been close, as in, the same-foster-home close. Later on, Rob had been there for him when cancer had robbed Antone of the thing he held most dear, his wife. Rob had seen the grief he'd lived and never pushed him to risk everything again. He was one of the only people who understood. Serious relationships were not worth the damage they could do. Not a second time.

"I know this is about Charlotte. You know as well as I do, nothing I do is gonna bring her back. And this thing with Evie, er, right now, it's nothing." Antone felt one side of his mouth kick into a grin. "I was thinking maybe we could come to an agreement, you know, keep things business."

Rob arched an eyebrow. "Yeah, that grin is all business."

Antone had a sneaking suspicion that that eyebrow was clearly testing the waters for how far Rob could tease, so he'd best shut it down now. "I'm sure I don't have to tell you how a Hartmann could help us with the political aspect of licensing, permit challenges, et-cetera. And if she's as business as the rest of her family, she's not gonna read into any smiles we might put on for the camera."

"You'd have more influence and more money if you stopped giving yours away..." Rob grumbled under his breath.

Not the point. Giving money to charity was one of the few things Antone did that made him feel worthy of the luck he'd had. He wasn't going to stop anytime soon.

"Seriously," Rob continued. "I mean, why can't she just be a date? Why does this chick need to be a means to an end? Don't you think it's time you gave someone else a chance?"

"You're pretty quick to defend someone you haven't

even met," Antone shot back. Subconsciously, he reached for the ring at his neck, a movement not lost on Rob, who swallowed and looked away.

Antone cleared his throat, regretting the heavy-handed gesture, even if it hadn't been intentional. "Look, don't overthink things, buddy. Evie owes me a favor. If I manage to launch the brand with the 'greatest of all time' vibe everyone seems to think is the best idea going, you know as well as I do that I need the right chick on my arm. Someone who won't get bummed about Charlotte, and about the fact that our smiles will be just for the camera, or the bedroom, but never for a wedding photographer." He grinned. "But you're right, I mean, I can give Evie a chance at some fun."

"You know that's not what I meant," Rob shot back, not smiling with his delivery.

Antone scratched his chin, then glanced at his Montblanc watch. Damn it. Only two hours before she, and their other guests, arrived. There was still loads to do.

"Just make sure you're careful. These society girls are different than celebs. Just want to make sure the player doesn't get played." Rob stood.

Antone nodded. His friend was right. Society girls could be trouble, and Evie's naive look didn't necessarily make her any different. "Do me a favor? Party planner ordered a bunch of flowers. You think you could pick them up?"

Truth was, the florist would have delivered them, but he needed some time on his own. He had a lot to think about. Rob nodded and walked away without another word, leaving Antone alone with his thoughts. Charlotte had been more than a wife; she had been a friend first. She'd been family, long before they'd made it legal, and a friend, long after their love had died. Maybe that was why he'd felt the loss so deeply, with such a visceral grief. She'd been family, and he'd loved her. Then lost her. And Antone Williams hated to lose.

He swallowed the feeling that began to creep up more out of habit than sincerity. If he wanted to stay relevant, make a difference and be worthy of the chances he'd been given, he needed a plan—*not a distraction.* He touched his necklace and fought the rising suspicion that the tall and curvy distraction that was Evie Hartmann might burn it all down.

"I can't tell you how honored I am that you would come to my birthday party," Joanna gushed. The birthday girl was dressed in a pink pantsuit, with matching earrings that dangled just below her collarbone. Everything about Joanna was over the top, including her enthusiastic appreciation for the evening's special guest, Evie.

Evie. Amelia had to remember she was there to play a part.

In contrast to Joanna's look, Amelia had opted for a strapless, pale blue dress made from modal cotton. Soft to the touch, the thin fabric clung to her body and left little to the imagination. Indeed, the only thing *she'd* imagined was that she lived in a universe in which she could pull off wearing such a dress. At the last moment, she'd paired the dress with a bulky blazer, which she now pulled around her ribs like a shield. Of course, the blazer did little to cover her legs. Damn Evie for suggesting this infernal ensemble.

"Legs for days. You simply have legs for days," Joanna fawned.

"I'm just tall, that's all." Amelia waved her off.

"I had no idea you would be so down-to-earth," one of Joanna's friends added. So, they traveled in packs.

Was this what it was like to be part of a girl gang? Mia smiled, praying her face didn't look as stiff as it felt.

"I mean, you think meeting a celebrity, that they'd be more... I don't know, unavailable?" More laughs from the friends followed.

"Down-to-earth, now, is she?" Antone's voice caused a fresh titter from the women, who parted like the Red Sea at his appearance. He carried a martini glass filled with a pink concoction—a cosmo, maybe?—and a crystal tumbler with what she assumed was whiskey, no ice.

She grinned. "How do you know I take my whiskey minus the rocks?"

Antone, dressed in a navy suit that hugged his muscled body, pursed his lips and shook his head. "You're all sorts of trouble tonight, aren't you, ma'am?"

"Ma'am? You're the one who is going to be in trouble." She grinned back, channeling all of her Evie energy. Somehow it felt natural to sparkle around Antone. His eyes were shining with appreciation, and in his presence, she felt every nerve in her system firing on all cylinders. Just like they had when she'd first met him, under the hot sun at the scene of her crime.

Their entourage howled in laughter, and a second man arrived, issuing a low whistle. Amelia recognized him as Rob, the best friend she'd been introduced to moments earlier.

"Rob, I brought you your drink." Antone offered up the pink martini, passing the whiskey to Amelia with a wink.

Mia accepted the tumbler with a wink of her own. Somehow, it was easier flirting as Evie. As though the persona gave her the freedom to be the kind of girl who winked at handsome NFL players, as opposed to an almost-divorcee who was prone to cry into a nonalcoholic beer, or more recently, Zinfandel from a box. For a minute, she regretted the forty minutes she'd spent staring at her phone, working up the courage to cancel. Not that it was ever really an option. She did owe him this appearance, not to mention the deal she'd already sold to Nick, the proposition regarding an endorsement for the resort that she hadn't even broached yet.

"I guess I am headed to pick up a drink of my own." Antone shrugged.

"I'll come," she started, navigating the flagstone path toward the upper patio of the modern ranch.

As Antone had advertised, the party was being hosted outdoors, with white lights strung across a polished cement and teak patio, the twinkle refracting off the glossy floor. The gigantic teak structure flowed to the edge of an infinity pool, lit from the bottom with large golden lights. Huge planters gave the impression of a leafy jungle, with oversize ferns and creeping flowers crawling up teak installations meant to keep the sun off the deck in hot weather.

The interior of the house, visible through floor-to-ceiling windows, was another question altogether.

Just then, Antone kicked over a bucket of dried plaster that was set against the patio and watched as a large crack split the side of the plastic. *Pffft.*

"I knew renovating would be huge when I bought this place, but I guess what I didn't expect was how long everything would take."

"You've been at this awhile then?" Mia clarified, pulling the edges of her blazer around her as though the realization had brought a chill with it.

Or perhaps it was the realization that her ask might be a little more within reach than she'd initially hoped.

"Yeah, the distillery needs a lot of updates too, so I had to take the team that was working here, and put both crews to work there. So, I'm sleeping in Rob's guest room."

"You are?" She bit back her surprise.

"I didn't want to attract press, and for sure, a month-long reservation in Big Sky, Montana, would end up in a few newspapers. I want the press to get excited about my distillery, so I need to be careful what I do and how I act."

"I guess you only have one chance to make a first impression," Mia agreed.

"Says the girl who rear-ended me yesterday." He grinned, then reached out and swatted her on her lower back.

She liked it.

"Wow, this really is...a work in progress." Amelia nodded toward the large sliding-glass doors.

"Yep," Anton answered, heaving the door open and walking through a jobsite to a bar fridge.

"Sorry?" Poking her head through the glass door, she balked as he waved her way.

"It's an open work site, better not come in just yet— I'd hate you to scratch up your 'legs for days.'"

Was that another wink? She waited, leaning against the frame of the custom door. Maybe her idea wouldn't be that much of a hard sell after all...

Moments later, Antone was at her side, stepping out onto the deck. "It was brutal getting the outside finished. Gotta admit, I flew in some help."

"So, when do you plan to move in?"

"Well, when the renos are done. Staying with Rob is fine, but I feel like a third wheel with him and Joanna sometimes. I am looking for new temp digs." He gestured toward the wrought iron bench partially obscured by a large fern. "Shall we?"

Desperate to avoid her newfound girl gang, Mia nodded.

As they walked toward the bench, Antone touched her arm, steering her toward the seating.

"So, you're looking for a place to stay?" she asked as soon as they were seated. *Could it really be this easy?*

"Like I said, I was planning to stay with Rob, but Joanna talks a lot more than I remembered," he rued.

"Yeah, looks like quite the project." She gestured

toward the glass doors separating the ongoing work zone from the party.

"I suppose I'm going to have to get a hotel. Staying with Rob and Jo isn't really workable—I'm the kind of guy who needs my own space." He smiled at her. "But I'd need something discreet."

Her stomach fluttered, and not just because she was on the receiving end of a grin that made her insides melt. *It was normal to melt and feel on fire at the same time, right?*

This was her chance. Except for one thing.

"Discreet?" she asked.

His mouth curved into a delicious smile. "Well, discreet, or on brand."

Mia had been in business long enough to see when she could go in for the close. He *wanted* her to ask. She could tell from the curve of his smile, and the cock of his hip. "You could stay at the ranch. I could arrange a booking…" It was awkward pitching the idea, but with such perfect timing, how could she not try? "I mean, I for sure owe you for the whole, selfie-with-the-cop scenario. I got the distinct feeling he wasn't gonna do me any favors."

"Stay at the Hartmann resort? You sure I can afford it?" he joked.

"Says the NFL player," Mia retorted.

"*Ex*-NFL player. Don't you follow any sports channels?"

"Proudly, not." She smiled again, this time relieved that it didn't feel nearly as stiff. It was easier flirting without an audience. She felt she had 100 percent of his attention, and to her surprise, she liked it.

"I mean, I'm sure we could work something out." He smiled at her, hard enough to provide a dimple. The man was too handsome for his own good—and definitely too handsome for her own good.

"Actually, now that you mention it, I, er, my sister could use your help." She spied a wrought iron bench by the hot tub, the steam coming off the whirlpool adding a fairy-like mist to the ambience. Raising her glass to the corner of the deck, she smiled. "Shall we take a seat over there?"

Antone grinned and walked toward the bench, light-footed as he navigated his way between the lit tapers. It was undeniably romantic, but Mia swallowed. This was her chance to be professional. To earn the position she had inherited by birthright. To show her family, and herself, that she was worth her paycheck.

Antone sat and smiled. "So, you were saying we might work something out? You know I was kidding, right? I'd be happy to pay for a suite at your resort, but I had a counteroffer for you."

Her stomach flipped. *A counteroffer? Was that sports talk for a sexy proposition?*

She sat beside the football player, amazed that they could both fit on the small bench. Her leg pressed against Antone's muscled thigh and she felt the heat of him through the thin cotton of her dress. It was impossible to think of anything else. "What's that?" she managed.

"I'm rebranding the distillery, rebuilding it from the

ground up. My publicist keeps stressin' how important it is for me to have the right woman on my arm, you know, keep the cool vibe for the launch. But I'm not in a position to be in a serious relationship right now, can't have any distractions. That, and I'm not available for what most women want."

"Distractions?" Mia choked out. Of all the things she'd been expecting, this was hardly it… She didn't let herself ask him to clarify what he thought most women wanted. She was still melting.

"I don't want is woman to think I'm offering any more than I am. You know, the high-maintenance type? I tend to attract them like crazy."

She felt her pulse in her throat. *What were the chances he could hear her heart beating right now?* She watched as he twisted his hands in his lap. There was something else. Something he wasn't saying. But did she need to know every detail of the *why* if the *how* was exactly what she needed? Him. Dating her. Or, Evie… She took a sip of whiskey and said nothing. A trick she'd learned in school. Leave the opponent enough room to say too much. Never be the first to break. Negotiating 101.

"Is this it? Your whiskey?" she asked, raising the glass in his direction.

"What do you think? Do you like it?" He studied her, his brown eyes unreadable.

She took another sip. This time, with her eyes closed.

"It's nuanced but subtle. Full-bodied, rich and somehow balanced, yet unexpected." She was parroting all the buzz words she could remember her brother using at their last *apéro*.

"All things I like," he said, his direct gaze leaving her wondering for a moment if they were still talking about whiskey.

"I'll stay at your resort happily, a big booking too. I figure there's at least a month of work left before this place is habitable."

There it was.

"I'd need more than a booking," she interrupted, the rush of words giving her courage. "I need the resort to be cool. Like, cool enough for athletes, I mean." She blushed, feeling the rush of heat color her cheeks. "I'm working on a rebrand too. Or rather, er, my sister is. If you could get your team members to come, maybe we could host the launch party for your whiskey at the Hartmann Lodge? I mean, you're gonna have a launch party, right? And if we date strategically, I can only imagine the media opportunities, especially considering your aversion to social media."

"You noticed, eh?" He sighed.

"Hard not to notice, I couldn't dig up much dirt on you, although it's not like I tried that hard."

Except that she had. Tried hard.

"Yeah, well, I don't like my social life landing me in tabloids, but my publicist says it's important for our launch. Nothing better than free publicity—"

"Exactly. We, er, Hartmann Enterprises, could use the PR boost too. Sounds like this arrangement could be quid pro quo."

"Quid pro quo?" He raised an eyebrow.

She nodded, unable to speak past her rapid heartbeat. *Was he pressing his leg into hers or was it in her head?* Finally, she found words to form a coherent question. "So, how do you figure we do this?" She swallowed. *Let him speak first. Don't break the silence.* She pressed her leg back into his.

He cleared his throat. "The easiest way to have the press believe we're dating? It's simple. We date."

"We date? You mean, for real?" She choked on the words.

"Right. But don't fall in love with me." He winked. "My first priority is always going to be the distillery, among other things."

"How romantic. Among other things—what does that even mean? I don't even know you."

"I can think of a good way to fix that," he said gruffly, placing a hot hand on her hip. *Nuanced but subtle. Full-bodied, rich and somehow balanced, yet unexpected.* Maybe she had been describing Antone…

"This feels a little, I don't know, transactional." She had to make him work for it. Couldn't agree too quickly. *Hard to get. It was important to always play hard to get.*

"Says the girl who wants me to give her resort a facelift."

He took a sip of his drink and smiled at her. "You know, we do some interviews, date in public… I mean, there are worse ways to spend a month."

"Worse ways to spend a month? So, there's a timeline already?"

It was working. It was actually working. She shifted

slightly, experimenting to see if a sliver of space between their legs might help her pulse calm down.

"But for this to happen, I mean, the way we can both benefit from it"—he gestured to the space between them—"people have to believe it. There's no way the press will print what they don't believe."

"Believe it, yes, of course. That's a good reason for your friends to come to the resort. Because we're, er, dating."

"Exactly. Dating as publicly as possible."

"And not falling in love." She raised a finger, more to remind herself than to clarify things.

"You better not." He winked again.

Amazingly, she managed not to wink back. Instead, she just stared, unblinking, into his warm eyes. He was going to help. Hadn't so much as batted an eyelid at her direct invitation to invite his NFL friends to the lodge and publicly call her his girlfriend. She felt dizzy.

"You'd have to move in. With me, I mean. For people to believe we're dating." *Was the precision for her own benefit or his? Maybe it was the whiskey. Yeah. Maybe the melting puddle of want inside her was fueled by whiskey.*

"You mean, your place?" He raised an eyebrow. "Sure. How about Wednesday? That gives me tomorrow to pack."

She nodded, biting her lip. It was fast, but she also had a timeline. She let her eyes fall down his body in a blatant once-over. He was wearing a fitted dress shirt with the top buttons undone and the sleeves pulled up to bunch at his elbows. Her gaze boldly traveled up his body, taking in the delectably muscled forearms, the impossibly broad shoulders, the solid wall of his chest...

That was when she saw it.

How could she have missed it?

The wedding ring. He was wearing a wedding ring, strung on a chain around his neck. She swallowed her disappointment and instantly felt silly. Her bold appraisal felt immediately inappropriate. But that was ridiculous. How could she be disappointed about something impossible?

He followed her gaze and fingered the ring on his chain.

"She's dead. It's been four years," he said simply.

That changes things.

Evie would have said something clever. Something to lighten the mood.

Mia just reached for him, putting a hand on his chest. The move felt right; however, the moment her palm pressed against his chest, she realized how intimate the gesture was.

How could she be so brutally awkward with men? Especially this man?

"Right. Sorry. *Ummm*, I just mean, sorry about all of it."

Then, to her surprise, he raised his large hand to his chest and covered hers, cementing the gesture with a squeeze.

"Look. Let's not talk about this here. The bushes have ears, and we need to chat up Joanna. But I'll call you tomorrow evening. Ask you out proper, like, and we can iron out the details of how we're gonna make this happen."

She nodded, at a loss for words. Just like that, she regretted her traffic infraction a little less. Crashing into Antone's Lexus might just be the best mistake she had ever made.

Five

You Did What?

Who left voice mails these days anyway? Only one person in her life was sadistic enough for that brand of tech torture: Scott.

Amelia knew she should delete it, but as she watched her phone blink with the menacing threat, she clicked the triangle play button. Clearly, she still hadn't outgrown her appetite for punishment.

"Mia. I can't believe you're gonna fight about chump change, mouse. You're anxious to end up alone, I get it. But if you think I'm letting you go without getting what's owed to me, you got another think coming,"

Mouse. The least sexy nickname in the world, but

his term of endearment nonetheless. He must need more money.

Then the thought rose, unbidden, and a flash of anger overcame the aching worry that he was right. *She might very well die alone.*

She pressed seven a few times and avoided managing to listen to the end of the message. She pushed back into the soft leather of her office chair, and organized the picture frames on her desk. Her horse. Her sister. Her momma. Evie, laughing at a premiere, looking chic in a strapless gown that left little to the imagination. Brothers: Nick, Jacks, Austin and his family. Austin and his wife had died a year and a half earlier in a helicopter accident—may they rest in peace—. So many people in her life, all enclosed in heavy glass frames. They were all perfect. And then there was her.

Reaching for the lower drawer of her desk, she pulled out the heavy, etched-crystal decanter. It had been her father's. When Nick was deep in the purge of all things Dad, she had sneaked the whiskey set, and it stayed under lock and key at the bottom of her desk. She needed a drink. A drink and a minute to reflect on the whirlwind of insanity that had landed her masquerading as Evie and fake-dating an NFL player while her twin namaste-d her way across the Washington mountains. She took a deep sip and allowed herself to admit that she liked it. Liked Antone. And she really liked the person she was when she was with him.

From her penthouse office, she enjoyed palatial views. Nick had the presidential suite, but she hadn't wanted it anyway, preferring to look out at the fields behind Bozeman, just visible at this height. She counted the snow-capped mountains that dotted the horizon. She ignored the zooming cars, so small they looked like LEGOs. Everything was small from up here, but it didn't make her feel bigger. She hadn't felt big in a very long time.

Not big like Antone. Antone, the most decorated wide receiver in the NFL. The same guy who'd asked her out. *Asked Evie out. Or more accurately,* he'd proposed they "help each other out." *Was that the same thing?*

She flipped open her laptop, pursing her lips as she relaunched her Google search on her fake boyfriend-to-be. No Instagram account. No Facebook page. How could someone so popular manage to ignore the social channels responsible for *making* most celebrities popular? Or was that it? Did his total nonchalance make him even more appealing?

She frowned. Maybe that was the thing about being truly great. You didn't need anyone to notice. You just were.

Her phone rang, and she drained her glass before answering.

"Hey." She'd answered fast. *It was Antone.*

"Evie. Sorry to call you so late."

Her eyes flicked to the top right corner of her computer. 9 p.m. *Was it late? She'd been waiting for his call all day. So, yes, she supposed it was late.*

"No, I'm still at work, actually."

"That so?"

She leaned back in her chair, letting the full weight of her body relax for the first time that day.

"It is. Work hard, play hard." *Except she wasn't playing.*

"Sounds like my coach." He chuckled.

"Cheerleader never was my best look." She pushed back from her desk and let herself spin around on her chair.

"All the best cheerleaders say that." *He was flirting with her. Dating her for real, but no chance for love. At least he was up-front about it.* She didn't answer. She hadn't even tried out for the high school cheerleading team. *But Evie had.*

"Where are you working? Are they filming in Bozeman?" His voice, deep and gravelly, held a flirty inquiry. *Or did she just hear what she wanted to hear?*

"No. I meant I was pinch-hitting at the family business. Er, helping my sister with the rebrand on her resort."

"*Ahh,* yeah, you were saying. Trying to make your place a bit less stodgy and a little more chill."

"For a man calling at nine at night, you are taking forever to get to the end zone." Maybe Evie wasn't usually this direct, but over the phone, Mia felt a little more herself. Maybe now, tonight, she was more a mix of who she was, and who she wanted to be.

"Pinch-hitting? End zone? You're mixing metaphors, darlin'."

Darlin'. Her stomach flipped. *He was flirting with her.* "And you're dodging the point."

He laughed. "You got me. I'm new in town. Just

wondering if you could recommend the best place to get a drink around here? See, I'd promised to take this girl out this evening…"

She looked at the crystal decanter in front of her. "My office." She'd meant it as a joke, but her voice had deadpanned.

"Hartmann Enterprises? Is that an invitation?"

Her stomach flipped again. She opened the second tab on her laptop, the one with the outline for the branding facelift she'd been furiously planning.

"It is."

She'd meant to say something cute. Something flirty. Instead, she was bold. *Fake it till you make it, indeed.*

"I'll be there in ten."

He disconnected before she could insist she was joking. Before she could suggest it was a bad idea. She thought of Scott's looming threat that she'd die alone. She thought of her own insecurities, that she was boring. That she was all the worst things she thought about herself.

Not tonight, she wasn't. Tonight she was Evie. And she was going to have fun.

What had possessed him to call her?

Likely the same urge that had him driving to her office at nine thirty at night, when he should be packing.

He found a parking spot for the Lexus, freshly repaired and good as new, around the corner from her building and marveled at the way the city changed at night. The streets had a different vibe after 9 p.m., and the financial district, where her office was located, was nearly empty.

In front of the building, a teen leaned against the polished granite of the facade. Beside her was a retriever, lying on a tattered gray blanket.

"'Sup." He nodded at the teen. It was a girl, her eyes rimmed in heavy black makeup. She'd placed a small backpack beside the dog and clutched a baseball cap, which she waved toward him. Antone paused, then reached for his back pocket. He took out $120 and slipped it into her hat, along with Rob's business card. "If you ever need a job, call my mate Rob. We're hiring at the distillery. It's a cool project, and it could be a cool opportunity."

The girl's eyes widened.

"We have staff housing too," he added, kneeling to give the dog a quick scratch behind the ear.

"Stay safe," he said to the girl before she could express her thanks. She nodded, appearing stunned.

"You're just giving them drug money," Charlotte used to say every time he left money with street kids.

That might be true. But if one of the kids he helped was a bit desperate, if a kind word or his pocket change could make a difference? It was worth it. It was one of the pillars of his business plan. Hire homeless and underserved people. Create jobs. Give people a chance. Give a man a fish, feed him for a day. Teach a man to fish, feed him forever. That was the thing rich people didn't get. Most people were just looking for an *opportunity* to fish.

Charlotte not "getting it" was part of what had

caused their marriage to fall apart. Which only made his guilt about her death worse. He'd loved her, then lost her. Without getting to say he was sorry. He thrust his hands in his pockets and walked on without leaving his mind much chance to overthink things.

The lobby was watched over by a security guard, who looked at him strangely as he made his way to the elevator. The uniformed guard passed him a badge in front of the elevator, situated at the far end of the lobby.

"This one will take you straight to the penthouse, sir."

The elevator, a mirrored replica with art nouveau styling, was quiet and quick. It smelled like her.

She was waiting when the doors opened.

"Kyle told me you'd arrived. Follow me."

It was nice to see that the company's stakeholders knew the names of the security staff by heart. He liked her a little more, just for that.

"Sure."

She spun and made her way down a hall. The office was lit with brass sconces, a modern interpretation of art nouveau if his hobby reading of architectural digest had taught him anything. They cast a dim shadow on the rest of the floor. Large vases held four-foot-tall flower bouquets, and all the flowers were white. Lilies, roses, white lilacs.

"Not what I expected of a cattle operation," he mused.

"I decorated. I mean, between movies," she said, faltering. "And Hartmann Enterprises is more than a cattle operation."

That, he knew. Sure, the Hartmanns were a Western family, but they had built an empire without an East Coast parallel.

She turned the corner and pushed on a heavy glass door.

"My office, at least for the time being."

The name on the door was Amelia Hartmann.

"Amelia is my sister," she started.

He raised an eyebrow. "And you're her decorator?"

"Among other things."

She was cute when she blushed.

The east wall of the office held teak bookcases, the midcentury-modern vibe accentuated with orange velvet accents on a white couch and a series of leatherbound books in white and orange, all featuring gold lettering. A Harvard business degree was framed by the door.

"She went to Harvard?"

She hesitated, then nodded. "Amelia always excelled in school." She nodded toward the framed degree, then added, "She's a nerd."

Evie made her way to the desk and lifted a large decanter, filling two rock glasses with whiskey. *How would she describe this drink? Full-bodied? Lush? Seductive?* He swallowed.

"You gonna tell me why you're really here?"

He balked. She was direct. Asked him the question while staring him down with her warm hazel eyes.

Evie looked even better than she had at the party. Every inch a businesswoman, she was his fantasy come to life, a fact unaided by the black spike heels that brought her to just shy of six feet. There was nothing like a tall woman who exuded confidence.

"I like your shoes." He smiled, dodging the question.

"Thanks." She smiled back but widened her eyes. Was she fallible after all? Small talk was the worst, but he knew the ball was in his court.

"I'm here about our chat. I mean, what we were talking about at the party. About dating. Dating you."

"I remember." *Was it his imagination, or was her voice breathier than usual?*

She walked toward the white couch and sank into the down cushions, drink in hand. Interpreting the action as an invitation, he sank into the couch beside her.

His mouth was dry, so he took a sip of his own drink. "You were saying you had the best drink in Bozeman?"

She laughed. A warm, throaty laugh he felt in his gut. And lower.

"Best drink in Bozeman is quite the claim to make to a man who is planning to open a distillery." He grinned.

She smiled. "Yeah, well, I know a thing or two about whiskey. Goes with the territory of three older brothers and a barn full of ranch hands. I learned how to drink pretty early."

A beautiful girl who could hang with the boys? She was exactly what his distillery needed. A down-to-earth heiress, the Princess Diana of Montana.

"I guess I still don't understand why you want to help me out, er, date me. I mean, I guess most women would be lining up for the job." She blushed, the heat coloring her cheeks making her even more alluring.

"The dating, or the helping?" he winked. Thing was, it wasn't just about having the right person on his arm. He felt comfortable with her. He wanted her. Maybe if they had this project together, it was okay to want her for a while.

"Yeah, well." He cleared his throat. "I guess I just get a good vibe from you. You seem like the real deal." He took another sip of the whiskey. *Damn, it was smooth.*

"Real deal," she repeated, eyes unreadable. "I bet, following that *GQ* article, you could get any woman to be on your arm for this launch—"

"That's the thing. I don't want just *any woman."*

"Don't you?"

His pulse sped up. He finished his drink and put the glass on the chrome side table next to the couch. "No."

"And why's that?"

"It's simple really. This distillery is more than a whiskey venture. I'm hoping to create jobs, hire people who didn't get a great chance at life. The renovation is taking a long time because I'm adding a large bunk house to the premises. I'm hoping to get people off the street, employed and empowered. I want Great-Whiskey to be more than a whiskey." The words had escaped him like a rush of air.

Apart from Rob, she was the only person he'd confided to about his bigger-picture vision for the distillery. His friends would call him crazy, hiring people with no experience, but Antone was sure of this idea. Sometimes people just needed a chance.

"I like that. 'Being a man is more than drinking the right *old-fashioned*?' Finally, you might have a whiskey women would buy."

She got it. She totally got it. More than a drink, being a man was about owning your choices. About giving back. About making something last.

"Right. I mean, I want to contribute to our society. Give people a chance. You'd be surprised at how many people are just looking for a leg up. For someone to bet on them." He had to stop now. He was going to share too much. There was something about her wide eyes that had him opening up. "And yeah. I like whiskey. A lot. I like the idea of creating something. Of wide-open spaces, and rugged country. Hell, I like Montana. So, here I am."

"And you think that our family could help you with the launch?"

She straightened, shoulders pushed back and posture erect. She wasn't happy about it.

He needed to minimize how much her connections might make a difference.

"If you were able to help us network some political support for the 'back to work' initiative,' great. The distillery is essentially a start-up. There's lots to do."

She relaxed a little. Good, he didn't scare her off. Then she licked a rogue drop of whiskey from her bottom lip, and his body tightened. Lucky whiskey. "I love the sound of your project. I am sure a lot of people underestimate how the right support can change everything. How easy it is to judge people."

Suddenly, once again, he liked her a little more. And he wanted to get to know her better.

"Well, that's my plan, anyway. Hire some people looking for a second chance. Get some families off the street. Create a distillery that gives something back to the community, and make *charity* cool again."

"Make charity cool?" she repeated. It was an interesting spin on public relations, and definitely a message the Hartmann ranch could get behind. He was confident about that.

"I think it's a win-win message."

She poured him a second drink and held the etched glass toward him.

"Cheers." He accepted it.

"You know, I don't need grants to make this happen." It felt awkward to point out, but it was true. He could fund the distillery a few times over, but getting the distillery's back-to-work ethos legitimized by government grants was important. He wanted his workforce to be seen. But he did believe in the project enough to fund it himself, and it felt important to share that with her.

She didn't say anything, just raised a glass in his direction.

He clinked it, then took a deep sip. *Damn. It was good. But he bet she tasted better.*

"So we try and get as much publicity—" she started.

"—on the back of our relationship. The press is al-

ways looking to write about who is sleeping with who."
He winked.

Who was sleeping with whom? The wink too? He might have been a bit more direct than he'd intended, but she hadn't even blinked an eye.

"I guess it all starts with getting to know each other better."

Was it just him or had she slid closer to him on the couch?

"What do you suggest? Twenty questions?" he grinned. At the moment all he could think of was one question, namely, *your place or mine?*

"Maybe we start with you telling me why you stopped playing? What little I know about football leaves me thinking you left at the height of your career, no?"

He exhaled. "Here we go."

She nodded; her eyes bright in the low light of the office.

"I guess I wanted to leave while I was at the top of my game. Hurt myself a few games back, nothing too serious, but it was enough to scare me."

She nodded again, but didn't say anything. Infernal woman had a way of getting him to talk without even asking a question.

"I mean, wouldn't you rather be remembered for being good instead of being not quite what you were? Not quite good enough?"

Her chin dipped a bit, and her lashes pressed into her cheeks as she closed her eyes. Damn woman had beautiful eyes, even when they were closed. Why was he spouting some nonsense of feeling not quite good enough?

"I mean, I'm the best in the game right now. And I'm gonna ride that success to my next project, where Imma be the best again. Whatever it takes."

"Even dating me," she said quietly.

"Yeah. Dating you. For our *mutual* benefit." He hadn't blinked as he'd said "benefit." True, he needed to keep things professional, but they could date as long as he didn't get distracted.

She maintained eye contact with a surety that was rare in most women. Then she nodded. "Right. Dating. But for it to benefit me, we need to also promote the resort. Something like"—she blushed, and he'd never seen anything so adorable, yet also, hot—"something like how Hartmann Ranch is the perfect spot to light a flame? And GreatWhiskey... can fuel it? Er, or whatever you think."

She stumbled, once again flashing her alluring blush in his direction, but when she raised her eyes to his once more, she smiled with confidence. "Are you okay now? I mean, when you got hurt?"

He put his drink down on a leather coaster centered on the end table. "Yeah, I'm okay."

He felt his mouth tighten. He could kiss her right now. Finally taste the whiskey from her lips. He let his gaze settle on the plump bottom lip that jutted out, tantalizing him in the low light of her office.

In the shadows, she looked even more beautiful. There was something about her that didn't translate to the screen. A sexy, wide-eyed quality he couldn't put his finger on. This wasn't the Evie Hartmann he saw on *Bridesmaid Heyday*; this woman was no laughing matter.

She didn't answer, just took another sip of whiskey. But then she inched closer, the three-seater couch feeling too large and too small at the same time.

"Just because we have to be serious doesn't mean we can't have fun," he added, turning to the brunette beside him.

"Fun? What's that?" She laughed, but her laugh was hollow.

He watched as she pressed her knees together, counting as the muscles in her legs squeezed repeatedly, tightening and relaxing in rapid twitches.

He felt the ring hanging heavily from the chain at his neck. The way he wanted her right now felt a little too serious, so it was good to see her pump the brakes. He eased away a bit to give her some space. But not too much.

"So slightly injured wide receiver at height of career decides to turn in his cleats for a cowboy hat and liquor license? Not only that but he's prepared to personally sponsor homeless people in a get-back-to-work start-up, making high-end and amazingly tasty liquor with a greatest-of-all-time branding, and needs an actress with Western heritage on his arm for the launch? Is that it?" She laughed. "Of all the ways I thought I'd spend October—"

"We'll have some fun, I promise. It can't be all work or the media will never want to cover it." He grinned. His hand fell to her leg, then immediately, he shifted it off. The last thing he wanted to put out there was a pushy vibe.

"Fun?" she repeated, her voice sounding a little husky.

He could think of a lot of *fun* things they could do together. He leaned forward, and without further thought, kissed her. Quick, firm, and with intention. There were all sorts of fun where that came from.

But instead of pulling away, she parted her lips, letting him taste her. He groaned, why did Evie Hartmann need to taste so good? Meeting her parry, the kiss lingered, until it became hotter for Antone than an office couch would permit.

"Erhem," he cleared his throat, pulling back. Fun was clarified, he needed to shake this off. Focus on the distillery. "I'll move in with you, and host the launch party at the ranch. We commit for a month and tie things up at a launch party Halloween weekend?"

Evie just stared at him, cheeks flushed and lips red. She was speechless. Then as though swallowing her determination, she nodded.

"A month. At mine. But just because we're sharing a space—" she blushed, and more pointedly, shifted her leg away from his.

He held up a hand. "Nothing is gonna happen that you don't want to happen, babe. Don't sweat it." Evie Hartmann was an enigma. A confident starlet that embodied a cautious ingenuity he found intoxicating. And her mouth? Addictive.

"To tomorrow." She raised her glass in cheers.

"And to a hell of a ride." He smiled back. *Ready or not, this was happening.*

Six

In for a Penny

"Can I help you?" A middle-aged woman dressed like someone from the cast of *Downton Abbey* opened the door, smiling at him. Twenty hours ago, Evie had given him directions to her private entrance, given that she was working late. Still, the side door to the "west wing" was imposing, the domed door made from oak, with a brass knocker in the shape of a buck. As he stood nodding at the housekeeper, it was hard to ignore that Evie Hartmann was every bit the Western princess that her brand promised. Now he regretted the text to Amy, his publicist, setting up a PR opportunity pre-Christmas with Sophia. He didn't need a backup plan, because this was going to work. Then he swallowed.

Evie Hartmann, the Western princess, might necessitate a backup plan. Not for his brand, but for his heart.

"I'm—"

"Yes, you must be Antone. Miss Evie told us to expect you around six. I'm Agnes. Could I help with those?" The woman nodded toward his bags, all business.

Antone was horrified. Let a woman only a few years younger than his foster mom heft his bags to his room? "That won't be necessary." He pulled his belongings away from her. "Please," he insisted, "I'll carry my own things."

"As you wish," Agnes agreed. "Follow me, I can show you to your quarters."

Antone nodded, glad for a moment that Evie wasn't there. The moving in felt a little too real and, more concerning, a little too comfortable.

"Right this way." Agnes was hopping up the stairs, taking them two at a time. "It's been quite some time since Miss Hartmann has had a guest of the male persuasion, but of course, you'd know that," she muttered to herself as much as to him.

"Sure. Well, we've been seeing each other for a bit now." Antone tried not to think about how natural his lie sounded, how easy it was to make, or how a very small part of him wanted it to be true.

Agnes led him down a long corridor, then stopped. "Miss Evie's closets are full; she instructed me to offer you this space for your affairs." Agnes pushed open the door to what he assumed were guest quarters. Antone focused on maintaining an expression of nonchalance but sucked in a breath nonetheless.

The room was spectacular, wooden paneling covering every square inch of the twelve-foot ceilings and walls, but unlike the paneling in the hallway they'd passed earlier, all the wood in this room was birch, the natural ash color offering a Scandinavian vibe to the room. There were three large windows, each featuring a deep window seat accessorized with pillows and cushions all covered in natural fibers—linen, velvet, silk, all in nature's palette of okra, mustard, cream and moss.

It took a minute to put a finger on what was missing; there was no bed in his bedroom. Instead, an imposing desk looked out at views fit for a king. There was a slim couch, which, in a pinch, could work as a bed should things with Evie not evolve as he hoped they would.

Through the windows, Antone could see the low meadows and valleys that abutted Yellowstone National Park. Bison and cattle grazed the endless fields; the mountains, already snow-capped in early October, reached for the sky; and the forest, nature's painting, was a tapestry of colors with its changing leaves.

"It's quite nice, isn't it?" Agnes followed his gaze, nodding out the window.

"It's all right," he offered with a dry laugh and a forced shrug.

"And the bedroom?" he asked, mouth as dry as his laugh.

"Right this way." She smiled, pushing at a birch

panel, gripping the brass knob and heaving the hidden door open.

Evie's room was in keeping with the rest of her wing. Light colors, natural fibers. What he hadn't been expecting was the four-poster bed.

"It's a California King, made special for her. She and Miss. Amelia have identical rooms. Identical rooms for identical twins... It's cute, but these beds are quite a nightmare to make in the morning. That said, I imagine it's not the least comfortable thing you'll sleep in." Agnes blushed, realizing she'd said too much. He kept his mouth shut.

"About dinner. Would you like it served here, in your quarters? Or the dining room?"

"I don't mind making dinner for myself," he offered awkwardly. He knew he sounded distracted; he was still taking in Evie's room. The faded rugs with heavy tassels at each corner, once again, a wall of bookcases, with a slim brass ladder on wheels, straight out of a French château but looking entirely natural here, in this bedroom. Vases housing arrangements of wildflowers sitting atop a tin-cased fireplace, and a mirror featuring antique mercury glass, spotted with age, but issuing a contemporary vibe in the fairy-tale space.

"Tsk, tsk," Agnes scolded. "Now, if you don't accept Pierre's cooking, he'll be out of a job. He's a fine chef. I'll bring you dinner. When would you like it?"

Antone studied the woman and nodded. "Maybe seven?"

Agnes nodded and spun on her heels, exiting the room before he'd even noticed her departure.

Eating beautiful food for a month was hardly the worst consequence to suffer in the name of a successful launch party. But for a moment, as he stared at the four-poster bed, he wondered if that was really why he'd come.

"Antone, are you here? Sorry, I was so late, I had drinks after work with my lawyer, and everything just went longer than I'd intended. I hate that I missed dinner your first night in."

He could hear her trek up the stairs and took a few steps back from her doorway. Looking around, he resumed his spot at the desk, picking up his pen and striking through his scratched notes. "I'm in here," he called back.

In the next room, he heard the dull thud of what he assumed was her purse hitting the floor. Then she was in the doorway, leaning against the same post his skin had pressed upon moments earlier.

"I had a hell of a day," she sighed.

"You look beautiful," he blurted. *Real smooth.* So much for Rob's advice to *"keep her guessing."*

She raised a hand to her head, covering her face. "I don't. I've been at work all day."

He stood and took a few steps toward her. "I didn't mean anything by it, but I just saw you standing there and… Well, truth is truth."

"Listen to you, talking about beauty and waxing on with the compliments. You sound like a lit professor and not a football player." She smiled and her face relaxed.

"I meant it." He winked. "And, don't forget, I'm an up-and-coming distillery owner now."

She laughed and it was like a gut punch. In the best possible way. "And I'm the girlfriend of said almost-distillery-owner, so we're good!"

She shrugged off her blazer, and pulled an arm to stretch, pressing it against her chest. He watched as her curves protested against her arching back.

"You still a bit hungry?" She asked, clearly unaware of her effect on him.

He wondered if it was the right moment to discuss the sleeping arrangements? It seemed the gentlemanly thing to do.

"I ate already." He gestured toward the tray Agnes had brought. *Another stretch like that and he might work up an appetite for something else altogether. But he wasn't sure she was on the menu just yet...*

"Right." She nodded. "I had liquid lunch and dinner, but I'm not hungry..." She spun and looked out the window at the river. "Fancy a swim?"

His stomach tightened. Evie in a bikini. It was a good start.

"Come this way." She sprinted forward, skipping with a childlike excitement he couldn't help but find endearing. The grass was damp with evening dew, and he could follow her steps as easily as he could follow the arc of a solid pass.

"Did you see that?" she exclaimed.

"What?" He laughed.

"The firefly!"

Stepping over a low, rough-hewn fence, she pointed to a clearing in the distance. "Right there, that's where I swim at night. It looks like a fairyland with all the fireflies, trust me."

How he wished he could. But he had learned a long time ago the only person he could trust was himself. He had Rob and Jean, and Charlotte, back when things were good, but it was different with women he'd dated as an NFL player. You trust someone too much, and they leave you.

"I saw the bed in your room. Wonderin' where I'm sleeping?"

His question, spoken over the water, hung heavy in the night air. She spun and faced him, shock clear on her face.

"Excuse you?"

He laughed. "I meant, Agnes dropped my things in your room?"

"I didn't think I'd have to explain that for this to be believable we'd have to sleep together."

"Excellent." He grinned, purposefully interpreting her words the way he wanted to.

"Together in the same bed. Not together-together. And no more kissing. I think it muddles the err, professionalism."

She was hella cute when she blushed.

"Your wish is my command." Deeming the timing perfect, he stripped off his pants, the black swimsuit he'd put on at the house slick on his skin.

"Is that so?" She took a step closer.

He didn't move. In a one-piece swimsuit, Evie Hartmann somehow managed to look sexier than a naked cheerleader hiding in a tour bus. Her demure sophistication, hazel eyes and supple flesh made him hungry in a totally unsophisticated way. A primal, instinctual way.

"Well, in that case, I guess we're sleeping together... Sort of." He said the words quietly, but meant them. *He should kiss her now. He wanted to, and from the slight part of her lips, he figured she did too. This time, he would take his time. Drink her in. Mean it.*

"Right. Perfect." The air was so thick between them, it forced a pregnant pause between each word. Then she walked to the edge of the water, as though unaffected by the electricity he felt sizzling between them. "Oh, and my assistant has started getting some interviews and press ops for us. You know, to make the most of our month together." She made the statement offhand, but instead of feeling excited, he felt annoyed. As if Evie was all business, and while he felt he *should be* too, watching her butt sway as she made her way to the edge of the lake left him decidedly distracted.

The water was warmer than he'd expected, but still cold. He was hardly going to say no to a chance to get to know Evie a bit better. He needed to know her in order to find the most efficient way for them to work together.

Yes. Efficiency. That was why he was headed to the private Hartmann lake with a woman he was wildly attracted to and "dating."

"So, is this part of it?" he mentioned, sinking into

file behind her as he made his way to the edge of the lake, pants and towel slung over his shoulder.

"Part of it?"

"Being late. Is it? Part of your plan, I mean."

"No." She laughed, which irritated him. That was the thing about Evie—she had him on a tightrope wire of emotion.

"Well, hardly seems like a good way to get people to believe we're in a committed relationship. Feels like you're more worried about booking some media events, as though a few articles will do more to sell our relationship than actually hanging out together during daylight."

She didn't say anything, just laughed again, this time, quietly.

He swallowed the rest of his complaints. It was hardly smooth, coming on heavy when she was making the effort of a swim now. And the flirting. Because if he knew anything, it was flirting, and the way she'd parted her lips earlier... They had a month, after all. He regretted the tirade. The tightrope walk was tripping him up.

Evie swatted some water in his direction, unaffected by his outburst. "Coming home late from work? That's likely the closest thing to a real relationship I've ever had anyway. And right now, we're spending time together..."

"Just wondering who you're faking it for." *She was altogether too nonchalant.* He flexed his arm, wondering if the muscle might draw her focus.

She shook her head, and her sincerity provoked a

moment of honesty from him in turn. She was feeling
it too. Whatever *it* was.

"What's fake? You said we were dating. I just had to
work late, I'm sorry." Her eyes dipped to his swimsuit.

There it was. She was checking him out. He allowed
himself a smile.

"No, I get it, I mean, Charlotte used to accuse me
of being lost in my work too." He didn't protest any
further; the fact that there was only one bed to return
to that evening took up all available space in his mind.

She stilled and turned to him, clearly curious about
his mention of Charlotte. But it was all part of his
plan: confide in her just enough to bring down her
walls. He swallowed, determined to get his head back
in the game. If she trusted him, she'd be more likely
to go on a limb and flex the Hartmann connections for
a distribution deal. He was, of course, willing to do
the same. If he had one thing down pat, it was a little
black book of pro athletes all willing to take a jet to
any private party he'd host. Ten years in the industry
had that benefit.

"I didn't know you were married until Joanna's
party," she said, pinning him with her trademark direct gaze.

"Most girls I date ask about the ring right away, but
you were kind. It meant a lot when you listened to me
the other night."

"Of course. I know what it's like to lose someone
you love." He knew her brother and his wife had died
in a helicopter crash. He gave her shoulder a gentle
squeeze but didn't pry further.

"Tell me about her." She said, swimming another few strokes toward the center of the lake. He followed, talking to the back of her head, which felt easier somehow.

"Well, there's not much to say. Charlotte and I were in the system together. I married her when she was seventeen, to get her out early. She was my best friend, and for a while, it was more than that. She was more than a wife; she was my best friend. Then she got cancer. It wasn't pretty."

Evie didn't say anything, just kept walking out toward the center of the lake. He waded up beside her. He felt a small hand reach for his and, to his surprise, found himself taking it. Sometimes saying nothing was better than saying the wrong thing, but Evie might be the first person he'd met who managed to understand that.

"I don't think I've ever said this much in one evening."

She squeezed his hand, again silent in her answer. Gave him space to talk. And space to be quiet. She was different than the other girls he'd been with in a way that was as troublesome as it was calming.

Perhaps it had been five minutes. Perhaps it had been longer. But soon, under the stars, she guided him back to shore.

At the edge of the banks, Evie let go of his hand and reached for her towel, still quiet. Antone followed suit, willing himself not to stare at her creamy thighs, phosphorescent in the moonlight. She was wearing a modest one-piece, but on her it was devastating. There

was something very sexy about a woman totally unaware of her own attractiveness. He hadn't meant to
tell her the truth about Charlotte. He never spoke about
her cancer. Or about the real reason he'd married her,
to get her out of the system. So much of how he felt
about her was wrapped up in how he felt about himself. He didn't need a shrink to tell him that, although
a few had.

He cleared his throat but didn't say anything. He felt
safe in the quiet space. Under the moon, he resolved
that, as planned, he'd use this distillery to help as many
other people as he could. And maybe, just maybe, Evie
would help him at the same time.

And in the meantime? Being close to her was a good
start.

"I guess we're—"

"—sleeping here?" Antone finished for her, eyes
darting to the bed. The walk back from the lake had
had the effect of a wind-up toy, with each step toward
the home, toward her bed, coiling the tension in her
lower belly even further. Now they were here, in her
room, and her guts were a mess of heat and excitement.

Amelia had always loved her bed. The custom kings
she and Evie had bought were her find, the wood hulled
from a nearby forest, and the mattress made to order.
But apart from the identical room, the deco was all
hers. Did he like it?

Antone shrugged, his towel slung low around his
hips. He'd slipped out of the swimsuit with lightning

speed, and it had taken all her willpower to turn away from the show.

Do not stare at his body. With great determination, Mia managed to keep her eyes north of his abs, but her gaze lingered on perfect pecs instead. Smooth. Delicious. This view was not any safer.

"Er, I'll have a shower. First, I mean. First, before bed." *Could she be more awkward?*

He nodded, alarmingly nonchalant, clearly not needing a cold shower of his own.

Once in the adjoining master bathroom, Mia headed for the bath, turning both taps to full force. In minutes, the bathroom steamed, and she felt a little less awkward at the blush tinting her skin pink.

How long did she have to stay in there for him to get ready for bed? What were the chances he'd be tired enough to fall asleep while she was soaping up?

She stared at her reflection and bit her lip.

No chance.

Instead of a leisurely soak, she shaved her legs. Not for him. For herself. Because even though she'd shaved yesterday, er, it was important. For hygiene. Or whatever.

Post bath, she put on a generous dose of body oil. Again, just self-care, nothing to do with the NFL athlete in her bed. *He thinks you're an actress. Little does he know that this is your role of a lifetime.* She wondered a moment about the guilt gnawing at her stomach.

Then she studied the clothes she'd grabbed to sleep

in. A tank top and shorts. Simple modal cotton, more Amelia than Evie.

She opened the bottom drawer of the master vanity, took one look at her sister's proposed pj's, and closed the drawer. Ironically, Evie was the virgin twin, but Mia was the modest one. Tank top it was. She dressed and stood in front of the closed bathroom door, willing herself to open it.

You've got this, she told herself.

The scene that greeted her on the other side of the door was hardly what she expected.

"What?" Antone quickly asked.

He was in bed, in *their* bed, but instead of watching sports or scrolling through TikTok, Antone was reading. And not just reading. Reading *her book.* She couldn't decide what battle to pick first, then watched as he dog-eared a page and closed the book, smiling at her.

"Are you seriously reading *Wuthering Heights*?" she choked out.

This time, Antone was the one to blush.

"Er, yes." He closed the cover. *It was her book. The nerve. Dog-earing a page of someone else's book...* Whatever generous, or arduous, feelings she might have had were fast evaporating.

She made her way to his side of the bed, and snatched the book off his lap, temporary anger helping dull the shock of electricity that spurted through her as her hand skimmed his hard chest.

"Just because you're living here, doesn't mean you

can go through my things. Or share my bed, for that matter."

His lips curled into a wide grin. "You're cute when you're angry."

"Keep it up and you'll see just how cute I can get." She marched to her bookcase, and took a step up the brass ladder she'd flown from a French castle on her last trip to Lyon. The classics were on the third shelf. Not that Antone needed a ladder. Then she paused. There, nestled beside *Sense and Sensibility*, was *her copy* of *Wuthering Heights*.

His deep chuckle reverberated in her bones. Damn. Just when she'd thought her blushes were behind her.

"You're reading *Wuthering Heights*?" She spun, still on the ladder. It was the last thing she'd expected of the hulking picture of masculinity.

He threw the covers off, revealing a tight pair of black briefs that appeared to be painted onto his hard body. This man was all kinds of trouble; December had never looked so good.

"I am." He nodded, his white teeth flashing again in amusement.

"And you bought the cloth-covered Penguin edition of the book…"

"As did you," he said, still smiling as he nodded toward their twin copies.

He held a hand out, offering a strong arm to help her step down from the ladder. She accepted his hand.

"I was reaching for the book." He winked. "My book."

She blanched. Then, to her relief, he laughed, and squeezed her hand.

"I hate you right now." She smiled.

Pressing the book against him, he trapped her hand to his chest. "You're forgiven," he said. "Wanna go to bed?"

"Whose bed would that be?" she retorted, freeing her hand. Sure, she'd expected him to share her bed. They'd talked about it in the lake, but she wanted him to repeat, if only so she could hear again that nothing was going to happen. Even though a part of her really wanted it to. Especially after he'd opened up to her about his past. There was so much more to him than met the eye. And that part was glorious too.

"Your bed," repeated without question, then turned and made his way to "his side" with alarming ease. "You coming?"

Somehow, the invitation was layered, and Mia was acutely aware of just how much she wanted to go to bed with Antone. But not Antone, the wide receiver. Antone, the reader of *Wuthering Heights*.

She spun and walked away from the bookcase, pulling back the duvet and crawling into her side of the bed.

"Sure. I'm tired," she managed.

Climbing back out of bed, Antone walked back toward her, putting his book on the bedside table before joining her again. She felt the heat from his body even though he was several inches from hers. Too many inches, according to the warmth in her belly, and not enough inches, according to her head. Infernal head.

It was awkward. She didn't know what to say. She

watched him flip onto his side, his chin resting on his hand. He was looking at her. Really looking at her, and it was unnerving. He leaned toward her, lips parted.

She sucked in a breath. Right now. She could have him *right now.*

Except she couldn't. For a lot of reasons, the least of which was simple and painfully unavoidable. This Brontë-reading, charity-giving Zeus of a man believed her to be her sister.

"Do you read a lot of Brontë, Zeus, er, Antone?" she managed to ask. She pressed her arm over the duvet, sealing it to the mattress.

He looked at her, eyes hooded and dark. Was he mad?

Easing back onto his shoulders, he closed his eyes. "What's a lot?"

The man was infernal. He seemed not to care in the least that she was sending frigid signals to thwart his attempt to test the waters. Frigid signals her own body was rebelling against. *Damn it.*

Shouldn't he try to seduce her? Or, rather, Evie?

"I don't know." Amazingly, she managed to talk books regardless of the turmoil in her head.

"Well, I'm trying to get through the one hundred top classics of all time. It's no *Frankenstein* if you ask me, but I mean, I do like it." Eyes still closed, he smiled.

"Right. Well, I guess you're going to sleep." Even to her own ears, the statement was fraught with disappointment.

"I pegged you for a clever one," he answered, a little

tersely. *Maybe the frigidity of her not-so-invisible line down the bed was affecting him more than she thought.*

"I am. Clever. And don't worry, I know exactly why you're here," she added.

With lightning reflexes, he shot up, pushing the covers off his chest and facing her.

"Evie Hartmann. I'm here because I want to be, not just for the distillery. I make my own decisions, and right now, I just want to sleep here, with you."

He was close to her. She could lean in and kiss him. Or she could lean away.

Instead of moving, she just froze, watching as his eyes met hers, unblinking.

"Okay, then let's sleep," she whispered. He was so close to her she swore she could feel his heartbeat. Or maybe it was her own.

"Right. Sleep."

But he didn't lean back. It was dark, yet she was aware of how close he was to her. Then, with a split-second decision she hadn't expected, her body willed itself forward, and she laid a kiss on the warm lips inches from her.

It was good. *God, was it good.* His lips moved with hers, warm, hard, tense. He groaned, and the sound pulled her out of the temporary madness.

"Sorry. We need to sleep. Not kissing. Big day tomorrow." She threw her body back onto the bed, forcing up a cold shoulder in the hopes that it might temper her own raging desire.

Would he touch her? Try to kiss her again? Make a move?

But no, they just lay there, side by side, in silence. The infernal man didn't even say anything, apparently unbothered by her goodnight kiss. When his breathing slowed, she tentatively let her leg cross the invisible line down the center of the bed. His leg was there. Muscled. Hot. He didn't pull away. He was sleeping.

Or maybe he wasn't.

But he didn't move.

Sleep was a long time coming indeed. Her mind tortured her, but maybe she deserved it for pretending to be someone else. Even if she'd felt more herself, more seen, during one evening swim than she'd felt in years.

Seven

Alluring Bedfellows

"What was it like? Falling asleep with him? Did any-thing happen?" Evie giggled into the phone, delighted with the news that her sister had taken the athlete to bed. Kind of.

"I can't believe you're awake, and what about the whole 'no cell service' part of this namaste retreat?" Amelia admonished.

"Haven't gone to sleep yet. No rest for the wicked, but I guess you'd know that?"

Amelia buttoned up her cardigan and reached for a pashmina. It was brisk at 6:30 in the morning, but the thought of being in bed when he woke up was too much to bear. She needed to ride. There were few things as therapeutic as riding bareback through the wild, and right now, she needed all the therapy she could get.

"You are not silent-treating me about your evening. We're not even fighting about this. But we could if that would help get details…" Evie was insistent. Insistent, and maybe a little tipsy.

"I mean, it was nice." Mia pulled at her cardigan again, pressing her fingers over the buttons. Seven of them. It was her favorite sweater.

"Nice? Are you seriously going to try to brush me off with a '*nice*'? You forget that I'm your twin. This is the guy who was literally ranked 'hottest man on the planet' and you slept next to him. So, don't tell me your first night together was *nice*. I will hang up on you."

Amelia held the phone away from her ear, not that the distance served to offer her any reprieve from the tirade Evie was issuing.

"I don't know, Evie. I mean, at first, it was awkward. He wanted to know why we were sharing a room."

"He didn't," Evie muttered. "Talk about looking a gift horse in the mouth…"

"No one, and I do mean no one, would believe that we were in a serious relationship if he slept in the guest room. I mean, it's not like I'm saving myself for marriage."

Evie answered with a shrill laugh, and for a moment, Amelia felt guilty. Evie *was* saving herself for marriage.

"After you explained, what then?" Evie pressed, perhaps anxious to move past the whole question of chastity.

"I don't know, I mean, we went for a swim and that was kind of awkward too. After, I was freezing... I don't know, Evie, we just went to bed."

Amelia kicked a rock in her path. It was still about ten minutes until she got to the stable. Truth was, she had no idea how to tell her twin what she was feeling. A storm of indecision, self-doubt. *Lust.* Yes, it was a good thing that he hadn't tried to make a move. After all, with no audience, there was no need for that. Plus, if this relationship ended before her resort turned around, it would be the most expensive mistake of her life. It would cost her her pride, what little she had left.

Still, it was weird that she wasn't telling her twin about the kisses, but an overwhelming feeling of guilt had hit her the moment she'd answered the phone. She'd kissed someone who believed her to be Evie. *And she'd liked it.*

"You just brushed your teeth and went to sleep?" Evie groaned into the phone.

"The question is, how can we get the most media attention possible on our charade? That's the problem at hand. Not Antone's abs."

She'd meant the question to be rhetorical but was interrupted by Evie's squeal. "You saw his abs?"

Amelia pulled open the wide plank door to the barn, revealing a busy crew, all consumed with a flurry of activity. The ranch hands usually started their day at five, and today was no exception. She smiled at the crew as they took their hats and tilted them in good morning.

"Shall I saddle her up?" Cody, the foreman, smiled at her.

"Yes, please," she said, eagerly anticipating her ride.

"So you're gonna host a gala? Is that it? That's what you're planning, isn't it? Such a Mia thing to do … if you make it for three weeks from now, I could come! Just think of all the people we could invite… Some of his teammates, for starters…" Evie was a sucker for galas.

"I was thinking of something a little more subtle, but a gala isn't out of the question," Mia interjected, wheels turning. "Maybe a few interviews? I already started the wheels in motion for a blind taste test following the launch party. It should drum up a lot of interest."

"Gala. Gala. Gala," Evie chanted, just long enough for Mia to smile. It *was* a good idea. "I just hope you don't have any doubts."

"Not for a second."

After saying her goodbyes, Amelia smiled and turned her phone off, sliding it into the cross-body purse she wore when riding. Evie was one downward dog away from being light-headed, but at least she was supportive.

Her side of the bed was cold when he woke up. He'd slept so well that when he cracked his eyes open, he felt hungover; such was the depth of his slumber. He'd been so aware of her in the bed next to him, it'd taken him an hour to fall asleep, her shallow breathing an intoxicating lullaby. One night down, twenty-something more to go, and then the launch party would be at hand.

Which meant they had twenty-something more opportunities to elicit some attention to their faux union.

His phone blinked 7 a.m. It was seven in the morning and she was already gone. Was she an early riser,
or was it that she hadn't slept half as well as he?

Swinging his legs out of bed, he adjusted the waistband of his briefs. Sleeping in underwear would take
some getting used to, but he hadn't needed to ask about
sleeping attire. One look at her in a white cotton T-shirt
and gray shorts and he'd gotten the point. It was pa-
jama party time. At least the pajamas had saved him
from losing himself in a fantasy that was well aflame
without further fuel.

Today he needed to rewrite the marketing plan,
along with an invitation to the state commissioner
to attend the taste test, which had been Evie's brilliant idea. The donation to charity, namely, his "off
the street" project, should entice a nice audience, and
nothing garnered media attention like a blind taste test.

He had an hour before he had to log on for his first
conference call with a marketing firm from New York.
But he had prepared his questions, which meant he
had enough time for a long, hot shower, even if a cold
shower was more in order.

In the adjoining bathroom, he peeled off his briefs
and stepped into the shower. Immediately, hot water
pelted his back from the spa showerhead. In his haste
to pack, he hadn't remembered shampoo and inspected
the myriad of bottles that lined the glass shelf of Evie's
shower with interest. There was a pink glass bottle with
a French label. He lifted a heavy stopper and froze.

It smelled just like her, rose and cardamom, fruity spice and everything nice. No, he put the bottle down. He was being childish. He likely only wanted her because he couldn't have her, the smell, and the feelings it evoked, was in his head.

He shut the water off, preferring to conserve a little H2O as he soaped up, and selected a bottle of chamomile shampoo. Much more manly. Then, midlather, his blood ran cold. There she was, in the bathroom, unbuttoning her cardigan.

"I'm in here," he started, eager to speak before it got weird.

She spun to face him, a normal reaction. It was something anyone would do, follow the sound of the voice addressing them. But he wasn't just anyone, he was naked and in the shower. He brought his hands down in a mild attempt at modesty.

"Oh my God. I'm so sorry, I didn't hear the shower running—"

"I turned it off. To save water." He shrugged and with that action, revealed a little more than he'd hoped to.

He played with the idea of turning around, but preferred to save the view of his posterior for another occasion. "I only need another five minutes," he added, offering up a sheepish smile.

Evie nodded, face crimson. "—please don't feel the need to rush." She pressed her eyes shut with a ferocity he could spot across the room, then left.

Antone turned the water back on and stepped under a torrent of hot water. As he washed the suds from his hair, he wondered what precisely she had seen. He wasn't a vain guy, but as he scrubbed off the soap, he smiled with the knowledge that he looked good naked. And she'd had an eyeful.

If it'd been someone else, he might've been mad. But strangely, he wasn't.

Evie, this idea was the worst. I just saw him naked.

Amelia stared at her phone, willing Evie to answer. All she could see were the three little dots indicating that Evie was writing.

You saw him naked? Evie had punctuated the message with an eggplant emoji.

An eggplant emoji? Seriously? What am I supposed to SAY?

You accidentally saw his eggplant?

He was in the shower. Help.

She could hear the water shut off in the room next to her, and she paced over to her fireplace, looking in the mirror above it. At least her appearance wasn't a total catastrophe. The furious blush actually looked good on her. Her phone pinged with an answer from Evie.

Make a joke.

She hated her twin. A joke? I asked for help, not condemnation.

You're on your own. Too early.

Amelia threw her phone onto her bed without so much as a "break a leg." Then in walked Antone, a fluffy terry cotton towel wrapped around his waist, eight-pack dripping and delicious.

"Hi, roommate," she started.

Roommate? Really? That was what she'd come up with?

"Hey, sorry, I didn't know the policy for the bathroom door." He smiled at her, apparently unconcerned with the peep show moments earlier.

"My usual policy is to lock it." She grinned for lack of a better thing to do.

"I'll have to remember that for next time." He grinned right back.

Do not stare at his abs. One would think she'd never seen a naked man before.

"I will just leave you to get changed." She flailed her hand around and stared at her feet. Anywhere but his torso.

"My clothes are in the next room, and I'm afraid I gotta skip breakfast. I have three back-to-back conference calls before lunch." He smiled, unperturbed.

Because of course he wasn't.

"Tha's perfectly fine. I have to get to work too."

She twisted her hands and cracked a knuckle. Then,

from force of habit, proceeded to crack every knuckle on her left hand. Twice.

"You okay?" he asked, concern naked on his face.

She straightened, forcing her hands to her hips. "Yes. I just have a big day ahead of me."

"Sure, but we could also have an early dinner, somewhere public?" He nodded at her, still unconcerned by his semi nakedness.

"Okay, I should be free around seven?"

"Yeah, all right, I'll text you."

Antone crossed the room and she stared at his muscled back.

"Don't worry so much, Evie, it's all gonna work out." Then he had the audacity to wink at her.

To her surprise, he walked toward her, put a hand on her chin and lowered his head to hers. He kissed her with a deliberateness that left no question as to whether he had wanted her last night. Struck by surprise, she parted her lips and kissed him back, letting her head fall back and her body press against him. His still-wet chest pressed against her tank top, and she felt her nipples harden in response to the contact.

This man was good. Too good. His hands were everywhere, strong strokes running over her riding gear, pulling her closer to him, as though there could be a "close enough." She wanted to melt right then and there, so they could melt together and be as close as two people could be—such was the electricity between them.

She let out a moan, which served only to fuel him

forward. Then, both his hands rose to her face, cradling her jaw as he withdrew, kissing her softly on her lips.

"Just wanted to say good morning properly," he added.

"If that was good morning, I guess good night is a showstopper," she answered, without thinking.

To her relief, he laughed. "I'm sure it will be," he promised.

"But, umm, you know, the kissing is fine now I guess... I mean, we're dating, and I know it has to look real—"

"Just try not to overthink things." He grinned again.

Then, he loosened his towel, turned and made his way to the adjoining room. Leaving her with thoughts of an eggplant emoji, of all things.

Eight

"**Y**ou're joking," Amelia exhaled, but Elsbeth shook her head. Two weeks later later and she still walked on eggshells around Antone, only to arrive to work where the same eggshells felt like hot coals. *When was this going to get easier?* She stared at Elsbeth and frowned. "We are not replacing all the toilet seats at the ranch. I don't care who this guy thinks he is."

"A prince with an ironclad contract to rent The Lodge, all the bells and whistles included?" Elisbeth frowned.

Amelia fumed. The worst part of this predicament was that it was her fault. It had been *her idea* to cater to the rich, but she hadn't been expecting the outrageous demands that accompanied a royal family. "I get your point. We will acquiesce, but make sure you charge them three times whatever we get quoted for this insanity."

Elsbeth nodded but made no move to leave the office.

"Can I help you with something else?"

"I just wanted to say that I did call a few of our contacts in the press. In addition to the two articles I told you about last week, people are interested. *Vogue* even offered a feature in their spotlight on Western fashion—how a new man is the best accessory for fall? But I wasn't sure if that was taking it too far. Their first idea was "The Athlete and the Heiress," but they are waiting for your all clear."

Amelia stared at Elsbeth, impressed but not surprised by her competence. *Vogue* was a surefire way to get in front of a lot of people. *The Athlete and the Heiress? It was an article angle that might sell, and a great opportunity to get Scott's attention... She knew exactly what to say to make him realize it was Mia behind the interview and not Evie... Which should prompt him to bribe her. Which was extortion and freedom all wrapped in the same felony.*

"Timeline?" she asked, hoping for ASAP.

"It's slated for January, but they have a hole in their editorial now. If Evie could manage the shoot this weekend, could drop you in the online coverstory this month."

It was too good to be true. But she would have to get Antone to agree.

"Confirm to *Vogue*, we'll do it. And check if they could do the shoot at the lodge. I'd love to have the publicity, and we don't have a booking until the Prince."

Elsbeth nodded. "You got it."

Amelia stared at her inbox. Nothing but new fires to put out, but she'd lost her appetite for drama. She stood. "Elsbeth, who do we know from the commissioner's office?"

Might be nice to focus on people who needed help instead of those who demanded toilet seat replacements or other infernal requests. Getting a few grants for back-to-work packages somehow felt more relevant and worthy than catering to a prince. And, Antone would be impressed—a nice bonus.

Elsbeth turned her attention to the iPad in her hands. "Barry Lopez? He's running up against the new commissioner but needs sponsorship if he is going to make any ground."

"Can you get me on the phone with his campaign manager? And I'm going to need to also get Nick on the line." It felt good to be working on something that mattered.

Amelia's intercom buzzed. "Nick on line one," Elsbeth said.

"Nick." She clicked the red, blinking line-one button on her desk phone. "I think it's time the Hartmanns got back involved in politics."

Nick chuckled on the line. "I'm here for the enthusiasm, but I wasn't exactly aware that we left politics? Austin had been networking on our behalf from New

York, investing in different people. I'm pretty sure I have a list somewhere." Nick's voice trailed off.

Amelia's throat tightened at the mention of her late brother. "If you could send it my way?"

"Sure, I could do that."

"And Barry Lopez, do you know anything about him?"

"He's running, but if we're talking politics, shouldn't we focus on getting Jackson hired as livestock commissioner?" Nick mused.

"Okay, Dad, I understand that's what you thought, but we run this family like a democracy, and I've already spoken with Evie. We both love the idea of focusing on employment opportunities for at-risk youth… And as you know, the current commissioner is not exactly sympathetic to our cause, so let's get behind someone who can line up with our values." She heard a deep exhale on the other side of the phone and pressed on. "Honestly, I don't see how helping street kids can hurt our family's brand."

"Alright, as long as it doesn't interrupt the cattle operation or reservation momentum, I'm with you. I'm just a bit surprised to see you so passionate about politics again."

Amelia laughed. "Well, I would've preferred support that wasn't predicated on an 'as long as,' but I'll take what I can get." She'd omitted the "again" She knew Nick had noticed her heartbreak, but he was stoic enough not to rub her face in it now. They had all made mistakes.

She sensed Nick's hesitation through the phone.

"What? I mean, I called you, but did you have something you wanted to talk about?"

"I just heard about Evie's beau? Sleeping over, if the wires didn't get crossed..."

This was why the shared room was so important. The help talks. Agnes was amazing, as predicted.

"Nick, are you listening to gossip?"

"Wouldn't have to, if my little sister was a little more open with me." She imagined him pouting in jest through the phone. "I'd have thought you'd have told me...you know he's still my number one draft—"

"Nice try—but he's retired. If you must know, yes, Evie and Antone are sorta dating."

"Well, this is news." Nick was smiling, she could tell from the way his tone had lilted up. "Does Jacks know?"

"I haven't exactly made a statement to the press," she joked. "Yet."

"I think we should have dinner. The whole family." Nick was descending into a tangent, and she could feel it.

"You mean with Mom and Evie too?" *That was not going to happen.*

"Depending on the schedule, I don't see why not. Maybe we could celebrate Thanksgiving together?" Nick suggested.

Thanksgiving. November. He would be gone. They'd said thirty days of dating.

"Let's put it on the books and play it by ear, okay? I am thinking about a Halloween gala as part of our promo—I'll keep you in the loop."

"Right. Later, then." Nick was off the phone. That was the nice thing about Nick. He wasn't chatty.

"Elsbeth, can you get Barry Lopez on the line? And find me everything related to *Sports Illustrated* and the commissioner's office." Amelia spun on her office chair, excited to finally have a new problem that didn't involve outrageous demands by royalty. It was amazing to concentrate on a problem she could actually solve.

As she stared at the blinking intercom, she somehow felt lighter for the first time all week.

Antone smiled at his team. "We have six minutes left—any of you have any questions?" He continued to smile at his crew in encouragement. "Yes?" He nodded at the redhead that had been scribbling notes furiously over the past hour.

"Er, I'm Leah, and I don't have a question, just wanted to say thanks for this opportunity."

Leah? He stared back at the girl, then recognized her as the kid with the dog from in front of the Hartmann office two weeks ago.

"Glad to see you made it out here. Welcome to the team." He smiled.

"Yes, Ellen?" He nodded toward another woman, in her midfifties. She'd been one of the first hires Rob had made and had been managing the renovation like the captain of a naval ship.

Ellen's face broke into a smile at being singled out. "All our licenses have arrived and are in order, and I've opened accounts with every vendor on your list. I think we're good to go. But I was thinking, why are we hosting the launch party at the Hartmann ranch? Shouldn't it be here?"

A gentle murmur of assent flowed through the crowd, and Antone spotted Rob grinning. *Had he planted the question?*

"Excellent question," Antone answered, scratching at his chin.

"When I was younger, Coach used to tell me, there are many ways to skin a cat. I try to approach all problems from that perspective, thinking about out-of-the-box ways to find solutions. Sometimes, the court of public opinion can influence large companies. It only takes one mighty foe to put a glitch in the machine. The Hartmanns are connected, and Evie has suggested we follow up the gala with a taste-test on-site, here. This gives us an additional two weeks to plan the media blitz, and a second chance to get in the press."

The team members nodded, taking notes with a seriousness that he couldn't help but find encouraging. They were almost ready. "I'll see you all Thursday."

The group broke off, with several of the original employees tipping hats in his direction.

His phone vibrated—so much for a little peace.

"Momma Jean," he answered.

"I hate to call you like this," his foster mom started. Antone turned and made his way to the glass-walled office behind him, taking in the picture-perfect views of the rolling hills and grazing cattle. He would never get tired of the expansive, rugged beauty of Montana.

"Can I put you on speaker? I'm just finishing up a

meeting and I have a dinner engagement." He smiled at the phone.

"Sure, of course. I won't take up much of your time. I hate to call with this. It isn't right, but I was wondering—"

"How much do you need, Momma?" he, said cutting her off. At least he could save her the embarrassment of having to ask. It felt like a small kindness.

"A few hundred? We can add it to my tab," Jean suggested in a small voice.

Restraining himself, he managed not to laugh, or worse, cry. "Mom, you don't have a tab. You know I played for the NFL right? I mean, really, I wish you wouldn't think twice about calling. Why don't you let me send you some real money?"

She'd disputed his first wire payment, objecting to her bank manager and refusing the transaction when he'd sent her ten thousand. Sure, it wasn't millions, but it would have covered the mortgage and utilities for a few months. Now she made do with the pittance she earned as a foster mom and whatever she earned from the occasional odd job.

"Why don't you come here? I could get you a spot at the distillery," he reminded her.

"Nonsense, you know I'm not going to leave New York."

He sat back down and took the phone off speaker, pressing it to his face as though the revised posture would make his mom listen. "I know you love New York, Momma, but Montana is beautiful too. We could even find you a cowboy." His stomach twisted at the thought of his elderly foster mom dating, but he figured it was worth a try...

"You're crazy if you think for a second you can hitch me with someone," she grumbled into the phone, clearly flattered at his offer. "Sweetie, just a few hundred and I'll be fine. As long as we have each other, I couldn't be happier. You know, sweetheart, I'm very proud of you."

"If you turn down my next wire payment, there will be no grandchildren, Momma. Really."

He stared at the phone, then wondered for a moment where the inspiration for grandchildren had come from. *Evie.* "I'll call you tonight."

"I'd love that." His mother sounded more uplifted already. "Please don't forget the—"

"I'm doing it right now. Love you."

There was nothing worse than the chilling truth of the matter. His mother's destitution was his fault. Well, the fault of the system. Because she'd abandoned her career as a social worker to raise him and other kids she'd seen suffering in the system. And somehow, that made it all the harder to bear. There was no time for second-guessing. There was no time for failure.

Amelia was too excited to eat. For two weeks she'd managed to temper her fever for the athlete roommate, and had focused instead on going over extensive SWOT analysis for his liquor launch. Anything to distract her from how sexy he looked in his trademark gray sweatpants and fitted white shirt.

But tonight? They had a date. She felt as if she knew

him better already, which helped her overcome her feeling of intense guilt every time he called her Evie. She had a big problem. She *liked* Antone.

"You dressed up." She grinned, eyeing him appreciatively. The first week of living together had passed without the need for texting any additional eggplant emojis, but the lack of a peep show did little to tamper how much she was starting to want him. The second week was tougher. Amazingly, there had been no more kisses. Now, sweatpants aside, he was dressed in a fitted black suit; he looked every bit the cover model she'd ogled online. She closed her eyes for a moment, picturing the calendar she'd splurged on. December indeed...

"Yes, well, I figured any boyfriend of yours would know his way around a *GQ* fashion spread. Pretty sure these pants are a little too tight, but I'm down for any sacrifice in the name of business." He grinned right back at her.

*

The restaurant was a French bistro, the only one in town, and it was buzzing with the populace of the after-work crowd. She passed four frenemies on the way in, while following the hostess to their table, one of whom was snapping a photo of them without much discretion. It was just as well: at this point, any publicity was good publicity.

But today? After just a few phone calls, a fabulous PR opportunity was in the works for both of them. It involved potentially the most influential fashion magazine in the world. It had been almost easy to ignore the three emails PJ had sent her, each one a tad more aggressive than the last. Their petition to dismiss the request for lump-sum payment to Scott had been rejected by the court. She was running out of time to keep her current lawsuit a secret. She was running out of time for a lot of things.

The hostess continued to lead them through the winding restaurant, eventually stopping to point at two tables. "Either of these, miss?"

"By the window, please," Antone cut in.

Mia smiled. She liked when he took the upper hand.

"I've had a productive day," she jumped in the moment they sat.

"I don't doubt it," he agreed. "Can't believe this place is so busy for an early dinner." He nodded at the bustling tables.

"I'm starving," he continued.

"Remind me to go over my menu ideas for the gala—it's now in two weeks. I mean, we need to scramble."

"I'm fast. Fastest feet in Texas, according to the sports journal you read.' He grinned.

Mia smiled but remained anxious about her bigger news. "There is this guy, Barry Lopez, a real do-gooder. You'd like him."

"Because he's a do-gooder?" Antone interjected.

"Because he's running for Commissioner of Montana, and he's now favored to win."

This got his attention, and Antone leaned forward, just close enough for her to smell soap and vanilla. Her shampoo. Was it weird that she thought it was cute that he used her shampoo? That, somehow, the implied intimacy of their shared bathroom made her nerves flutter? The scent brought her right back to her fated interruption of his first shower, and for a moment, she fought the heat that spread up her cheeks. "Er, he pointed me toward some very interesting studies."

"That so?" He took a deep inhale, then let it out.

Reminding herself that this outing was about getting attention, she reached for his hand across the table and gripped it. Her stomach fluttered at the contact. *This was just for show, right?*

His jaw tightened, but only for a moment. Then she watched as his Adam's apple bobbed with a swallow. As she watched him begrudgingly accept her public affection, she felt her stomach turn. *Why was she really doing this? To avoid a payout with Scott she could well afford? To avoid humiliating herself in front of her family? Or was she really doing this because she wanted this charade? Because she wanted to be Evie, dating Antone, and being her best self...*

She squeezed his arm, then released it, reaching for her purse and pulling out the papers Elsbeth had printed and collated. She passed them across the table, biting back a smile. *He was going to love this.*

Antone accepted the papers and studied the first page, scanning it with his finger. Then his face broke into a beaming smile. "If I'm reading this correctly," he started, finger skimming the page as he pressed it against the table in front of him, "then there are no less than seven grants we can apply for to fund additional hires, assuming our business plan is accepted. Er, rather, the distillery's business plan," he corrected.

After four evenings spent poring over the SWOT notes he'd left with her, her stomach betrayed her with another flip at his Freudian slip. *Our business plan.* It certainly felt that way.

"I got the news from a family friend." She grinned. "These grants will announce for fourth quarter, and if we move quickly, we should be able to pair our media blitz with the coattails of the commissioner's campaign. Grants are a shoo-in!" She felt her cheeks twinge with her wide smile.

"Family friend?" He pulled his eyes away from the document and studied her, his brown eyes searing into her with an intensity she'd been unprepared for.

"A judge."

He shook his head. "Sounds like a plan. And I've got something for you...twenty footballers and thirty cheerleaders, all coming to our launch party, and all ready to post about it." He looked like a little boy, as delighted by her discovery of the new grants as if she'd just given him a glow-in-the-dark fidget spinner. And she? She felt alive and relevant in a way she'd missed. Too bad it wasn't real.

Over appetizers, they shared ideas. Petitions they could write to get more funding for an off-the-streets initiative, influential politicians she could connect them with. Then they brainstormed ways to crack the distribution of GreatWhiskey, including a few of the connections Evie had in hospitality. It was easy. Easy and light, and all the best parts of dating with none of the pain.

"Open wide," Evie teased, offering a bit of her pasta.

Cocking an eyebrow, he agreed, not immune to the scrutiny of their ever-present audience. He chewed thoughtfully, then reached across the table to touch her nose. Their audience oughta love that.

"Maybe we should take a selfie? I assume you still have an Instagram?" he suggested. Might as well live up to his part of their arrangement—she was certainly delivering on hers.

She smiled at him, then shook her head. "I'm good for the selfie, but I deleted my social media after college."

He stiffened in surprise. *Deleted her social media account?* "An actress without an Insta? Is it uncool of me to admit I've seen your account @EvieHart?"

She blanched. "I never thought I'd see the day. The NFL player with no IG admitting to a little stalking." She shook her head. "And for the last time, I'm not just an actress."

He raised his hands in apology. "You're right. You're so much more than that.""

"I mean," she blushed. "I have a work IG, but not a personal one. You know, I only post for work."

"Right. But isn't this work? Wasn't that the point?"

If possible, she turned a deeper shade of vermilion.

"You're absolutely right. Let's take the selfie, and I'll send it to my agent. Er, she manages the IG account."

He smiled at her. "Sure."

"What?" she pushed.

He took a sip of his draft beer and smiled at her. "Evie Hartmann. You're not who I thought you were."

"Not sure if that's a good thing or not."

"A surprisingly good thing." he mused. *Surprising indeed.*

"Er, before we finish up here, an opportunity landed in my lap that I just couldn't say no to. I hope you understand."

"I'm afraid you'll need to elaborate," he insisted, a little nervous at her umbrella definition of opportunity.

"Vogue."

"As in, the magazine?"

"Is there another *Vogue*?" She smiled. She picked up a fork and tapped it against her napkin in a quick succession of rapid movements. "An opportunity came up, for an article, something on the lines of *The Heiress and the Athlete take the Wild West*, and well, they agreed to feature me. Feature us. I already agreed, and I'm sorry I didn't ask first, but—"

"No, it's okay. *Vogue*, eh? Not exactly my target market, but I'm sure I can do a little photoshoot. When?" He wasn't angry; she was so nervous with her request that he felt the urge to immediately reassure her it was fine.

"When the photography team frees up, they're gonna call, but it will likely take place this weekend. On the ranch."

He nodded. He'd known what he was signing up for when he'd agreed to their fake relationship. A relationship that was beginning to feel real. That was why he'd stiffened at her touch earlier. Simply because it had felt too good, too…right?

"Just let me know when and where, and I'll be there."

"Thanks, Antone, this should work. I mean, the feature on *Vogue* will get picked up by other magazines. We can assume this will snowball into a lot more press, and everything might—"

He had to stop her. "You don't have to explain. I'll do it." *Fair was fair.*

He watched her as she inspected her water glass, then brought her napkin to the rim to wipe it off. He said nothing but noted the event. It wasn't the first time she'd been a little odd. The tapping, of her hand and her foot, it was impossible not to notice, not that it mattered. It was one of the little things that made Evie, Evie. And he was beginning to appreciate the whole package.

Nine

"Darling, you look sensational," Raoul insisted. Vogue's stylist was French and over-the-top in every way that mattered.

"You don't think it's too much? I don't feel ready for this, I only confirmed this shoot four days ago!" Amelia stared at her reflection, hardly recognizing herself. Her eyes were rimmed in cobalt liner, which only served to make her hazel eyes shine like fresh honey. Her lashes were teased to a volume she'd never imagined possible. Her pouty lips were skimmed in nude lipstick, which she'd thought would wash her out, but if anything, the makeup made her look even more alluring than she'd thought possible. Her face, contoured and blushed to a smooth sheen, felt as light as it looked natural.

"Magnifique," he assured her. "Now, for the wardrobe."

The lodge had been transformed to a mobile dressing room, with rolling rack after rolling rack of designer dresses. Raoul flipped hangers, fingering an Ellie Saab before selecting a Jenny Packham. "This one is a British designer, so dreamy."

Dreamy it was. The dress was an illusion of crystals and sequins, exuding a 1920s *Great Gatsby* vibe, but with a contemporary twist. The sequins and tulle offered the allusions of nudity, and there was no way Amelia was putting it on.

"I think you're confusing me for someone who would actually wear a dress like that," she started, infusing what she hoped was insistence into her tone.

"Figure like yours, it's a crime not to show it off." Raoul thrust the dress forward. "Champagne tulle, ombré to a blush sunset, this dress is perfection. Lavish elegance against a stark horizon, the article will write itself." Raoul nodded toward the bedroom. "Go, and put it on."

Partly because she recognized a lost battle when she saw one, and partly because it was the most beautiful dress she'd ever seen, she accepted the gown and closed the door to the bedroom she'd been sequestered to.

The dress had two parts, a floor-length champagne slip with straps so thin they looked to defy gravity in their construction, and a bedazzled tulle overlay. The overlay surprised her with its weight; tulle was light, or she'd thought it was, but the stones and sequins accounted for at least eight pounds of glitter. Twisting vines of leaves in copper and rust married platinum leaves with soft gold flowers. The dress was spectacular. The back had a series of small satin-covered buttons, but the neckline was wide enough for her to step through it.

Raoul pushed the door open without waiting for an invitation and applauded her.

"The clapping isn't necessary," she assured him.

"Oh, darling, it is." He winked. "The team has texted me. Your *monsieur* is ready and waiting outside. They are taking light samples by the water. I'd say you have at least fifteen minutes before they will want to shoot." He blew a kiss at her and issued a wink in the way only a flamboyant Frenchman could get away with.

"I left shoes on the couch, size thirty-nine. They are a must with that dress, *croyez-moi*!"

Suddenly, without waiting for a reaction, he was at the front door, peering out.

Her newfound friend was right about one thing: the shoes were perfect. Manolo Blahniks in a dusty-pink matte leather with a studded heel. Five inches, but it didn't matter one whit. Antone would still tower over her.

Antone. She reached for her hair, pulling at a loose curl. What was he going to think of all this? She looked over-the-top, that was for sure.

Looking around the main room of the lodge, she decided there was no time to second-guess. When *Vogue* offered to fit you in at the last minute, you trusted them.

And so, she joined Raoul at the door and pushed it open, letting the setting sun hit her dress and greeting the team with a smile.

It didn't take long for Antone to question every truth he'd held. Agreeing to a public circus of a relationship was one thing, but a feature in *Vogue*? A nationally distributed magazine, with a photoshoot pulled together at the last minute? The stylist assigned to him had frowned all afternoon. First at his buzz cut. "Hair like this and you can't even be bothered to deep-condition it from time to time?" he'd said, tutting his disapproval. Then, incredulity at Antoine's indifference when faced with a rack of suits.

"A blue one?" he'd suggested. The request had given rise to another scowl.

"Blue one?" The stylist had frowned reprovingly. "Sacrilegious, if you ask me. Build like yours and to have no interest in fashion whatsoever."

"Well, I don't think I was. Asking you, that is." Antone had smiled. He was impervious to judgment and didn't care that he preferred blue jeans to suits. If it was good enough for the educated elite, that was all that mattered.

Finally, he'd agreed to a Zadig & Voltaire slim-cut suit. The thin wool had a drape even he could appreciate. Truth was truth, and the suit was incredible. Then came the shirt, pressed to a crisp white, followed by the cowboy hat. Always a Stetson, this time an oiled brown to match a pair of Italian shoes. He was starting to feel like he belonged in Montana. The cowboy hat helped.

"You can keep it all, compliments of the designers." The stylist smiled.

Antone nodded, not that any of it mattered. Still, the hat was pretty cool.

Hair washed, freshly buzzed and styled, and he was ready. He'd accepted the shave, marveling in the luxury of someone else shaving his scruff. It was a far cry from the typical barber chair, but ambience aside, it was quite nice.

When his attendant deemed him ready, he'd agreed to wait outside, feeling far too polished.

Then he saw her, and forgot everything else.

The sun was setting behind the ranch, and it back-lit the angel that was pushing through the door of the lodge. Her dress sparkled, but it was her face that trans-fixed him. Then the smile, shy at first, then so genuine it hurt. She was so beautiful that he didn't think about the reasons why they couldn't *really* be together. Didn't think about the past and his promises, of what was at stake, and how important success was. He thought only of her, looking like an enchantment. What wizardry was this? He was bewitched.

With his eye contact, she straightened, reaching for the balustrade to steady herself. Then she took a step down the porch toward him. Antone swallowed, the vision weighing heavily in this throat. He was struck with emotion. It was impossible to look at her and not see the girl he'd sat beside at Joanna's party. The awkward teetering and clumsy drinks they'd shared. The moment he'd stood a hair too close, and fought all the instinct in his body to refrain from kissing her. It was impossible not to remember the smell of her hair, the notes of persimmon and spice flooding his memory, both that night and now.

Staring at her now, it was impossible not to see a perfect picture of the best parts of his life and what they could build together. He felt like a groom staring at his bride, imagining all that could be. *If things were different. If he didn't know exactly how much love like that could end him.*

"We have fifteen minutes," she said after she closed the space between them.

"Fifteen minutes?" he repeated, as though she was speaking another language. Before he could stop himself, he effused compliments, wishing he was capable of finding words good enough for her. "You look incredible. Beautiful. You could stop time if you tried hard enough, I'm sure of it." He smiled at her reaction, mirroring her happiness with his.

"They're watching," he said, nodding toward the writers and photographers.

"Right." She backed away.

"That's not what I meant." He took a step toward her. "I think we need to give them the show they came for." He softened. With a hand on her hip, he pulled her toward him, pulling her against the cock of his hip. She felt slim and small against him, the prickling sequins scratching against roughened hands.

Nodding, she licked her lips. A subconscious movement perhaps, but it lit the fire in his belly just the same. He let his hands wander up her rib cage, over her shoulders, cradling her head and bringing her closer to him. "Are you sure about this?" he whispered, his mouth so close to hers he could almost taste her.

She pressed her lips against his in answer, pushing her body toward his, melting into him with an effortless lean. Gone was the question of whether they should be doing this. No kiss had felt so right, no joining more necessary.

A flash brought him to the present, and he pulled back, aware their audience had crept nearer. It was a camera, only a few feet from them.

"Are you still hungry?" The French photographer laughed. "Might we get some work in before we lose the light?"

Evie laughed, nodding.

"Keep it up, just like that. We want to photograph love. The possibilities that unfold with a second wind. That's the article. Hartmanns finding a second wind. Second love. Second chances. Second careers, and second success. It's poetry with the two of you looking so *magnifique*."

Antone reached for her hand, finding it warm yet small. "Where do you want us?"

The group was led to the edge of Yellowstone and positioned against a wooden fence.

"Hands on her hips," the lighting assistant instructed.

"Tilt your head closer, lean your forehead on hers," another suggested.

He was distracted. "Where should I put my hands?" The question felt as ridiculous as it sounded.

"Here." She took his hands and placed one on her hip, the other on the top plank of the fence.

"Don't stare at her like that," the helpful lighting aide suggested.

"Why don't we look out to the horizon?" Evie smiled.

Pops and flashes hit from every direction. It was hard to focus on the beauty of the landscape with all these people everywhere.

Evie, on the other hand, was a natural. She inclined her head back and laughed with an ease that relaxed him, but instead of staring at the horizon, all he could look at was her. It shouldn't surprise him that she was so comfortable: she made a living in front of the camera.

Her glittering eyes, which met his, helped the rest of the world slip away, as though the advice were but a running commentary set for their amusement.

"Pretend you like me," she whispered into his neck at the urge for them to "be more intimate."

"Why would you think I don't like you?" He pulled away, to the chagrin of their entourage.

"Antone," she muttered. "Now is hardly the time." She winked.

Whether her flippant dismissal was for the cameras or for him, he wasn't sure. "I just need a minute," he asked of the crew.

The photographers dissipated, granting him a well-earned break. Flexing his back against the fitted suit, he placed his hands against the top rail of the white-washed fence.

"It's beautiful here," she said, her voice coming from behind him. Moments later, she was at his side, stepping up onto the bottom beam and boosting herself up to his level.

"Yeah." He turned and offered her a sidelong glance. "I don't know what to say. I thought this would be easier. I want everything to look natural, but I feel so rigid with everyone watching me."

"I know. That's how I feel all day, every day. How I've felt my whole life."

"Really? I never would have guessed."

"I suppose it's because I haven't felt that way with you." She smiled at him. He saw past the makeup and the hair. Past the sequins and glitter. But what he couldn't see was a trace of the girl he saw on screen. He pressed his eyes shut and tried to remember why he was here. *This wasn't real.*

"Hey, it's just a photo shoot. I'm sure we can work some publicity for the distillery. If we play this right, we could probably even spin this article into a love letter to opportunity."

Love letter to opportunity, it did have a nice spin.

"But we need to work on this. Need to sell us a little more, like that first kiss. That's what they want to see." She put hand on his arm and squeezed so he could feel the heat of her touch through his suit.

"What's your biggest turn-on?" he asked, dead serious.

"I beg your pardon?" She squeezed his arm. "Not

that kind of photoshoot, I assure you." A faint pink betrayed her embarrassment, provoking another pang of desire in his gut.

"It's gotta look real. If we're gonna sell this. So, what can I do to make you swoon?" He shuffled sideways, leaning a little closer. "You can whisper if it makes things easier." He smiled. He liked this shift, her shyness and his being in charge once again.

"Okay, Antone. I'll bite."

"Please do," he interrupted, grinning.

She pulled her hair away from her neck and dragged a finger from the side of her neck to the spot where her jawbone met the top of her throat. Just below the ear. He watched, eyes transfixed by her purposeful movement. "Here. It really turns me on when I get kissed right here."

His mouth was dry, but he swallowed anyway. He'd never wanted to kiss a woman's neck more than in that moment.

"What about you, Zeus?" she asked. "Fair is fair."

He hadn't thought of this. The question was predictable—why hadn't he seen it coming?

"You guys feel ready to shoot again?" the photographer called across the field.

Evie nodded. He had an out. Didn't need to answer, but he wanted to.

"I like your little moan. When you sighed into me between kisses earlier. It was very sexy. A huge turn-on."

She bit her lip and nodded. The lip biting was pretty hot too, not to mention when she called him Zeus…

The nickname only served to remind him how he'd like to make her feel closer to God, in private.

"Let's shoot a few against this fence, when you're ready," the photographer said, smiling. Two aides carrying lighting equipment moved toward them and Antone grinned. "Ready, set, roll."

"The proofs are amazing," Raoul assured her. "I had a peek. Really spectacular."

"I'm sure it's easier with such a beautiful model," Antone added casually.

Her stomach fluttered with the compliment. The beautiful model had always been her sister, but today, it had been her arms wrapped around the beefy biceps of a newly minted cowboy, and she'd felt every bit the princess.

"Let me see." She hovered over the laptop, instantly mesmerized by the images.

"Could you send me a few of them?" she asked the attendant.

"We're really not supposed to do that, miss," he said.

"Marcus, don't be so uptight. Can't you see these lovebirds want to hang on to a little piece of today?" Raoul swatted the tech, who relented with a surprising speed.

"I suppose a few would be okay."

Antone had a flash drive in his hand before Mia had heard the request. "I'll share them." He grinned at her. "If you're good."

If she was good.

"I told you this dress was the one." Raoul, still hunched over the laptop, was drooling.

"Can I get a few minutes with Mr. Williams?" It was Caity, the journalist.

She was dressed exactly how you'd expect a journalist to be dressed. Casually but with an effortless, chic charm.

"Sure," Antone agreed, pulling himself away from the proofs and shooting a devastating smile in her direction. "I promise not to tell *all* our secrets, babe." He winked.

Such a troublemaker.

"You can stay here with me." Raoul grabbed her by the arm. "They like to interview the couples separately for the features. They'll also take a few candid shots in case the page count is approved for a larger interior spread. I can only imagine that with a Hartmann and an NFL hero on the cover, they will want a bigger article."

Mia balked. "Cover? My aide said it was a feature in an article on men being the most desired accessory for fall?"

"That was before. An attractive couple like yourselves, the pitch team loved the idea of a second-wind careers feature on Mr. Williams. Not to mention the second-chance love angle for the heiress and the athlete. Divorcée has a second chance with the right man...!" Raoul glowed with glee at the thought of it.

"That's not really what we talked about." Amelia felt sick to her stomach. Her guilt was back with a vengeance.

"You didn't think *Vogue* would fly a whole thing out here just for a column? Must I remind you that I come at a hefty price?" He grinned.

It was a small comfort. Amelia stood, suddenly feeling dizzy. "Please excuse me, I need a moment in the ladies' room."

Moments later, she locked the door behind her, putting both her hands in the sink. Turning on the water, she washed her hands, scrubbing while she counted to seventy-seven. Cover article? Last-minute? This whole thing had gotten so out of hand. She felt like such a fraud.

Turning off the water, she dried her hands on an Egyptian cotton towelette. Then, following the rich baritone of Antone's voice, she crouched onto the ground and pressed her ear against the vent that connected the bedroom next door.

"You met her following a car accident?"

Her stomach flipped. The last thing she needed was her deception to come out.

"It wasn't quite like that. I mean, you could say we had a little run-in, but from the minute I saw her, I knew she was different. There's something about Evie."

Amelia felt her cheeks flush at the memory.

"You expect our readers to believe it was love at first sight?" Caity pressed.

"I don't expect anyone to believe anything. I'm not here to impose any beliefs, and I think how I feel about Evie is my business, not the business of your readers."

Mia frowned at the terse tone of his voice, but she

was struck by the conviction there. Could he have real feelings for her?

"My research shows that you were married once."

So the reporter had found about as much as she had.

"Couldn't have been hard to find. Aren't marriage licenses a matter of public record?"

Amelia sucked in her breath, not wanting to miss even a word of this interview. It was hard enough to accept that she'd missed the first few minutes.

"Sure, that's true. So, you don't deny it?" This reporter was worse than the cops; this interview sounded more like an interrogation from Mia's side of the vents.

"Deny that I got married fourteen years ago? No, I don't deny it." He laughed, and his ease handling the questions was reassuring. And sexy.

"Let's talk about you and Evie. She's had her fair share of public breakups. Would you say that that gave you common ground?"

Amelia pressed her face into the HVAC vent, as though the few millimeters of space might help her hear better.

"It was never a question of common ground between us. Sometimes connections are undeniable, that's how it was for me. I guess I'd say that, for me, Evie Hartmann is magnetic. As unequivocally elegant and beautiful as she is smart. She's like the sun."

He cleared his throat and Amelia pulled her face away from the grate rubbing her cheek. It felt wrong, somehow, listening to him.

Wrong, but oh so right.

A sharp knock on the door reminded her of her obligations. "Did you fall in?" Raoul, her stylist/minder, rapped the door again, this time more urgently. "We're wrapping up here. Did you have a few minutes for Caity?"

Amelia pinched her cheeks and rubbed her face, hoping to scare some color back for the impromptu shots she knew would follow the interview.

"Yes, I'll be right out." First, to turn the water back on and let it run just long enough to wash her hands for seventy-seven seconds.

She had been there a long time. Surely, it was longer than his interview, but he supposed it made sense. She was a Hartmann.

Antone took a brisk walk to the door to the study; he could hear the interview and fought the desire to listen. Anything she wanted him to know she would tell him, that he was sure of. Still, a man could pace.

"What advice would you give our readers? Any words to live by?" the interviewer pressed on.

Antoine leaned toward the door, curious of her answer.

"Words to live by? *Have courage and be kind.* I can't tell you how often I repeat Cinderella's mantra."

"Cinderella's mantra?"

"Sure. I love that movie."

"I'd have thought you'd pick a line from one of your own movies." The interviewer laughed.

Evie paused, then he heard her laugh back. "No. If I'm being honest, the words I live by are too serious to use for a self-promo. I can't tell you how often I've said them, and the dark days they've seen me through. I truly think the world would be a better place if everyone *had courage and was kind.*"

A muffled agreement passed through the door.

"Did you know that Antone described you as the sun? What do you think he meant by that?"

He paused midstride, overcome with curiosity about her answer.

"I don't know much about astronomy," she started.

Antone stiffened; she was going to dodge the question. A bit predictable. Then, to his surprise, she continued.

"I'm sure Antone knows more; he is one of the kindest and smartest people that I know." Evie paused, maybe to take a sip of water. He flirted with the idea of moving closer, to have a better angle on their discussion, then quickly dismissed it.

"When I think about the sun—I think about the sun as the center of the solar system, with everything spinning around in perfect synchronization. But I can't think about the sun without thinking about the earth."

Another pause, and to Antone's surprise, he had to remind himself to breathe. He crouched down.

"I think about the dance of our universe and about how the earth turns and rotates on its own axis with as much precision as the sun does."

"I can't say I'd ever given it much thought," Caity answered, her voice muffled by the door. Antone briefly thanked the fates for putting Evie within earshot; he could hear her clear as a bell from his position.

"Really?" Evie laughed. "I can't tell you how often

I've wondered if the sun shines brighter for its audience."

"Does it matter?" Caity wondered.

"I mean, I know I've started to feel brighter around him. I feel stronger, like the best version of myself, when he's there to see it. I won't say anything as trite as I'm the sun and he's the moon, so please don't print that."

"We're just talking, Evie. The goal isn't to print salacious gossip—say what you were going to say," the reporter assured her.

"Well, I guess I would say instead that I'm the sun and he's the earth, and we've been dancing since we met. Unless you think that's even sillier?"

"I think it's wildly romantic," Caity said instead.

Antone stood and shook his head. Trouble was, he found it wildly romantic too.

Ten

Kiss Me, I'm Cute

It took less than twenty minutes for the team to leave. The lights, makeup cases, rolling racks of couture and suitcases of shoes were all packed into the back of a cargo van with the efficiency of an ant colony.

Antone was in the library, fingering the series of leather-bound books and talking out loud. *Or was he?*

"It's really not a problem. I want to, I promise."

No, he was talking on the phone. She felt like an intruder, but her feet were rooted in place.

"I won't hear another word about it. The money will be in your account tomorrow morning."

She didn't want to feel jealous, but she did. *Was he on the phone with an ex-girlfriend? Bookie? Did it mat-*

ter? For the past two weeks, she'd felt that Antone was too good to be true. Maybe she'd been right.

"No, thank you, Momma."

His momma. He was sending money to his momma. She stepped back, acutely aware of the fact that she had come unannounced, and then a floorboard creaked in betrayal.

"I'll call you tomorrow. Thanks for the update." He turned, delivering the line to her, unsurprised by her presence.

"I'm sorry," she started. "I'm not exactly a light-footed ballerina."

"That's okay, I was just talking to my mom."

"Right." She nodded. "I gathered as much when you finished your last sentence when you referred to her as 'Momma'." She smiled.

"Hard to get one by you, isn't it," he agreed, but his tone was light.

"I thought we could just talk a few details about the gala? The launch party?"

"Right. Sure." He smiled.

"My team have arranged most of the details and invited a *lot* of press."

"And I've coordinated with Rob. The food is going to be spooktacular and Halloween themed. Rob has promised a menu to raise the dead."

And she had no doubt that Rob would deliver. He and Joanna were the best. "It's just hard to believe the party is ten days away. Our time together has breezed by. It just all went by so fast."

* * *

He didn't say anything, just nodded. She'd taken care of 90 percent of the details for the party, with his only responsibility being food and drumming up an athlete-studded guest list. The RSVPs had been pouring in, and, truth be told, he was looking forward to reuniting with his team.

She nodded and took another cautious step into the library. "My mom found these bookcases in a French château. Had the whole library disassembled and shipped over here. Took four months to strip it all and install it. A team worked around the clock."

"Quite the project." He nodded, keeping his face unreadable.

"My mom spent every day over here. I was nine. Now, she escapes on boats. She's cruising the med as we speak." Her fingers traced the molded wood, skipping over the ridges with books and touching down on favorite spines with the precision of someone who had spent far too many hours in this place.

"I see." Antone nodded. "It's nice to learn a little more about you," he added, this time punctuating his remark with a warm smile.

"You say that to all the girls." She laughed.

He took a step toward her and stopped her hand from its cautious exploration of the bookshelf. "I don't, actually…"

"You're the one who's a closed book." She added. "You never share anything with me. Nothing outside the distillery. And the few words about Charlotte. I mean, I thought your mom was, er, dead." The lines between fake dating and falling were blurring, but he couldn't stop himself. She was intoxicating.

"About that." He maintained his close proximity but released her hand. "I wondered if you wanted to bring that basket to my place. Now, *that* would keep the staff gossiping." He smiled conspiratorially.

The idea was born the moment he'd seen the packed basket, a thank-you prepared by the staff at *Vogue*. It was easy to forget the limits they'd set, easier still when they were dressed as the Princess and Prince Charming. Now, in the library, an invitation had been issued before he'd realized it.

"Your place?" she repeated, eyes wide. "The renovation?"

"It's not finished but there's enough done that we can be comfortable. Plus, I'd love to get your opinion on the state of things."

She was difficult to read.

"If you want?" He infused his offer with a casual air, careful not to give away how much her answer mattered.

"I want." She nodded.

He felt her admission with an electricity he felt in his belly. *He wanted too.*

After she gathered her overnight things, he loaded the basket, along with his duffel bag and her stuff, into his truck, then helped the princess climb into the passenger side, careful to include all of the layers of her dress. The lodge was on the west end of the property, cutting the forty-minute commute in half, but the anticipation of getting her to his place for a night left his foot heavy on the gas.

"I'm actually so excited to see the process on your place!" She smiled. Then, to his surprise, she reached out and settled a hand on the crux of his arm. He felt it there, hot as a brand, but if her touch was a brand, it was one he'd wear willingly. They were both still dressed in their finest, not wasting a moment even to change. That was the thing about wanting to get right to the good part of your night—all the steps in between were easy to ignore.

"It's nothing really. Only the master bedroom and living room are done. I still have carpet in the bathroom..." He felt sheepish, wishing for a minute he had something grander to welcome her to. But he'd build it. And it helped to remember she wasn't permanent, so what she thought didn't *really* matter. *Did it?*

"That actually fits." She nodded.

He stole a glance at her, but she was looking out the window, smiling at the moon. Then he took a hand off the steering wheel, which had the unwelcome effect of displacing her grip on his arm. She held her hand high, but he caught it, taking her hand and twisting his fingers with hers. She fit perfectly.

As he pulled into the drive, he slowed. "I saw deer come right up to the patio the night before I moved in with you." And he kept his voice quiet as though the volume was somehow linked to a potential animal sighting.

He parked several yards away from the garage, preferring to walk up to the patio in the hopes that they might cross some more of Montana's wildness. He wasn't in the Bronx anymore. He reached for her hand. He'd already decided. If she was the sun and he was the earth, then tonight they danced. You could only fight gravity for so long.

"Milady," he jested.

"Why, thank you," she breathed, hand cool against his arm. "It's spectacular here," she said, her voice heavy with her own breath.

"Just my little slice of heaven," he agreed, pleased that she liked it.

"Do I hear the water?" she asked as they walked up the twisting driveway.

With a little pressure on her lower back, he diverted their course, walking toward the thicket of birch on the left. The leaves rustled as they walked—yellow, red and orange marrying together in a harvest of color.

"Fancy a dip?" he dared her as they stood at the edge of the river.

"Always." She met his challenge with one of her own.

"I've got a bag." He let the duffel fall from his shoulder to the ground. "I took the liberty of packing your swimsuit. It was hanging in the bathroom beside mine, so I grabbed them both."

"Thanks," she said, giving no indication she was upset. It was one of the great things about Evie: she was so easygoing. "Could you help me? The beaded part is its own layer. I'm not sure I can get it off by myself."

His fingers were stiff, clumsy with the small buttons, but he managed. Then she spun to face him and, with cool deliberation, let the beaded tulle overlay fall from her shoulders. She stepped out of it, folding the gown into a compact and heavy bundle and holding it forward for him to put in his bag.

Standing in front of him in her floor-length silk slip, she was a vision.

"I'll change over there." He nodded toward a cluster of Douglas pines. Amelia agreed, stepping behind the screen of birch to change in parallel.

Once in the water, they swam in silence, a few strokes out toward the center of the lake, lit by the moon hanging low in the sky. Underwater, his hands brushed her back, and he felt the twist of electricity light a fire in his belly.

"Do you often send money to your mom?" Evie blurted in the face of his touches. Was he getting to her? He hoped so.

"I owe her a lot more than what I send." His hand moved away from her back. He couldn't talk about his mom and touch her. It felt wrong.

"Why is that?"

Typical Evie, always ready with the hard-hitting questions. "She's not really my mom. I mean, she is, in all the ways that matter, but she fostered a lot of other kids. Gave up a lot to take us in and raise us." He plunged underwater, then resurfaced, shaking the water from his hair.

"I'd rather not talk about it, not now. I don't want to talk about anything that could take me out of this moment here with you."

"I see." She bit her lip. "But that's what I like about this moment. Getting to know you better."

He let himself sink into the water, grateful for the moment of punishing silence. Punishing because he was forced to confront his own thoughts. He surfaced, preferring to be with her, even if it required a nakedness he was unfamiliar with.

"My birth mom was a working girl. It's not public knowledge. Not something I'm proud of."

She didn't say anything. That made it easier.

"I'm ashamed though. I mean, she didn't have a lot of options. It's hard to get out of the life. She overdosed when I was four. The social workers found me with her."

"Antone."

She said his name without pity. And he felt a cold arm circle his waist.

"I shuffled around a lot. Sports were everything for me. I was determined to make it out. To help. Sports kept me clean. Kept me disciplined. Sports, coaches, and eventually, on my fourth foster family placement, Momma Jean."

The hand on the small of his back pressed against him. It felt good saying all this. To her. Too good.

"Sounds hard."

"Hard is not having another option," he corrected. "Now I'm here. I built this, and I want to share it. I want to help make opportunities, help be part of the solution."

She didn't say anything, just nodded. There wasn't anything to say. Nothing to add. It was just his truth.

They were interrupted by a chilling howl, a wolf, singing to the moon.

"I think I'm ready to get out now," Evie said, plunging her head underwater and swimming toward the shore.

He waited a moment before following her. Treading water in the same place, he considered his options. On the one hand, if things were to get more serious, he risked investing a lot more in Montana than he'd intended: his heart. On the other hand, it wasn't the first time he'd taken a woman to bed, and perhaps if he bedded her, there was a good chance he'd get her out of his system. Maybe he'd gotten it all wrong and she wasn't the sun.

He watched as she stepped out of the water, legs long in the moonlight. He swallowed, fighting the certainty that one night wouldn't be enough. Right now, one night was the only thing he was ready to promise.

Maybe she wasn't the sun.

"Antone," she called.

Maybe she was the moon, because, right now, he fought the sinking feeling he wasn't strong enough to resist gravity a second longer. Not one second longer.

"Are you coming?" Evie smiled from the shoreline.

She led the way, making a beeline for the glass doors that opened to the master bedroom, singular in her objective, or so it seemed. When a sprinkle of rain fell, she hurried her pace, but all he could do was follow.

"Thanks for the swim," he said. Inside his room, everything about him seemed bigger, if that was possible.

"Thanks for showing me…all of this." The bedroom, the lake, his past, *his* corner of Yellowstone. The bedroom was minimalist but sleek; but the most imposing part of the room was the king-size bed. There were maps pinned all over the wall, boxes of cleats and football gear, and books were stacked haphazardly on every flat surface. So, he'd been coming here to work, the bedroom doubling as an office.

"I think better here. Away from the hustle of the distillery." He shrugged, bathing suit dripping onto the floor.

His tastes ranging from Thoreau to Grisham, the man was a bookworm. It was hard not to feel closer to him, hard not to see the corner of his soul that he bared here in this bedroom, which was so undeniably Antone.

"Are you cold?" he asked, his eyes scanning her body with surgical proficiency.

"No." A one-word answer, to prevent her from saying more. It felt too familiar. She debated taking a step away from him, given that she was too gun-shy to take one forward.

It was Antone who leaned toward her. "You smell like the rain," he whispered. There was a heaviness to his voice. A languid confidence she lost herself in.

"I smell like a swamp," she corrected quietly, pulling her arms across her chest. "Do you have a towel?"

"I don't." He shrugged, still not moving away.

She slid her hands against his chest, intent on delivering a playful swat, but the moment her palms dug into his muscled pecs, she couldn't pull them away. So, she left them there, pressed against him, the heat of his body warming her fingertips all the way to her center.

"Evie," he warned, "what are you doing?" His voice was gruff and low, growling a warning she took as permission.

Now it was her turn, and without moving her hands, she took a step closer to him. Took a step across the line they'd been so careful to protect over the past weeks.

"I want you." She said the words aloud. No flowery sentiment to dress up her admission, just the truth, as raw and naked as she wanted to be.

"Evie," he warned again. "Maybe this is a bad idea."

"Why?" She pressed her hands up his chest, curling them behind his neck. "Why is it bad? You're not married, neither am I." Then, she released his neck. "Or is it because you don't want me back?"

Her words were small, and she hated herself for not making them stronger. She knew why it was a bad idea. Because he thought she was Evie, and she wasn't. She needed to stop this now, before he hated her.

He caught her wrist with a leopard-like reflex and brought it back to his chest. She flattened her hand over his muscle and he pressed an open palm over it, fingers curling around the edge of her palm. "No. I want you."

Then he released her hand and pulled her toward him, crushing her body into his, pressing his lips against hers. His skin was hot against her cold swimsuit. His mouth, soft and hard and insistent.

Antone was thorough in his kisses, his hands cupping her head and pulling her close to him as though any space between them was too much. It felt like magic being this close to him. She felt more feminine than she'd ever felt in her whole life as his hands roamed her body with a possessiveness she'd only hoped for, only dreamed of.

She wanted to cry. She was feeling so much, but the feeling overwhelming her the most was relief. Relief that he felt the same way.

"I can't not kiss you," he whispered, "With three words, you compel me."

"I. Want. You." she tried them again, this time punctuating them with nips to his lip that elicited a guttural growl.

His hands moved to her hips, fingers searing into the tops of her thighs and slipping under her butt. He lifted her against him, and she wrapped her legs around his waist, pressing herself to him as close as she could.

"You're so beautiful. It was hard to bear it when I saw you step out of that lodge, when you stepped out from behind the birch trees, looking like a nymph come to life," he whispered into her neck.

He took a few steps back and pressed her against the edge of his bed. "If you don't want this, you need to leave now," he managed to say, his breath ragged. "You can take my car, and we don't have to ever talk about this again," he promised.

As if she could manage leaving now. "Not want this? I've wanted to feel like this my whole life. Maybe longer. I want you more than I've ever wanted anyone." But then she pulled away. He was good and kind and strong and dead sexy.

He thought she was Evie.

"I have to tell you something. Something that might make you...not want me."

He closed the space between them, hands back on her face. "You don't have to tell me anything. There is nothing, I repeat, nothing, you could say that would make me want you less right now. I want you more than I want to breathe."

Was it permission? Permission not to tell him? He rained kisses across her collarbone. She'd never been kissed like this before. His lips were hot against her skin, and she felt each touch reverberate in her bones. *She felt alive with him. And more herself than she'd ever felt before.*

"Don't tell me. Show me," he asked.

Then her body went slack, and she surrendered. She wanted to feel good. She deserved this. At least for tonight. Mia kissed him, then lay back on his bed, enveloped in the smell of him, and of rain, looking out the domed window of his master bedroom and thinking for a brief moment that everything about this moment was perfect. She didn't need him to profess a binding love or passing promise, she just needed *him*. Needed that piece of him that was raw and real and without pretension. She needed him to lose himself in her, and she longed to do the same. Maybe if they both got lost, they'd find each other, and she dreamed of it with the ardor that had been unparalleled in her life thus far.

He paused, his delay maddening and provocative, then he crawled over her, heat emanating off his body and warming her to her center.

"I have wanted you just as long. Just as hard."

Digging deep, she found a boldness she'd hoped for and sought to clench him in her grip. His swimsuit was wet against her hand, the rest of him achingly hot.

He peeled back her swimsuit without pause, pulling it around her waist and feasting on her breasts, his rough shave coarse against her most delicate skin. "You are spectacular," he whispered into her chest, hands roaming her body with the same intensity.

And she? She was touching him with the same fervor. His hard chest was the perfect opposite to hers, smooth against her hands, delicious muscle in perfect ridges up his rib cage. "I guess I shouldn't be surprised that you have a body like this," she said, panting, hoping he wouldn't take his mouth off her long enough to answer. It was an unanswerable question anyway, a question for higher powers.

"All the better to serve you with," he promised. Then he lifted off her, and she moaned a moment, mourning the loss of his ardent attentions. Then she felt the tug of her swimsuit scaling down her legs, and just like that, she was naked.

"Your turn." She smiled, eyes widening. He slid off the bed, keeping eye contact with her. His eyes were piercing black with desire and she wondered for a moment if he could see right through her. If he could see how much this meant. She quieted the part of her brain that reminded her she was signing up for heartache. If he was just using her, so be it. At least she'd have tonight. She'd use him too.

He laughed, stripped off his swimsuit and threw it at her.

Then he caught her foot and dropped to his knees, kissing the inside of her ankle. He followed the kiss with another, leading a trail of hot kisses, each more insistent than the last, up her calf, to the back of her knee.

"Hey, why don't you come up here?"

She joked because she was nervous. It was one thing to fantasize about Mr. December, it was quite another to have him. *You can't lose what you never had.* She pressed her knees together as he pulled up to the tops of her thighs.

"You're not gonna go shy on me now, are you?" He kissed the crest of her hip, then pushed both hands up her stomach, past her ribs, to cup her breasts.

"I wasn't planning on it," she said breathlessly.

As he crept up onto the bed next to her, it was impossible not to notice how hard he was. She reached for him, but he pinned her arm back, pressing it against the mattress. "Not so fast." Once again, he kissed the inside of her wrist in what was becoming a signature move. "I'm not done with you yet."

Holding both her hands pinned over her head with one of his, Antone let his rogue hand trace her body, fingers skimming lazily over every aching inch of her. When he stopped, finding her slippery and wet, he stroked her, a torturous, slow exploration as he fueled her with an aching need for more.

"I didn't know you were a sadist." She panted as he played her, startled by his carnal knowledge. "Why are you so good at everything?"

"I just like to touch you." He kissed her on the collarbone, then again, higher. She fought against his entrapment, wanting to touch him too, but he held her pinned beneath him with ease. Then he released her, needing both his hands to cup her face.

Wasting no time, she stroked his back, reveling in each delicious ridge of muscle, pausing at the small of his back, then tracing the most glorious ass she'd ever seen; she pulled him against her.

He slipped off her only long enough to grab a foil packet next to his bed. Then he sheathed himself in her. He pushed deeper, giving her the excruciating fullness she craved. She felt the bed shifting with each push in and raised her hips to meet his with eagerness to actively participate in their joining. If he could be closer to her, she wanted it, needed it.

Then he kissed the spot on her neck. The spot she'd told him about in a moment of weakness. His lips hot against her skin, his body pressed against hers, she exploded.

*

He didn't move right away. Couldn't, even if he'd wanted to.

"I'm sorry," he managed to say, breathing the apology into her neck.

"Sorry?" she parroted.

"I was a brute. Taking you like that, I should have been more gentle, more, I don't know, since our first time together, I've thought about you so often... I just lost it." He frowned. "You stir something in me I can't explain."

"You're disappointed?" She was so quiet he almost didn't hear her.

"Disappointed?" Drawing every ounce of strength he could muster, he pulled himself up to lean on a cocked forearm. "Only in myself," he ground out.

She smiled, relief palpable on her face, then heaved up and kissed him. Her kiss was lazy and undemanding, until she bit him. "It was perfect. Everything was perfect. You are perfect."

If he was so perfect, why was he questioning everything he thought he knew?

Eleven

Ancient Herstory

It was their fourth night holed away in his unfinished place. Forgotten were the IG photo ops at the ranch. There was only sex and lust and nakedness between hurried meetings and work obligations. They got home, stripped, and got to know each other in all the carnal ways he'd hoped for.

He wasn't sure what woke him up. Squinting, he noticed the desk light. Through half-lidded eyes, he wondered what she was up to as she sat scribbling furiously at the desk.

"Go back to sleep," she hissed. The desk light threw a delectable shadow under her breast, which awakened every instinct he had to fight sleep.

"What are you doing over there?" he asked instead, rolling over to face her.

She closed her notebook and smiled at him. "I'm just jotting down some notes. Ideas for our party. The Halloween theme is risky, but you know how much *USA TODAY* loves featuring different Halloween costumes. I was thinking we could make up different mixed drinks, all featuring your whiskey, and name them after different outfits and clichéd costumes."

"The naughty nurse." He grinned.

"The pervy pirate," she countered.

"The old-fashioned," they said in unison, despite the fact that he wasn't too sure how you'd dress up as a drink.

"Exactly." She smiled. She reached for the desk light and turned it off. "I'll come back to bed now."

She climbed in beside him, rumpled, her hair messy. She was perfect.

Without the desk light, the room was lit only by the moon, which hung low in the sky. They were only a week away from Halloween *and* their gala.

He was very aware of her body lying so close to him. He reached out and pulled her against him. She fit into the crook of his torso and melted into him, but instead of letting his hands roam her body to coax their spark into becoming a flame, he just held her. He was hungry for something else.

"Tell me something about you no one else knows."

He felt her stiffen. It was slight, but undeniable. There was a chance she'd refuse; it wasn't a part of their deal. No falling in love. And secrets, especially the soul-baring kind, had a sneaky way of leading to more. But then he felt her soften and he smiled despite himself. If this was being sneaky, he was ready for it. In the dark, it was easier to pretend this wasn't anything more than a fling.

"I've been married before. I'm getting divorced. No one knows about it. It was an elopement, and everything about my marriage was awful."

Of all the things he'd been expecting her to say, this wasn't it. Was that what she'd wanted to tell him earlier? When he'd been distracted with his desire for her?

"It was worse than awful." She sniffed.

"Worse how?" he asked, saying the words cautiously, as if they might scare away more secrets.

"Worse like, I was a means to an end—"

"The bastard." He tightened his arms around her, as though the reflex might undo time. Might protect her. *She was so much more than a means to an end.*

"Sometimes it's hard to feel like you deserve more," Evie said simply.

There was so much he wanted to say. That no one deserved to be treated like less than they were. That she deserved only the best. But didn't she deserve more than what he was offering? So he didn't say anything.

"I stayed with him for seven years. I didn't want people to know about my mistake. Like, admitting it made it real. I told my family the divorce was finalized. But it's not. And now it's a mess. He's suing me for spousal support. It's a nightmare."

"I had no idea you were married," he said simply, surprisingly refraining from a scoff and a joke at the mention of spousal support. He knew what it was like to not want to admit things. He didn't want to admit how he felt.

"Separated now. And divorced as soon as my lawyer is through with things. But it's bad. I've been hoping that Scott sees the articles and makes contact. Like, I can talk some sense into him, or..." Her voice faded and her hands curled around the hand he had pressed at her waist. "I don't want to talk about him anymore... is that okay?"

He pressed a kiss onto her shoulder. "It's okay," he assured her.

"And, Antone?"

He pressed another kiss onto her shoulder. Chaste but comforting, or so he meant it to be.

"Don't tell anyone."

"I'm glad you told me." He kissed her again, this time on her forehead. "I like you. A lot."

She wiggled against him, and he held her tightly until her breathing slowed.

I like you a lot. It was feeling a little too real indeed.

Twelve

Zeus

"**B**igras in da house!" Biggie, the fullback, arrived to the ranch, entourage in tow. He'd booked four rooms for two weeks. Definitely a good friend.

"Love, love, love this place. It's so cute!" His girlfriend, Pricilla, was wearing a pink cowboy hat with matching pink cowgirl boots. She was as opposite to Evie as possible, but he was still grateful she'd come. She had 700,000 followers on Instagram, and she absolutely loved a good photo op.

She was snapping pics and taking selfies without being asked, and Antone watched as Evie smiled at the guests. "I'm so thrilled you could come to our party."

"Love Halloween, and love this guy. Gotta admit,

though, we played together for four years, and I never saw him drop the G word on a date."

"G word?" Evie asked.

"Girlfriend," Pricilla clarified.

"Well, she's someone very special to me," Antone said. He tamped back the thought that it was not for show, that it was true. She *was* someone very special to him. A little too special. For real.

The athletes arrived over the next forty-eight hours, and Evie's team handled the resort business with ease. Everyone loved the accommodations, and the Instagram following of @HomeIsWhereTheHartIs, Evie's new IG feed, blew up with all the celebrity tags. The distillery was finished, and their evenings were spent hunched over distribution contracts and employee files. Evie was more than a media opportunity: she was becoming a confidante, and to his surprise, he liked it. Maybe it was okay to need someone. To be someone that was needed. He'd been single for the better part of thirty-two years, but now, he felt like it might be ready for something more.

He'd woken her in the night stiff with want of her once again. The second course was even more appealing than the urgent fever that had exhausted them both the first time around. This time, he made sure to take things slow. Watching her back arch under him was rousing, and he found that he craved her cries more than his own release.

Now, in the light of day, he wrestled with reality.

How could he want her so much? *He didn't want to need anyone as much as he wanted her.*

She'd been dressed before he even woke up. The light streamed through the half-domed window, falling on her cheek, creating a stained-glass shadow of blue and green on her skin. The room was quiet, no bustle of staff, no ringing phones, just the singing of birds and the soundscape of the forest. It was heavenly. All he could ask for, and maybe more.

"I've got to go, babe. I'm finalizing the last changes for the lodge today, and I have a luncheon call with the commissioner. I'm going to tell him about our spread in *Vanity Fair*." She smiled.

This got his attention as he cracked open his other eye to focus it on her. "*Vanity Fair*? I thought we shot for *Vogue*?" *Vogue, Vanity Fair,* they blurred together.

"That little darling, Raoul, the makeup artist? He texted me this morning. He was talking about our shoot at the after-party and was overheard. The stylist for *Vanity Fair* fell in love with the idea."

"The idea?" He paused.

"Our story. A lot of people think it's pretty charming, *The Heiress and the Athlete,* it's embarrassing but catchy."

"Well, I think *you're* pretty charming." He pulled her toward him.

"I have to go," she whispered between kisses. "Haven't you had enough?"

"Never," he promised, realizing with a twinge that he meant it.

"Tonight," she promised, pressing a swift kiss onto

his mouth and twisting away. "I'll bring dinner," she said as she slammed the door. "Let Agnes know."

Just like that, she was gone, leaving nothing but the scent of her on his sheets and in his mind. What had he done? And what had she hesitated to tell him?

He got out of bed, glad it was a Friday. He didn't have any meetings until ten and felt he needed at least that long to clear his head. His phone beeped with new messages, but all he could do was think about her. His favorite distraction.

"Someone is in a good mood." Elsbeth grinned. "I guess dating a pro athlete has its perks?"

Amelia didn't even blush, she just nodded and agreed. "It does," she said simply. So, Elsbeth had worked it out. She knew the truth, and in many ways, it was a relief.

"How did you know?" Mia asked, truly curious what had given her away.

"Your interview. In Vogue. *USA TODAY* sent the article over. And this—" she tapped at the magazine "—is not Evie."

Mia felt her stomach roll. "You think people will know?" she asked quietly.

"That's all you're going to ask me?" Her assistant laughed. "No. I don't think people will know. I just figured it out from a few of your answers. Quoting *Cinderella*? 'Have courage and be kind?'—that's so *you*."

She'd known, of course; that was why she'd said it. She'd repeated the quote at every interview. Scott would read that line and know immediately it was her.

Mia uttered the words like a mantra every time he'd put her down. Every time he'd made her feel less than enough.

Amelia threw her purse against the back of her chair and forced herself to stare at her computer screen, but, try as she might, she couldn't keep the grin from her face. "He's pretty wonderful."

"Well, you're going to love me. I got you lunch with the Hyatt resort chain. They are interested in some cross marketing at their international locations. For his distillery."

While there were other things she'd have preferred to do over lunch, an afternoon delight with Antone for one, this seemed a pretty strong second. She squeezed Elsbeth's hand. "Thank you."

Elsbeth took a step back, giving her a sly smirk. "You really care about this distillery, huh?"

Amelia looked up at her, eyebrows shooting up in surprise. "Er, yes? I mean, he's doing his part. With only a few Instagram posts, bookings are filling up at the estate. The least I can do is help where I can with regards to drumming up demand for his whiskey."

"Well, the launch party looks amazing." Elsbeth let out a low whistle. "Everything came together so quickly. I can hardly wait to see it in action."

"I know. I hope he likes it." Mia smiled.

Elsbeth nodded, all the while looking at her strangely. "I'm sure he will."

Once alone in her office, Mia hummed as she worked. Filing emails as she addressed them, she frowned as a familiar name bolded in her inbox.

Scott Altman.

She clicked on the email. Short. Terse. She supposed word of her new relationship had hit his circle too.

Mia,

When you're done acting like a petulant child, get back to me.

I know what you're up to. You will not get away with this. You should be spanked for this.

Scott.

"Elsbeth," she called. "Can you get PJ Banks on the line?"

"Sure thing, boss," Amelia heard in the distance.

This email was nothing her lawyer couldn't address. And the only spankings she was interested in were from Antone.

"Banks," he answered on the first ring.

"PJ, this is Amelia Hartmann, I'm just wondering where we stand on the divorce?" She infused all the sweetness she could into her voice.

"His lawyer is contesting, and your petition has been denied. I've told you, a settlement is your cleanest option. At this point, we're going to court."

"Can he even do that? I mean, in a marriage, if one person doesn't want to be married...they get divorced, right? I don't need him to agree." A sick feeling began to mount in her throat.

"In principle, yes, but there are a lot of ways to slow the process down. Abusing the discovery process, asking for continuances, false accusations, and forcing several motions to be filed… It does complicate things, but nothing we can't handle."

He was legally allowed to make her life hell as he'd been doing for almost a year. Unless she could stop him.

"There's nothing to do now but stay the course."

"How long a course is this going to be?" The last thing she wanted to do was mar the upcoming launch party with any negative publicity.

"You could accept his offer of a settlement."

"I really don't think settling is good for our image." *Anyway, Nick would never go for it.*

"I was thinking about that. What if we were to include a confidentiality clause? Some sort of legally-binding addendum ensuring that any plaintiff accepting our settlement must sign an NDA?"

Mia hesitated, taking a moment to consider his suggestion. In her fingers, she twisted a little Montblanc pen, reveling in its heaviness as she flicked it round in circles. Around and around and around and around and around and around and around. But settling had a second effect, a new consequence she wasn't quite ready to face. With the bookings at the resort through the roof, the need for an over-the-top and public relationship was over. The launch party was next week, and that was as far as they'd discussed…but would Antone still want her when he didn't need her anymore?

"I see where you're going, but I'm still not sure about it." She exhaled, happy to have deferred the decision.

"Why don't you let me draft something up? I could have it in your inbox by the day after tomorrow. If you like it, we send it to opposing counsel. Worst case, they refuse. Best case, this divorce is finalized, with no one the wiser."

"All right," she agreed. "Go ahead, draft something up," she answered without pausing to think what it might cost.

"Thanks, Ms. Hartmann. I'll do that," he promised, his silky voice imbued with self-satisfaction.

He wasn't a bad lawyer, especially if he'd succeeded in getting her to reconsider her position, which she'd hitherto believed to be unshakable.

She stared at her inbox. Seventeen emails from the Prince's team, and all she wanted to do was work on the gala.

"Elsbeth," she said, and her executive assistant arrived before she drew her next breath.

"Have you seen—"

"—the latest round of requests? I have. My favorite is the email requesting our assurances that all the fruits and vegetables served at the lodge are organic."

That didn't seem like the most unreasonable request made to date.

"And that all the meat served was butchered within twenty-four hours of being cooked."

Yep, it was ridiculous.

"Just make sure—"

"—to charge them three times whatever it costs, I

know. I'll manage, don't worry." Elsbeth issued a short bow and left, humming to herself.

Amelia felt sick to her stomach. Catering to these people was demeaning and utterly unfulfilling. She flipped through her emails again, deleting all the requests on which she'd been cc'd. Elsbeth could handle them.

Then she opened her spreadsheet. The plan of attack to launch Antone's whiskey into foreign markets. It felt amazing to use her brain for something other than catering to a prince's every whim. Amazing, and energizing, and not only because it was what mattered to *him*. But first, she needed to sort out her divorce.

"I've got Indian," she howled up the stairs. For a moment, she let herself miss the cramped intimacy of his partially renovated ranch, but it felt good coming home and seeing him. Even if she did need to come clean.

"Give me a minute, just brushing my teeth," he shouted down. *Brushing his teeth, so he was likely fresh out of the shower.* The image too tantalizing to ignore, she took the stairs two at a time.

Her room was humid, and she hesitated a moment before barging into the bathroom. Then she smiled. He was listening to his voice mail, on speaker, multitasking like a boss. This was what she'd missed all day long. And she could hardly wait to tell him about her plans for their star-studded gala.

"It's Mom. Thanks for the money, I appreciate it. I do hope you're tracking all these loans, because I am going to pay you back one day."

Amelia smiled at his mom's insistence, liking the woman already, although they'd never met.

"Message saved," the phone spoke back, the tinny voice echoing through the door.

"Antone, it's unacceptable that you drop off the face of the earth for three weeks. I've made commitments, promises, and you? You don't even have the guts to call me back. If you want me to dump you, just say it."

She heard the message through the door and instantly wished she was anywhere but there. But she couldn't move. Couldn't even breathe. The woman sounded mad, and likely had every right to be. Almost a month of dead air? She swallowed the acrid taste of bile, wishing for a minute she could unhear the truth and keep living the lie. Once a player, always a player, and from what she knew, NFL players were the biggest in the world.

He pushed his way out of the bathroom, towel slung low across his hips, and smiled at her as though she hadn't just overheard the damning voice mail.

"I thought you'd never come home." He winked at her.

"Never come home?" she repeated dumbly, still in shock.

"You brought the food up?" He nodded toward the paper bag she clutched in her had.

Amelia nodded, then found the strength to walk over to her desk. Issuing an icy stare, she looked at him, then threw the bag of Indian into the paper waste basket with vehement force.

"Hey, what was that for?" Antone asked, confused.

"As if you don't know." She kicked the wastebasket, then reached for her foot, rubbing the instant numbness that accompanied the hurt.

"I'm not sure I do?"

She tapped her hand against her thigh. Tap, tap, tap, tap, tap, tap, tap. But it didn't help. Didn't make her feel any better. This betrayal was bigger than anything a few manic taps could remedy.

"I heard her. Heard about the promises, the commitments...is that what you want? You want to get dumped? Well, let me beat her to the punch. Whatever *this* is, it's *over*." She felt her eyes sting with hot unspent tears and willed them away. She wasn't sad, she was pissed.

Antone looked at her, blank faced, then tilted his head toward the bathroom. "You mean Amy?"

"Amy? *Yes, I mean Amy*." Amelia swore, and added a stamp to her expletive.

Then, Antone's face cracked into a smile, and he unleashed an infuriating laugh.

She felt it then, the new emotion, unfamiliar but for its force. Hatred.

Antone took a few steps toward her, reaching for her arm, but she shook him away. Then he laughed again, this time softly. "She's my agent, Evie. Manages my speaking engagements, endorsements, shoots, that kinda thing. Babe, I'm not seeing anyone else. That would totally ruin our launch, and the gala is only days away. Why would you think the worst of me so easily?"

As quickly as her jealousy had risen, it faded, and in its place came a quiet sadness. His agent. Of course he had an agent, didn't all athletes? But still, she felt defeated.

"I'm never going to know you, Antone. Not really. And you're never going to know me. Not really." She pressed her chin into her chest, staring intently at the pattern on her rug.

"Why would you say that?" His arms were around her, her face, pressed into his chest. It felt good, but it was a lie. She was the liar, and because of her dishonesty, it was all a lie.

"Sorry I overreacted. I don't know what came over me. I just—it's been a long day." She said the words on autopilot, wishing they were true. She had known exactly what had come over her. The crushing realization that Antone was in this for the PR and nothing more, and that as real as this relationship felt to her, he was here for a reason, and it wasn't a dying desire to be her boyfriend. *Babe, I'm not seeing anyone else. That would totally ruin our launch.*

Well, maybe she'd ruin it first.

Antone was fishing the Indian out of the trash. "This smells heavenly, Evie."

She didn't answer right away. Didn't say the words thundering in her head. *"It's not Evie, it's Mia."*

She couldn't. Because the moment she said them, whatever this was would be over, and she wasn't sure she could bear it.

So instead, she wrapped her arms around the athlete's waist, and pressed herself against him. "You do indeed."

And they forgot all about the Indian feast.

He started at her neck, pressing a kiss into the hollow of her collarbone. The kiss was followed with another, then a third, fourth, fifth…her head lolled back and she stopped counting and only felt. Maybe she was fake dating, but at least *this* was real. These kisses. The searing heat of his hands roaming her body as if they owned it. And didn't they? Wouldn't she do anything for him just to keep touching her?

She moaned as he pulled the straps of her camisole off her shoulders. No bra—it had been a strategic choice—and he bit his lip in appreciation.

Antone captured a nipple in his mouth, teasing it to tautness with a tongue that promised more exquisite torture. His hands were now on her skirt, urging it up her thighs into a tight bunch around her waist. He released her breast long enough to whisper, "Take it off," the command leaving little room for protest, not that she had an ounce of fight in her anyway. She slid the skirt off, hesitated, then removed her panties.

She wanted this. Wanted it with a desperation that came with the sure knowledge that whatever this was… it would soon be over. Her hands went to his waist and pulled at the buckle of his belt. He was hard, and the fact made her burn even hotter for him.

"Your, er… I mean, you are…you have…you're just…" Each statement was punctuated with a gasp as he touched her, intent on interruption.

"I'm what?"

"Sexy." The pronouncement was followed by a guttural moan as his fingers slipped inside her.

"Sexy, am I?" he whispered, into her ear. Then he bit

down on the lobe and pushed deeper into her, his fingers winding her up. "Nothing sexier than you. Right now. Pink and bothered and sweaty and wet." He teased her with another nibble to her ear.

"This isn't fair," she managed to protest, her hands pressing against him. "Let me touch you." She was pinned beneath him now, his body covering hers, both her hands caught above her head in his lazy grasp, and her legs apart. She couldn't stop him, not that she wanted to. He was solid muscle, and enjoying himself far too much.

"I want to watch you explode. I want to feel you shake under me."

"Get inside me," she said simply. "Get inside me, *now.*"

He kissed her, this time fueling his kiss with urgency.

She widened her knees and, with a forward thrust, sought his hips with her own.

She rocked against him, reveling in watching his eyes roll back as he lost himself in her.

He didn't say anything, just kissed her. Kissed her as he thrust into her, deeper than she'd been touched by anyone. She felt him in her heart.

In one fluid motion, he flipped her onto her back. She was hardly a slight woman, but considering the facility with which he maneuvered her, she felt like a plaything. Like his sexy plaything.

Still inside her, he covered her body once again with his, his hands everywhere at once.

His pace quickened, and Mia felt the coiling tension of an explosion in the making.

"Antone," she said, panting. "Don't stop."

"Shake for me, baby," he asked of her, kissing her neck.

And she did.

Thirteen

Black Ties and White Noise

The day they'd both waited for arrived in a flurry of activity: the gala. Last-minute taste tests and texts to his friends. There would be 300 guests, each invited for a reason; the guest list was as catered as the menu. None of this would have been possible without her. Evie was amazing and had more than delivered on her end of the bargain. Pricilla, the wife of one of his favorite teammates, had delivered too; every hashtag under the sun was exploding with #Hartmannlove. Together, Antone and Evie had achieved perfect synergy. She'd shooed him away at three o'clock. "Give me a minute to collect my thoughts." she's asked.

Four short hours later, he was back, a black tie in

a sea of white noise. The party they had dreamed up was already in full force.

"C'est original!"

Antone recognized the accent. Frenchmen were hardly common in Bozeman, let alone wandering the Hartmann estate. *"Nom de bleu, le deco est magnifique,"* the stylist added, clapping his hands together as he took in the space.

"Raoul, good to see you again." Antone extended a hand, amazed at having been able to place a face to a name.

"Ah yes, Monsieur Antone, so good to see you again." Raoul drew Antone's hand up to his lips, and, to Antone's surprise, planted a kiss square on the backside of his hand, provoking a blush.

"Raoul," Evie called out. Raoul dropped his hand like a hot potato.

"The student has become the master." He winked at her unapologetically.

"Evie." Antone nodded toward her. It was surreal, standing next to her at this gala, pulled together at the last minute. She was beautiful in a sequined gown, a mirage of sequins that spilled to the floor in cascading sparkle, with a skirt made from a luminescent silver taffeta. She was dressed as an angel and, quite literally, she looked every bit the part. The only thing out of place was her despondent expression. Something had been off with Evie, not that he could blame her; it had been off with him too.

"Antone," she said, nodded back, barely moving her lips. Raoul was a wizard, no denying it—she was breathtaking. But she always looked breathtaking, perhaps even more so in the graphic tees and slouchy sweaters that no one outside her service team ever saw. Her service team, and him. Antone swallowed, wishing he knew what else to say. Wishing he knew how else to feel. This tension was wretched.

He knew better than anyone that *this*—their time as a couple—was almost over. He couldn't, wouldn't, lose himself again.

"You've outdone yourself." He gestured to the ballroom, entirely transformed with a majesty that was awe-inspiring. When they'd decided on a Halloween party, he'd expected... Well, not this. The theme of the evening was black-tie Halloween, but it was the white noise that had him off balance.

Still, this evening was beyond his imagination. It was incredible that she had pulled this together in a matter of weeks. Sure, she'd had a staff, but there were pieces of Evie sprinkled all over the room. The ballroom was decked out as a secret garden, complete with papier-mâché trees, but they were all leafless, nature's skeletons setting an eerie vibe to the evening. The midnight-forest installation featured trees varying from six to twenty feet high. Moss-covered arches woven with white flowers added to the dark fairyland mystique, and smoke machines blew fog and mist into every corner of the room. The drinks were all cooled with dry ice, and smoking martini glasses featuring Campari cocktails and charcoal-activated mixed drinks made for an orange-and-black drink menu the guests were eating up.

The guests were a story in and of themselves. Antone was not usually impressed by glitterati and celebrities, but Evie had pulled out all the stops. Commissioner Barry Lopez was chatting up several judges and other politicians Antone knew only from the society pages. In another pod were the celebrity A-listers, currently being entertained by a devil that bore a striking resemblance to his own angel. Must be Amelia, her twin. Then there were the athletes, not only from the NFL but the popular Western rodeo circuit. The Hartmanns sponsored the PCRA—Professional Cowboys Rodeo Association—he knew that, but there were a lot of cowboys present, even for a Hartmann event.

Everywhere, people were drinking and partaking in the stunning array of passed hors d'oeuvres, courtesy of Rob and his food truck team. At the back end of the room was a large screen, on which a thermometer was pictured, depicting their fundraising progress of the evening. It had been Evie's idea: fundraise among the guests for the off-the-streets project behind the distillery.

Whoa. "Two hundred thousand already?" he said aloud, as much to himself as anyone else.

"The night is just getting started," Evie promised him with a wink. He hadn't even felt her approach.

"Little sis, this is incredible." A tall man in a navy suit reached over and hugged Mia in an awkward posture.

"Thanks, Jacks." She smiled back. "I got the local art institute to make these trees. Each one is bespoke for our space. They are wired too, thus the lights. Isn't it amazing?" Evie beamed, but he knew he wasn't imagining the shadow in her eyes.

Jacks. As in Jackson Hartmann. Looks like the whole clan was here tonight.

"Nice to meet you." Antone extended a hand. "Antone Williams." He smiled.

"I know." Jackson smiled. The redhead on his arm unleashed her own grin and Antone fought the feeling that the attractive couple were precisely the sort of people he enjoyed spending time with—quick to smile, and a tad awkward in social settings. He swallowed, then frowned. Evie was pulling at his arm, urging him away from her brother.

They worked the room, greeting benefactor after benefactor. Evie played the room with ease, massaging donors and sprinkling every conversion with insinuation and suggestion. And the guests ate it up, adding donations electronically, through apps, and handing over folded checks with a practiced efficiency. Antone pounded drink after drink, numbing his distaste for these events—or, more likely, the realization that his time with Evie was coming to an end—with an alcoholic anesthetic, and it was working. Evie was magnificent, but the truth just made it harder to bear. This was almost over, and he only had himself to blame, for letting himself believe it couldn't ever be anything more.

"I have a surprise for you." Amelia squeezed his arm. Watching him, a stunning standout in a room of celebrities, and she couldn't help but feel now that she'd approached this whole relationship wrong. She should have come clean sooner. Tonight was a mine-field, and she was terrified of getting caught. Evie had flown back for the party, anxious to do her duty, and a little too excited about it. They'd made a pact to stay away from the people they knew well, and as far as she could tell, people were buying the switch. And as for Antone? She would confess in the morning and beg for forgiveness. What was it that Antone had said time and time again as they'd planned this evening? Better to ask forgiveness than permission?

There was no right, no wrong, when it came to love. She swallowed, sure of herself. Was that really how she felt about him? She forced a smile through her confusion.

"Surprise? What's that? You're gonna let us leave early?" Antone's face broke into a relaxed grin. He was on the other side of four drinks and finally looking a little more comfortable. "You look good enough to… you know…eat." He delivered the last syllable into her ear, and Mia was far too aware of the cameras click-ing. She pulled back.

He looked at her with a hunger she did her best to ignore. She needed to be careful with Antone. He'd caught her off guard. Still waters might run deep, but she needed to remember that with Antone, she could drown if she didn't protect herself better. Still, it was hard not to swim in his smile. Because, well, damn.

"Sweetie, I can't tell you how proud I am of you." The small woman smiled as she turned to face them. Her surprise, right on target. Antone's mom.

"Jean, it's so nice to meet you in person. I am

thrilled you could come tonight." Amelia extended a hand, doing her best not to focus on how surreal this experience felt. She thought about all the moments she'd imagined meeting Antone's family. And now the time was finally here. She'd invited his foster mother and her best friend, flown them both first-class and put them up in a comp room in the The Lodge. Jean was beside herself and clearly starstruck by the party.

"Mom?" Antone's voice had an odd, strangled quality.

"Your girlfriend invited me. Even sent me a copy of the articles you guys have been in. The girls at work thought I should bring *Vogue*, ask you both to sign it, now that you're a famous social activist." Jean reached for Amelia's hand and smiled conspiratorially. "Don't worry, I would never actually do that." The elderly woman's face pinked at the thought she'd try something so embarrassing.

"Momma," Antone grumbled. "You could have told me you were planning on coming."

Amelia looked at Antone, then back at his mom. The two were an odd couple, his mom a smaller woman, with pale yellow hair. This was a side of him that was dangerous to see. Dangerous because it made him even more charming, the way he cared for his foster mom. He was the antithesis of Scott.

"Why don't you get us each a *spooktacular* drink, darling?" Mia asked of Antone. This was the perfect time to ask some questions to one of the people who knew Antone best. Maybe she could try to understand his reluctance to be serious. His aversion to falling in love.

"What a splendid idea." His mom smiled, spinning in a floor-length orange tulle skirt. The copper sparkles shone with the movement; Mia had seen to all the details.

"Sure," Antone agreed, looking fleetingly from woman to woman before walking off to get drinks.

"Evie, can you point to your twin? I'm dying to meet her." Jean asked.

"The devil by the cake—she's the one with the pitch fork." Mia smiled.

Jean giggled like a schoolgirl, before spinning in her new dress once again. "I really do love this outfit. Thanks a lot."

"I can't tell you how much I appreciate you coming," Amelia started, thankful for the space to breathe, apart from Antone.

"I'm the one who oughta be thanking you—this dress, the invitation, not to mention how happy you're making my son." Jean smiled, and Amelia sucked in a breath, glad it hadn't been too much.

"You both have the same smile," she said.

Jean let out a laugh. "I do hear that a fair bit." She smiled again, lifting a hand to cover her mouth.

"I can't believe you managed to get Rob to come cook. The food turned out wonderfully, and I've already heard plenty of folks talking about the chef." The woman was doing her best to make her feel comfortable, and to her surprise, she was.

"You really think Antone is looking happy?" Mia

couldn't resist. The band, a popular country group from Elsbeth's connections, was strumming away some soft pop, and she tapped her foot anxiously. Seven taps then a pause, then seven taps again.

Jean put a hand on her arm. "I'd say he's looking very happy indeed."

Mia couldn't hear her. She could only hear her own heart as it beat in her ears. Her mouth was dry, and her tongue, thick and flaccid in her mouth. She pressed her eyes shut and tapped her foot again, focused only on the vibration as her heel met the floor with a click. Then six more: *click, click, click, click, click, click.* She was nervous. Nervous about how he felt. Nervous that this was her Cinderella moment, if only Cinderella had been a twin, and her Prince Charming connection, fake. But anyway, it wasn't midnight yet. *Tap, tap, tap, tap, tap, tap, tap.*

"Two spooktacular drinks for two spooktacular ladies," she heard Antone announce through her closed eyes.

Click, click, click, click, click, click, click.

His hand was on her lower back, and she focused on the heat of the pressure, hating herself for finding comfort in it.

She forced her eyes open. Then, with the laser focus of a person who saw their own hangman for the first time, she said the two words aloud that would invite midnight a little earlier than anyone wanted: "He's here."

It was amazing that she was able to keep her voice so level.

Antone squared his jaw. "He?"

"I can't do this tonight. Not here." She gestured to Scott, who was lurking near some potted plants across the room. She knew what she had to do—find him, get him to try to extort her...but she couldn't bear the thought of it, and the scene it risked. Scott might be more keen on revenge than money, and if he wanted to ruin things for Antone... Maybe her plan wasn't worth it. If her options were to end her pending lawsuit via accepting the settlement, or ending her facade with Antone on bad terms, she'd rather live the lie a few more days. Whatever the cost.

"I need to get out of here. I can't face him. Not now. He'll make a scene. Ruin the night."

"That's your ex?" He followed the line of her eyes and saw Scott lurking by the caterers.

"In the joker outfit. Very droll." It occurred to her that she was shaking.

"I'll take care of it," Antone assured her, his hand continuing to add pressure to the small of her back.

The thought of Antone defending her honor made her feel worse. If she could count on Scott for one thing, it would be ruining everything good in her life. Scott would make sure he didn't leave without taking her down first.

"My brother. Please let my brother handle this. Jackson. With the redhead. Go tell him I asked him to escort Scott out. Jackson. Not Nick."

"I remember which one Jackson was." Antone smiled. He pressed a kiss on her head and disappeared. She didn't worry that he'd find Scott. He was the kind of guy who did what he said he was going to do. He was the good kind of guy. But her stomach turned for something else. The fact that she'd knowingly traded her ace in the hole for a few more days with Antone. Pathetic indeed.

"This drink is amazing," Jean said, oblivious to the tension.

To her amazement, Mia was able to maintain small talk until Antone returned, unperturbed.

"Mom, I'm afraid I'm going to have to steal Evie away for a moment. Can I leave you here?"

Mia loved the tenderness with which he cared for his mom. "She has a plus-one," she managed to add.

"Right, Betty. She's around here somewhere, probably chasing down a football player, begging for an autograph, or a date, ha ha." Jean shrugged and made her way into the crowd, eyes scanning the heads, a wide smile on her face.

Antone grabbed her by the arm and led her through the crowd with an artful efficiency.

"Do you really think finding a dark corner is going to make this exit any easier?" She sighed.

"I don't think any part of you is easy." He smiled.

They exited the main ballroom, and Antone pulled her aside, taking cover in a wood-paneled office. Her dad's old office. Then he kissed her. He kissed her with the heat of a thousand kisses, then followed his kisses with a possessive touch on her lower back.

"You know, Antone, I'm struggling with what you want. There's no press. This is private. Who is this even for? What are we even doing?"

"I want you," he started, but there was a thinness to his voice.

"For how long?" she asked bitterly.

"You have to trust me."

"Can I?" she answered.

Mia felt a rush of heat flush her face. "This was all your plan. Date, but don't fall in love. Then cavort along to the press to show that we are. And yes, initially I thought there was a chance Scott would turn up, and I wanted it to make the divorce a bit cleaner. But the thought of him making a scene here? I just couldn't. Tonight can't be about that." She swallowed, hating to bring up Scott's name.

His mouth tightened into a thin line, and Mia watched as the muscle along his jaw twitched. She didn't want to do it. Didn't want to cause everything to come crashing down. But she had to. At least, this way, she controlled the when. She controlled the how. The gala was shaping up to be an outrageous success. The bookings at the ranch were zero vacancy for the rest of the season, and the Hyatt chain had picked up his whiskey, along with the Sky Alliance of airlines committing to serve GreatWhiskey in the clouds globally. They'd achieved what they'd set out to achieve, and in a month nonetheless. It was time to come clean.

"I know what tonight was about, Evie," Antone said, hands back at her cheeks. He pressed a kiss onto her mouth and she stifled a sigh.

"That's the thing, Antone. You don't. To start with, my name isn't Evie."

Fourteen

Band-Aids Suck

"What do you mean it's not Evie?" He choked.

Mia didn't answer. Just took a step toward him, then two steps back. He turned and repeated the question. Her dad's office at the lodge, a room that had felt gigantic all her life, at once felt suffocating.

"I mean"—she twisted her hands in front of her, wishing for a moment that she hadn't worn this ridiculous dress—"I was going to lose my license. And my job."

"Don't you *work* for the family business?" His voice had an unfamiliar chill, and she set her jaw. Now was the part that hurt. Now was the part when she lost everything.

"It's not that easy, working with family," she started. As though that reality excused her lies.

"Try not having one," he cut in. His face was unreadable, jaw set in a determined frown.

"Antone—" she started.

"—you used me," he finished.

"Used you? Kinda like you're using me? What happened to quid pro quo?" She crossed her arms in front of her.

"Evie was meant to get me some press opportunities."

It was insulting. That that was the first thing he'd objected to. "You think—you think you didn't get enough press?"

"Sure, I guess you run this twin switch all the time. You must have thought I was pretty stupid."

He paced the length of the room. Then, heading to the desk, he picked up a stress ball and tossed it from one hand to the other.

"Pretty stupid? Well, I do right now. I tried to come clean, and you kissed me anyway. Said it didn't matter."

"Nice, Evie. Before we made love, you should have come clean. I didn't give you a carte blanche to hide your identity, so don't throw that evening back in my face like it somehow excuses you." He blushed.

"It's Amelia. Mia." She took a step toward him and he thrust out his hand.

"Don't."

"What? I can't touch you now?" She faltered.

He didn't answer, just walked out of the room, pausing at the door. "The gala is still going on. I trust Scott is gone—your brother seemed pretty pissed. So, let's finish this. Put the show on for the cameras. I'll do what I have to do to hold up my end of the bargain. But I won't let you in again. This, whatever this was between us, it's done. We're done."

She felt the dismissal like a cold shower, waking her up in the rudest way ever. But she deserved it. This was still better than Scott outing her. She was glad she told him herself, even if it was humiliating.

"Sounds like exactly what you told your publicist. Exactly what you assumed would happen, right from the start."

"I really don't think you're in a position to throw anything in my face, Amelia." He held his head high and left.

She let him have the last word. He deserved it. His footsteps grew fainter as he went down the fall. *She cringed at the way he'd said her name. Amelia.*

It was over. They were over.

But there was still the gala. Maybe if she made the end of the evening more successful than he imagined it could be, it would be enough. *She* might be enough.

She chased the thought away as suddenly as it had appeared. He'd never wanted Amelia. No one did.

"What are you more mad about? The fact that she played you, or the fact that you care?" Rob poured a beer from the keg that had been set up at the distillery. The renovations were done ahead of schedule, and the inside of the distillery was officially Western chic. His decorator had done a stellar job with Joanna's party, and Antone was the first to admit she'd outdone herself once again. But Antone felt empty.

"The fact that I care. Damn it. I'm mad that I care."

He'd thought about lying. About telling his friend he just didn't like being played, but the truth was, it was *her*. He didn't like being played by her.

"I thought we had something good, something real. I don't know, for the first time." He paused, unsure if it was okay to bring her up.

"You never gave it a chance to be real."

Antone didn't say anything, just took a deep drag of his beer. "I guess I did say that. But people don't always mean the things they say."

"So say what you mean." Rob asked. "You've been happy. Talking business with the heiress. Scheming ways to hire more people. And Mia? That's her name, Mia, right? The way she gets you. This whole thing might have started as quid pro quo, but I think you both know it went a good deal farther than that."

"How do you mean?"

"You're in the end zone, buddy. You fell for her, now you just need to be man enough to admit it."

Man enough to admit it? The woman had lied to him. Their whole relationship, or whatever you wanted to call it, was based on lies. "I don't think you get it. She duped me."

"About her name. But what does a name even mean? Take yours. Williams. That name isn't yours, but you wear it well. We picked our names the day we turned eighteen, but what makes us who we are isn't our name. Why are you letting it define your girl? Doesn't she deserve better than that? A chance to explain herself, for example."

Antone didn't say anything, just took another drag of his beer. He spun the Super Bowl ring on his pinky around and around, seven times. Damn it. His friend was right. He needed to be man enough to admit it. The thing that brought him peace was seven seconds thinking about her.

She wasn't there when he stopped by their house. Her house. Then he saw the two bags, packed neatly by the door. *Agnes, but on her orders, he had no doubt.* He hadn't come for his things; he'd come to talk. Clearly, she had a different chat in mind.

He felt…empty. Picking up the two bags, he made his way to his Lexus, heaving them into the trunk. Then he hesitated. Maybe he could leave a note, something more personal than a text.

Back inside, he made his way to her desk, shuffling through the papers in the top drawer in search of a blank sheet. That was when he saw it. The batch of correspondence from her lawyer.

He knew he shouldn't read it. It was private. But there was something that caught his eye.

"PJ Banks. Atorney-at-law."

What kind of self-respecting lawyer misspelled at-torney?

* * *

"What do you mean he's in LA?" Mia asked angrily.

The girl at the bar didn't raise an eyebrow, only shrugged. "I mean, Mr. Williams is in Los Angeles."

The girl resumed wiping down the bar, then nodded toward the patrons seated at the far end. "If you don't mind, we're kinda busy."

Mia looked around. Two days post gala and they had opened the tasting room of the distillery. It was busy indeed. Really busy. The space was packed to the brim, the din of chatter deafening. Perhaps it was the overflow of famous athletes. Her guests were all here, drinking Antone's whiskey and having their photos taken for the "Athletes' Corner" by the bathroom. She couldn't help but smile.

"Is Rob here?" she shouted into the crowd, having made no headway with the guard dog at the bar.

"Here," he called out. How he'd heard her over the noise of the bar was something.

Rob looked like a new man, smiling, with a dishrag slung over his shoulder.

"Mia. You're lookin' for Antone? Is that it?"

She smiled. At least he hadn't chased her out of the bar. "I am."

"He left. Something about a celebrity endorsement, bottle service, I'm not sure. He's gonna be back for the taste test next week, but that's all I got." His hands fell to his hips, and his eyes darted away before he added, "He's pretty upset."

Her stomach fell. "Yeah. I know."

Rob leaned on the edge of the bar and put his hand

on her shoulder. "You don't, actually. That man is hurting, but only because you've made him question everything. He's been an island for a long time. And in one short month you've gotten under his skin."

Her heart stopped. Maybe there was still a chance.

Fifteen

Unmasked

"I'm telling you, doesn't make any sense." Antone paced as he ran hands over his chin. He stopped in front of his desk, pouring himself another tumbler of whiskey. The room was short, and with Rob sitting on the lone two-seater couch, Antone could hardly pace to the extent he wished. He'd flown back early from LA. Heck, he hadn't even made it out of the airport.

"Don't you think you've had enough of those?" Rob raised an eyebrow in the direction of Antone's drink.

He eyed his friend and drained his third glass of scotch, putting it down, squarely in the center of a leather coaster, only to uncork the bottle and refill it.

"That guy, PJ Banks? There was a spelling mistake on the envelope of his last invoice."

"You're reading her mail now?" Rob met him with another hooked eyebrow and put an arm on the back of the sofa.

Antone blushed and thrust his hands into his pockets. "She left it out," he lied.

"And you what...you proofread it?" Rob pressed, scratching fingers along the upholstery in protest of the lie.

"What kind of lawyer misspells 'attorney'? I'm telling you there's something off about this guy." Antone swore.

Rob pulled his phone from his pocket, swiping the screen as he scrolled. "This site looks pretty legit." He frowned.

"Not like it's hard to pay someone to set up a nice website. Especially if you're running a con. That's probably the first thing I'd do." Antone swore again.

"I love how that's what you jump to—running a con. Once again, totally blind to how your so-called girlfriend lied about who she was for the duration of your relationship. But what you're worried about is a spelling mistake on the header of her lawyer's stationery? Yes, I can see how *that* is cause for tremendous concern..." Rob laughed, but it was a laugh entirely devoid of empathy. "You might not be as different from her as you think. You're both nuts."

Antone stopped his pacing and fell into the chair. He opened his laptop, clicking on the bookmark to PJ Banks's website. The website looked good at first glance—nice font, professional graphics—then he frowned. He left-clicked on one of the banner images, then popped it into a reverse search on Google. Stock photography. The whole site was stock photography—the office, heck, even the photographs of other partners, were all stock photography.

"I need to call her," Antone started, stomach turning. "No. First I need more facts. More research. What exactly *is* the con?"

"I guess you didn't read *all* her mail?" Rob held his hands up and shrugged. "You do you, buddy."

Antone chuckled. "Always." He held up the bottle of whiskey, offering it forward.

"Yeah, thanks, don't mind if I do, I think I'll take my drink outside, though, if it's all the same to you."

Rob accepted the bottle, rummaged for a glass of his own, then offered Antone the grace of a few minutes of unasked privacy.

Twenty minutes later, Antone stepped outside. "You're not going to believe this," he said, just loud enough to draw Rob's attention away from the sunset across the lake.

"You were busy long enough for me to drink just the right amount of scotch." Rob smiled. "I think you'd be surprised at just how much I believe right about now…"

Antone drew a second teak chair out and sank into it. "Yeah, well, it's not what I thought, I'll tell you that much."

"Easy, buddy, I get it, it's a tough situation." Rob tipped his glass toward the surroundings. "Silver lining, you've got a heck of a beautiful spot to mourn in."

"I'm not mourning anything." Antone clenched his jaw. "Now's when I start to fight for what's mine."

Unbelievable. Amelia stared at her phone, not believing it was him. On the fourth ring, she answered.

"What?" Her voice was terse and tight; she wanted him to feel like he was the last person she wanted to talk to, even if the opposite was true.

"We need to talk," Antone said simply.

"Do we? You want to go over the details for the taste test?" Amelia countered. Part of her wanted him to say something unrelated to work, so she could apologize and beg for his forgiveness.

"You know, I don't believe for a second that you haven't already made your mind up about whatever it is you want to *talk* to me about," she added. "But let me give you a hint—there's nothing you can say that would make me forgive you."

And nothing you can say that would make me forget you either, she thought, pressing her eyes shut.

Mia hadn't been to the office in three days, not that he had any way of knowing that. Things were not good. Instead of working, she lay in her bed, staring at the top of her cotton canopy. Lying on the Egyptian cotton sheets, she was the worst version of herself, trying to convince herself that it was enough. That this house, this company, this land, that it was all enough. The reality, that it all paled in comparison to her four weeks with Antone, was impossible to escape.

"Can I come by? After work?" he asked.

After? "What time would that be?" She did her best

to sound disinterested, cursing her optimistic heart for jumping at his suggestion of a meeting.

"Mia, please, don't be like this." Antone's voice was measured. Calm. Always the cool athlete. She'd love it if just for once he'd seem as lost as she felt. But silver lining; he was calling her Mia.

"Fine. You can come. I'm staying in tonight and can see you if you're going to insist."

"Thanks."

She hung up and stared at her phone, impressed that she'd managed not to cry.

Then her phone buzzed. Antone, again.

"I canceled my meetings. I need to see you sooner. I hate this," he insisted.

She smiled at his urgency, tears momentarily at bay. "All right," Mia agreed, mirroring his calm demeanor. She felt alive on the phone with him. "Meet me at the office. I need to go into town this afternoon. I could meet you at three?" She glanced at her watch, nodding to herself.

"Three. At your office. Okay, thanks, I'll be there," he agreed, sounding lighter with the meeting confirmed.

Ending the call, Mia got out of bed, finding an energy that had failed her for the past three days. She pressed the intercom at her bedside, and moments later, Agnes was at her door, as prim and proper as always.

"Thanks, Agnes—can you call for the car? I'm going into the office."

Agnes nodded. "Of course, ma'am, straight away."

Amelia felt the buzz of her phone and pulled it to her ear a nanosecond later. "You again." She smiled.

"You can't imagine how pleased I am that you're so happy to hear from me," PJ answered, voice dry.

Just like that, her stomach flutters vanished. "Banks, sorry, I thought you were someone else." She blushed, grateful this wasn't a video call.

"Not today," her lawyer replied.

"Well, how can I help you, Mr. Banks?" she answered, happily taking her stairs two at a time in her eagerness to get to work. It was just after 1 p.m., so she had enough time to get to her office and look appropriately busy before Antone came to see her.

"I've heard back from the opposing counsel. Do you think you could discuss their response? It's time-sensitive." He lingered on the disclaimer just long enough for her to appreciate the urgency.

"Right. I mean, yes, I could. I'm about thirty minutes outside of town, but I could meet you for a late lunch? But it needs to be quick. I have another meeting at three." The minute she suggested food, her stomach twisted in hunger. In addition to wallowing in self-pity, she hadn't eaten much in the past three days.

"Yes, perfect. Half an hour at Mona's Bistro?" PJ suggested.

Mia agreed. "See you shortly. If you arrive before me, I'll have the Rösti."

*

Mona's Bistro was a bustling joint, and PJ was already seated by the time Mia arrived forty minutes later.

The waiter noted her drink order, an old-fashioned to stiffen her nerves, and she sat.

"Thanks for seeing me on short notice." PJ nodded toward the leather folio case between them. "I heard back from Scott's lawyer and thought we'd better respond to their offer before it expires."

"Before it expires?" she asked.

"Right. We have a little less than twenty hours. I must add, it's a very clean proposal, shouldn't take long for us to review, but you'll need to make the wire transfer before end of day."

Mia nodded, wondering if two drinks was too many to have pre meeting with Antone. She wanted her wits sharp but her nerves dull. Maybe paying Scott off in order to get a quick divorce was worth it just to move on to the next chapter of her life: spinsterhood.

"I don't like making decisions on a tight timeline," she answered on autopilot. All she could think about was Antone. She stole a glance at her phone clock. Two twenty, forty minutes until he arrived. *What did he want to talk about that was worth canceling a meeting for?*

"Thanks again for meeting to discuss this urgently," PJ started, voice silky and hypnotic.

"I hadn't yet eaten, so it worked out on all counts," she stated magnanimously.

"I ordered the moment I arrived, for us both." He smiled stiffly. PJ shifted in his seat, taking off a black cowboy hat and putting it on the table. Odd, she didn't see many lawyers in cowboy hats. She smiled to herself, thinking that, before this month, she hadn't seen many football players in cowboy hats either.

PJ fingered the folio, unsheathing the documents and straightening them in a tidy stack. But he didn't push them toward her; instead, he leveled his gaze on her. "Communicating on your behalf, as your legal representative, has allowed me the opportunity of negotiating a very profitable settlement."

"How can a settlement be profitable?" she pushed, immediately on edge.

"If we can avoid a costly and drawn-out litigation, it's profitable, no? A dollar saved is a dollar earned."

"Is that how you think of it? Might be more apt to say that a dollar paid is a dollar lost." She reached for a breadstick, snapping it in half and tidying the crumbs with the side of her knife, organizing them into a thin line.

"This litigation is going to move forward whether you like it or not. Unless we make it go away, today."

"Quite the confident statement from a lawyer who has thus far been unsuccessful in getting the opposition to budge." She eyed the portfolio. "What's the price tag?"

In the dim light of the bistro, his paleness was still obvious, and PJ raised a napkin to his brow, dotting the few beads of persistent perspiration that had arisen. *He was stressed.*

"What?" He scowled at them. Then he refocused on Mia, his cold eyes calculating. "You think it's easy? As I remind you, your husband has every right to see his day in court, and here I am, working to protect your reputation."

"About that." She held up a finger, angling to pull this conversation back to present. "I got a message from my assistant that your offices called inquiring as to the latest round of invoices? I find it hard to believe we've exceeded the first retainer." She matched his scowl, but refrained from her own insistent tapping and flailing. This was, after all, a nice restaurant.

"You can hardly expect me to work for free." PJ gestured for the waiter, swinging his glass for a refill.

"Begs the question of who is extorting whom, at your rates," she muttered.

"I hadn't pegged you for the type to nickel-and-dime, regardless of what they say about you Hartmanns in the press," PJ shot back.

"Can we get back to the matter at hand?" She took an exaggerated glance at her watch, then narrowed her eyes at her lawyer.

"Five hundred thousand, as promised." He pushed the paperwork toward her and she accepted the pages without seeing them. *There was a reason everyone hated lawyers, and right now, Mia totally understood it.*

Her phone vibrated in her pocket. She reached for it, and read the text preview on her home screen. From Antone.

Picking up lunch, have you eaten?

She stared at her phone under the table, only to be distracted by PJ clearing his throat.

"Please excuse me." She stood, bumping into the table with her stomach. "I need to go to the bathroom."

Mia had been to the restaurant before and made a beeline to the bathroom with the proficiency of someone who wanted the privacy of a stall.

Thanks, she texted, I'm actually at Mona's meeting with the attorney.

She wanted to be mad at him. To stay mad at him. It was easier to hate him than to miss him, but lately, she'd been doing plenty of both.

In the bathroom, she put both hands on the side of her sink, turning the faucet of cold water to full throttle. Mia splashed the water on her face, hoping the coolness would push back the rising heat in her cheeks.

Her phone buzzed again. I'm coming.

Two words. Two words and her head spun. That was the thing about Antone; it was all or nothing, and for the past few days, she'd been terrified it would be nothing. What if it was destined to be something even more frightening? What if she was going to get it all?

I don't see you. Her phone buzzed with his statement.

You're already here? She typed faster than she could think, then stared in the mirror again. This was it.

Then she exited the bathroom, just in time to see Antone Williams land a punch square on the unsuspecting jaw of PJ Banks.

Sixteen

Devil's in the Details

"Antone!" she gasped, both embarrassed by his outburst and slightly enamored with the possessiveness.

What was he doing there?

"Do you want me to call the cops?" the elderly
woman seated in the neighboring table asked.

"No, no cops," PJ managed to say.

"I bet you'd like that," said Antone. "Yes, please,
ma'am, call the cops."

"Antone, what are you doing? That's my lawyer."
Mia didn't know what to make of the situation before her.

"He's not a lawyer, are you?" Antone threatened.

"And I bet Scott is just around the corner. Any monrey the two are running this scam together."

"You're literally insane," Mia muttered under her breath. *Was this what her world was coming to? Was she so wrong about Antone?*

"Call him," he said, directing the request at PJ. "Call him now, or I'll call the cops myself."

"I don't know what you're talking about," PJ started, getting up off the ground and straightening his suit.

"Don't you?" Antone pulled out his phone.

"Okay, okay, I'm calling him."

"Madame." The server came to them, and Mia busied herself apologizing, pulling out her purse, and moving to the back of the restaurant to speak with the owner regarding possible damages.

Then she took a few minutes to find some space and clear her head. It was past time she got in touch with the family lawyer. Pride be damned.

By the time she'd made her way back to the table, it was surreal. There, seated at their two-seater table, were Scott, PJ and Antone.

"This was a scam." Antone nodded toward her ex-husband and PJ. "They were from the same frat." Sneering, he looked at Scott. "Did you really think it would be this easy?"

"We can't all sleep our way to the Hartmann fortune," PJ hissed.

Amelia felt sick. She was being played. Maybe if she'd given Antone a chance to explain, let him in on all the details, let go of the pretense of having it all together, she could have avoided this humiliation.

"If you think I won't hit you again, you're wrong," Antone said in a dry tone. He was stretched out in his chair, his large frame, usually languid and casual, now with the coiled tension that promised to spring at the first given opportunity.

"Easy, tiger," Scott muttered.

"What, were you waiting next door? Hoping to cash in on your ruse?" Mia sputtered. "What's the problem, Scott? You're pissed I told Antone the truth about who I was? Can't blackmail me now, can you?" She was angry, shaking and ready for her turn to hit the men, all three of them.

"PJ here thought he could run a different scam your way," Antone added, lifting an eyebrow in heavy skepticism.

"A different scam?" Mia frowned. "Antone? What are you talking about?"

"This supposed lawsuit you're being sued for? The petition for lump-sum alimony? PJ isn't a lawyer, he's a frat boy. They were trying to talk you into a settlement for a case that doesn't exist. Scott never filed for lump-sum alimony. He never filed for anything."

"I can still get a lawyer," Scott interjected.

"You'd have to actually pay a retainer, you know that, right, Scott?" PJ hissed.

"Sure, maybe PJ isn't a lawyer, but it doesn't change the facts. If we go to court, I'm gonna win something, *Evie*. Or maybe I could just sell my story to the press? How the princess impersonated her twin to sell some booze for her boyfriend..." He brandished a newspaper in her direction.

Antone hit the tabletop with his hand, and the bickering peanut gallery quieted. "You can stop, Scott. You're not selling anything to the press. I'm no lawyer, but I do have a great legal team that works for me, and I'm sure this fake lawsuit has ramifications far worse than a smear campaign on the Hartmann family. Extortion is criminal, as is impersonating a member of the bar." Antone's voice left no room for doubt of his seriousness, and Mia felt a shiver up her spine she was sure Scott felt in his heart.

"You can't be serious," Scott started. Then he reached for PJ's water glass, untouched before the two of them, and took a deep sip, shaking his head.

"As serious as a heart attack," Antone promised.

Mia took another step toward the table, aware of the wide berth left to them by the serving staff. "You. You manipulated me." She jabbed a finger into PJ's chest.

"To be fair, we wrote a demand letter. If you would have agreed to a settlement, that's your own free will. There's nothing in the law that prevents a citizen from writing a demand letter."

To think she had once found him attractive.

"Now you're an expert in all things law?" PJ opened his mouth to speak but she silenced him with a cool stare. "Just get out."

"And you," she said, turning her attention to Scott. "There might not be a lawsuit right now, but there should be. I promise you this. If you ever threaten a lawsuit again, to me, or the man I love, I will sue *your* family, and I won't stop there."

Scott cleared his throat. "Leave my folks out of this. We can still divorce like adults." He paled.

"Scott, you've gotta know it would be best for everyone if you crawl back under that rock you've been hiding behind. Until you work your shit out. And yes. You're going to agree to a no-contest divorce, effective immediately."

Mia was still so mad she was shaking. She took a sip of water, proud of herself for managing not to wipe the glass first.

Scott eyed her, nostrils flared, and picked up a napkin, throwing it with all his might. It fluttered with an airy descent to the table. "This isn't the end," Scott threatened. But there was a feebleness to his tone.

Mia smiled. She didn't care anymore. He could have the last word, just not his way.

"I assure you, it is," Antone answered angrily, clearly not okay with Scott having the last *anything*.

"If you have any further questions or concerns, I invite you to talk to my lawyer. My actual lawyer. I won't be shamed or manipulated, by anyone, anymore." Mia smiled, this time allowing her statement to sink in to all the parties present.

Scott left without another word, fuming. And just like that, her legal trouble walked out the door.

Mia drew her chair closer to the table, taking another sip of water. Antone, opposite her, stared at her.

"Are you just gonna stare or what?" she asked, feeling like a bug under a microscope.

"Is that true?" he asked, quietly and calmly.

"What part?" She blushed, realizing that there wasn't a need to clarify: it was all true. "Yes, it's true."

"The man you *love*?" Antone said the words thoughtfully, as though hearing them aloud gave them a new meaning.

Mia pushed her shoulders back. "I'm finished running after princes and trying to impress everyone. Marketing campaigns for guests. Social media campaigns I don't really care about. The last few weeks, I've had fun. I've been more myself, more free, than I've felt ever before in my life. I've felt alive. And yes. I love you. I know I promised I wouldn't fall. And shit. It's really embarrassing that I did. But don't worry, I won't hold you to anything. You can go, and there are no hard feelings. Really. I mean that." She pinked. She was blabbering.

"No hard feelings? What do you mean?" His voice was quiet, and she had to lean in to hear the whispered question.

"It's simple, really. Everything that happened between us, I wanted it, and I wanted more. I still do."

"Simple, is it?" He smiled. "Mia Hartmann, that's where you're wrong. There is nothing simple about you."

He wasn't getting up and running out the door. That was a good thing, she supposed.

Then he stood and her blood ran cold. This was the part where he left. She steeled herself, but instead of turning away, he reached for her, pulling her to her feet. Then he enveloped her in his arms.

"There's nothing simple about you, except for my

feelings. See, the thing is, I love you too. Even if it's a bad idea. Even if loving you means you can hurt me more than anyone, you also make me happy. I want to be with you. Beyond any measure of time or limit. I want to wake you up with kisses, and hold you as you whisper truths you haven't admitted to anyone before into my ear. I want to watch you shake as I kiss your neck, and do as many ridiculous photoshoots as you need."

"I might hold you to that."

"The photoshoots?"

"The neck kisses."

His hands tightened around her waist. "Rob is going to love this," he said.

"Not as much as I will," she promised.

He kissed her and slapped five one-hundred-dollar bill on the table, anxious to leave.

"For your time and inconvenience." He nodded to the server before pulling her away from the restaurant.

"Where are we going?" she asked.

"Anywhere," he answered. "I'd follow you anywhere."

Epilogue

"One of these whiskeys is the Johnnie Walker Blue Label. And one of these is GreatWhiskey." Antone was proud to serve his drink and even more proud of the woman at his side.

Mia was bursting with excitement. "Don't worry, Commissioner, *both* whiskeys are expensive."

The members of the press laughed.

Antone swallowed. He was nervous. Who wouldn't be?

"We should have started with the Glenlivet," he muttered.

"Babe, you can go top-shelf with this crowd, don't worry." Mia squeezed his hand.

One squeeze and he felt calm. That was the effect she had on him. He squeezed back and watched as

Barry Lopez took a deep sniff of one snifter, then the second.

The room, filled with the distillery's staff, thirty members of the press, the Hartmann family, and at least twenty football players, was quiet, with every eyeball focused on the commissioner.

The first sip, then the second.

Antone reminded himself to breathe.

"I think the first whiskey is the Johnnie Walker."

Antone wasn't sure which of his friends let out the first hoot, but what he was sure about was that his girlfriend let out the second one. Mia clapped "That's the GreatWhiskey, Commissioner! Well done—it definitely *tastes* more expensive."

She had the best way of turning the experience on its side and making the politician at ease for his pronouncement.

"Indeed—congratulations are in order." Barry extended a hand toward Antone, and he shook it, eyes blinking at the flurry of camera flashes that followed. The press from this would have far-reaching implications for both the distillery and their nonprofit.

"You made this happen," he said, turning to her, feeling the rest of the room melt away.

She looked at him and smiled. "We did."

"I have something to ask you."

The pro athletes hooted and howled, and he waved them away. "Guys. It's been six weeks. I'm not going to propose."

She frowned, and a piece of him blossomed. *"Yet,"* he corrected. "I'm not going to propose yet."

Mia's face broke into a wide smile. "What did you want to say?"

"I think you should join me. That we should run this business together. A real team. I know it's a lot to ask. That you've got the family business—"

"I'd love to." She interrupted.

He didn't hear anyone else. Didn't see anyone else. Didn't feel anyone else. Only her.

"You know," he said, unable to resist. "I just can't believe this all started with a would-be ticket."

* * * * *

Don't miss Evie's story,
available Summer 2023!

Get 4 FREE REWARDS!

We'll send you 2 FREE Books plus 2 FREE Mystery Gifts.

FREE Value Over $20

Both the **Harlequin® Desire** and **Harlequin Presents®** series feature compelling novels filled with passion, sensuality and intriguing scandals.

YES! Please send me 2 FREE novels from the Harlequin Desire or Harlequin Presents series and my 2 FREE gifts (gifts are worth about $10 retail). After receiving them, if I don't wish to receive any more books, I can return the shipping statement marked "cancel." If I don't cancel, I will receive 6 brand-new Harlequin Presents Larger-Print books every month and be billed just $6.30 each in the U.S. or $6.49 each in Canada, a savings of at least 10% off the cover price, or 6 Harlequin Desire books every month and be billed just $5.05 each in the U.S. or $5.74 each in Canada, a savings of at least 12% off the cover price. It's quite a bargain! Shipping and handling is just 50¢ per book in the U.S. and $1.25 per book in Canada.* I understand that accepting the 2 free books and gifts places me under no obligation to buy anything. I can always return a shipment and cancel at any time by calling the number below. The free books and gifts are mine to keep no matter what I decide.

Choose one: ☐ **Harlequin Desire**
(225/326 HDN GRJ7)

☐ **Harlequin Presents Larger-Print**
(176/376 HDN GRJ7)

Name (please print)

Address _____ Apt. #

City _____ State/Province _____ Zip/Postal Code

Email: Please check this box ☐ if you would like to receive newsletters and promotional emails from Harlequin Enterprises ULC and its affiliates. You can unsubscribe anytime.

Mail to the **Harlequin Reader Service:**
IN U.S.A.: P.O. Box 1341, Buffalo, NY 14240-8531
IN CANADA: P.O. Box 603, Fort Erie, Ontario L2A 5X3

Want to try 2 free books from another series! Call 1-800-873-8635 or visit www.ReaderService.com.

---

*Terms and prices subject to change without notice. Prices do not include sales taxes, which will be charged (if applicable) based on your state or country of residence. Canadian residents will be charged applicable taxes. Offer not valid in Quebec. This offer is limited to one order per household. Books received may not be as shown. Not valid for current subscribers to the Harlequin Presents or Harlequin Desire series. All orders subject to approval. Credit or debit balances in a customer's account(s) may be offset by any other outstanding balance owed by or to the customer. Please allow 4 to 6 weeks for delivery. Offer available while quantities last.

Your Privacy—Your information is being collected by Harlequin Enterprises ULC, operating as Harlequin Reader Service. For a complete summary of the information we collect, how we use this information and to whom it is disclosed, please visit our privacy notice located at corporate.harlequin.com/privacy-notice. From time to time we may also exchange your personal information with reputable third parties. If you wish to opt out of this sharing of your personal information, please visit readerservice.com/consumerschoice or call 1-800-873-8635. **Notice to California Residents**—Under California law, you have specific rights to control and access your data. For more information on these rights and how to exercise them, visit corporate.harlequin.com/california-privacy.

HDHP22R3

HARLEQUIN
PLUS

Try the best multimedia subscription service for romance readers like you!

Read, Watch and Play.

Experience the easiest way to get the romance content you crave.

Start your **FREE TRIAL** at
<u>www.harlequinplus.com/freetrial</u>.